FINDING H

"*Finding Home* is a poetic, sweeping, and transportive story of Jewish returnees seeking to rebuild their lives after the war. In a world where prejudice and greed haven't ceased, and where displacement continues long after liberation, Cycon gives us a powerful and emotional read, with faith, music, and beauty central to the search for home."

—**Jennifer Rosner, award-winning author of *The Yellow Bird Sings* and *Once We Were Home***

"The image of Eva Fleiss playing imaginary keys at Auschwitz to contain the madness that surrounds her is the epicenter of this beautiful novel. Like Ulysses returning to Ithaca, she will face a variety of tests that will define—for her and for us—the meaning of *home* in a disrupted world. A powerful debut!"

—**Ilan Stavans, Lewis-Sebring Professor at Amherst College and editor of *The Oxford Book of Jewish Stories***

"In his debut novel, *Finding Home*, Dean Cycon delves deeply into the seldom-explored story of Jewish life after the Holocaust. As survivors return home to the ruins of their former lives, they must rely on the restorative powers of hope, courage, and art as they work to heal their souls and repair the world. Cycon tells a tale that must be told with great passion and historical dedication."

—**David R. Gillham, NY Times Bestselling Author of *City of Women***

"*Finding Home* by Dean Cycon is a rollercoaster ride of deep emotions as six Holocaust survivors—five men and a teenage girl—are returned to their hometown in Hungary directly after the war. The anger and resentment from the townspeople who had taken over all of the Jewish houses and businesses is palpable and disturbing. This is a truth-telling historical novel at its best, where the author has not flinched and the reader cannot put the book down."

—**Jane Yolen, author of more than 400 books including the Holocaust novels *The Devil's Arithmetic, Mapping the Bones,* and *Briar Rose.* Her book *Kaddish* won the Sophie Brodie medal in 2022, the same year she won Sydney Taylor Lifetime Award.**

"*Finding Home* examines the plight of Jews returning to their homes in Hungary after the end of World War II—their relations with the post-war gentile community, the complexity of the emotions and issues involved, and the search for hope among ruins. I cared deeply about these characters, particularly the ambitious and strong-willed musician at the book's center, and my eyes filled with tears—not just of sadness, but of love—many times. I loved this novel, and recommend it highly."

—**Mitchell James Kaplan, author of *Rhapsody, Into the Unbounded Night* and *By Fire, By Water***

"A heart-wrenching story of Auschwitz survivors longing for home, who are forced to create the fabric of new lives woven from brittle threads of suffering, continued loss and fear, and the hope that acceptance and the power of music might heal them in the end."

—**Karla M. Jay, author of *The Puppet Maker's Daughter***

"Dean Cycon brilliantly depicts post–World War II Budapest in his debut novel. Through the careful and documentary-like depiction of contemporary Hungarian musical life, we can gain an insight into the forgotten world of the Liszt Academy of Music in Budapest. Heroes, victims, criminals: the author captures the potential for music to be a transcendent force for good in this sad but ultimately uplifting tale."

—**Peter Barsony, Professor, Liszt Academy of Music, Budapest, Hungary and University of Music and Performing Arts Graz, Austria**

"It is often said that it is difficult to convey the feelings and emotions of music in a novel. In his debut, Dean Cycon has done that admirably. His protagonist tries to use music to heal both her own trauma from the war, as well as that of other survivors. She further attempts to harness the power of music as a transcendent force to combat hatred, with heart-rending results. *Finding Home* is a sobering yet beautiful exploration in which Cycon speaks with a strong, literate, and powerful new voice."

—**Howard Jay Smith, author of *Meeting Mozart* and *Beethoven in Love, Opus 139***

Finding Home
(Hungary, 1945)
by Dean Cycon

© Copyright 2023 Dean Cycon

ISBN 979-8-88824-075-5

Published by

köehlerbooks™

3705 Shore Drive
Virginia Beach, VA 23455
800-435-4811
www.koehlerbooks.com

FINDING HOME

(HUNGARY, 1945)

DEAN CYCON

VIRGINIA BEACH
CAPE CHARLES

TO JACK TERRY (Z"L)

(Jakub Szabmacher)

Born March 10, 1930,
who passed away peacefully on October 30, 2022.
Concentration camp survivor, psychiatrist and psychoanalyst
who sought answers to why and how it could have happened,
healer of those who suffered, and dear friend.

AUTHOR'S NOTE

How do we return home when home no longer exists? This question kept coming up as I researched what happened when Jewish concentration camp survivors sought to restart their lives immediately after the war. In most popular accounts, reports, and novels, the story jumps from the camps to the survivors' new lives in America, Great Britain, or Palestine. Yet the journalistic and academic literature tells a deeper tale. As I explored papers written by researchers around Eastern Europe, I came upon multiple accounts of survivors trying to return to their original homes. There were interviews with survivors, townspeople and town officials, factory owners, and union members—all revealing the emotional, moral, and economic complexity of the interactions between the survivors and the populations of their hometowns. *Finding Home* is based on dozens of these real-life interactions. I think you will find it a reading experience that is difficult at times, heart-warming and sobering, yet ultimately hopeful.

CHAPTER 1

The black locomotive chugged heavily south toward Hungary through the ruins of a defeated Germany. The four wooden cattle cars that followed lurched roughly and rhythmically, like an orchestra conducted by a madman. The metal wheels gave off the same steady *clunk—clunk—clunk* as the metronome atop the piano that waited for Eva at home. She felt the tingle in her fingertips, the dry pain in her throat, the blurring of her vision. She grunted as her fingers dug into the wall, desperately clinging to reality as she spiraled toward another delusion. The sounds of the train dulled and what little light remained in the world dimmed and disappeared. Eva clawed toward home as a thick darkness swallowed the tracks and closed in on the train.

A metallic bump from the cars behind hers jolted the young woman. She emerged from her vision, feeling the scratchiness of the dull woolen skirt and threadbare gray sweater the Red Army soldiers had tossed to her as they had ridden out of the open gates of the abandoned camp at Auschwitz. Her precious fingers—dirty, bruised, and scarred—rested on the ledge of the cattle car's barred window as if ready to caress a piano keyboard. She hadn't played an actual piano since the day before the deportation. Yet moving her fingers across imaginary keys kept her remembering and sane in the camp, allowing her a small hope of salvation. Fingers trained since age four to bring light and hope, ordered to assemble instruments of death in the camp munitions factory.

During her nine months in Auschwitz, Eva never dreamed. Death danced mockingly around her. Hunger and anxiety ate away at her from within. Survival kept her mind sharp and focused. There was no room for dreams. After the Russians liberated Auschwitz in late January, 1945, Eva was sent to a displaced persons camp. Only then did her dreams return. They were not the pleasant nocturnal images of her once comfortable childhood. Rather, troubled visions of her lost family and friends assaulted her at random hours of the day and night, as did macabre imitations of her piano performances. The visions clung to her like a mourning shroud. The more she fought to free herself, the more entangled she became until she slumped to the ground in defeat. The British army doctor at the displaced persons camp had checked her ears, throat, and pulse, then pronounced that when she reached the sanctuary of her home, the dreams and visions would fade away. But Eva was not home yet. She stood locked in this cattle car, transiting a liminal space between horror and hope.

The lurching movement of the train and the measured clicks of the wheels signaled to Eva that she was returning to life, to her large house and exquisite Bosendorfer piano, to whatever friends from high school were still alive. When Professor Sandor came back from the Terezin camp, she would continue her preparation for attending the Ferenc Liszt Academy of Music in September. She had been accepted before the deportation. Eva focused on the letter she was desperate to write the Academy upon her return home. Thinking about her promising future helped push away the horrific memories of the year she was leaving behind.

Eva turned and looked around the car. The wooden walls were rough and splintery, except where they were polished smooth by years of cattle jostling and rubbing on their way to the slaughterhouse. Five ragged mannequins rocked pensively against the walls or stared blankly back at her from the hay bales that provided the only physical comfort during their journey. The baker, the butcher, the young Hassid, and the two farm hands—all who remained of the three hundred Jews of Laszlo.

The clothes they wore came from Jews stripped and murdered in the camps. The baker wore a banker's silk vest atop rough spun woolen trousers and muddy farm boots. The others wore an odd assortment of fancy and common garments. Eva picked at a loose thread on her sweater and thought fleetingly of the young girl who must have worn it last. She hoped some surviving Jewish girl, somewhere, was wearing the nice clothes the Germans had stripped off her.

Eva gazed out the window at the passing landscape. It was late May. The gray and black of her world in the camp had evolved into a riot of green on the trees and in the fields, and the exquisitely blue sky of a Hungarian spring. Blue was her favorite color. It was the color of her mother's eyes and the color of hope. The air inside the car reeked of the human and animal odors that clung to the walls in a last cry for remembrance—dirty bodies, sweat and the pungency of blind fear. The air that entered through the barred window battled between the choking smoke of the locomotive ahead and the liberating vernal scents from the fields beyond. As the train rounded a curve, sunlight shot directly into the window. Eva shut her eyes against the glare but welcomed the warmth on her face. The comforting heat spoke of another time, a time of butterflies and clover in the fields, picnics, and friendships. That first shared cigarette with Andras, the handsome boy in her graduating class. He had toyed with the yellow Star of David patch she and all the Jews had to wear. Closer and closer, inches away from her first and only kiss. A sweet idyll shattered by the sound of a loudspeaker atop the police van.

"Attention! Attention! All Jewish residents of Laszlo will report to the Town Square tomorrow at eight a.m. for processing. Only one valise of personal items will be allowed . . ."

Nine months in the hellish torment of Auschwitz. Three months in the surreal safety of the displaced persons camp. Three days locked in this train. Now the nightmare, the earthquake, and its aftershocks were finally over. The train was slowing down. They were home.

CHAPTER 2

The station master of Laszlo drummed his stubby fingers on the desk, waiting for the two o'clock Special Train. He could feel the rumble in the small station building before he could see the train. That usually thrilled him, even after thirty years on the job. But this time was different. He shifted uncomfortably in his chair. The Jews were coming back. Who would be among them? He knew a good number of the town's Jews and had felt uneasy watching them being loaded onto cattle cars like animals by the town police and the German overseers. Until then, the government had done a good job of resisting German demands to deport all the Jews during the war—too good a job. Hungary had the largest remaining Jewish population in Europe. Even though they were allies, an impatient Hitler invaded. Eichmann himself passed through Laszlo by train on his way to speed up the deportations.

Like most of the townspeople, the station master had thought the Jews were being sent to a work camp. Many Hungarian Jews before them had been sent into forced labor battalions to build roads and trenches, releasing more soldiers for combat. But the labor battalions had always shipped out on Hungarian passenger trains with Hungarian crews. The deportation train was a long line of cattle cars pulled by a large, black engine from Deutsche Reichsbahn, DR, the German company. The first and last cars were full of heavily armed German soldiers. It was only after the train left that a drunken SS guardsman who supervised the loading laughed at his naiveté. He said these Jews were being shipped to a concentration camp called Auschwitz, where Hungary's "Jewish problem" would be solved forever.

The station master had never heard of Auschwitz. He should have protested there was no such problem. The Jews of Laszlo were assimilated and productive members of society. Most Hungarian Jews were. Hungary wasn't Poland. Yet he didn't protest. What could he say to armed men? Who would listen to an aging railway station master in a small town when the whole world was aflame? It all happened so quickly. The SS swept in like a killing frost. The Jews were taken away. Some nights it haunted him so deeply, he lay awake stiff as a corpse and soaked in sweat.

These Special Trains gave him a headache. Dozens had been rolling through Laszlo over the last few months. Day and night they came, shuttling Jews from the four thousand work and concentration camps the Germans had set up throughout Poland, Ukraine, Czechoslovakia, Romania, and Germany itself. It was as if the new postwar government was in a hurry to deliver the Jews here and there and get things back to normal. To forget. The state could cut away the past and start fresh. The station master could not. As the screech of hot steel brakes announced the arrival of the train, he cinched his tie and straightened his hat.

The conductor dropped from the still-smoking cab holding a clipboard.

"Good afternoon, Johann," the station master said. "Quite a small train today."

The conductor surveyed the train with a bored look and shrugged. He held out the clipboard to the station master. "Sign here, Josef."

"And what do we have today?" the station master asked, trying to mask his discomfort.

"A cargo of six DPs. Nothing more."

"DPs?" The station master focused on the clipboard, avoiding the heat and recrimination that shimmered off the train.

"Displaced persons."

"Oh, you mean the Jews returning to Laszlo."

"Call them what you will, Josef. To me, they are just cargo. And I am not responsible for their condition, either. Six DPs were packed alive three days ago and the door has not been opened since." He tapped on the clipboard. "Sign here and be quick about it. I have other cargo to deliver."

The station master took the clipboard with a shaking hand and looked at the list of Jewish names. He recognized a few. The baker, the butcher, and Jacob Fleiss's daughter. He remembered Jacob's annual ritual of taking his daughter to Budapest to attend concerts. The station master would bow and present her with a flower before Jacob picked her up and put her on the train. He continued to do it even when she was a teenager, although it embarrassed the girl. It was their private moment. The baker and the butcher never rode the trains, but the station master had bought the pastries and meats they produced and known the men all his adult life. He was relieved they were returning. Seeing them would remind him of what he had done, but at least they were alive. He struggled to blot out the surging memories of those Jews who did not appear on the clipboard. It wasn't his fault. He signed the bill of lading.

"I thought there would be more." He handed the clipboard back to the conductor and sighed. "Six DPs it is. Received."

The heavy iron bolt resisted, but the large wooden door soon rumbled open. Eva and the others gathered protectively at the opening. She squinted through the residual smoke from the still-huffing engine and stepped out on to the sunny platform. Her home and the piano she yearned to play waited a half hour's walk up the hill.

Her heart sank. Beyond the smoke, a group of armed, grim-faced police fanned out at attention behind a captain. Her hands began to shake at her side. The smoke enveloped the car again. When it dissipated, snapping dogs lunged at the shrieking people tumbling from the train. Sharp whistles pierced the air. Were they at the camp again? Eva's balance deserted her. She stumbled backward into the car and huddled in a corner, her fingers searching through the dirty straw for the keyboard. The barking and screaming faded slowly. Someone crouched besides her and spoke gently.

"Don't worry, Eva, those men won't hurt you. The war is over," Yossel the baker said.

"The war will never be over," grumbled Oskar the butcher.

Yossel helped the others down from the train. Eva came out last. She watched as the baker stretched his back with a groan and turned to the familiar faces of the town police—the same policemen who had loaded her and her father and the rest of the town's Jews onto the cars the day of the deportation. Yossel tipped his frayed cap to the captain and cleared his throat, while Eva shrank behind the other returnees to avoid the officer's stares. What could he possibly say to these men?

"Hello Captain Szabo, Sergeant Ritook, Gronski, Boros. Hello Zoldy, Corporal Miklos."

The policemen looked at each other. Eva could see they were perplexed by the gaunt man in a silk vest before them, whose skin hung on him like an oversized suit.

"When I reopen my bakery I trust you will stop by in the mornings for bread and jam, as always."

Eva heard the nervous edge underneath the baker's attempted camaraderie. She did not want to stand here confronting policemen. She ached to go home.

The captain peered hard at the man in front of him. "Yossel the baker? Is that you? I can hardly recognize you." He shifted his weight uneasily and scanned the list he held in his hand. "Yossel Roth, baker, Oskar Lazar, butcher, Mendel and Herschel Fischer, farmworkers, and Eva Fleiss, student. All from Laszlo." He looked up after each name, discomfort flickering through his officious demeanor as he went down the list. "Final name. Naftali Nachman, from Kosveg."

Eva shivered as if a heavy spring storm were about to break. Sometimes, she could try hard and compartmentalize what happened at Auschwitz. The vicious German guards had caused those horrors. But these ordinary Hungarians standing in front of her, the local police of her hometown, had not only sent her to Auschwitz, but the very next day committed the unspeakable at Kosveg. Eva had known little about the orthodox Hassids in the hill towns surrounding Laszlo until the surviving young men from Kosveg arrived on the selection platform a day after she did. Eva had always considered the local police to be her friendly protectors, like uniformed uncles. In the end, they were just like the guards in Auschwitz. They took their orders from the SS, whose black leather gloves and trench coats controlled men like reins and saddles controlled horses. She noticed the different reactions on the policemen's faces, ranging from disdain and haughty stares to guilty avoidance.

The captain cleared his throat into his fist. "It is late in the afternoon and you must be tired after your . . . journey. The mayor has requisitioned the former Armin Hotel for your comfort, and the people of the town to welcome you back with donated clothes, personal items, food, and everything else you will need to get back on your feet. The town has provided new mattresses and pillows for the hotel to insure your comfort."

Eva startled at the mention of new pillows and mattresses. When her head was shaved that first day in Auschwitz, the Jewish barber pointed to the mountains of hair that surrounded the inmates. He said her hair would be mixed with that of other prisoners, turned into stuffing for bedding or woven into socks and sold to support the German war effort. Were they to sleep on the hair of murdered friends and relatives? Eva feared she would hear the muffled screams from deep inside the pillow. She swallowed hard to push down the nausea that roiled up with the thoughts. The displaced persons camp doctor said she needed to avoid seeing everything in terms of the gruesome past in order to move forward. But it was so hard. She had only been one week out of high school when she was deported. She had so little life experience through which to judge and counterbalance the deaths, the hellish behaviors she had lived through at Auschwitz.

Eva followed Oskar's gaze past the policemen. The platform and the street leading to the station were deserted. Oskar gave a sardonic smile and nodded his head.

"Yeah. A warm welcome by the town."

The captain stiffened as he glanced behind him. "The people of Laszlo are trying to get back to normal, too. It is the middle of the afternoon. They are at work. Be assured they welcome you."

"What do you mean, the 'former' Armin Hotel?" the butcher asked.

Captain Szabo grimaced and recovered. "Ah, yes. The hotel was taken by the town a few months ago for failure to file annual reports and pay taxes. The owner can't be found."

"You mean Armin Epstein? Of course he can't. He's dead! The old man was gassed and incinerated like the garbage you thought he was. Right off the train!" shouted Oskar, taking a step toward the captain. The policemen grabbed for their batons, except for Corporal Miklos, who fell back as if pushed. Shock and sadness spasmed across his face. Eva was stunned by Oskar's rage. She feared it would only anger the police. The guards would have shot him immediately for such an outburst at Auschwitz.

"Calm down, Oskar," the captain warned. "We've had no notice of his death. Things are very confused because of the war."

"He was dead the moment you shoved him onto that train. They all were. My wife and son, Eva's father, Naftali's entire village, all of them." Angry tears surged down his cheeks. Yossel put a hand on Oskar's shoulder and looked pleadingly at the captain.

"Captain, please, we just want to put the horrors behind us and go back to our homes. We don't need to stop at the hotel."

Some of the policemen stirred anxiously, but the captain held up his hand and they snapped back to attention. "I'm afraid that won't be possible right now. Please, everybody, go settle into the hotel. Get some rest and some food. Tomorrow at ten o'clock come to the town clerk's office and your situation will be explained."

Oskar wiped his nose on his sleeve and studied the captain warily. "Situation? What situation is that?"

"The town clerk will explain tomorrow. Now, please come with us in the van."

Eva looked at the police van, noticing a shadow under the fresh red paint. Crossed green arrows on a circle of white—the Arrow Cross insignia. It lurked like a suppressed infection waiting to burst to the surface again. When she was in high school, the Arrow Cross was more like a gang of angry young thugs and petty criminals than a real political party. She heard that the Germans put them into power after the mass deportations. With no Jews left to terrorize in the countryside the Arrow Cross turned their bloodlust onto the Jews of Budapest, murdering tens of thousands in random roundups. Bile burned in her throat and her hands shook again. The Arrow Cross was supposed to be gone now, a rogue wave that crested, broke, and disappeared. But the insignia sneered at Eva. She spoke in a barely audible voice. "Are we under arrest?"

The captain looked at the girl as if seeing her for the first time. She saw a twitch of regret in his eyes. His gentler tone betrayed his discomfort. "No! Of course not. You are free citizens of Hungary." He regained his formal manner as he addressed the group, "You are home now. Let us escort you to the hotel."

Oskar defensively held up his hands. "No thank you, Captain. We know where the hotel is. The last time you escorted us somewhere it didn't end well, did it?"

CHAPTER 3

The small band of survivors trudged up the hill toward town, automatically forming the lines they had been forced into every day by the guards. Eva and Yossel led the group, followed by the grumbling Oskar and the taciturn Naftali. The Fischer brothers lagged behind, the younger Mendel leading the older Herschel by the elbow as the larger man blinked in confusion at the surroundings. The red van roared past in a spray of stones and dust as it returned to the police station in the center of Laszlo.

Eva sneezed as a mist of early blooming *parlagfu* ragweed invaded her nose.

"*Gesundheit*," said Yossel. "The smells and sounds of late spring at home, right?"

"Home," Eva replied, visualizing her beautiful house. "I don't understand why I can't go to my home."

Suspicion laced Oskar's voice. "Who knows what they've got planned for us."

"Oskar, keep an open mind," the baker calmly responded. "We'll find out what's going on tomorrow. I'm sure everything's fine."

Yossel cast a protective glance at Eva. She knew he was trying hard to keep their homecoming positive for her sake. When he thought she was asleep on the train he had whispered to Oskar that the poor girl had lost everything and gone through too much for one so young and innocent. But how could anyone who survived

Auschwitz be called innocent?

The road to town was too empty for a late Thursday afternoon. Where was the welcome the police captain promised? The few people they did encounter turned away or put their heads down and hurried past. Eva wondered what the townspeople saw—the usual peasant families who wandered into town from nearby Romania looking for work or handouts, or a phantasmal reminder of what they had done.

"Where is everybody?" she asked, peering around the deserted, dirt streets as a trickle of sweat ran down her back.

"Like the captain said, they are working," Yossel replied. "We can't expect the world to stop for us because we've returned."

Oskar's voice rolled over their shoulders like distant thunder. "Why not? They owe us a lot more than a welcome."

Eva heard the labored breathing of the Fischer brothers behind her. Those young men had been in the same rotating Jewish labor battalion as Oskar's oldest son. They had shipped out and come home on leave together several times before the deportation. But the brothers came home alone the last time. Eva noticed in the cattle car how they avoided Oskar's anguished stares. It was clear he couldn't bring himself to ask about his son, and they wouldn't volunteer anything. In the camp, Eva heard that the Laszlo battalion had been ordered to Russia to join the German sneak attack on its former ally. The entire Hungarian Second Army and unarmed labor battalions had been slaughtered at the battle of the Don River. The camp gossip was that all members of the Second were declared heroes and their families would get privileges after the war, but not the Jews who served in forced labor. There was no one to honor their memory except whoever remained of their shredded families.

As they continued, Eva thought of the last time she had walked this road. The day of the deportation. Crowds lined both sides of the street. So many faces she knew peeled back to reveal their true selves. Little children joyfully and mindlessly waving miniature Hungarian flags, jeers from many of the onlookers, shock, embarrassment, sadness, and tears on other faces. Her father kept trying to take her hand, but teenage girls did not hold their father's hands in public. She remembered the smug faces of the high school girls who used to taunt her after class. Looks that she returned. How petty and meaningless that all seemed now.

 A mother and child appeared as they neared the hotel. The small boy waved to Eva. She sucked in a breath. Eva didn't recognize the mother, but the child looked familiar—had she played with him in the park or been his babysitter one afternoon? She returned an uncertain smile, realizing it was the first time she had smiled since the night in the displaced persons camp when the inmates first assembled by hometown. The night she saw Oskar and Yossel. It was a joyous occasion at first, as families and friends gripped each other in tears and laughter. Yet by the end of the assembly the groups were so small, even from the bigger cities like Debrecen and Miskolc, that the magnitude of the disaster sank in. Her father, her teachers, shop owners, and friends. Every Jew she knew was gone.

Suddenly, Eva remembered the child's name. "Izidor?" she called out. The boy turned his head and studied Eva wonderingly. The mother yanked the child roughly in the opposite direction, tearing Eva's smile away with him. She turned to Yossel in bewilderment. "I know that little boy. How could he be here? He's Jewish. How could he be alive?"

Yossel watched the woman walk briskly with her child until she met a man down the street. Their faces registered anxiety as they stared back at the Jews before hurrying away. "No, Eva, you can't know him. You are only seeing shadows."

"But did you see how the parents looked at us?"

Oskar barked out a harsh laugh. "What do you expect? We're the stuff of nightmares, creatures from Grimm's fairy tales. I'd run away if I saw us coming, too. The smell of the camp still clings to us. I bet it always will."

Yossel spoke up as the couple and child faded away. "They all have to be feeling shame. Even the ones who didn't do anything, the ones who stood by and let the deportation happen." He removed his cap for a moment and wiped the perspiration off his balding head with his other hand.

An elderly couple passed by. The man curled his lip when he saw the Jews, revealing ancient teeth turned yellow by a lifetime of resentment. He waved an ivory-topped cane toward the survivors. "Look. See what a Jew looks like shorn of his fancy clothes and arrogance. Underneath they are all demons."

His wife clung to his arm. She spoke to him but her eyes never left the group. "I thought Eichmann exterminated all of them."

Oskar met the old man's stare and returned the angry look. After the couple walked away he spit on the ground in their direction and turned to Yossel. "Shame? Nah, they just don't want us back."

Eva detected the low murmur of Naftali's *niggun,* the wordless melodies the orthodox Hassids chanted incessantly in Auschwitz. She clenched her fists, disturbed by the memories evoked by the sound and by Oskar's constant muttering. She quickened the pace when she spotted the Armin Hotel further up the hill. She was anxious to get to the old, familiar building, get some food and a decent night's sleep, and return to her home in the morning.

They walked on, Eva noticing that each of the survivors seemed lost in his own muck of memory and anguish. She searched for something to say to Yossel, to get the sight of the child and the words of the old couple out of her head. "You were so brave back there, speaking to the police the way you did."

Yossel waved a hand cavalierly. "Me? That was nothing. I have known most of those men for years. I've baked cakes for their weddings and promotions, given them bread and hot tea on cold mornings. I have to act like everything is normal with them. That's how we start the healing with the town." He appraised the young woman. "You are the brave one, Eva. Smuggling gunpowder out of the factory into the camp under the guard's pointy Aryan noses. When the bombs exploded in the crematorium it was like God saying 'Hold on.'"

Eva shrugged. "It was a small act. The older women organized it. I just did what they told me. At that point, I didn't feel I had anything to lose. I didn't feel anything at all."

"Still, it was a brave thing. Maybe you didn't feel anything in your head or even in your heart, but deep in your soul a little spark of life was flaring up to say even in that hellhole you mattered. And you do."

The door of the Armin Hotel had been left unlocked. As she entered the small, musty lobby of the traveler's hotel, Eva could smell the despair from the last guests, probably out-of-town Jews who never finished their business in Laszlo nor advised their families they would not be coming home. The grey rug was threadbare from years of shuffling salesmen, and the cream-colored walls could not hide the mold of neglect. The dusty incandescent bulbs in the wall sconces gave off a tired yellow glow. Framed photographs of Charles IV, the last King of Hungary, a few politicians, and some sportsmen hung askew on the walls, their smiling faces unaware of what the war had done to their hosts. The lobby was clogged with boxes labeled "clothes—men" and "clothes—women and children."

Oskar gave a ragged laugh, edged with bitterness. "Guess they thought some children were coming back with us." The butcher squeezed his eyes shut for a long time. "Mine didn't." He exhaled angrily and dug around in a box until he found a belt. He held it up in triumph. "Finally! I can stop holding up these oversized pants like some Romanian country beggar." Eva stared at the buckle. She never thought something so small could give someone such a sense of dignity.

Oskar pulled a pair of three-quarter length trousers out of the box and put it against his body. "I'd look like a starving Russian peasant in these."

Yossel shook his head. "Be careful, Oskar. People in Laszlo might think you're a Communist if you wear those."

"I'm not, but why shouldn't I be? The Russians were the only ones who helped us. They pushed the Germans back and captured Budapest."

"Just the same," Yossel said. "We don't want to stand out or give people cause to talk about us."

Oskar threw the trousers back into the box, his face twisted in disgust. "I'd rather look like a Russian peasant than a Hungarian."

Mendel grabbed a red dress with puffy sleeves and a wide collar from one of the women's boxes and held it up. "Eva, this would be good at your new school."

Eva hid her reaction to the ugly dress. She did not need these used clothes, except for something to wear in the morning. Her closet at home was full of dresses, skirts, and blouses. "I might need something that loud to take people's minds off my playing. I'll need a lot of practice to be good enough for the Academy." The men stopped rummaging through the clothing and stared at Eva. Yossel gave her a surprised look.

"You are a wonderful pianist, Eva. I remember seeing you play on Revolution Day before we . . . were taken away. A little practice and you will have all those professors dropping their monocles in their teacups, just like before."

From the back of the room Herschel stuttered as he tried to speak. His words boomed across the room. "Yu . . . yu . . . you have to be great, Eva. You ha . . . have to make us proud."

Eva was taken aback by the first words she had ever heard from the lumbering Herschel. She thought that the last beating he received from the fleeing guards as the Russians advanced on Auschwitz had rendered him dumb. He seemed so docile, yet there was such conviction in his plea. She took in the hopeful faces of the men in the room, except for Naftali, who never glanced her way. She should have been comforted by such a show of support, but it settled on her shoulders like a heavy winter cloak. The women in the camp said Jews mitigate the distress of loneliness through communal compassion, but except for the baker, Eva didn't know any of these men. What did she represent to them? A lost daughter or sister? A community that no longer existed? She didn't want to be their Jewish hope for the future, she didn't want to be anybody's anything. Maybe she was being selfish, but the weight of her own grief was hard enough to bear without being responsible for anyone else's happiness.

Her silence hung in the room while Herschel waited expectantly for a reply. When none came, Eva and the men continued to open the boxes. Naftali stayed back, announcing he didn't want any of the clothing. Yossel went behind the reception counter to find keys for the rooms. Since the floors shared common bathrooms, it was decided that the men should stay on the first floor and Eva could have the second floor to herself. Naftali began to walk toward the door.

"Naftali, where are you going?" asked Yossel, standing with his hands full of keys.

Naftali turned and stared at the floor. "I must go home to Kosveg."

"Now?" Oskar protested as he adjusted his new belt again. "It'll be dark in a few hours. Wait until morning and some of us will go with you. The roads may not be safe for us yet."

Naftali refused politely, but agreed to take some bread that Oskar retrieved from the kitchen. After he left, Eva took a key from Yossel and walked toward the stairs.

"Do you think Naftali didn't want to stay in the hotel because a woman would be here? I've heard that the Hassids are strict about separating men and women. I hope he didn't leave because of me."

"I don't think so. He's haunted, like the rest of us. Naftali not only lost a family, he lost his entire world." He jingled the keys in his hand. "The Hassids up in Kosveg and those other little villages didn't have much to do with us before the deportation. Then one day they are snatched up, and when the door opens again they are with us in Auschwitz."

"They thought they were better than us, holier than us," Oskar murmured offhandedly as he poked a finger through a hole in an old shirt.

"And we thought we were better than they were, too. Right?" Yossel countered. "One thing we found out was that our petty differences didn't matter in the end. The Germans treated us all equally."

Oskar shrugged. "God treated us equally, too. He ignored the Hassids just like He ignored us." He picked up a hat embroidered with *Egon Pig Farm* and threw it to the floor. "What's Naftali hoping to find in Kosveg now? There's no one there."

Eva shook her head slowly. "I don't know. Maybe he's going to say goodbye."

CHAPTER 4

Naftali strode the few kilometers through the undulating hills between Laszlo and Kosveg, holding his bread tightly and humming a melancholy *niggun*. He was glad to be away from Laszlo, where modernity had tempted so many Jews away from the path of righteousness; riding and smoking on the Sabbath, mixing freely with women, ignoring the rituals. Coarse fellows like the butcher and the baker could barely read Hebrew and did not fast on *Yom Kippur*, the Day of Atonement. Even in the hell of the camp, men like them had denied what little Jewishness they kept in their lives. They died without repenting or chanting the required deathbed confessions. As the last Hassids in Auschwitz perished, Naftali could not find ten righteous men to form a *minyan* for proper prayers—these fallen Jews from town couldn't create the spiritual vortex needed to open the gates of Heaven. He had no one with whom to argue the finer points of Jewish law, *halacha*. There was no one left to share the mysteries of the *kabbalah*, the deep meanings of the numbers and the letters, the insights of the great rabbis of the past. His family, his friends, his teachers, the traders, the gossips—all consumed in the fires of the death camp. Although Naftali returned with the small band of Jews from Laszlo, he felt completely alone.

But now he was almost back in Kosveg. How many times had he travelled this dirt road accompanying his father, the Rabbi of Kosveg, to town to buy supplies? They would pass old men and their sons,

Hassids all, traveling the road from their small *shtetls* in the hills surrounding Laszlo, their carts full of wool to be processed, old kitchen utensils, clocks, and tools to be traded. Their black clothing, broad-brimmed hats and wild beards announcing their allegiance to the Hassidic path, a life of strict observance in thought and deed that brought awareness of *Ha Shem* into all things at every moment. The ruts of their carts remained like a worn trail of memory, although the spring rains had dulled the remembrance. This day neither the creaking of ancient, wooden wheels, the braying of mules, nor the harsh sound of country Yiddish challenged the mournful stillness. Naftali heard a rustling in the bushes and the occasional hush of whispers off the road, but paid no heed. It was surely the *mazzikin*, the forest goblins the local woodcutters conjured up to scare the children of Kosveg. They were following him, preparing some trick to add to his humiliation and despair.

The young man stopped at the top of one hill and surveyed the valley below. He tugged on the short, scraggly beard he was urging to grow back, hoping to pull some wisdom out of it as his father had always done. Why did the holiest of men, the Satmar Rebbi and the Belzer Rebbi, who guided their Hassidic courts, tell them everything would be fine and to stay in Hungary, only to flee to the Promised Land as the deportations began? Why did they go to the Promised Land by boat, when all of Kosveg went as ashes in the wind? Why did nothing terrible besides a few beatings and lack of food happen to Naftali in the camp? Why wouldn't *Ha Shem* let him suffer the same fate as the others? Why was he the only Hassid from the horror of Kosveg left alive, a lone cedar standing? What mission had *Ha Shem* prepared for him and when would it be revealed? The questions burrowed under his skin as tenaciously as field ticks in the summer.

Naftali continued laboring up the road until he climbed the last hill overlooking Kosveg. As he crested the hill, the low sun hit him hard in the eyes, a fierce, burning ball of judgment forcing him to his knees in supplication. He shielded his eyes with his hands and saw

Kosveg below. All twelve houses in the tiny hamlet were destroyed or heavily vandalized. Roofs and walls blackened by fire. Doors and windows ripped out or hanging on broken hinges on the few houses that stood by *Ha Shem's* grace. No smoke rose from evening chimneys or cooking fires. Neither sounds of prayer nor marital discord, nor the squeals of well-worn fiddles drifted up to greet him. He reached for positive thoughts, but the rush of memories and images merged Kosveg and camp, overwhelming Naftali. The weekly bathing in the men's *mikvah*, cleansing the body before the Sabbath. Men and women stripped naked and herded into showers together in the gray light of the camp. The *shofar* and clarinets played at Cousin Esther's wedding celebration in the village last spring mixed with the high-pitched screams of mothers being torn from their children while the inmate band played, and the trains muscled into the camp. The pungent smell of Sabbath dinner. The acrid odor of burning flesh. Prayers and holy chants. The repetitive thud of a baton on a lifeless body. The universe turned a searing red. He dropped to his knees, thrust his face into the dirt and screamed.

Naftali gathered himself off the ground to face what he most desired, yet dreaded. He wandered aimlessly through Kosveg, picking up a ladle here, a mauled prayer book there. Naftali thought he heard a wretched moan from the cool afternoon breeze, beseeching him to bring the *ruach*, *Ha Shem's* breath of life, back to the dead *shtetl*. He shivered, but ignored the plea. He had nothing to offer. He was as hollowed out as the village. He passed the wreckage of Shmuel's dry goods shop, the only one in the village, where he and his childhood friends would plead for a piece of licorice and receive a kick instead. He glanced into Feivel's smithy, but the clang of the hammer against the anvil and the pungent odor of rotting manure from the small stable were gone.

A small object half buried in the dirt outside the smithy caught his eye. It was a wooden block inscribed with *Aleph*, the first letter of the Hebrew alphabet and the first sound produced by *Ha Shem* breathing the universe into being. He knew that village parents soaked these blocks in honey so their children would associate learning with sweetness. He popped the block into his mouth and sucked hard, hoping for a trace of that beloved memory. It lay deep within the grains of the wooden block, or perhaps within his imagination. Naftali smiled and rocked back and forth, humming a *niggun.* He let the tangy sweetness expand throughout his mouth, his throat, his face, until his whole body delighted in the message from *Ha Shem* that under the dirt and decay, sweetness and joy always waited to be uncovered.

Naftali put the block in his pocket and summoned the courage to approach his home. One wall had collapsed, bringing the roof down to a slant, making the house appear like a decrepit shelter where lonely woodsmen lived deep in the forest. He walked up the three steps to the porch where his father, the rabbi, sat every Friday evening, his pockets jingling with coins for the town's children. He recalled his father crying out "Heavenly Father! Please send me poor Jews who I can give these coins to!" A last good deed before the family welcomed the *Shabbos* Bride, the *Shekinah.* Then the light of holy *Shabbos* would dispel the darkness of the world and peace would reign over all existence for a full night and day. Until the day it didn't. The day the German soldiers and the Laszlo police arrived. The day they herded the villagers and all the Hassids from the other *shtetls* surrounding Laszlo into the brick factory. The day the men were taken away on the trains and the women and children remained.

"I'm scared. I want to go home," Janos mumbled miserably.

"Quiet, you baby! He'll hear you," Viktor, the son of Sergeant Ritook, said as he threw a stick at the boy's head. "And watch where you're walking. Don't you remember anything about forest tracking?"

"Sorry." At six years old, Janos was four years younger than the other boys. "But the man looks so sad."

"He's just sad because he lost the war," Viktor said. "My father says the Jews were trying to take over the world so the Germans and our brave Hungarian army had to stop them. That's why we had a war."

"But didn't we surrender?" Gyorgi, the newest scout, adjusted his glasses and kept his voice to a whisper, less to alert the Jew than not to anger Viktor.

"Yeah, but at least we stopped the Jews, that's what really mattered."

The four boys crept stealthily through the woods, following the tall, skinny Jew as closely as they dared. They froze each time he stopped and turned around, but he didn't seem too interested in them. Viktor put up his hand, motioning for the boys to stop. He waited a few seconds until Naftali had gone further down the road, then he turned and grabbed the ear of Janos.

"Lucky for you he's too busy thinking about his buried treasure, otherwise he'd come over here and steal you for your blood."

Janos went pale. "For my blood?"

Viktor hissed angrily at the little boy. "Of course, stupid. Don't you know that Jews drain the blood of Christian children to make their bread?"

"Oh, stop scaring Janos," said Peter, who was taller than Viktor but not nearly as beefy. "Let's go back. That's enough for today."

Viktor gave Peter a withering look. "So you don't believe the Jews take children's blood? Everybody knows it's true. My father told me just last week in some town in Poland eighty children were murdered for their blood."

Peter laughed. "Yesterday you told me it was thirteen."

Viktor furrowed his brow and reached for a response. "They found more bodies!"

Gyorgi stepped between Viktor and Peter. "Come on, scouts. We should be getting back. You know our parents said we're not supposed to go near the old Jew town."

Viktor backed away from Peter and kicked at a stone. "Yeah, that's so we won't find the Jew's treasure before they do." Viktor hated being too young to help out in the war like his older brother. He couldn't even do messenger duties. Now he had an important mission. Find the Jewish treasure. "We all swore an oath to uphold our mission, right?" He looked at each boy for an answer. "Janos! What's the mission of the White Stag Scouts?"

The little boy stood at attention as straight as he could. "To pursue the White Stag for the joy of the chase, and onward to new trials and adventures."

"Good man. We know the Jews were all wealthy and hid their treasures before leaving, just like the ogres in the stories." Viktor watched as Janos's eyes widened. "That means our mission is to find their treasure before anyone else does." He puffed up his chest. "And who is the leader of our pack? Who is the only scout here who has the Wood Badge?"

"You are, Viktor," said Janos. Peter and Gyorgi looked down at the ground and mumbled their assent.

"That's right. So whatever I say goes. And I say that we keep watching that Jew until he leads us to his treasure."

CHAPTER 5

It was the same dream almost every night. The bright lights illuminated Eva's long fingers as they danced across the Bosendorfer keyboard in Budapest's Grand Hall. She felt elegant in the cerulean gown her mother had made, complemented by her luminescent gold and pearl necklace. The attention and adoration of the full house embraced her at the periphery of her awareness. Bach's *Brandenburg Concerto No. 3 in G-Major* filled the hall in three-quarter time.

sol fa Sol / re do Re / sol fa Sol / si la Si

As she performed, other sounds began to infiltrate the hall. The deep, slow rumble of a kettle drum did not distract her at first. Yet it grew louder, joined by *basso profundo* voices seeming to emanate from the ground beneath the stage. Eva fought to concentrate as the guttural assault from Wagner's *Twilight of the Gods* invaded her body. Men in SS uniforms filled the hall, chanting debased hymns while Wagner's warring Gods writhed in all-consuming flames above her. She struggled to continue but was overwhelmed by the furious sounds that engulfed the hall.

Eva woke to the crackle and smell of frying eggs. Even after the troubling dream, she didn't want to leave the rough comfort of the bed. It was the first time since the night before the deportation she had slept alone, with a real mattress, a sheet under her and a soft wool blanket. No prying eyes, no fetid breath from faces forced close together at night, no lice hopping from head to head, no whimpering or screaming during the night to escape a nightmare that couldn't possibly be worse than the realities of the daytime. But those horrors were over. The scrape of a spatula against the hot skillet brought her back. They were real eggs, not the powdered gruel prepared in the displaced persons camp.

She lay for a few minutes in her comfortable cocoon, humming Beethoven's *Spring Sonata* to accompany the movement of her fingers against the mattress. She warmed at the thought of how proud Professor Sandor would be to learn she had followed his advice to practice in her head when not at the piano. Even though he meant it for vacations or days off, the professor's advice kept her skills sharp and was essential to her survival at Auschwitz. It covered up the unending sounds of camp life. It took away the loneliness and filled up the rare silence when memory and loss would storm in and tear her apart.

Today Eva would play her piano again, working hard to be ready for Professor Sandor's return. He was strict and demanding, but the brief smile and nod he offered at the end of a good practice was worth the effort. She thanked God the SS officer at the selection had recognized him and sent him to Terezin to perform with the Jewish orchestra there. That guaranteed his survival. The SS officers laughed dismissively when the professor had pleaded to send Eva with him. They said there was no need for young pianists at Terezin. The Germans could choose among the best Jewish composers and musicians throughout the conquered lands. One officer took her hands in his reptilian grip, toyed suggestively with her long, delicate fingers, and said that instead of playing piano she was suited for the precision tasks at the munitions factory or the brothel.

Music had saved both their lives. Otherwise they would have joined her father and the other older men and women who clutched their small children as they were forced to run, run, run straight from the train into the "delousing" showers. *Move, Move!* Nobody questioned. Nobody had time to think. Gassed before anyone knew what gassing was. It happened too fast for Eva to understand it was the last time she would see her father. She never said goodbye. Her chest ached, but it was more than a physical pain. It was an emptiness starting somewhere outside of her and coalescing like a yawning chasm in her heart. No one else from Laszlo had come back from Auschwitz yet. She knew no one would. The entire community was gone. Professor Sandor was the only thread binding her past to her dreams for the future. She longed for his return.

Eva reluctantly got up and scanned the empty room. She was relieved she only had to stay one night in the sad hotel. Tonight she would sleep in her own soft bed, surrounded by the folk dolls of her childhood, the trinkets and souvenirs her father had bought on his frequent travels, her awards from piano competitions, and the photographs of her family during their many happy times. She wouldn't see her parents. She would never see them again. She hadn't really thought about what it would be like to live in her big house all alone. It would be full of photographs and memories. And her piano.

Eva sighed and chased the bittersweet images from her head for the moment. She knew when she let the feelings and thoughts overwhelm her, she could hardly move one foot in front of the other. It took a supreme act of will to free her mind. That was one of the gifts Professor Sandor had given her. Focus and willpower to practice when sick, to overcome the anxiety of a major performance. A skill that served her well.

She noticed a small, beveled mirror hanging on the wall. There were no mirrors in the camps, and her reflection in the puddles only warped her wan, bedraggled appearance. She steeled herself to see her own face for the first time in over a year. Her light brown hair had sprouted like shoots of spring grass since leaving the camp. It could almost pass as a fashionable bob. Perhaps she could walk the streets of Laszlo without a kerchief and not be self-conscious when she saw her friends from high school. But she was still so thin, her face so gaunt. She looked forward to retrieving her make-up kit from her room when she got home. Some rouge would bring color back to her cheeks. Eyeliner might take the hollowness out of her eyes. Eva realized she hadn't thought about make-up since before the deportation. She didn't care how she looked in the camp. Nobody noticed except the guards.

When Eva came down the stairs the men were already gathered at the few tables in the dining area, seated on old wooden chairs that squeaked and complained beneath them. She nodded and gave a slight, shy smile to each, and sat next to Yossel. He had set a fork, knife, and a cloth napkin at every chair as if the dingy hotel were a fine country inn. Eva hesitated to pick up the knife. There were no knives in the camp and the fear of punishment for having anything sharp hovered at the edge of her awareness. She willed herself to pick it up and spread butter across a slice of bread. Simple butter, fresh bread. How wonderful it tasted. She slipped a small piece of bread into her pocket.

Yossel gave her a sad grin. "You don't have to do that anymore, Eva. We are home and food will always be available."

Eva flushed and put her head down, but not before noticing Oskar had taken two pieces, stuffed them into his shirt and given her a wink while Yossel spoke.

The two farmhands babbled energetically at another table. Mendel stood and addressed the room. "We are going to the farm. When we get our jobs back we will bring you some fresh vegetables."

Herschel stared upwards with a dreamy look on his face. "I can't wait to see my Zsuzsa again. I hope she remembers me."

Yossel raised his eyebrows at the big man. "Herschel, I didn't know you had a girlfriend."

Herschel tilted his head in confusion. Mendel grinned and replied for his brother. "Zsuzsa is his cow, but he does love her a lot."

Yossel beamed. "And I can't wait to go to my bakery. Eva, it's on the way to your house. Let's walk together through town. We can go as far as the end of the square and head our separate ways. We need to be back at the town hall by ten." He rambled excitedly about rolling out *matzo* dough for the cutters to shape and perforate. He would bake French-style breakfast rolls, loaves of seeded rye and a few special pastries for the most valued customers. Eva's frown broke his reverie. "Let's not dwell on what happened, Eva. There is nothing that can be done except honoring the memory of our loved ones. Go back to your home. Play your piano again. We need to think of the future." He thumped his fist on the table. "And our future begins today."

Eva and Yossel stepped outside of the hotel. The professor said there was always music if you listened hard enough. Whether it is the wind swirling leaves on the sidewalk or birds' wings beating through the air, everything that rubs together creates a vibration, a sound. Often they are beyond our ears' range, he had said, but it is still important to know the music exists. Eva could rarely hear those kind of sounds, this subtle music, and she didn't spend much time listening for it. There certainly wasn't any music in the camp. If there was, it was drowned out by the sounds of suffering and inhumanity, alongside the noises of industrialized murder-trains screeching, metal doors sliding open, the low but constant background roar of gas ovens. How could anyone hear music in that?

They turned up the street toward the town square. The few people they passed either ignored them or gave a pleasant nod. Eva relaxed as she realized Oskar had been right—they were such a dirty, disheveled sight getting off the train that people recoiled from them. Now that they were cleaned up, rested, and dressed in ordinary clothes they blended back into Laszlo.

Eva looked up at the older buildings, some dating to the 1700s. They appeared to be off center by a degree or two. The barely perceptible, odd angularity made her feel uncomfortable. It was as if the balance of the world that had been thrown off by the war, by the camps, and everything was still askew. She wondered if it had always been that way.

"The town feels different, Yossel," Eva said as she continued to look upward and around. The doorways and window frames bent away from them at odd angles. The buildings either leaned in to loom over them in menace or shied away in alarm, whispering to each other in secretive tones, "Look! The Jews are back."

Yossel gave her a sympathetic, reassuring look. "The town is the same as it ever was, Eva. We are seeing it through different eyes."

Eva stopped to give the buildings time to become accustomed to her presence. Something else was wrong. She glanced at the different shops along the square. "Look at the names of the shops. Where are the Jewish names? There is Moises Shoes, but the sign says Schultz Emporium." She blinked and rubbed her eyes, hoping the vision would evaporate. But it didn't. She looked wildly around, her breath quickening. "And the old shops with the Yiddish signs on the other side of the street—the dried goods store and the fabric shop. The signs are in Hungarian now."

Yossel took in the shop names. Eva could see he was trying to remain calm, probably for her sake. "Well, there have been some changes since we were here last," he said. "That happens with businesses, especially during a war. Most small businesses only last three or four years anyway. Let's move on, we have happier places to go."

They walked closer together without realizing it, and soon entered the main square. The early morning light created long, jagged shadows across the square. Eva surveyed the square uneasily. She saw families huddled over small suitcases, looks of fear or resignation on the faces of the adults. Some women stood in clusters, fanning themselves and speaking in hushed tones. Children clung to their mothers' legs or ran around the square unsupervised and unaware. She tried to shout "Run! Run now!" but phantoms don't react to human voices. Something like a giant scythe sliced through the square and swept the vision away. Eva became disoriented and stumbled on the uneven surface of the cobblestones. She looked down and gasped.

"The paving stones! Why do they have Hebrew letters on them?" She bent to examine the stones. They differed in size and shape and were patched together over a small area of the square. Eva looked around to see if anyone was watching them as they crouched on the ground. "I can't read the letters. What do they say?"

Yossel squirmed. "They are old paving stones, I think. Probably needed during the war to repair the square. Temporary, I guess, until the town gets hold of regular pavers."

Eva sensed Yossel's discomfort. She pressed him. "Look there, a small angel. And here, some sort of scrolled border pattern." She choked out the words. "They look like broken up gravestones. Please tell me the truth. Don't try and protect me."

Yossel sighed. "They are gravestones. Must be from the old Jewish cemetery north of town." He ran his finger over some letters. "Here is a family name. 'Leib.' It means 'lion' in Yiddish. And there is the image of a lion above the name." He moved to another stone. "Here is some family's coat of arms." He shook his head wearily as he rubbed his chin. "Jews thinking they were royalty. That shows how much they felt accepted into Hungarian society."

Eva's stomach churned. She wanted to go to her home. She slipped on the slick marble surface of the gravestones as she started to get up. Yossel grabbed her elbow firmly, steering Eva off the gravestones and onto firmer footing.

They continued toward the other side of the square. Yossel wished Eva an enjoyable morning playing her piano and reminded her to be at the town hall by ten. He turned and hurried away, disappearing through a small crowd of people entering the square on their way to work in the early morning.

The wispy ground fog crawled through the square and snaked

around Eva's ankles. A tendril rose up and slithered down her neck. She felt a chill and began to shiver. Alone, she turned up Kossuth Street, passing the women's clothing store where her mother had bought her a green dress for a competition. It was the last time they went shopping together before her mother became completely bedridden. The styles in the windows did not seem different from a year earlier but the hems were almost to the ankle and the colors less vibrant. It was as if a prudish schoolteacher had ordered the girls to pull their skirts down to a prim and proper length.

The little music shop where Eva went to buy the scores required by Professor Sandor was abandoned. The sign over the door had been torn down. She peered through the dark window and saw the disorganized stacks of sheet music that covered every surface. There was Mr. Schenk, who could reach into those piles and find a Mahler score like a magician plucking the right card from a shuffled deck. A small boy stood at his side, holding a child's violin. Was that Izidor? Mr. Schenk turned to Eva and held up a sheet of music. Eva squinted to see it. Why was he showing her a Wagner score? Eva shook her head and blinked. The store was empty and dark. Of course it was, she thought as her heart clenched. Mr. Schenk had been in the same cattle car as she and her father. He had kindly stood with his back turned along with her father to allow Eva a modicum of privacy to use the overflowing toilet bucket in the corner of the packed car. Eva craned to see where the violins and violas hung from the ceiling, but hues of gray and black shadows hid anything remaining in the shop. She pulled herself back from the darkness, feeling the world tilting again. The shops, the square, the buildings—nothing felt familiar. She needed to get home before she was unable to remember the way. She hurried up the road.

Several young people sat on a bench in Orczy Park, just beyond the business area of town. Eva could not be sure from the distance, but she thought she recognized a few high school classmates. They would just be returning from their first year at university. The tallest girl with blond braids looked like Hanna, who sometimes played chess with Eva after school. They glanced toward Eva and then returned to their conversation. Eva realized she was not ready to see anybody she knew from before the deportation. Anyway, they would not recognize her short hair and haggard face. If they were younger, they might think she was *Babak*, a witch, and run away. Small children giggled and screamed with pleasure on the metal swings and the seesaw, but Eva didn't recognize any of them. She turned onto Alpar Road, named after the architect who designed the grand houses along the wide street, and saw the whitewashed stone wall that surrounded her family home. She quickened her pace until she stood in front of the white, two-story house with marble angels on each side of the polished oak front door. The muscles in her jaw relaxed. She was finally home.

Eva could see her room on the second floor to the right, shaded in part by a large lilac bush in full early bloom. Her father would shake its branches, liberating sweet-smelling purple flowers as Eva spun around beneath the magical shower. Her brief smile at the memory was wiped away by the realization she would never have that experience again. Her father was gone. She could not use any other word. *Gone* was clean and emotionless. It was all she could take in for now.

Eva approached the front door. She tried the handle but it was locked. She rapped on the heavy brass knocker and waited for the housekeeper, Mira, to open the door. Had the knocker always been a fist? It was the clenched leather hand that smashed her father to the ground and sent his thick glasses flying when he tried to hold on to Eva at the selection. The fist pulsed, eager to grab her hair. She blinked and it turned static again. She heard the approach of footsteps, the *click-step click-step* of high heels against the hardwood floor in the entryway.

Eva remembered her mother's elegant shoes making the same sound when she walked through the house before she became bedridden. Her fingers twitched out the Brahms lullaby she played to bring peace to her mother during those last hard months before the illness stole her away. Eva was still mourning the loss of her mother when the deportation brought all love and remembrance to a dead stop. She missed her mother terribly, but was grateful she had died before the deportation and didn't have to perish in the madness that followed.

The door jerked open. Eva saw her mother standing before her, wearing her favorite pinstriped dress, the one she had worn to Eva's recital before becoming too ill to attend any others. She wore the gold and pearl necklace she had promised to give to Eva one day when she performed in Budapest. But Eva's mother was dead. Eva's vision blurred. Her heart beat painfully fast and hard. She grabbed for a rational thought, but her mind and body stood frozen in place.

The phantom eyed her coldly. "Can I help you?"

Eva tried to speak but nothing would pass through her suddenly swollen throat. She motioned toward the necklace. "M—M—Mother?"

"We don't give to beggars, and we have no work here."

The curt comment snapped Eva from her strange vision. A vaguely familiar, squat woman confronted her. She was wearing Eva's mother's clothes and jewelry. The woman began to close the door, a dismissive look on her pinched face.

Words burst from Eva's mouth. "I am Eva Fleiss! I live here!"

The woman stopped with the door half closed, hesitated, and opened it again. She squinted at Eva and her face paled. "You . . . you can't be Eva Fleiss. That girl is dead. All the Jews of Laszlo are dead. What a cruel joke. Have you no shame, girl? Go away!" She slammed the door shut.

"No! This is my house! I am Eva!" Eva screamed as she pounded on the door with her fists. "I am home. You must believe me. Please! They took my father and me away, but I came back!" A wave of nausea and dizziness crashed over Eva. She crumpled to the ground, leaned against the door, and sobbed heavily. Her hand stroked the door, pleading with the house to come to her aid. "I need to come in.

I need to play my piano to go to the Academy. I need to be home."

After a few minutes, a cautious voice came from behind the door. "What kind of piano is it?"

Eva stirred from her tears, sat up and wiped her nose on her sleeve. She was so drained that her response was monotone. "It is a black Bosendorfer grand. *Bosendorfer* is written in gold script on the front. There is a small gash in the *B* where the movers scraped it."

"Wait." The voice said sternly. The *click-step click-step* slowly faded, but returned shortly. The door opened again and the woman stared down at Eva with a face contorted by a mix of consternation and anger. She exhaled sharply, as if blowing a mosquito away from her face. "I don't know what to say to you. The war changed everything. This is my house now. My husband, the mayor, bought it when your family left. We have the deed. You have to talk to the town clerk if you want to understand any of this. There is nothing I can do for you. I am very, very sorry." The door closed firmly and did not open again.

CHAPTER 6

Yossel wandered in the opposite direction down Kossuth Street, where so many of the Jewish shops had been. As before, the names were changed with no evidence of their former Jewish owners. The *mezuzahs* that announced Jewish homes or shops had been torn off, leaving little shadows of unpainted surfaces on the door frames. Even the Hebrew letters inscribed in the granite of some of the older stores had been chiseled away. Yossel struggled to remember what shops those had been. He noted the absence of the salted herring sellers and the wagons full of used goods that lined the early morning streets. No hawkers' cries filled the air. A chill crept up his spine. In a generation, nobody would remember that Jews ever lived in Laszlo.

The baker tried to smile and nod as people passed. His efforts were infrequently rewarded with an ephemeral smile, but mostly people ignored him as if he weren't there, or visibly shrunk away as if he were a lost, wandering spirit. The Wandering Jew of Laszlo. Yossel unconsciously touched his heart, where the yellow star had been on his clothing a year before. He passed the synagogue on his right. The building was abandoned and deformed as though the claws of a monstrous *verevolf* had scraped across its beautiful, sculpted facade. His heart sank as he considered that some of his neighbors and customers might have looted and defaced the exquisite sacred space. He stood staring at the synagogue for a long time, wondering which of the people passing him had thrown the stones that shattered the beautiful oval stained glass above the door. A tingle of fear came over Yossel as he considered the people on the street. Who had been a member of the Arrow Cross? Who kept silent? Who felt shame and who didn't care? Yossel realized that he couldn't read the people walking by; everything was locked behind masks of politeness or indifference, or obscured in the morning half-light. Were people lost in their own thoughts of family and work or were they trying to hide their sins? He had no bearings in Laszlo anymore. He needed to get to his bakery.

Yossel smelled the baking bread a block before reaching the bakery. He could tell they were almost ready, and wondered if his assistant had properly oiled the loaves before putting them deep in the wood-fired oven. As he approached the front of the bakery he let out a long nervous breath—the *Yossel's Bakery* sign was still intact. It was the only Jewish shop sign he had seen. He smiled and thought perhaps things weren't as bad as they originally seemed. He pushed the shop door open to the tinkle of the small bell he had placed over it to alert the employees that someone had entered. The racks behind the counter were half-full, indicating that the usual customers had picked up bread on their way to work, but the pastry shelf was empty. Where were the raspberry cream roulades, the seven-layer chocolate tortes, the honey walnut *kolachi* rolls and the simple *kiffles* that were the gems of Laszlo? Yossel made a mental note to twist the ear of his young assistant for being so lazy when the morning was the best time to sell his popular pastries.

A grumble of "I'm coming, I'm coming" drew Yossel's attention to the curtain separating the shop from the kitchen. A chunky, beetle-browed man with hairy arms covered in flour emerged with a limp from behind the curtain. The baker recognized him as Krauss, the man who delivered flour from the mill every week. Yossel was more confused than upset that the man was behind his counter.

"Krauss, what are you doing in my kitchen?"

The man startled and put out his hands defensively. "Your kitchen?

Who the hell are you? This is my kitchen." He staggered back a step when he recognized Yossel and saw his stunned expression. "Oh my God, Yossel! What happened to you? What are you doing here?"

"I . . . I have come back to my shop." He looked around the bakery.

Krauss frowned and wrung his hands together, raising a small cloud of flour. "Look, Yossel, you have to understand. The place was deserted, the flour was rancid and rats were living in the grain bins. You shouldn't have stayed away so long, Yossel. The place had gone to hell. The town condemned the bakery." He wiped the beads of sweat from his brow with his apron, creating a streak of white paste like the Christian ashes from Lent. "When I came back from the Russian front with this leg wound I bought it cheap. It was a benefit for wounded veterans. I can't straighten my leg so I couldn't drive the delivery truck anymore. I have spent all my savings and taken out a big loan to bring this place back." His face softened. "I kept the name out of respect for you."

Yossel stepped past Krauss and stuck his head through the curtain into the kitchen area. Three people splattered with flour stared up from their stations. Yossel didn't recognize any of them. They were all making wheat bread. Nobody was rolling out the unleavened dough for the *matzo*, nor rolling the perforator over the dough to guarantee its uniform drying. His *matzo* tools hung forlorn and ignored on the wall. He walked back toward the door on wobbly legs and leaned against the doorframe for support. The *mezuzah* was gone.

The door opened and the little bell tinkled as a large woman entered the bakery. She seemed flustered and in a hurry, immediately demanding her two loaves of rye. As Krauss scurried behind the counter to grab and wrap the breads the woman glanced at Yossel. She turned away indifferently but quickly looked back, her eyes bulging.

"Yossel! Is that you? Thank God you've returned. Are you baking again? I have missed my *kiffles* so much." She put a hand on her generous middle. "Although you wouldn't know I haven't had one in a year," she carried on gaily.

Yossel was warmed by her enthusiasm. "Thank you, Mrs. Gondor. It is good to see you again. How is your husband's gout?"

The woman smiled broadly. "He is well, Yossel, and thank you for asking. You always cared about your customers." She looked sternly at Krauss, then returned her pleasant gaze to Yossel. "And your breads and pastries are the best in Laszlo. I am so looking forward to your baking again. Everyone in town is, I'm sure."

An awkward silence hung in the air as the woman left the bakery to the tinkle of the bell. Krauss wiped the counter with a rag and straightened some loaves of bread on the rack. Finally, he turned to Yossel.

"I am not a baker, Yossel. And I am not a manager. For the past six months I have heard nothing but complaints from the customers. 'This doesn't taste like Yossel's bread,' or 'Why isn't there more powdered sugar on the tortes?' I can't make them happy and I can't stand the criticism. All I wanted was a business to support me and my family. Yossel, I never wanted to do you any harm. I felt awful when you Jews were taken away, but what could I do about it? I didn't want to join the army and fight the Russians either, but what could I do about that?" He looked at Yossel imploringly. "You know all of these people. You know what they want and how to bake so many things. Yossel, maybe you could come and work with me, maybe you could be the manager. What do you think about that?"

Yossel was stunned by the turn of events. Of course he wanted to bake again and take pride in the reaction of the customers, *his* customers, to what he created. Maybe this was God's plan after all. Yossel had suffered, survived, and now was being rewarded. Yossel knew in his heart that people were good. The war was an aberration, a plague of German locusts that swept across the land and had finally abated. He wanted to rebuild his good life.

A young boy came out from the kitchen carrying four loaves of bread. He stopped and regarded Yossel with curiosity for a moment, then placed the loaves on the shelf and retreated to the kitchen. The baker watched the boy and turned back to Yossel.

"That's my son, my assistant. He will be a great baker when he grows up. Maybe you could teach him. This will be his place someday. All I ever wanted was for my son to have a trade, maybe own a business so he wouldn't grow up poor and disrespected like his father." He stared sympathetically at Yossel. "You're a bachelor. You never had children, did you, Yossel?"

Yossel and Oskar arrived early for the meeting with the town clerk, eager to get their property back. They sat on the hard wooden bench outside the office as town employees bustled past them with barely a notice. Yossel listened to the loud tick of the Vienna Regulator wall clock over the bench.

"Where are the others?" the baker asked.

Oscar rubbed his unshaven chin. "The brothers are off to Karosi's farm to see if they can get their jobs back. I haven't seen Eva this morning, but I heard her crying in her room. I didn't want to bother her. I figured we could share whatever we learned with them later."

Yossel explained the visit to his former bakery. "You see? There are good people in Laszlo. We had to wait for this hatred to pass and now we can live again in harmony."

"You have it backward, my friend. We have to wait for the harmony to pass before the hatred returns. You can have a good life until the next tragedy." Oskar kept balling his fists as his eyes expressed increasing anger. "I went to my apartment and got chased away by the new tenants. They told me all my things were gone, either stolen or thrown away. My whole life, Yossel. My wife, my two sons. Anything I could hold onto. Thrown away." He reached up and pushed away a tear. "Then I went to old Schiff's butcher shop. It's being run by that *goy* Egon who has the pig farm out of town. He said there's no call for a kosher butcher in Laszlo anymore, but he has some work for me. Maybe more as business picks up. I need the work, I guess. Pigs are better than nothing. He said I could use a corner of the kitchen for kosher if I wanted it. But if my only customers are the few of us I might as well use the kitchen at the hotel."

Yossel smiled hopefully. "It would be nice to taste real chicken soup again."

"Maybe. To me, any soup will taste of ashes for a long time." The butcher scratched his head. "Something is going on here in Laszlo. I don't understand it and I don't like it."

"My friend, I know how much you have suffered, but you've got to clear the blood out of your eyes and see some of the good around us. The town clerk will help us figure out how to get back our properties and move forward. Please, please just be a little patient."

The office door office opened abruptly at the stroke of ten. A stiff-backed woman with thinning brown hair pulled into a tight bun directed the men into the office. Tomas Kador, the town clerk, nodded politely and motioned them to pull up chairs and sit before his desk. His face displayed no emotion.

"Gentlemen, let me be blunt. The return of our Jewish citizens to Laszlo presents certain administrative challenges. First, the question of housing and welfare. Fortunately, the good people of Laszlo have provided you with housing, food, and clothing until you are back on your feet. That, of course, is a temporary solution. The World Jewish Congress—"

"The what?" Yossel cut in.

"The World Jewish Congress. It is an international support group for resettling Jewish refugees, among other things. The Congress has made funds available for you, a portion of which the town is using for non-Jewish war veterans as per our agreement. Of course, the rent and expenses for the hotel have been deducted. The funds will allow you to recuperate from your experience and make arrangements for transition to more suitable locations. The Congress will help you locate relatives or friends in England, America, or elsewhere, arrange transportation and so on. Any questions?"

Yossel's head was spinning. "Wait, wait. Why are you taking money meant for us? And we aren't thinking about going anywhere. We are Hungarians, not Englishmen. We are from Laszlo. We are home." He looked at Oskar in confusion. The butcher shook his large fist at Tomas.

"You deported us as Jews, then welcomed us back as Hungarians? Now you tell us to leave again? We've lived in this town all our lives and our parents and grandparents before us. We belong here and are going to stay. We want our homes and our businesses back."

Tomas took off his glasses and cleaned them on his narrow tie. "Please, you must understand our difficult situation. The war upset all our orderly processes. Old laws, new laws, missing deeds, lost contracts, who is alive, who is not. It's an administrative nightmare." He blinked several times and returned his glasses to their proper place. "Of course, as citizens of Hungary you have the right to live anywhere in our country you choose. But given the realities of the situation, the town thought it best if you were resettled somewhere with more opportunity and a more . . . *similar* community. You must know that many of the Jewish citizens of Hungary are leaving. It is understandable and it is our civic obligation to help you. When you are ready we will begin to process you—"

"Process us!" Oskar yanked his left sleeve up to reveal the tattoo *3594-A* carved into his thin, hairy, shaking arm. "We've been processed enough!"

Tomas pushed backward in his chair at the sight. "Please, put that away."

Yossel felt like he was being herded into a corner, but he needed to remain calm and not alienate the town clerk. He watched passively as Oskar struggled to control himself. The butcher seemed to be gasping for breath or comprehension.

"Is that why you stole Yossel's bakery and all our property while we were in the death camp, to leave us no choice but to go away if we ever came back? Or did you just hope we'd never return?"

"Oh, oh. No!" Tomas put his hand to his heart, a pained look spread across his face. "Nothing of the sort. You must understand. Any property abandoned by its owner, whether business or personal, is subject to confiscation by the state or the town. Property must remain in productive use for the good of the community, for health reasons, for the tax base, and so on. This is not aimed at our Jewish citizens. This is the law for everybody."

Oskar raised both fists before him. "Not aimed at us? We were barely gone for a year and you know why. Because the good people of Laszlo gave us to the Nazis. How sad they looked as we were marched away, except for the ones who jeered at us. How quickly they turned around and grabbed everything we owned." He unclenched his fists and exhaled a chest full of anguish. "Look, Mr. Kador, what do we have to do to get our properties back? Yossel needs his bakery. All of us had apartments or houses. What do we do about those?"

Yossel noticed Tomas was sweating heavily under his suit jacket. "There are procedures for reclaiming property, and very specific procedures for reclaiming Jewish property confiscated after abandonment in the war. Well, actually, those new rules are going through the legislative process in Budapest but should be enacted soon."

"And what do the rules say about my family photographs, my child's toys, the touch of my wife's hand, our memories?" Oskar's eyes bulged. Yossel could see the butcher's rage building again. He put his hand on Oskar's arm to calm him.

"How do we get them back, Mr. Kador?" the baker asked.

Tomas stiffened. "I can only suggest you retain a lawyer to assist you."

"Who?" Oscar blurted, "Jacob Fleiss? He was the only Jewish lawyer in Laszlo and he was gassed and murdered as soon as we got to the camp."

Tomas cringed. "I'm sorry. I really don't know anything about that. You might find legal counsel in other towns. There are many good lawyers in Hungary, you know." He stood up and motioned toward the door. "Now please, I have other appointments today."

The men left the office with shoulders slumped. Yossel turned back to Tomas. "One other thing, if I may, Mr. Kador. On my way here this morning I walked on top of Jewish gravestones that were broken up and used to pave the square." Yossel imagined the names, dates, and family histories inexorably being ground away under foot, wheel, and hoof. A subtle, sure way of erasing Jewish memory from Laszlo.

"Yes, an unfortunate incident that happened when the Arrow Cross was in control."

"Well, we would like them replaced and we want to return the gravestones to our cemetery."

The town clerk pursed his lips. "Of course, of course. I will notify the planning board and if they approve at their next meeting they will put in a work order to the road department."

Oskar swelled with frustration. "Why don't we just dig up the headstones ourselves? You can fill in the holes when your meetings and approvals are done."

Tomas looked astonished. "You can't just dig up a public way. There have to be permits, funds allotted. There is a procedure that must be followed and a long list of public works that take priority over paving projects. The rules are the rules. They apply to all Hungarians equally. If we made a special exemption for our Jewish citizens, the whole town would resent it. We certainly don't need to create bad feelings at such a tenuous time, do we? Now please, I must get on to my next meeting."

CHAPTER 7

Mayor Kodaly came home for lunch on Friday after a long morning reading ministerial reports on reconstruction, listening to complaining pensioners and ex-soldiers, and trying to reconcile the town's shrunken revenues with its growing needs. He sat down wearily at the long antique oak table in the dining room, next to his wife. She dished some goulash onto his plate, careful not to chip its delicate edge with the heavy silver ladle. The mayor inhaled the scent of braised beef, vegetables, and a touch of red wine in the thick, steaming stew. The moist scent revived his sagging spirits. *Marhahus gulyas*, beef goulash, was his favorite meal.

"And how has your day been so far, dear?" The mayor asked, as he always did.

"Actually, Ferenc, a disturbing thing happened to me this morning."

Ferenc put down his spoon and gave his wife a look of concern. The end of the war had not calmed her nerves as he had hoped. She seemed to have gotten more high-strung since it ended. Perhaps seeing so many haggard young soldiers returning, or the new threat of Russians occupying parts of the country so close to Laszlo. He had become increasingly afraid to confront his wife about anything for fear of a volatile response. "What do you mean, Greta?"

"Well, I had a visit from a young woman. She frightened me because she was so unhealthy looking and her clothes were so ill fitting."

"A Romanian beggar?" The war had turned the occasional visits by wandering Romanians into a flood of ragged refugees. Budapest had promised assistance, but despite the mayor's constant telegrams, it fell to Laszlo to offer meagre food and clothing. The town had lost many of its own sons to the war in body and in mind, there was little appetite to help the stranger.

"That's what I thought." She ladled more goulash onto her husband's plate. "But then she said she was Eva Fleiss. Imagine my shock. Eva Fleiss, alive and at my door. Did you know she was coming back to Laszlo?"

Ferenc briefly choked on a chunk of beef. "I knew a few Jews were returning yesterday, but I didn't know who. Frankly, I have been so busy I didn't have time to welcome them back yet." He gazed off, hearing the girl's sweet music envelop the room as it had so many times when he had reviewed legal documents with Jacob at this very table. "Young Eva. And Jacob? Is he back as well?"

"I don't think so. She was alone and didn't mention it, though she was quite hysterical." She sipped at her wine. "She said this was *her* home and she wanted to come in and play *her* piano. She said she had to go to the Academy in Budapest. Isn't that strange?"

The mayor cradled his chin in his hand. He remembered how elated Jacob had been when Eva was accepted into the Academy. She was the first student from Laszlo ever to be offered admission. "But dear, this *is* her home. You know we only took ownership until Jacob came back. I didn't want his property to be vandalized and plundered, or fall into the hands of anyone else, especially those who pushed so hard to deport him and the others." He thought of the roving bands of men and women who ransacked Jewish houses almost before the deportation train had left the station that sad day. "You know how many people coveted this house. Jacob signed it over to us specifically for that reason."

Greta's face flushed with emotion. "But Jacob isn't coming back and the girl is too young to own and maintain a house."

Ferenc looked apprehensively at his wife. Over time, Greta had gotten increasingly comfortable in the house, and in Miriam Fleiss's clothing and jewelry. Miriam had passed away six months before the deportation, and Jacob was honoring the Jewish custom of remembrance that lasted a full year, including keeping all of her worldly possessions in place. When they moved into the house, the mayor felt like he was visiting someone's sacred space. He tried to speak gently.

"You know, my dear, we will have to return the house and all the Fleiss's things. It was my promise to Jacob. It is our Christian obligation."

Greta threw down her spoon, cracking her plate. The stew juices leaked over the table. "No! I won't! I donated all of my clothes to the war refugees last winter. These are the only clothes I have now." The mayor's wife smoothed the dress lovingly with both hands. "These are my things, my house now. We have cared for them all this time and Jacob is gone." She began to weep, her tone pleading but her eyes accusing. "I never had things as nice as these. You weren't as clever as the Jews who became lawyers and doctors and owned all the businesses. They were always better off than we were. I refuse to let this go. Tell the girl to go away."

"But Greta, think of what the girl has gone through."

"Think about her? If it weren't for the Jews, the Germans never would have invaded. The war would have stayed out there in Romania and Poland. Things have finally settled down now that the terrible war is over. Why do those Jews have to come back and upset everything again? Ferenc, please send them away." She put her face in her hands and sobbed uncontrollably. "Send them away."

The Jews were returning. It was the mayor's most fervent hope and his biggest fear. He had tried to maintain normalcy in Laszlo when the war started by ignoring the changing laws that forced Jews to sell their property, and limited their attendance at universities and ownership of businesses. He dismissed the dehumanizing propaganda claiming the Jews had started the war. But it was like trying to hold back a flood. Even a minor town like Laszlo, so far from the capital, felt the seams of society ripping apart. Jewish slurs became more frequent, schoolyard bullying increased, neighbors began to avoid Jewish neighbors. It all happened so quickly. Hungary's sophisticated society simply collapsed.

Still, Ferenc held out hope that Laszlo, with its highly assimilated population of middle class and professional Jews, would be spared. Laszlo was an island of peace in the eye of a storm of blood. Yet, a week after the German invasion, Jacob and all of the Jews were rounded up at the town square with little warning. The mayor barely had time for a clandestine meeting with Jacob the night before the deportation to sign the deed over, his firm handshake sealing a solemn promise to an old friend.

Ferenc put his hand on his wife's shoulder as she cried. He knew she was lonely in this big house. They had left their old community of close friends to move into this affluent Jewish section of Laszlo. Their new neighbors were a random assortment of townspeople who had moved into the big houses quickly. Greta had become infected by the same disease as many in Laszlo. Grab the easy wealth. Tear up the floorboards, dig in the basements and fields for the mostly imaginary treasures. Forget friendships, ignore the gruesome rumors about the camps. By law the Jews were no longer Hungarians, no matter how many generations they lived here or how long ago they had intermarried.

After the coup, when the fascist Arrow Cross became so emboldened, Ferenc could no longer ignore their demands. Overnight the entire apparatus of the state united in one goal—rid Hungary of the Jews. The deep well of greed, fear, hatred, and envy that was always beneath the surface when it came to the Jews rose up. It drowned the decency and the social order that kept people's baser instincts checked. What would it take to push it down again? How could Jews once more find a semblance of justice and comfort in Laszlo? Was there even a place for Jews in Laszlo anymore?

The goulash had gone cold. The mayor took his wife's broken plate into the kitchen. As he passed through the dining room, he could see into the library that housed Jacob Fleiss's impressive book collection, and the piano that held his daughter's dreams.

CHAPTER 8

When she returned to the hotel, Eva tore off her donated clothes and plunged under the covers of her bed. In a troubled sleep, she performed *Danse Infernale* from Stravinsky's "The Firebird" at the Grand Hall. Her fingers disappeared in a blur of overlapping octaves as she brought the composer's exotic pallet of colors and textures to life. Again, she played to a full house of German officers, but this time she was wearing a white silk gown. As the tempo slowed she looked down and noticed the small red spot forming in her lap. *No, no, not now!* She couldn't allow the audience to see the spot. Almost all the women in her barracks had ceased to menstruate within a month or so of incarceration. There were no menstrual pads and few opportunities to wash the blood off the striped smocks they wore. An older woman in her barrack said that the Germans wanted to make sure there was no possibility for reproduction, no "making more Jewish vermin," and that was why the guards would beat women who bled. Nobody knew if it was the poor camp diet or their bodies' innate sense of survival that stemmed their monthly flow. Eva had been terrified when she bled that first month, but some of the women helped her clean up and hide it for the next few days. She hadn't bled since. Even though the war was over the same dream visited her regularly. Eva startled awake, whipped off the blanket and searched for the spot. Nothing.

Eva spent the whole of Friday afternoon paralyzed under the

blanket, not knowing what to do. She fell in and out of deeply distressing sleep. Her mind careened randomly between family memories, her mother so pretty in her pinstriped dress, the smells and sounds of the camp, and the surreal, disturbing visit to her house. She didn't want to leave the bed. Where could she go? There was no one left for her in Laszlo. She did have an aunt in Belgium somewhere, if that family survived the war. Should she wait for Professor Sandor to return? She had to. They could go to Budapest together. After all, there was nothing left for him in Laszlo either. Most of his students had been Jewish. As she imagined going to the Academy with the professor, Pachelbel's *Canon in D* began to drift into her ears. It soothed her. She played along with it, her fingers picking out the melody as she hummed softly. She slowly surfaced from her drowsy state and realized that the music was real. She got up and threw water on her face.

Eva wandered down the stairs, through the dining area and into the kitchen. The music was coming from a small Orion Nepradio in a brown Bakelite housing that perched on the counter. Yossel hummed along to the silky Pachelbel piece as he kneaded dough on the steel table in the middle of the room. He looked up with a sad smile.

"It's the BBC. We can finally listen to music again."

Eva remembered how for months before the deportation, her beloved Radio Budapest played less and less music. Instead, increasingly strident special news reports told of Jewish politicians betraying the government, and Jewish businessmen stealing their employees' wages and sending the money out of the country. The barrage was relentless. Eva was forbidden from listening to the broadcasts, but she sat hidden behind the large newel post on the stairway every night after supper, frozen in anxiety at the announcer's voice. Her father tried in vain to tune in the BBC but the Germans were jamming foreign broadcasts, replacing elegant music with harsh static. Now, she was comforted that the music had returned.

Yossel looked down at the dough. "Have you ever made bread,

Eva? I am making *challah* for tonight. It's *Shabbos*."

Eva shook her head meekly. "We weren't that traditional." She admitted that her family rarely observed the Sabbath, only when they had guests who expected the Friday night ritual. When they did they bought the *challah* from Yossel's bakery. Yossel smiled and motioned her over to the table. He took a large knife and cut the dough in half, placing a lump before Eva.

"There's value in keeping traditions alive, even if you don't fill them with meaning. Maybe one day your child or grandchild will wonder what's behind this ritual and will search it out. Jews who light candles and eat *challah* on *Shabbos* are the keepers of memory even if they don't know it." She plied the dough uncertainly, her fingers one at a time gently poking as if trying out a new score. "Now put those talented fingers to work. Knead the bread firmly, roll it over and knead it some more."

Eva massaged and stretched the dough, becoming more confident in her movements. Yossel continued humming the melody from the radio.

"And as this is *challah* for *Shabbos*, while you are kneading think about all the people who've made this bread possible, all the hands that have touched it. The farmers who broadcast the seed, tended the field, and harvested the wheat. Think of the rain and sun that God sent to nourish the plants. Then there is the miller who cleaned and processed the wheat into flour. And the man who delivers the flour to the baker." A shadow crossed his face briefly. "Now think about our hands as we knead the dough and shape the *challah*. That's why at the end we braid the *challah*, to remember and honor all those hands working together to bring this to life."

Eva worked the dough methodically, turning and pressing, turning and pressing, until it became elastic in her hands. She let out a deep sigh and felt herself relax a little as she massaged the dough. Usually, her fingers bore down on hard piano keys not soft, pliable surfaces. It was comforting.

"These are the kind of daily miracles we overlook when we are so busy. This is why keeping *Shabbos* is so important. It gives us a moment to let go of the pain of the world. It reminds us that we are not alone in anything we do. It nourishes our souls."

The *challah* had merely been a beautiful bread before this moment. Now, Eva felt the connection Yossel spoke about. She realized Professor Sandor had talked the same way about music; her playing was part of a continuum from the composer, through the teacher, and out Eva's fingers. Just as with her weekly practice with the professor, working and then braiding the *challah* with Yossel was creating a personal bond between them. She was not alone. After Yossel put the braided dough into the oven, Eva told him about the visit. Why was the woman so cruel? How could Eva get her house back and play her piano? The baker sighed and turned down the radio.

"Eva, the world is so chaotic right now. The war is barely over and everyone is just trying to move on or make sense of the madness. We have suffered so much, but the people of Laszlo are in shock, too. Many of them lost sons and brothers in the war. Imagine being on the other side of that door for a moment. What a shock that woman must have felt when she opened it and realized who you were. We need to give this time. We must have faith that our neighbors will come to their senses and give us the justice we deserve. We have to be sensitive to their pain just as we want them to be sensitive to ours."

"Sensitive to *their* pain?"

Yossel and Eva turned to see Oskar charge into the kitchen.

"Their pain is nothing compared to ours. When we do *Shabbos* tonight and I reach out my hands to do the blessing over my children, no one will be there to receive it." He placed his hands out before him, then clenched them and drew them in to his chest. "I have nothing." His longing permeated the air.

Yossel tried to placate the distressed butcher. "Oskar, please, we were only—"

"And who's gonna come to their senses? The police are the same ones who loaded us away. The men who worked with the Arrow Cross and the Germans are still walking the streets in Laszlo. Their lives haven't changed—they just ditched their uniforms and put on street clothes. And those people who stole our homes and everything we owned? They will never give anything back. Did you tell Eva what the town clerk said? We are trapped in this damned hotel."

Eva gasped as a bolt of fear hit her chest. "They won't give my house back?" She looked at Yossel wild-eyed.

The baker moved his hands in a soothing motion, as if he was kneading the air. "Oskar, you heard the town clerk this morning. If people don't return our property, we have legal means."

Oskar barked a protest.

Yossel continued. "I know, I know. It won't be easy and it will take time, but there are good people in Laszlo. If we are cautious and follow the rules, we will recover what we've lost." He turned to Eva. "You'll see. And you will play your piano in your own house."

The butcher picked up a slab of dough, stared at it until his anger seemed dulled by sorrow, and thumped it back on the table. "You are right in one thing, Yossel, we have to be smart how we go about things. Some of the townspeople want to forget and move on, some may feel bad about what happened. But I'm telling you, the war may be over but hatred never surrendered. It was here long ago and will be here past our lifetimes. There are still plenty of people out there looking for an excuse to get rid of us once and for all."

Yossel let out a long, slow breath. "It's true, Oskar. Our people have been living with the fear of the next resurgence forever. That's why we hold on to hope, isn't it? Because we know that at the end of each torment is a period of sweet peace and prosperity. Round and round it goes. It's our inheritance. You can focus on the bad, or you can focus on the good. Tonight is *Shabbos*. Join us. Let's focus on the good, alright?"

"Alright, alright," Oskar mumbled as he sniffed the air. "If that's what it takes to eat that chicken you are cooking."

Eva stared down at the motley clothing on her bed. The only times she had participated in a Sabbath ritual the men wore dark suits and the women wore white. It was supposed to be a sign of purity, she guessed, but she didn't feel pure or innocent after Auschwitz. She grabbed a threadbare white sweater that was too small, but would at least pay homage to the ritual.

Four small tables had been huddled together in the dining area and covered with a white tablecloth. Two half-melted candles sat waiting in unadorned metal holders. Between the candles, Yossel's *challah* was under a white napkin. Eva remembered the host family letting the youngest child pull off the cloth when it was time for the blessing, asking "Who wants to wake up the *challah*?" Was that a tradition or just something that family did to keep the children engaged? She was self-conscious that Yossel would say that tonight. The baker was clattering away in the kitchen with final food preparation. The heavenly smell of spiced, roasted chicken permeated the air. The farmhands finished setting the table. Herschel put the knife and fork together on the right side of the plate while Mendel set the fork on the left and the knife on the right. Oskar was absent. Eva wondered if he was avoiding the ceremony but would come later for the chicken. She turned at the sound of muttering and heavy footsteps behind her. Oskar was fighting with a necktie, pulling it into a semblance of a Windsor knot like her father used to wear. Yossel came from the kitchen carrying a large chicken on a platter. He set it on the sideboard between bowls of potatoes and root vegetables. He was wearing a worn, collarless white shirt and his banker's silk vest. He turned around and smiled at the small gathering.

"We've all had a rough homecoming but here we are at our first Shabbos at home. Well, in Laszlo, at least. It is time to let go of the darkness of the world and enter into the holy light of *Shabbos*, where

God grants us peace." He looked at Oskar and shrugged. "For twenty-four hours, anyway."

Eva surveyed the faces around her as they took in Yossel's words. What did "peace" mean? It couldn't mean quiet in the world. Since the deportation, Eva knew nothing of the world except violence and the survival instincts of ordinary people. Maybe peace was something personal, internal. Just like what music offered in the worst times—if she could only access the feeling.

Yossel's soft voice interrupted her thoughts. "Eva, it's time to light the candles. As the woman in the house you have the privilege of reigniting the holy sparks." All of the men were staring at her, smiling. Were they expecting her to take on that role every week? The woman was the foundation of a Jewish home and she was the only Jewish woman in Laszlo so far. She wasn't going to stay at the hotel and didn't want to commit to going back there every Friday night. Or was Yossel just trying to respect the tradition? She could politely refuse. *Light it*, she commanded herself. *It's only a candle.* A box of wooden matches sat at the base of the candlesticks. She removed one match, rolled it around in her fingers and took a deep breath. Striking the match, she lit the first candle and moved the match to the second. The match burned down quickly, scorching the tips of her fingers. Eva stepped back and stared at the candles. The men looked at each other. Yossel cleared his throat.

"Let's close our eyes. Let the light fill the room and chase away this sad world, leaving only the light of creation that exists within all things at all times." The room became still. Yossel continued. "Eva, do you know the blessing?" Eva's heart began to pound. She didn't really know the blessing because her family didn't celebrate the Sabbath and she vaguely listened when others did it. In the camp, on the rare occasion a candle could be made or stolen, the blessings were barely whispered so as not to attract attention from the guards.

"I think I do," Eva stuttered from behind closed eyes. She began to mumble in an unsteady voice.

"Baruch ata Adonai, Eloheinu melech ha olam . . .
Asher kid'shanu bemitzvotav . . . V'tsivanu . . . v'tsivanu . . ."

Herschel thundered happily, *"V'tsivanu l'hadlik ner shel Shabbat!"*

Eva slowly lowered her hands. She peeked through loosening lids. It was as she feared. Beyond the glow of the candles, everything was the same. Yossel swayed with a beatific smile. Oskar seemed to be ruminating, chewing on something and deciding whether it was palatable. The two farmhands stood respectfully, Mendel apparently lost in thought and Herschel smiling as he rolled his head from side to side.

"I can see the light even with my eyes closed!" Herschel observed with wonder.

Yossel stared at the flames. "It is good to see the light again. And to have real candles. What a blessing! I remember in the camp, someone hollowed out a rotten potato and stuffed it with a rag soaked in machine oil from the factory. We lit that smoldering, foul smelling thing. And it brought light. Even within the rot and wretchedness, the light is always there." He blinked, rubbed his eyes, and looked toward Eva. "Were you able to light candles in the women's barracks?"

Eva furrowed her brow. It was so hard to wallow in the mud of painful memories from the camp, and yet, she did see a light there. "There was one woman in the barrack. She took the margarine they gave us once a week. You remember, less than a spoonful. She saved it up and when she had enough she took a thread from the hem of her smock and rolled it inside the margarine into a little candle. I don't know how she knew when the Sabbath was. Every day and every night were the same. But she knew. She lit the little candle and we gathered around. Someone whispered the blessing. That was all we could do, and it wasn't every week. But I do remember how the women seemed to breathe deeper when the candle was lit." Eva stared at the sputtering candlelight. "I guess there is light behind the darkness. But it is so hard to see."

Yossel held up a small cup filled to the brim with red wine. "*Kiddush*. Blessing the fruit of the vine. This wine represents all of the abundance in our lives that God has given us. Look, even at the worst of times, no matter how difficult it is to feel grateful to God for this life, we are overflowing with grace." He held the cup higher.

> "*Baruch ata Adonai, Eloheinu melech ha olam*
> *Borei p'ree ha gafen*"

Eva watched the candlelight glisten off the top of the wine as Yossel took a sip and passed the cup to Oskar. The butcher struggled with some mumbled words, took a sip of wine, and passed it to the farmhands. When the cup came to Eva, it was half full. *I can't see my blessings overflowing,* she thought, *but I guess I am grateful to be alive.* She looked around the table at the few surviving Jews of Laszlo as she brought the sour wine to her lips. Each of them was probably struggling with similar thoughts. Oskar reached out with his eyes closed as if to bless his missing children.

Without family, without friends, without anything, it was hard to feel gratitude. But Eva did have her house and piano at least, even if it would take a while to get them back. And she had the professor's return to look forward to. She had more to be grateful for than the others.

Yossel removed the covering off the *challah*. "I know we're supposed to have two loaves, but this was all the flour I had in the kitchen. We can be grateful for at least that." He held up the *challah*. Everyone recited the blessing.

> "*Baruch ata Adonai, Eloheinu melech ha olam*
> *Ha motzi lechem min ha'aretz*"

Eva thought about how her life had been braided together with these men at this moment. Shared tragedy, shared survival. But this was only temporary. Step by step, she needed to braid a new life without her parents and friends. The piano and the professor were the only ingredients she had to work with.

CHAPTER 9

Early Saturday morning the mayor walked to the hotel. He would have preferred to drive the shiny, powerful red Chrysler Imperial in his garage, but it had belonged to Jacob Fleiss and although Ferenc used it every day, he didn't want to upset Eva when they met. Oskar answered the knock on the hotel door. He looked warily at the visitor. The mayor carried a box of fresh pastries and a friendly smile.

"Good morning. I am Mayor Kodaly. I have come to officially welcome you home." As the men came out of their rooms, Ferenc's brightness contrasted sharply with their reticence to speak. He made some generic comments about how valuable the Jewish citizens were to Laszlo. Finally, he said "I understand Eva Fleiss has returned as well. May I see her?"

Eva came down the stairs and sat with the mayor. He had expected the shy, pretty girl he remembered from her stunning piano performances and his visits to the Fleiss household, but the drawn waif who appeared shocked him. Thick-lidded, dull orbs that guarded whatever was within had replaced those blue-green eyes that sparkled when she played. She was thin, as were the others who came back, but Eva's posture belied something else—a sadness or sickness lodged deep within her. Ferenc felt a welling up in his eyes and a tightening in his throat. He had seen Hungarian soldiers coming back from the war dirty and disheveled, but these were the first Jews to return to Laszlo. If the rumors were true, they had experienced unimaginable horrors. He had heard that they all carried dehumanizing numbers tattooed on their arms hidden beneath their sweaters, but their trauma and grief were clearly etched in their faces, especially Eva's.

Ferenc felt a greasiness in his gut as he realized that maybe what he thought were his acts of resistance by dragging his feet on implementation of the anti-Jewish laws hadn't accomplished anything in the end. By letting the gossip spread and the propaganda against even his friends go unchallenged, was he ultimately complicit in the results? Feelings of shame began to tug at his awareness. He tried to look around the room with a cheerful expression to break the sorrow that was overtaking him. Yossel put the pastries on a tray and brought a small coffee for the mayor. Yossel and Oskar hovered for a minute until it became clear from the silence that Ferenc wanted to talk to Eva alone. They begrudgingly went into the kitchen. The mayor sipped at his coffee and placed the cup on the end table next to his chair.

"I was just looking at your piano this morning. I remember you playing at the high school graduation and some of your other performances. I remember how proud your father was."

Eva winced at the mention of her father. "I don't understand. You were my father's friend. Now you are living in my house. My father . . ." Eva couldn't force another word through her swollen throat. Her vision blurred with tears.

"Eva, please." Ferenc reached out and put his hand on her arm. She stiffened at the touch and he withdrew. "Things are very confused and disorganized now that the war has ended. Your homecoming was unexpected because we heard that . . . well, we heard that nobody survived. We all need time to adjust. I took your house because your father asked me to. He knew it was the only way to protect it from the looters after you left." The girl put her head down. Ferenc quickly realized that everyone Eva knew and loved was gone. How could she tolerate all the loss? "It must seem as if you are deserted and alone, but you are not. I promise you will be taken care of." He looked toward the kitchen, where he could see the shadows of Yossel and Oskar on the wall as they listened to his conversation with Eva. "I promise all of you will be taken care of."

The girl clenched her fists but didn't look up. "I don't have time to adjust. I need to play my piano to prepare for the Academy."

Eva's intensity unsettled the mayor. Perhaps the piano was her way of getting past the pain and moving forward. Perhaps she felt she could honor her father by succeeding at the Academy as he had wished. He looked at her with new respect. She wasn't a child anymore. "Eva, the property issue will take time to resolve, but my wife has agreed that you can come every day and practice on your piano. She was shocked to see you at the door and wasn't thinking clearly. Please find it in your heart to forgive her. We can walk to the house and you and Mrs. Kodaly can talk. Come to the house with me and practice."

It was clear to Ferenc that the girl was conflicted about seeing his wife again. Her fingers were twitching at her side and her jaw worked side to side as if chewing over clashing thoughts. He knew there was more going on than Greta had told him. But he also saw the urgent, burning desire in her eyes to play her piano. "Come and practice. It's going to be alright; you'll see."

They left the hotel in silence, but as they headed up the hill the mayor began to talk about the changes to Laszlo because of the war. He mentioned many of the young men, some who had been in high school with Eva, who were lost on the Russian front. He talked about the sadness of the families of the fallen soldiers. When they came to the square, Eva stopped and stared at the headstones in the pavement.

"Mayor Kodaly, can you please do something about this?"

The mayor sighed and shook his head. There was so much to undo, so much to rebuild both physically and psychologically for the townspeople and for the Jews. This could be a small but significant place to start. "The Arrow Cross. We will take care of it immediately. I am sorry you had to see that."

As they crossed the square people looked at them. Some smiled and nodded to the mayor, some peered quizzically at Eva. Ferenc realized that being seen so publicly with the once popular young Jewish girl might provide an opportunity for the mending he so desired for Laszlo. He thought about taking her to the coffee house, where Jewish and Christian businessmen always congregated before the war, reading the newspapers, playing cards, swapping gossip and family news. He turned to Eva, who still carried a vacant, guarded look in her dull eyes. She needed so much healing before she would be ready for that. *One day at a time*, he reminded himself.

The mayor's wife opened the door and offered an awkward yet gracious welcome. The insincere gesture was lost as Eva focused immediately on her mother's floral dress. She tried to hide the anger that flashed within her by looking past the woman and into her house. Mrs. Kodaly led the girl into the library and gave her a chair within feet of the piano. Seeing the massive black shining instrument calmed her, just as the doctor at Bergen-Belsen had said. Sanctuary. Eva looked around the library. All the furniture was the same as she remembered. The red Persian rug laid at her feet as before. Strauss's *Blue Danube Waltz* played softly on the big Audiola radio in the corner.

Mrs. Kodaly walked over and turned the radio off. Eva remembered how every New Year's Eve her father would roll up the Persian rug and she would dance the *Blue Danube Waltz* with him as the Vienna Philharmonic Orchestra gave their annual live broadcast. First, she stood on his toes, but as she got older and more confident her father would sweep her around the room on her own two feet as her mother clapped joyfully to the downbeat of the waltz. The memory was painful, but Eva swore to herself that she would not cry in front of the mayor and his wife. She had learned in the camp to keep her emotions hidden, especially in front of someone who had power over her. The mayor and his wife were occupiers in Eva's home. Oskar was right. The war was not over yet.

Her father's floor-to-ceiling book collection sat unmoved on its shelves, all the great Jewish thinkers like Einstein and Freud managing to hold their places of honor in spite of being banned, in spite of what happened to their kin. How often the library was full of her parents' friends; men and women discussing the novels of Ferenc Kormendi and Andor Endre Gelleri, or Bela Szolt's essays debating whether Jews should or even could assimilate into Hungarian society. Eva remembered the meetings turning from polite discussion to passionate, angry debate as the war raged on. "The assimilating Bundists and the passionate Zionists," her father used to say, although Eva never understood what that meant. However, until the deportation it was only talk, and Eva preferred to read in her room anyway. Now she wondered how many future Einsteins, Freuds, and other great Hungarian minds had been denied to the world by the atrocities of the war.

The room seemed frozen in time, only the framed photos of her family were missing, replaced by generic, bloodless still-life paintings of fruit and woodland scenes. But it was the lack of familiar odors that Eva noticed most. No smells of her mother and Mira cooking or the thick, sweet smoke from her father's pipe. Nor were there familiar sounds. No prattle from Mira. No radio playing classical music nightly after dinner. No noisy friends or visiting clients. Now that Mrs. Kodaly had shut off the music, the house was as quiet as a mausoleum.

Mayor Kodaly looked at ease in her father's large brown leather armchair with his legs crossed and his hands clasped together lightly in his lap. How many times she had curled up in her father's lap in that chair when she was younger. How often she fell asleep in the chair waiting for her father to come home on the days he traveled to Budapest. Mrs. Kodaly chatted amiably in her slightly grating, nasal voice about the beautiful spring weather and the flowering lilac in the yard. Eva tore her eyes off her mother's dress to steal a glance at the

Bosendorfer. The mayor followed her gaze, then cleared his throat.

"Greta, Eva is very excited to practice on the piano and regain her skill level for the Academy. Shall we leave her to play?"

Mrs. Kodaly maintained a frozen smile, but Eva noticed her hard brown eyes.

"Yes, we want to do everything we can to help you regain your skills. I understand how important it is for you to practice." She picked at some lint on her sleeve. "And as soon as you have fulfilled your household responsibilities you may do so."

Eva looked at the mayor, who had a stunned expression on his face. She turned back to his wife. "Responsibilities? I don't understand." She tried to retain a polite demeanor, but her gut was starting to clench.

"Well, I don't think it is fair for you to come into my house every day and play our piano without giving something in return." Mrs. Kodaly surveyed the room with satisfaction. "Really, young people can be so selfish."

"Greta!" the mayor blurted. "We've already discussed this."

Mrs. Kodaly raised an eyebrow. "We did talk about it, Ferenc, but I have been troubled by it ever since. I have spoken to my friends and they all agree. I simply don't think it is fair for her to take advantage of us in this way. I think she should earn the privilege of playing our piano."

"It is not your piano, it is mine! It is not your house either!" Eva shook with anger and shock. Had the world gone mad while she was in the camp? Mrs. Kodaly maintained her poise, smoothing her dress with her hands. She stared hard at Eva.

"Young lady, if you wish to use the piano, you must earn your keep. Come here every morning and help around the house. Then in the afternoon you can practice. It's not a lot to ask, is it? I'm sure you had to help around the house before, didn't you? It should help you get back to your normal routines, I should think. You can start on Monday. That is the end of it." She stood stiffly and left the library.

Eva stood up and walked around the library fuming. She saw the big book of Grimm's fairytales her father would read to her when she was younger. Was she to be *Aschenputtel*, a Cinderella, forced to clean her own home by a wicked stepmother? Eva turned a fiery gaze at the mayor, who sat in ashen silence. "Was this your plan? Is this how I am welcomed back to my home? Is this how you will take care of us?"

"No, honestly Eva, I am utterly surprised by this. Please, let me talk to her. I am sure I can get her to reconsider." He rubbed his face vigorously with both hands to calm himself. "But if she refuses to budge, do you think you could come and help out around the house? It won't be so bad. You'll be able to practice. Isn't that the most important thing?"

Eva approached the piano that had enriched so many hours of her life. Her body buzzed with anger and her vision blurred with the onset of tears. Was the mayor right, or were he and his wife trying to manipulate her? What did it matter? She could not let them keep her from her piano. She noticed a bit of dust on the top of the piano and gently swept it off with a finger. She ran her right hand along the top of the closed fallboard, looking at the golden Bosendorfer signature. The professor would demand that she practiced no matter what. She needed to prepare for his return. She felt the vibrations of the keys only inches beneath her fingertips, calling to her, waiting impatiently to come alive under her touch. Her fingers stretched longingly toward the keys underneath the fallboard. *So many hours . . . such a beautiful sound.*

CHAPTER 10

Naftali wandered the wreckage of Kosveg all morning. He entered each house, touching the *mezuzahs* nailed to the door frames and bringing the holiness to his cracked lips. There must have been some imperfection in the *mezuzahs*, some mistake in the sacred lettering, some impure hands defiling the scrolls before sealing them into their little arks. It must be so, Naftali thought, otherwise a *mezuzah* would have protected each house in Kosveg from the devastation. He found moldy potatoes and onions in the bins of some kitchens. How often his family survived on these foods during the week, until somehow, by magic, a bottle of red wine, pots of stew, and fish with walnut sauce appeared to grace the *Shabbos* table.

He gathered pieces of a shattered life together. A torn, muddied prayer shawl. A child's *yarmulke*. Black trousers and a white shirt. He found one-half of a pair of *tefillin*, the leather box and straps every man in the community wore for morning prayers, as commanded by the Torah. In each home he asked permission to enter, and begged forgiveness for taking anything that might help him rebuild his identity as a Hassid.

Yet as he scavenged, he was bothered by the feeling it didn't matter. At the camp all outward manifestation of his obedience to God was stripped and shaved away. There were no prayer shawls, no Torah scrolls, neither beards nor sidelocks. The holiest people in the camp were as beaten and humbled as the greatest sinners. The

Hassids and the reformist Neologs, the fallen and the non-believers all looked the same. Some of the most devout said the Jews were being punished because they didn't pray hard enough, didn't conform strongly enough. But Naftali couldn't help but wonder if it was the arrogance of separating each other by what they wore and how they prayed that had led to this. If the Jews all believed in the same God, shared the same Book and rituals, wasn't that enough? Wasn't anything that classed some Jews as holier than others mere hubris?

Naftali could not let doubts and confusion interfere with what he had to do. No one else was alive to mourn the dead Hassids of Kosveg and the other *shtetls*. He would have to do that before he could worry about anything else. He would have to go to the brick factory and say the Mourner's Kaddish for each of the six hundred or so elderly, women, and children who never left the site after the train departed.

Naftali wore the mismatched outfit he had pieced together that declared him a Hassid. He gently wrapped the *tefillin* in the prayer shawl. He took a shortcut through the woods toward the brick factory, allowing him to stop by a stream to wash himself and the dirty prayer shawl, take a drink and say a prayer of purification for the sacred task ahead.

> "Baruch ata Adonai, Eloheinu Melech ha—olam,
> asher kidshanu b'mitzvotav
> vitzivanu al netilat yadayim."

He rejoined the main road further on. The heavy tread marks of the government trucks that carried the entire village down to the brick factory were still scrolled into the road. He remembered the smell of fear permeating the sweet spring air as he and thirty other men were forced to stand in a truck pounding along the road, followed by other loaded trucks. How could birds sing and butterflies dance alongside the trucks when the terrified and brutalized Hassids were being taken away?

The *mazzikin* followed him now through the woods, whispering

and cracking branches behind him. He walked along in the ruts until
he came to the entry gate of the brick factory. The sign overhead
declared its Jewish ownership, but the factory had been closed since
it was confiscated by the state after Hungary joined the German
war. He wrestled the iron gate open to the complaints of rusted
metal and respectfully entered the property. On his left loomed the
three-story, windowless brickmaking building. It was made of the
same red bricks it had fabricated since before Naftali was born. Long
escalators brought the raw clay and sand up to the top of the mixing
bins and down into the blistering kilns below. The large warehouse
that held the bricks for rail transit stood directly before him. He
saw the railway beyond the warehouse, where he and all the young
men of Kosveg had been crammed like those bricks into cattle cars
for transit to Auschwitz. He looked at the field to the right where
the women, children, and elders had been sequestered as the train
departed. The field was covered in the light red dust of the bricks—or
was the soil so soaked in blood that it oozed to the surface? He heard
the wailing of prayers and the screaming of names of loved ones and
of *Ha Shem*. The railway doors slammed shut with metallic finality.
He heard the shots. They were so loud at first he thought they were
aimed at the train. Everyone in the car tried to duck down but there
was no room to move. Yet no bullets pierced the wooden walls of
their rolling prison. The sounds of gunfire and murder persisted,
dying, dying, dying down as the train picked up speed and left the
brick factory behind.

Naftali sighed deeply and buried his face in his free hand for a
moment. Then he took the prayer shawl and swept it high. Usually, it
fluttered down softly onto his head and shoulders, but the wet fabric
flopped down on his head like a damp towel at the ritual *mikveh* bath.
Another humiliation. Yet having the shawl was blessing enough. It
still blotted out the remembered sights and imagined sounds around
him. He breathed in the silence under the shawl and calmed himself
for prayer. He took out his one *tefillin* and wrapped it around his left

arm seven times, covering the number tattooed by the Germans, and recited the proper prayer. His hands started instinctually to wrap the second *tefillin* around his forehead until Naftali realized there was no *tefillin* there. From the sanctuary created by the shawl, he surveyed the killing field through wet eyes and began the Mourner's Kaddish.

> "*Yitgadal v'yitkadash sh'mei raba b'alma di-v'ra*
> *chirutei, v'yamlich malchutei b'chayeichon*
> *uvyomeichon uvchayei d'chol beit yisrael, ba'agala*
> *uvizman kariv, v'im'ru: amen . . .*"

CHAPTER 11

Eva sat slump-shouldered on a stool between the two men in the hotel kitchen. Automobiles and trucks chugged past the hotel as the Saturday food market drew vendors to the streets of Laszlo from surrounding towns and farms. So many of the out-of-town sellers used to be Jewish, with their wild beards and theatrical arguments over quality and price. Eva loved to walk the impromptu stalls with Mira. Sadness and fury swirled around the memories, fueled by her treatment by Mrs. Kodaly. Her anger found a ready ally in Oskar. The butcher chopped vigorously at the chicken on the counter before him, visibly fighting to hold back his rage as she described her latest encounter with the mayor's wife. He grabbed the bird by its headless neck and shook it. "No, no, no! You can't do it, Eva! Don't let them humiliate you like that. We'll find another piano. We'll find another way."

She waited until Oskar's storm passed. Anger didn't help; she had to be practical and focused. "There is no other piano like mine in Laszlo. I guess I could practice on that old upright at the coffee house, or even the one at the Jewish Home for the Aged, but how would playing those poor instruments improve my skills?"

Yossel kneaded a mound of dough methodically and quietly, creating the golden *bilkalach* buns so beloved by his lost Jewish customers. "No. Eva needs to play her own piano." He spoke to the young woman in a soothing tone. "Maybe that's why God had your father put the piano in the hands of the mayor, so it wouldn't be stolen or sold. It would be here waiting for you. You have to honor that. And if making a bargain with that she-devil is the only way, just do it. It's not the worst thing, is it?" He turned back to Oskar. "If Eva doesn't do what that woman wants she'll be nowhere at all—and nowhere is not such a good place to be in the world right now."

"You know I don't believe in God anymore," Oskar said bluntly. "And what about her dignity? This is an insult."

"Such a small slap compared to what we've all gone through," Yossel replied. He looked at Eva. "But, Eva, it's your decision. And whatever you choose, we will support you. Right, Oskar?"

Oskar whacked a thigh off the bird, exhaling a sound somewhere between a sigh and a growl. "Yeah, right. Of course we will."

Eva's heart warmed as she looked at the butcher and the baker. They were the only people in the world besides Professor Sandor who cared for her. But they didn't really know her. Nobody in Laszlo did anymore. It would be different when the professor came back. He would know what to do. He would help her. But he wouldn't be coming back until at least next Tuesday or Thursday when the Special Trains rolled through Laszlo again. She silently prayed he would be on the next one.

"Let's stop at the coffee house around the corner before we go to the house. They have the best Linzer torte in Laszlo and the coffee is excellent." The mayor dropped his casual air and lowered his voice. "Besides, by walking in together we can show the people of Laszlo that our Jewish neighbors are back and are welcomed."

Eva kept a static smile on her face as the mayor spoke. "Yes, I would like to go to the coffee house. My father took me there sometimes." She avoided his remark about the Jews. She didn't want to be the representative of the Jewish people for either the mayor or the other Jews at the hotel. She just wanted to practice, wait for Professor Sandor, and leave Laszlo for the Academy. There was nothing left in the town but clouded, sad memories. Without her parents, her house seemed like an inert museum of remembrance. Except for the Bosendorfer, the key to regaining her music. She would have to go along with the mayor's idea to access her piano. Focus and willpower.

It was early Sunday morning and the coffee house was crowded with families. The waiters in their white shirts and black bowties bustled around carrying small plates of sweets and cups of coffee. They wove in and out of the mass of patrons, raising and lowering their plates and cups in a comical ballet. Eva smiled at the spectacle. Her father took her here sometimes after work when the tables were full of businessmen and town officials eating heaping bowls of beef goulash with thick noodles and dollops of sour cream. She had never been here during a weekend, when the staid atmosphere of the work week gave way to such clatter and high spirits. The end of the war seemed to unleash joyous energy in Laszlo. At least for the Christians. The thought surprised her. She had never considered people in Laszlo as Jews or Christians before—no one in her family had. Hopefully, that kind of thinking ended with the war. They were all just Hungarians again.

They were seated in a far corner, allowing Eva to observe the commotion of the coffee house as Mayor Kodaly gave a running commentary on who was who and what people were up to. He was charming to older women and businesslike to men. In turn, sympathetic and analytical. Maybe he had to be like that to be a mayor, like a conductor handling the many pieces of an orchestra. Or maybe he was two-faced and manipulative. Was she just another instrument in his Laszlo ensemble, or could he be trusted to take care of her and the others like he promised? She didn't have to like him or trust him, but she did have to deal with him and his wife if she wanted access to her piano. Eva had agreed to Mrs. Kodaly's terms, at least for now.

Maybe she would talk to the town clerk about how to get her house back, but after hearing about Oskar and Yossel's troubling conversation in his office, she had concluded that was a dead end. Besides, he would probably tell the mayor, and Eva did not want to take a chance on angering the man who had such power over her.

The occasional *clunk* of billiard balls ricocheting around the tables in a side room broke through the noisy chatter that surrounded Eva. She remembered her father's teaching the first time they visited this place. *By law, you must have two billiards tables to call your establishment a coffee house; otherwise, it is a mere coffee shop.* Eva relaxed a bit, nibbled at the torte, and took small sips of coffee. She hated the watery coffee she drank every morning in the camp, her first experience drinking the stuff. This full, rich taste was different and surprisingly appealing.

A steady stream of people stopped by their table and chatted with the mayor, occasionally smiling or acknowledging Eva without recognition. Some looked at her nervously, talked too fast or had fear in their eyes. Eva wondered what she represented to them. Lost friends? Guilt or shame? A few sought to relate to Eva's suffering by telling their stories of loss during the war. Eva tried not to listen. She had pain enough of her own. Something else about the patrons troubled Eva. They seemed enormous after a year surrounded by emaciated people. She watched them speaking through mouths full of food, their engorged bodies seeming to expand with each forkful of torte. They might fall over in front of her, dead from overeating, like the people at the displaced persons camp who stuffed their bellies after months, years of starvation. She pushed her plate away and examined her arms. They were as thin and delicate as a doe's.

As the mayor conferred with a businessman about some sort of permit, Eva continued to survey the coffee house. At the far end of the main room she saw several town police officers gathered at a table. She shuddered and turned away. Out of the corner of her eye, she thought she saw the couple with the little boy Izidor, if that was, in fact, who he was. She suppressed the urge to get up and follow them. Instead, she merely peered through the crowd, unsure if the people quickly leaving the coffee house were the same couple. She hailed a passing waiter.

"Excuse me," she said, pointing at the couple. "Do you know those people?"

The waiter peered through the crowd. "That's Mr. and Mrs. Frigyesi."

"And their child," Eva said. An urgency in her voice made the waiter blink and look at her more closely. "Do you know his name?"

"Child?" he stuttered. "Oh, yes. His name is Karl." The waiter excused himself and left quickly, apologizing for how busy he was this morning.

As the couple exited the café, the child waved to her again, as he had in the street. Was he real or a vision, a specter of the lost Jewish children of Laszlo? Suddenly, Eva became dizzy and nauseous. There was too much noise, too many people. Her breath began to quicken and she started to shake. Eva gripped the edge of the table as the light began to fade. She told Ferenc quietly that she needed to leave immediately.

The mayor led Eva out of the coffee house, passing a table of the town's businessmen playing cards. They nodded cordially at him and Eva in turn. He invited them to convene a meeting of the Laszlo Business Promotion Council to discuss some ideas he had concerning the return of Laszlo's Jewish citizens. After they left, the men looked at each other and shook their heads.

"What do you think the mayor is up to, parading that Jewish girl around?" asked Mor, who had taken over the former Weiss furniture shop after the deportation. He wondered if more Jews would return.

He didn't really have anything against Jews, but if Weiss returned, he could demand Mor give back the shop, like the Jewish baker had done. The town was buzzing with the news. His beefy hand picked up his coffee cup, and he smelled the shot of brandy surreptitiously poured into it by the waiter.

"He wants Laszlo to move on, forget the war, and rebuild," said a sallow-skinned insurance salesman with a large moustache. Mor noticed that he had abandoned the toothbrush moustache style favored by Hitler when it became obvious the war was lost. Mor had started as a salesman in Weiss's store, but now that he was an owner, he detested the oily, ingratiating behaviors of people like the salesman. Always trying to please, neither backbone nor principles.

"Well, that's how you attract investment," said Andor, the banker. "The Allies have a lot of rebuilding money. They know we were reluctant participants in the war. After all, we only wanted to get our old territories back and restore Greater Hungary, not conquer Europe and get rid of the Jews. We are not like the Germans."

"Sure, sure," Mor added. "I don't like what the Germans did to the Jews either. So unnecessary. The labor battalions were hard enough, but to kill so many of them . . ."

Andor waved his hand dismissively. "That's what the Jews want you to believe, but it's just propaganda. I heard that hardly any Jews were killed. They're moving on to Russia to be with the other communists or America to join the bankers. The Allies know we protected the Jews until the Germans invaded us and the Arrow Cross took over the government."

Mor looked around nervously. "Be careful what you say, Andor. They may have slipped out of their uniforms when the Allies came, but the Arrow Cross are still among us. They are in the factories, the police." He shot a hard look at the insurance salesman. "Even at this table."

"Don't look at me!" the man protested as he withered under Mor's gaze and coughed out a crust of bread. "We all waltzed with the Arrow Cross when it was in power. Business is business, right?"

Andor readily agreed. "Right, business is business. That's why the mayor was smart to get a share of their recovery money. The Jews of Laszlo may be poor, but their friends in America and Britain are rich. They still have some use to us. I'm curious to hear his ideas."

"I'm not so sure," Mor said thoughtfully. He was grateful to Weiss, who had taught Mor everything he knew about business over the years. The morning of the deportation, the old man gave Mor the keys to the shop and the combination to the beautiful Dottling safe, begging Mor to care for the business until he returned. But that memory was fading, replaced by Mor's fear of losing his business if Jews swarmed back into Hungary and grabbed everything. He had grown the business over the past year. It was his now. "Getting in bed with Jews is a dangerous game. Once involved they always scheme to take over. Now they are plotting with the Russians to take over our government again, like they did in 1918. Whether they wear a yellow star or a red star, Jews will never truly be Hungarians."

The salesman leaned into the table, his moustache twitching. "I am less concerned with the Russians taking over Hungary than I am with the Jews trying to get their property back right here in Laszlo. I heard the Jewish baker was harassing Krauss to give him the shop. Can you imagine? After all the money and sweat old Krauss put in to bringing the bakery back to code? And a wounded veteran at that!"

"That's just the beginning," said Andor, as he patted the confectioner's sugar from his lips. "We are talking about a lot more than a few stores. Almost every Jew in Laszlo owned a house. Who's going to kick out all the good citizens who moved in, especially the ones who lost sons or husbands in the war? Every house had furniture, paintings, and jewelry that disappeared. Who's going to find all that and return it?" He quieted as a waiter slipped past with a tray. "Half the businesses in town were started by Jews. Every business had inventories, property, and accounts receivable. I've seen the banking records. It's a mess."

Mor began to perspire. He wondered about old Weiss's two sons. Arrogant young men. What if they came back and tried to claim the furniture store? What about Weiss's daughter Elena? Mor used to flirt with her in the old days, before he was married. Might she come back, as well? He lifted the cup to his mouth again to hide his frown and take a few deep breaths. He didn't want his nervousness to show. That would be like admitting he had done something wrong. And he hadn't. He just continued the business when Weiss left. Someone had to. "We all have losses from the war. We all have disruptions," Mor concluded in a stentorian tone. "I say everybody has to forget and move on. Jews included. The mayor is stirring up a hornet's nest if he thinks we're going to return to the way things were before the war."

The salesman's hand slithered up to his mouth to hide his words from a passing couple. "My wife says the mayor's wife refuses to give anything back to the girl."

Mor nodded sagely. "I think your wife should encourage her. Mrs. Kodaly is setting a fine example for the rest of the town. The sooner the Jews realize there is nothing left for them in Laszlo, the better for all of us."

Andor chuckled and took a sip of coffee. "It will be soon enough. I've seen the draft law for return of Jewish property. It is a tangled, bureaucratic maze."

"As I am sure it was meant to be," the salesman interrupted with a wink.

The banker stiffened at the overly familiar gesture, then continued. "It would take enormous amounts of time and money to get a simple painting returned, let alone a business. I don't see any of these Jews having the stamina or the resources, even with help from the Allies or the foreign Jewish groups. Besides, now that Christians own the shops they stay open on Saturdays. I like that. More time for commerce."

The banker's words gave Mor some comfort. If Weiss or his family came back, they would have to go through that cumbersome legal process to try and regain ownership. Someone else had taken their house and lands. With no home, no work, and no resources, they might just go away. All of the returned Jews would be forced to leave soon. "We should remember, we are not anti-Jewish, we are pro-opportunity." Mor raised his cup. "A toast, gentlemen. To the end of the war, and the beginning of our prosperous Hungarian future."

Sergeant Ritook's eyes followed the mayor as he left the coffee house with the Jewish girl. Laszlo had finally gotten rid of the Jews and now, not only were they coming back, but the mayor seemed to take delight in it. What was he up to? What was the point of the war if Hungary lost all the land it had recovered thanks to the Germans, and the Jews simply came back? The national government was rapidly dismantling the anti-Jewish laws it had carefully constructed for over a decade. Ritook was proud that Hungary had such laws long before Germany. They were meant to provide opportunity for real Hungarians by limiting Jewish participation in professions to the percentage of the population they represented. Why should Jews, only 6 percent of the people, be half the doctors, lawyers, and business owners? But at the end of the day the Jews had won.

"Ritook! Play your hand," Corporal Zoldy urged the Sergeant. "Quit daydreaming."

Ritook groaned at the cards in his hand. *Piss poor*. He discarded a ten of spades. He didn't particularly care for the Hungarian game *Kaszino*. Since the war ended nobody wanted to play the more sophisticated German card games. "Just thinking about the Jews."

"Again? We've got five beaten-up men and a girl. Why do they bother you so much? You should be more worried about our brave soldiers coming back with no jobs, boiling because we lost the war." Zoldy threw a ten of diamonds on top of Ritook's card and swept them into his pile. "The streets are full of thieves and drunks."

Ritook couldn't tell if it was the Jews or the cards he held, but his anger was rising and he needed to control it. "They bother me because it's just the beginning. That's how they do it. They sneak in and soon they own the businesses and are making demands. Already that girl is twisting the mayor around. She's probably after his big house. And who knows what he wants from her in return." Ritook ground his jaw as he thought about the large white house on Alpar Road. The mayor grabbed it while Ritook was doing his duty at the brick factory. All he got was a small apartment and some used furniture. "Then the baker convinced old Krauss to make him the manager of the bakery. And that butcher is nothing but trouble. One of these days he's gonna do something violent. He's an angry, vengeful Jew." He looked at his remaining cards and realized he had been dealt a bad hand. He threw the cards on the table with a loud curse that caused a few patrons to glance his way and quickly turn back to their tables. He always got a bad hand.

CHAPTER 12

Eva listened to the chirping of woodlarks and the cooing of mourning doves through the open kitchen window. The familiar sounds softened her anxiety from the crowded coffee house and gave her a moment to collect herself before seeing the Greta Kodaly again. It was clear to Eva that she was not going to be handed the keys to her house immediately by this woman. She needed to understand her and the mayor better and figure out a smart way forward. Fortunately, Mrs. Kodaly appeared to be in a pleasant mood. That was a good start.

"All you need to do this morning is clean the kitchen, lightly mop the floor, wipe the counters and perhaps polish some of the daily use silverware." Mrs. Kodaly handed a written list to Eva. "That's not very much, is it? And then you can practice the piano for a few hours. I will even prepare you a nice lunch."

The knot in Eva's stomach slowly unwound as Mrs. Kodaly twittered on and Eva walked around the house more freely. She shut out the sound of Mrs. Kodaly's voice. For a brief moment it was her house again. Maybe she could go up to her room later. That might help her feel more settled, even as she stayed in the old hotel. The house was simply too big for one couple to occupy fully, so Eva was certain that her photos, clothing, and mementos would be more or less as she left them the morning of the deportation. She longed to wear her own clothes again. Especially the dresses she wore at recitals and competitions. Many of them were made by her mother. Wearing them would bring her mother closer. She hoped that even with the mayor and his wife living in her house, her room would be the sanctuary she craved.

Her budding comfort was interrupted when Mrs. Kodaly moved a cast iron pan off the stove and it scraped and clanked into another pan. The metallic sound brought memories of Mira preparing dinner, and her mother bustling around directing the housekeeper to add more paprika to the chicken or to be less heavy-handed with the salt. Her mother was such a good cook. Even after she was bedridden her mother would read cookbooks and manage Mira's efforts. She tried so hard to maintain normalcy and a sense of order in the house right until the end. The memory was as bittersweet as Mira's *lecso*, her special vegetable stew spiced with smoked paprika from Szeged. Eva's stomach tightened once more in a twinge of hunger as Mrs. Kodaly banged pots and pans together as she straightened up the kitchen. Her father used to call it Eva's Pavlovian response to the food preparations. He loved to tease her, his blue eyes twinkling under his glasses. A hand shook Eva's shoulder firmly.

"Are you paying attention, young lady?" Mrs. Kodaly's polite but suspicious voice brought Eva back to the present. "I will be upstairs if you need anything. Just come to the bottom of the stairs and call for me."

Eva began working in the kitchen. It was good to have something physical to do. Touching the pots and pans, silverware, and other kitchenware gave her a sense of connection to her family, even though she would never see any of them again. Seeing the Bosendorfer in the other room reminded her there was something positive ahead. Mrs. Kodaly came downstairs just as Eva was finishing and overloaded Eva with compliments on her work. Eva smiled. Although the mayor's wife saw her as merely cleaning the house, Eva could feel herself reinhabiting it. Mayor Kodaly came back from his office to share lunch on this first day. Eva was certain he was there to insure a semblance of harmony in the house. After a quick meal of potato bread, cold ham, and spicy *Csabai kolbasz* sausage, Mrs. Kodaly asked Eva to do one more kitchen chore before practicing.

"Gas for the stove has been hard to come by since the war," Mrs. Kodaly said. "Fortunately, the stove uses either gas or wood." She blinked and reddened. "Of course, you know that. I think we should clean out the wood chamber. It shouldn't take you long at all."

Eva nodded her assent, hoping these little additional chores would not be the norm and she could have the time she needed daily to regain her skills at the piano. She remembered where the ash bucket and small shovel were kept and retrieved them from the utility room off the kitchen. The mayor and his wife retired to the living room. Eva opened the chamber on the left side of the white enamel stove. She pulled out the metal bin that collected the ashes under the wood fire and began gently shoveling them into the bucket.

Eva worked carefully, yet the air around her steadily filled with minute flecks of gray. Eva stopped her work and looked up as a shaft of sunlight from the kitchen window illuminated the small particles. She watched them settle on her arm. Her eyes were drawn inexorably in the direction of the two tall chimneys looming above her. The structures belched ash that rained down upon her and the professor as her father was hurried toward the low buildings beneath the chimneys. Soon Eva was trudging through a snowstorm of ash, a dull gray storm that never seemed to abate during her time at Auschwitz. She tried to brush the ashes off her arm, but the storm picked up in intensity. She was soon buried to her waist. She struggled to run but the ashes were too deep. She could no longer see her father. Professor Sandor disappeared along with everyone on the platform. She was drowning, suffocating in the burned remains of the once living and loved. She opened her mouth to scream for help but the ashes flooded in, pushing further and further down her throat, seeking to smother the small flame of life that glowed at the core of her being. An arm broke through the cinereal sea, grabbed Eva, and pulled her to the surface. She coughed and opened her eyes to see the mayor crouched next to her, holding her arm. Mrs. Kodaly stood over his shoulder with a wary and frightened look on her face. The mayor helped Eva to her feet and into a chair in the living room. Eva was coming back to consciousness as he and Mrs. Kodaly went to the kitchen to get her a glass of water. Though they kept their voices low, Eva could hear their conversation.

"What's the matter with that girl, Ferenc? Did you hear her scream? Is she mentally ill? I don't know that I can trust being alone with her in the house. This is too much for me. Perhaps we should forget the whole thing."

"Shh, Greta, keep your voice down. These Jews have suffered things we cannot even imagine. I have no idea why she passed out. Maybe inhaling the ashes made her swoon or maybe she is having bad memories. Let her play the piano this afternoon. I will stay here and keep an eye on her. If she seems all right, we can try again tomorrow. Let's just take this one day at a time, shall we?"

"Do you think she feels the work is beneath her? Jews and young people can be so prideful. We are being more than generous to her, but I don't want to put us in danger if she goes mad or becomes vengeful."

The mayor spoke in a benevolent whisper. "Day by day, Greta. Day by day."

Confused and vulnerable, Eva spent a half hour recovering from her experience with the ashes in the kitchen. The dry, bitter taste was still in her mouth when she sat at the piano bench and stared at the scratch in the Bosendorfer name. She lifted the fallboard and took in the keys. She whispered to the piano, "Help me. Please help me." Her quiet voice unlocked a heavy door inside her heart. She pushed hard against it to gain a small entrance to a place that hadn't felt warmth since the last time she played her piano. She tenderly poked at middle C with the pointer finger of her right hand and hesitatingly added fingers to make an A-Minor chord. Its melancholic tone spoke knowingly to her deep sadness. She placed her left hand on the keyboard as well and began a series of arpeggios to warm up her fingers. The resonance of the piano was familiar and welcoming. Her body began to feel solid again. Each chord produced a memory as well as a sound. Consoling images of practicing with Professor Sandor, playing for her parents in the evenings and performing at the Jewish Home for the Aged, the high school, and her many competitions. She blinked away the memories. This was time for practice.

Mrs. Kodaly's voice came from behind her. "It is obvious you haven't played in a while. You are going to have to practice long and hard to merit the honor of attending our prestigious Liszt Academy." Her face registered hope mixed with doubt. "I do wish you luck." She shook her head and retreated into the kitchen. Eva wanted to rage at Mrs. Kodaly. She was trapped in the camp. She was trapped in the hotel. Now she was trapped again, a prisoner to this mean and fickle woman. She would have to ignore Mrs. Kodaly so she could concentrate on playing. She decided to think of her as an elderly consumptive hacking away in the audience at a performance.

Eva was aware that the mayor sat in her father's brown leather chair not five feet from where she was, yet he and his wife left her consciousness as she began to reconnect to her keyboard. After twenty minutes or so of technical warm-ups from her years of study, Eva began to play longer melodies. She wasn't particularly mindful of what they were. It was as if her fingers needed to play these short pieces disconnected from the professor's formal practice regime. When her mother died, Professor Sandor had tried to comfort her by telling her that suffering in life led to breakthroughs of profound emotional depth, and that great pain was a rehearsal for greatness in performing. His words didn't soothe, as Eva was consumed by the grief of her mother's death, something she had never felt in her comfortable life. She told the professor she was sorry she disappointed him, but he had replied that he was not disappointed. Rather, she was simply too young and inexperienced to turn the pain into learning. Eva thought back on the deportation and her time in Auschwitz. So much death, so much pain, such a sundering of what she thought she knew about people. When the professor returned she would finally be able to translate her experiences into deep and meaningful performance. He also told her music opened a gate to heaven, the only place where there was truly no suffering, hate or danger. Eva longed for her music to take her there. Even with her eyes closed, she felt the presence of the professor next to her.

Suddenly, she was conscious of the mayor standing behind her. He spoke to her softly.

"What are you playing, Eva? I am not familiar with those short pieces."

Eva kept her fingers on the keyboard while she considered his question. "These are pieces I played in the camp."

"Oh," the mayor said brightly, "you had a piano in the camp? That's good."

Eva cringed inside. Didn't anyone in Laszlo know what they went through in Auschwitz? She didn't want to be angry at people's ignorance all the time, but she didn't want to have to relive her experience constantly either. But she needed the mayor's support, so she allowed him inside her troubled world for the moment. "No, I played in the air, on my bunk, or with my hands at my sides. I held on to the music as much as I could, otherwise I would have gone mad." She remembered the suicides. "Many people did."

She played a mournful melody in a minor key. "This is what I would play when the trains arrived and I saw the people whipped and clubbed, pushed from the platform, and herded into the gas chambers. It is Mahler's 'I've Become Lost to the World.'" Her fingers began to burn as she played. She moved on to a soft, fluid piece.

"This is Mendelssohn. His music is so soothing. This is called 'Spring Song.' I played it when the new arrivals who survived the selection wandered blinded by grief through the barbed wire and into the camp. I played Mendelssohn almost every day as I looked around and saw the confusion, pain, and despair." She continued to play, her eyes closed but the images in her mind softened by the vibrations of the Bosendorfer. "Sometimes at night I would hum these melodies to comfort the women around me. I stopped when one of them complained to the guards. If she couldn't find comfort then she didn't want anyone else to, either. People in the camp could be like that." She took a deep breath and changed the melody to a more strident, forceful sound.

"And what is that piece?" The mayor said, his voice quiet and seeming strained.

 Eva continued to play but remained silent. She didn't want to talk about it. She would not use this as a bargaining chip to gain his sympathy. He had seen enough of her insides for the moment. The experience was too intimate, too painful to share with anyone just yet, especially a man. This was what she played when the guards pulled women out of the barracks and used them. "The War of the Huns" by the great Hungarian composer Ferenc Liszt. The battle was so furious that for three days people could hear the screams and war cries of the dead as they continued fighting. The anger in this piece kept Eva from curling into a ball of humiliation for the women, for herself as a witness, for her shameful gratitude that the guards never chose her. Afterward, the guards would give the women extra bread or a piece of cheese, which they would offer to share with Eva. She wanted to crush the guards' gifts under her heel in the dirt, but the food would help someone else survive another night. Humbly, she took it with gratitude and gave it away.

Eva had to respond to the mayor's question. She stopped playing "War of the Huns" and began striking a single chord, quietly then with more force and passion. "Did you know many composers use this as the sound of hunger? It's A-flat minor." She switched to another. "And this is D-minor." She banged the keys and held them down so the sound roared and faded across the room. "It signifies death."

The room was enveloped in a humid silence. Eva opened her eyes and looked at the mayor. His face was buried in his hands. He seemed to be weeping.

CHAPTER 13

The station master checked his pocket watch when he heard the deep mechanical rumble in the distance. The Tuesday two o'clock Special Train was right on time. He had to be at his post as each Special Train passed through, per regulation. Since his assistant had not returned from the war and no replacement had been found, the station master was forced to workdays without a break. He spent foggy nights at his desk, finding a needed boost from the bottle of local *palinke* apricot brandy he kept in the top drawer. The trains slowed down as they passed through the station and picked up speed again beyond. He often glimpsed hollow, blackened eyes staring out from the shadows of the cattle cars. It was hardest for him when they came in the middle of the night, when there was nothing between his conscience and those eyes.

He hadn't thought much about the different Jews of Hungary being deported on the trains. The German and Czech Jews who lived in the border regions, they weren't real Hungarians anyway, so nobody objected. He only paid attention when the Jews of Laszlo were brought to his station and shipped out on the German train, but by then it was too late.

There were no DPs destined for Laszlo on this train, but it would still slow down as it went through the station. He looked down the tracks. Several of the newly returned Jews were waiting, staring at the approaching train. He felt profound pity for those people. Especially the girl. She was so young and alone. Were they hoping someone would get off? Should he tell them the train wasn't stopping? No, it was none of his business. Yet the memory of her father tugged at his heart. Jacob Fleiss was a decent man, always ready to help as a lawyer or as a neighbor. How many times had the station master sold him a ticket to Budapest so the lawyer could represent someone in Laszlo against the government for some injustice or another? Jew or Christian, it didn't matter in those days. He always took the ticket with a smile and returned with a triumphant story to share. The station master wished he had a flower to give the girl.

The train slowed as it approached. Eva ran alongside, shouting into the windows to the shadows within. Yossel and Oscar stood dutifully nearby, like concerned uncles, there to protect Eva as she waited for someone to return.

"Has anyone come from Terezin? Do you know Professor Sandor?" Eva searched the blackness within the cars. "Any musicians from Terezin on board?"

She was met with blank stares or piteous looks. Occasionally someone shouted back to her. "No! Don't know him." Or simply "Sorry!"

Eva ran down the tracks and followed the last car. She cried out frantically. "Please help me! Has anyone come from Terezin?"

The station master watched Eva and felt a heaviness in his chest. He thought of Professor Sandor, who traveled to the capital regularly to teach or give concerts. Yet he always made time for Eva and other students here in Laszlo. He had no idea if anyone else was coming back, but what did he know of the displaced persons camps? These trains were still coming twice a week. Every Tuesday and Thursday at three o'clock. Maybe one would stop and let off the professor or some other survivors.

"*Josef!*"

The name rang out sharply as the metal wheels of the departing cars sliced through the air. The station master looked down the tracks. Yossel and Oskar were comforting the sobbing girl, too far away to have shouted so clearly to him. He looked up as the last car rolled slowly past.

"*Josef!*"

Nobody could have cried out his name. He didn't know anybody on the train. All he could see were shadows and stares that felt like hot judgment. Those damned hollow eyes! He didn't do anything wrong. There's nothing he could have done. Why were they judging him? He put his hands against his temples and pressed hard, hoping to squeeze out the penetrating accusation.

"Josef!"

The station master twisted quickly to see Oskar approaching.

"Josef, when is the next train coming?"

The station master realized that his heart was pounding powerfully. The bottle of *palinke* in his office would calm him down. He put his hand to his chest and took a deep breath. "Oh, Oskar. You startled me. Thursday, same time."

that her mind could go elsewhere, seeing the Special Trains rolling by without stopping, their steel wheels keeping time with her metronome. Thursday, Tuesday, Thursday. It had been over two weeks, yet Professor Sandor had not returned. The mayor advised her to be patient; everything took time. There were so many camps to empty, so many Jewish ex-prisoners to process.

After a half hour, Mrs. Kodaly walked over to the piano with her friends. She spoke in her usual gay way, under which Eva always detected a note of insecurity. "Eva, dear, my friends wondered if you might play something a little less somber, perhaps some Hungarian folk music." The women gathered around, smiling in anticipation.

Eva looked up from the keyboard. "I am really sorry, Mrs. Kodaly, but I don't know any."

"Well then," Mrs. Kodaly went on cheerfully, although Eva could hear the pinch of exasperation in her voice. "Why not some popular Hungarian songs from Annie Fischer or Vali Racz. They were Jewish. You must know something from them?"

"I have only been trained in classical music, and as you pointed out, I need much practice."

"But you must have seen Vali Racz' latest movie, *White Train*? She sings so beautifully and looks just like Marlene Dietrich. Every Hungarian girl wants to be like her. Am I not correct?" Mrs. Kodaly's friends smiled and agreed.

Eva gave a stony-faced reply. "I don't think I saw it. We didn't go out to the cinema in Auschwitz very often."

Mrs. Kodaly's eyes bore into Eva's, but her voice did not betray her anger. She turned to her friends. "I am so sorry. It seems the child's musical education is quite limited. Maybe she can work on something for your next visit." Mrs. Kodaly shuffled the women to the front hallway to say goodbye. Eva clenched her jaw tightly as she overheard their parting conversation.

"If my maid spoke to me like that I would slap her."

"Well she has been through a lot, so Ferenc and I put up with her outbursts."

"Greta, you are a saint to take the Jewish girl in and tolerate her rude behavior. They always act so superior."

"It is a hardship, but it is our Christian obligation, as I need to remind Ferenc now and then."

"I hope we won't have any problems with her or those other Jews. There's a lot of talk in town that they are stirring up trouble everywhere they go . . ."

When the door closed behind her guests, Mrs. Kodaly charged back into the library. "How could you embarrass me in front of my guests?" Her breath was sickly sweet from the *Unicom*.

Eva looked squarely into the woman's eyes. Mrs. Kodaly's false, imperious comments to her friends were too much for Eva to tolerate. "I am not your maid. You are not being charitable to me. This is my house and my piano."

Mrs. Kodaly's mouth dropped open and her jaw trembled. "I was only trying to get my friends to appreciate your music, to see you as one of us again. I am trying to make your return easier." She struggled to continue, turned, and fled up the stairs.

Eva followed Mrs. Kodaly with her eyes until the woman disappeared. It was so hard to hold her tongue as she tried to navigate this strange situation. If she angered the mayor's wife, she could be cut off from the piano. But the injustice of being treated like a servant in her own home was hard to bear. Yet maybe Mrs. Kodaly was sincere, trying in her fumbling way to show kindness to Eva and to get the women of the town to support her. She squeezed her eyes shut for a few moments, pushing the confusion of how to deal with Mrs. Kodaly out of her mind. She turned back to the keyboard. Her fingers felt stronger, more confident. Her timing and pressure were improving so much. She had written to the Academy. As long as Eva had access to the Bosendorfer and Professor Sandor returned soon, everything would get better.

That evening, Eva once again sat at the piano in the Grand Hall. She looked out over the sea of German uniforms in the audience. Strangely, she did not feel intimidated. She concentrated on the keyboard and released an energetic rendition of Beethoven's Seventh Symphony, the master's intoxicating paean to creativity and rebirth. When she heard the rumblings of Wagner coming into the Grand Hall she increased her tempo and pressed harder onto the pedal to anchor her into the instrument. She banished Wagner to the margins of her awareness. As she played, she looked down, noticing the small red spot appearing on her white dress. *I will not stop. I will not be silenced*, she thought. The spot grew larger as she continued. It soaked her lap but she did not stop, nor did she awaken as she had always done. The blood flowed out of her and washed across the stage. The audience began to shout angrily at Eva but she kept playing. The blood filled the Grand Hall as the officers scrambled to escape the deluge. Eva played with a ferocity she had never embodied before. Nazi salutes became flailing arms and hands as the blood engulfed them all. She heard a seismic rumbling from the piano as the audience disappeared under the red tide. She finished the piece, bashing the final note with a concussive crack.

Eva woke in her hotel bed to the awareness of warmth between her thighs. Her fingers explored between her legs and felt the viscous fluid, the womanhood that had been denied to her for so many months. She reveled in her connection to the very pulse of life itself. She felt physically weak and psychically strong. The feeling was so overwhelming and comforting that, even though she should get up and clean herself, she simply surrendered to it. Her measured breathing, her heartbeat, and the surge of blood through her veins created a symphony of renewal within her.

Eva heard movement in the kitchen as she lay in the darkness. She got up and washed herself at the sink. She folded a small hand towel the way she was taught by the women in the camp and tucked it into fresh panties. That would have to do until she could get some menstrual pads at the pharmacy. She tiptoed carefully down the stairs. Yossel sat at the steel preparation table making little figures out of dough. He looked embarrassed when he saw her.

"I am making gingerbread men."

"In the middle of the night?" Eva cocked her head at the baker and raised an eyebrow. She embraced herself against the midnight chill.

Yossel kept making the little figures and finally stopped and looked at Eva with a shy smile. "Alright, alright. The truth is I am making Golems."

"What is a Golem?"

"It is a creature made of the earth," Yossel said, adding with a wink, "and a few special ingredients." He arranged a dozen or so on a tray and placed them in the oven. "According to the *kabbalah*, a Golem can be made to protect Jewish communities in times of trouble. I thought we could use a little help here in Laszlo."

"And you believe that? Where were the Golems during the war when we needed them the most?" It came out angrier than Eva meant it.

Yossel's shoulders slumped. "Do I believe it? No, not really. But I thought it couldn't hurt. Anyway, I don't know the magic words that make them come alive. I don't think anybody does. And if they don't come to life, at least we will have fresh gingerbread cookies for the morning."

Eva shook her head at the baker's foolishness. She returned to her room and fell back asleep. A short while later she woke to a clatter in the kitchen again. She went down to tell Yossel to go to bed, but there was no one in the kitchen. A scratching noise came from the oven. Eva thought a mouse might have gotten into it and slowly opened the oven door. Twelve little figures lay on the baking tray. Seeing no mouse, she took the tray out and placed it on the prep table.

Yossel's Golems, she marveled, as she pondered what could be the incantation that would bring them to life. Eva thought about the day, about how angry she was at the mayor's wife for being so insensitive to her. She thought about her confused opinion of the mayor, for his lofty promises that everything would be fine, that they would all be taken care of when so little seemed to be going well for any of the Jews of Laszlo. She leaned on the table and began to cry. A tear landed on one of the Golems. It popped up to attention. Eva fell back and stared at the figure. She wiped a tear and lowered it on another of the small gingerbread figures. Once again, the figure popped up and looked at Eva. She laughed through her tears. Finally, someone, something was going to help her. She placed a tear on each of the Golems. The little cookie men lined up in a military formation, seeming to wait for instructions. Eva stared at the strange creatures before her. *I wish they would punish Mrs. Kodaly and kick her out of my house forever.*

The little men exploded off the table and ran for the door. They climbed on top of each other to open it and charged into the street. Eva was alarmed and chased after them. The Golems went up the street and across the empty square. They stopped and pulled up the Jewish gravestones, piling them neatly on the street. Then they charged up Kossuth Street in the direction of Eva's house. When she caught up, they had already smashed open the front door and entered the house. The fist doorknocker lay dented in the foyer, the brass fingers twisted together. Eva followed the trail of gingerbread crumbs into the house. A shriek from upstairs made her dash to her parent's former bedroom. She pushed open the door and screamed when she saw the little Golems in her parents' bed, smashing the heads of the mayor and his wife.

"Stop! Stop! This isn't what I wanted! It's wrong! It's wrong!" It was too late. The faces of the victims were pummeled into pulp, yet in the shadows of the room their eyes remained open. Eva saw the same hollow look she had seen on the camp inmates. The Golems ran out of the room, out of the house and back toward the hotel.

Eva leaped up from the bed. Her breathing was heavy and her nightgown soaked with sweat. It was morning. Schumann's "Fantasy in C" was playing on the kitchen radio. After catching her breath, Eva threw water on her face and pulled a large sweater over her nightgown. A warm platter of gingerbread men waited at the bottom of the stairs on the largest of the dining room tables. She sat down and rubbed her eyes, staring at the cookies for a sign of movement. When nothing happened she gingerly picked one up. The morning newspaper was on the table. Eva glanced at the headline as she chewed on the gingerbread. A note of salt played on her tongue.

"Mayor Orders Repair of Kossuth Square—Jewish Stones to be Removed."

"This is wonderful!" Eva said. "The mayor is doing what he said he would. He is taking care of us."

Oskar lumbered up and snatched the paper from the table. "Yeah, he is, isn't he? But read the article, Eva." The butcher scrolled a stubby finger down the article, stopping and tapping on the third paragraph. "Look there, he says 'it is time to turn the page on a dark era in the history of our great nation.' He doesn't mention Jews once. He could be talking about fixing up an old playground. Worse, there's a bunch of quotes from locals saying he is doing 'special favors for the Jews,' and that the town has more pressing needs than 'tearing up the square for the Jews.'" He jabbed a finger at the paper. "And look at the photo of the mayor with his hard hat and shovel. This is more about him being a good politician than righting the wrongs done to us."

"Maybe he is trying to do the right thing by us, but not upset some of the townspeople," Yossel said in a tentative voice. "The war is barely over. We've seen the mixed reaction we've gotten in Laszlo.

I think he's trying his best."

Oskar dropped the paper back onto the table. "I know you think the mayor is well-intentioned. Maybe he is, but this just gives people another excuse to spit on us. There is so much hatred under the surface, always has been. We have to be real careful we don't feed into it." He pointed to the paper. "Even by accident."

Yossel smiled ruefully. *"Der top rufn di kesl shvarts."*

"What does that mean?" Eva asked.

Oskar frowned at Yossel. "'The pot is calling the kettle black.' Yossel thinks my anger feeds into the hatred, but I think his *tuchus*-kissing does. Seems like anything any of us does just makes people hate us more. There's no way out of this."

Was Oskar right? Was there anything Eva could do to get the mayor and his wife to return her house? Her angry outburst didn't help, even if it was warranted. But if she didn't stand up for herself, Mrs. Kodaly would continue to treat her like hired help. There was never a moment to talk about the issue as Mrs. Kodaly had each day tightly scripted. Work, lunch, practice, leave. The mayor was rarely there. Were they avoiding the subject of Eva's house?

E va rummaged through the women's clothing boxes, finding a knee-length white cotton sailor-style dress outlined in blue with a low waistline. It seemed a bit old fashioned, but was clean and nicely pressed. She didn't want to be seen in the same clothes day after day, partially because she didn't want to reinforce the image of herself as the poor Jewish girl wandering town in sad, old clothes, but also because Oskar's remarks about people hating them upset her. Why would they? People liked her playing and she was clearly part of the community before the deportation. She sighed heavily and went upstairs to change, determined not to let Oskar's negativity weigh her down. When she returned the men were still arguing in the kitchen. Eva leaned against the kitchen counter as Oskar complained bitterly about the receipt he found in his room.

"They used our money to buy the new mattresses for the hotel from Mor, the *momser* who stole Weiss's furniture store. And look at how much he charged!"

Yossel glanced up from the dishes in the sink. "At least they are modern ones with springs, not lumpy cotton or horsehair like Armin had."

"It was our money. They could have gotten the cheaper ones. We won't be here forever."

As Yossel tried to parry Oskar's litany of woes, Eva grabbed some of the World Jewish Congress money out of an envelope in the kitchen drawer and slipped out of the hotel. She intended to buy menstrual pads at the pharmacy, even though she had never bought them herself before. They were always in the upstairs bathroom cabinet. Her mother would call over the wife of the pharmacist whenever she needed to buy *personal items*, as she called them. But the ownership of the pharmacy had changed. The sign no longer said *Getz Pharmacy*. A larger one proclaimed *New Laszlo Pharmacy*.

Eva peered through the pharmacy window on her way to the house in the morning. The displays were the same, carved walnut shelves full of face creams, shaving razors, and popular hair ointments near the make-up counter. Instead of old Mr. Getz behind the counter and his wife perched on a stool off to the side, a young man with slicked down hair and a crisp white lab coat who sat puffing a pipe seemed to run the pharmacy. He signaled Eva to come in. She entered the pharmacy and surveyed it casually, then wandered down an aisle toward the make-up. The young man followed her, smiling. Eva picked out a lipstick, not too red, some pancake that matched her skin tone and some mascara. She hadn't intended to buy these things, but with the young pharmacist watching she needed time to figure out where to find the pads without asking this man. Even though it was a ruse, it felt good, so normal, to be buying something luxurious, just for herself.

"May I help you?"

"No, thank you," Eva replied absently. "Is it just you running the pharmacy now?"

Pride brightened the young man's face. "Yes! I graduated pharmacy school last year. My father owns a pharmacy in Debrecen. I often worked there as a boy. When this place came on the market, it was such a steal! Father bought it and I run it."

"Why such a steal? It was always a good business for Mr. and Mrs. Getz."

He smoothed down his hair and chuckled. "A girl your age probably doesn't know much about business. The shop was listed as surplus Jewish property. The owners were ordered by the Ministry of Health to run a pharmacy at a labor camp. It was their patriotic duty during the war. But they haven't returned and can't be found, even though they were notified at their last known address."

"Their last known address was Auschwitz concentration camp," Eva said dully. Did this young man or his father not understand why the pharmacy was "surplus"? Did they care?

The young pharmacist was startled. His eyes darted to the side, avoiding Eva's glare. "Oh, you must be the Jewish girl people are talking about. Well, welcome back to Laszlo."

Eva couldn't tell if there was embarrassment, irony, or nothing at all behind the voice. She took her make-up to the register. As the pharmacist rang up her purchases, Eva looked behind the counter, hoping to see the pads. "Isn't there a woman here to help with . . . women's purchases?"

The young man raised an eyebrow. "Miss, it's 1945. I am a trained pharmacist. There is nothing I can't provide you." His eyes shone slightly as he smiled at Eva. "What can I do for you?"

The look on his face reminded Eva of the guards at the camp. She wouldn't be surprised if he had scales instead of skin. "Nothing at all. I was only wondering."

The final *ching* of the register broke their interaction.

"That will be fifteen *pengos*."

"That seems like a lot, are you sure?"

The pharmacist smirked. "Young lady, the value of our money shrinks weekly. I have heard that the government will soon replace the *pengo* with a new currency. I shouldn't have to say this to a Jew, but if I were you I would spend all you can now before it becomes worthless."

"Not today. Thanks for your advice." Eva said as pleasantly as she could through a clenched jaw. As she left the shop, she realized she would have to find another way to get the pads. She would never ask this young man for help. His sense of superiority and his innuendo were disturbing. Besides, her situation was a woman's business, not any of his.

Mrs. Kodaly appeared relaxed when Eva arrived at the house after the visit to the pharmacy. Eva asked if she wanted her to clean the upstairs bathroom and hallway. She had not been allowed to go upstairs yet. Mrs. Kodaly seemed leery of letting her get too close to her old bedroom, and hovered behind Eva as she swept the polished wooden floor in the hallway. After a while, she seemed satisfied and left.

Eva finished the hallway and moved on to the bathroom. She noisily cleaned the toilet, bath and sink so that Mrs. Kodaly would feel comfortable that Eva was working hard, but between tasks she furtively opened the cabinets under the sink, the medicine cabinet, and the closet, looking for the pads. When she moved some old cleaning supplies in the back of the closet, Eva noticed an open package of pads. She reached for them but hesitated. She had never stolen anything in her life. But was this stealing? They were most certainly her mother's. If not, taking a few pads was small recompense for allowing Mrs. Kodaly and the mayor to live in her house. She could surely replace them when things settled down. Eva's moral compass spun wildly. She reached inside for the courage she had when she smuggled the gunpowder out of the camp factory, glancing to see if Mrs. Kodaly had returned. Feeling safe, she grabbed two of the pads and put them in the cleaning bucket.

"What are you doing?" Mrs. Kodaly's stern voice stabbed into Eva's back. "What did you take from that closet?"

Eva blushed deeply. She hadn't thought of a lie to cover her actions if caught, and nothing came to mind. She reached inside the bucket and took out the pads. She held them out with a downturned face.

The mayor's wife looked at the pads and stiffened. "You are stealing from me?" Then she saw the anguish and embarrassment on the girl's face. Mrs, Kodaly softened. "Oh. Don't you have any pads of your own?"

Eva burst out in tears. She told Mrs. Kodaly how the women in the camp were beaten and lost their periods, and how after almost a year she had only begun to bleed the night before. She talked about how her mother would always buy the pads, and Eva's discomfort at the unfamiliar ownership of the pharmacy.

Mrs. Kodaly stood straight and unblinking as Eva spoke. Finally, she cleared her throat. Her words came out strained, yet gentle. "Well, you should have asked me instead of taking the pads. But given the circumstances I forgive you and will not mention this incident to my husband." The women stood together in silence. Mrs. Kodaly spoke quietly. "If you need more than what is in the closet, let me know and I will buy them for you." Then she quickly added, "Of course. You must pay me back immediately."

Mrs. Kodaly's small kindness lifted Eva's spirits. Further, lunch was more than the usual cold meats. Instead, Mrs. Kodaly served Eva a chilled gooseberry soup with potatoes and sour cream. After lunch, the music flowed out of Eva for the first time in a year. Precision and timing were returning to her fingers. She grew increasingly able to sight read the complex classical transcriptions she found in her piano bench. Soon she would be racing comfortably and unconsciously across the keyboard without missing a note. All she needed now was to reconnect with Professor Sandor and prepare for the Academy.

The Tuesday Special Train would be pulling through Laszlo soon. Eva hurried through a series of exercises the professor always made her perform before finishing a practice. They were odd combinations of notes with no particular harmony or flow, chords that floated disconnectedly from the keyboard. He insisted on these short segments without any explanation. "Sometimes there are *why's* beyond our comprehension," he would say before closing his eyes and going far away, signaling the end of the lesson. Eva often wondered if they would add up to a complete composition, just as the small movements in her childhood ballet classes evolved into sweeping dances when combined later. She missed a note, smiling as his voice urged concentration in her ear. *Stop banging the keys as if you were hammering nails into wood. This is a glissando. Let your fingers skitter gently across the keyboard like a little mouse.* She thanked a surprised Mrs. Kodaly as she ran out of the house and toward the station, not wanting to miss the train. Intuitively, she knew today was the day.

As Eva passed the park, she became aware of her high school friends again. This time she clearly saw Hanna. A young, blond-haired man stood next to her, smoking a cigarette. *Andras.* She stopped suddenly and felt her heart racing. She wondered if he had thought of her, missed her while she was gone. Would her friends welcome her back if she approached them now? Professor Sandor's train would not be arriving for fifteen minutes. She would be able to hear the whistle of its approach from the park. That would provide an excuse to break from the reunion if it wasn't comfortable. As she weighed the possible outcomes, she found her feet had made the decision for her. A herd of small children led by a young nun in a black habit raced between Eva and her former classmates. Eva closed her eyes as they passed, resisting the urge to search the group for children she had known. There were no Jewish children in Laszlo.

Eva braced herself, trying not to stare at Andras. The broad expanse of lawn and the dark copse of trees reminded her of their last meeting. Their near kiss in that very spot was the last recollection of anything resembling joy she could find. Yet she didn't see him at the deportation, nor had he tried to contact her since she had returned. At first, Andras did not appear to notice her. Then their eyes met and he gave a tentative smile before putting his head down. Did he not want to see her or did he simply not recognize her? She felt so ugly, so thin. When she was ten feet away he looked at her again. This time she could see recognition in his eyes. He offered his familiar smile, revealing the shining white teeth that had attracted her so.

Besides Andras stood Hanna and Ilona, two girls who were best friends in high school. They were statuesque, beautiful. Aryan. Eva felt so much lesser than these two. She fought the urge to flee in embarrassment. Hanna was always friendly to Eva, but when these two were together, nobody else mattered. Hanna spoke first, wide-eyed with surprise.

"Eva, is it really you? We heard you came back."

Ilona crinkled her nose. "What did you do to your hair?"

The four stood awkwardly for a brief moment until Eva forced out a few words toward Hanna, ignoring the other girl.

"Yes, I am back." How could she begin this conversation? She looked around the park. It was exactly as she remembered it on her last day with Andras. "So much has changed in Laszlo."

Hanna and Ilona looked at each other, perplexed. Ilona cocked her head at Eva. "Really? How?"

A giant hand thudded against Eva's chest. "Are you serious? For one thing, all the Jewish stores are gone and all the names have been changed."

Ilona flipped back her long brown hair and shrugged. "The war's over. That's the most important thing."

"Don't you wonder what happened to all the Jews in town?" Eva gasped. "Don't you know what happened to me and my family? Don't you want to know?" Eva's self-control was evaporating.

Hanna put up her hands, a note of pleading in her voice. "All we heard was that the Jews were sent to work camps and then just moved away after the war ended."

"How could anyone believe that? How could you not know or even ask what happened to all your teachers, your doctors, your neighbors, your friends? What about all the other Jewish students at school?"

"Actually," Ilona said, "remember Mr. Horvath, our science teacher? He lost his leg in the war."

Eva was startled by a sudden memory. She gritted her teeth. "Last time I saw Mr. Horvath he was pushing families toward the train with his blackboard pointer like he was sending children to the principal's office instead of to their death."

"Mmmm," Ilona replied thoughtfully, as if Eva had never spoken. "A couple of boys from the class ahead of ours were killed and a bunch didn't come back."

"Some boys from our soccer team didn't come back either," Andras added.

"It's so sad." Ilona shuddered. "But I really don't want to talk about that."

Eva's world was turning ashen. She felt a wave of nausea and anger. "What do you want to talk about? Hanna's pretty dress? Her new hair style?"

Ilona's mouth opened and closed indignantly. "Oh, so now you are jealous of Hanna? Is it because you're so skinny and pale?"

Eva took a long, slow breath. What was more important, being self-righteous or reconnecting with her only friends? "No, I'm not jealous. It's just that those things aren't important." She was swept away by a sudden surge of emotion. "Not as important as losing my family—losing everything I loved and being totally alone."

A heavy silence ensued. A train whistle in the distance split the tension. Eva looked toward the station and back at Andras. "I need to meet the train. I am waiting for Professor Sandor, my piano teacher, to return."

"Can I walk with you a little ways?" Andras said hesitantly.

Eva shook off her anger and confusion. She felt like she was on a different planet than her former classmates, but she was so desperate for a connection. "Sure. I'd like that."

They turned and left the park without looking at Hanna or Ilona. Their hands brushed as they walked toward the square. Eva wondered if she should reach out and take his hand as a gesture that there was something to hold on to. But she didn't. In the camp she learned that trust must be earned, it was too easy for someone to betray a trust. Andras offered her his cigarette. She took it and drew on it slowly. It felt like it did in the park, except he wasn't looking at her. With a shaking hand she passed the cigarette back to Andras. He took a deep drag, then sighed through a cloud of smoke.

"I'm sorry, Eva, I really am, but this hasn't been easy for us either. After you left and the Arrow Cross took over, everybody who had Jewish friends was suspected of being disloyal to Hungary. People whispered about each other and made accusations. I got taken into the police station. They slapped me. Can you believe it? They slapped me! Then they questioned me about our relationship. They said we kissed and why did I kiss a Jew? They said that my blood would be polluted if we went any further."

"And you believed them?"

Andras's face flushed. "No, of course not. It's hard to explain. When the police, the Germans, the teachers, everybody in authority tell you something is true over and over again, even if it doesn't convince you, it confuses things. It makes the truth and the lies sort of equal."

His eyes turned downward as they crossed the square. "Look, Eva, I just don't know what to say. Even before you left . . ."

You mean before my family was deported to a concentration camp. She wanted to scream out the bitter words. She was so angry at people tiptoeing around the issues that had deformed her life, but she didn't want to alienate Andras. They had almost kissed once.

". . . it was on the radio every day. Everybody was talking about it at school. Constant, constant bad things about Jews. Pure Hungary, free from Jews, bright future. It was on the newsreels and in the newspapers. It kind of took over. Even at the university." His eyes begged Eva for a sympathetic response. None was given. "Anyway, now that the war is over and you are back, I would like to walk with you from time to time."

Eva looked down, noticing they were walking where the Jewish tombstones had been. Andras's explanation struck her as weak. Are people so easily swayed into betraying friendships? "So even when we shared that cigarette and almost kissed, you disliked me because I was Jewish?"

"No, I was struggling. I really liked you. I just didn't . . . like . . ."

"Jews?" Eva's heart became a block of ice. Her demeanor remained soft as she tried desperately to hold on to her threadbare connection to Andras, but her insides were deadened. The gap between her and Andras felt too wide.

Andras changed the subject. "So, your professor is coming back. That's great. How is your music coming along?"

"My music?" She chuckled sardonically, the dead feeling rising closer to the surface. "When my life was stolen and I was sent to the death camp, I felt like I had slipped down into hell. Music was the only thing I could control, even if it was only in my head."

The young man shook his head slowly as he whistled a long note. "I can't imagine what that was like."

No. He couldn't.

CHAPTER 16

The Special Train slowed to a halt. The station master met the conductor, but no clipboard passed between them. They talked for a moment, then the station master approached the group of Jews waiting on the platform.

"We have to hold this Special Train here until the track ahead is clear. No DPs from Laszlo today, sorry." He gave a fleeting glance to the disappointed girl standing before him, turned briskly on his heels, and strode away.

Eva followed him toward his office. "Wait, please. Did you say none of the passengers are from Laszlo? Nobody is getting off?"

The station master was startled by Eva's language. *Passengers.* He realized that he had unconsciously been calling the Jews on the Special Trains *DPs* to keep them at an emotional distance, to prevent himself from facing the consequences of his and the town's actions in shuttling their friends and neighbors to their deaths. He looked at the confusion in the girl's face. Pain seared his heart. She was there every Tuesday and Thursday. Each time he saw her waiting for her professor, he prayed for his return as well. He had even started to believe the man would be on one of the next trains. He had to be, for the girl's sake and for his own. "No, young lady, nobody is getting off today. But the train is going to be held up. All the . . . *passengers* . . . will be able to get off and stretch their legs." He saw the ray of hope in her eyes. "I know who you are waiting for. I am afraid Professor

Sandor is not on this train."

He gave Eva a strained smile and walked quickly back to his office. It was bad enough to stare into those accusing eyes and to hear his name in whispers or shrieks from the trains as they passed through the station, especially at night. It would be harder to see these other Jews close up. He didn't have a choice. The shabby, skeletal passengers who jumped from the train gazed at him as he worked his way through the gathering crowd toward his office. At first he ignored them, keeping his eyes fixed on the sign that read *Station Master* ahead. They pressed in on him. His heart pounded furiously and he elbowed his way toward the calm of his office, swimming upstream against the condemning current. He was the epicenter of guilt. He had heard some stories of the horrors of the camps from different conductors. Yet they heard the stories from others because Hungarians only took the trains as far as the borders. The Germans took over from there. Hungarians were always making up tales to show how inferior and brutish the Czechs, Slovaks, and Germans were. He couldn't believe those stories. He didn't want to.

"Please!" he shouted. "Let me through! I am not responsible! I couldn't stop the trains!" The station master burst into his office, slamming and locking the door behind him. He sat down heavily and allowed his heart to slow. Then he reached for the half bottle of *palinke* in the top drawer of his desk.

Eva watched the passengers jump down off the cars. Mismatched clothes and vacant stares, disheveled and lost. *That's what we must have looked like,* she thought. She tried hard to block the images of the camp forming in her head, concentrating instead on practicing with the professor again and waiting for a reply from the Academy to her second letter. Instead of yelling her questions at a slowly passing train, Eva grabbed the chance to speak to these survivors directly. Somebody must know when the people from Terezin were coming back. She approached a small group of passengers as they stretched and peered around in confusion.

"Excuse me, but were any of you in Terezin? I am looking for someone. Professor Sandor, a musician." At first, the group shrunk away from Eva, but soon recognized her as a fellow survivor. No one had any information about the professor. She repeated her entreaty to other groups along the five cars of the train. Blank stares, slowly shaking heads, disinterested or sympathetic looks. Heartbroken, she turned away from the last car to return to Yossel and Oskar. A man's voice came from behind her.

"You are looking for a musician from Terezin?"

Eva leaped at the hope carried by the question. "Yes, yes! Do you know anything?"

The man grimaced, looked down at the ground and spit. "Musicians in concentration camps. What a mockery! They debased themselves. They stayed alive by playing music for the Nazis while our families died."

Another voice emerged from the group. "Everybody did what they could to survive. So what if they got an extra piece of bread or didn't have to carry dead bodies around, they still suffered. Let them go in peace."

The first man's angry voice rose up. "They played while the Nazis marched our people to the gas chambers. I was in Auschwitz. I heard them. I saw them. How could they do that?"

"No!" Eva shouted, shaking. "Professor Sandor wasn't in Auschwitz. He was sent to Terezin. There were no gas chambers there. He didn't do that. He wouldn't do that."

The angry man snorted. "Musicians who played in any camp perverted music. They used our beautiful music, our great composers, to lie to us, to distract us from the horror of our lives." He turned to the emaciated man next to him. "Do you remember when we marched back from dragging the bodies, digging the ditches? The orchestra played 'Rosamunde'—what do they call it now? 'Beer Barrel Polka'? They mocked our suffering. The music destroyed our spirits as surely as the ovens destroyed our bodies." His face turned purple. "I was a music teacher before the war, but I will never listen to music again."

The words struck Eva hard. How could music be perverted so? All her life, music was beautiful, life affirming. But then images that were locked deep inside her emerged. The blue sailor uniforms of the camp women's orchestra. Buoyant marches playing as the new prisoners arrived at the selection tables. Music giving false hopes. Long lines of shuffling men and women returning from hard, horrid labor while another band played uplifting Bach pieces. Music Eva associated with family and good times used to degrade and break the human spirit. She had blocked out these memories, determined to keep music pure and hopeful in her mind. Eva put her hands on her knees and breathed deeply until the roiling nausea passed.

A woman's voice called from the crowd. "Terezin? Terezin? He was a musician in Terezin?" Eva searched for the voice. It came from a crowd of a dozen or so people, gathered in the shade of an overhanging station sign. She spied a woman's haggard face in the afternoon shadows. Her heart quickened. Someone knew the professor.

"Yes! He played piano. While I was in Auschwitz I heard he was conducting the children's orchestra at Terezin." A long, tense silence draped over the crowd like a shroud. Eva was confused. At last, she pleaded urgently, "Can you help me find him?"

"Oh, you poor girl," the woman said back to her. "If he was the children's conductor, well, I can only tell you what I heard." She pushed herself to the front of the crowd. She was as thin and haunted as death itself, yet she managed to give Eva a pitying look. "Back in September, the SS put on a performance for the Red Cross at Terezin to show the world how well we were treated in the camps. They let the children's orchestra perform a piece of their own choosing.

They performed '*Brundibar*', or 'Bumblebee', a simple opera about the triumph of helpless children over an evil tyrant. The fools from the Red Cross loved the show and told the world that Terezin was not such bad a place for Jews."

"Every camp was hell, a disaster for us," another voice added. "How could the world not know what was happening?"

The woman's strained voice continued. "The Germans had never seen the opera before, but they soon understood the performance was an act of defiance. The bumblebees even wore black and yellow striped outfits that mimicked what the children were forced to wear." A long silence followed.

Eva hesitated before launching her next question. She felt queasy, and hugged her stomach tightly with both arms to calm herself. "Please, what happened?"

Some of the passengers on the platform turned their heads toward the older woman. Many bowed and closed their eyes, mumbling prayers. "After the Red Cross left, the Germans took all forty of those precious little bumblebees. They grabbed the conductor, the musicians, even the poor simpleton who turned the pages for the pianist. They marched them to the train to Auschwitz and directly into the gas chambers."

"*Hier ist kein warum*," grumbled the angry man. "That's what the guards said in Auschwitz. Remember, girl? 'Here there is no why.' Your professor probably ran right past you into the showers."

Eva remembered the rainy, cold morning the inmates were forced to stand at attention and watch as three men and a woman were hanged for some untold infraction of unknowable rules. Behind the dangling bodies, she saw a train arrive. Just another in an endless series, but this one had a car full of brightly costumed children. The dogs were snapping and barking, the children screaming in terror. She saw them being whipped and shoved toward the gas chambers with a smaller group of adults. It was such a painful sight that Eva had turned her face away. She played a Brahms lullaby in her mind, trying to take herself far away from that morning of impossible inhumanity. But now she wondered. Did Professor Sandor search for Eva through the barbed wire? Did he shout to her? Had she missed her chance to say goodbye by turning away and blotting out the ugly scene with music? Was he in the ashes that rained down upon the camp that afternoon, his soul reaching out to touch Eva's cheek through the incinerated gray remains of his body?

"Everybody back on board!" cried the conductor. "Let's go! Quickly!"

The blood drained from Eva's face as her entire body began to vibrate. The world shattered into a million shards of sharp, twinkling glass. Her vision darkened as she crashed to the ground, her fingers frozen and unmoving at her sides.

CHAPTER 17

Oskar took the bucket of bloody chicken guts outside. The garbage cans were nearly overflowing and drawing swarms of flies in the hot, moist June air. Their incessant buzz taunted Oskar. The town was supposed to pick up the garbage at the hotel every week, but the collector had refused, saying that Armin still owed him money from before the deportation. The butcher poured what he could into the last can and threw the rest behind some bushes, knowing it would attract rats and other vermin. He had no choice. He tried to talk to the town clerk and gotten the usual confusing explanations and impossible administrative remedies. His frustration swelled when he went to the hardware store to buy a shovel so he could bury the waste. The owner told him he had none to sell—in spite of the fact that a half dozen were in plain view beyond the register. He thought about talking to the mayor himself. *Yeah, the mayor can get another headline*, he fumed. *"Mayor Saves Town from Filthy Jews."*

Oskar clasped his hand on his stomach. He could feel the anger burrowing like a worm deep within. If it wasn't a worm, it had to be some other kind of infestation. Maybe something he got at the camp. It was in his gut, but other times it crawled through his brain. Sometimes it wound painfully through his heart. It hurt most when he thought of his wife and children. Without his apartment, photographs, or any material representation, it was as though their lives had been erased. His existence was meaningless. The red-hot worm corkscrewed deeper inside with every hostile stare or indifferent sideways glance. Being hated made him angry. Being pitied made him angrier. But being ignored was the worst. It made him invisible and that rendered his rage impotent. Oskar growled and cursed a God he didn't believe in. He went back inside the hotel to grab the last bucket of garbage to toss in the bushes. Yossel was setting the dinner table.

"How's the girl?" Oskar said. Thinking about Eva took his mind off his own misery, if only for a moment.

"She's resting. She'll be alright." Yossel replied. "She's made of pretty tough stuff."

"Tougher than me. I am ready to kill someone for what they did to us."

"Don't even joke like that, Oskar. Eva's a strong girl and she's got something to hold on to. Her music. Losing her professor was a hard blow, but she still has the Academy to look toward. We have to support her any way we can. And that includes watching what we say about our own problems, right?"

"Yeah, I know, I know." Oskar squeezed his fists together. "Look, Yossel, Eva's got her music. You've got the bakery. I've got nothing. No family, no apartment, no job." He looked down at his mismatched clothes and muttered miserably, "not even any clothes of my own."

"What do you mean no job?"

Oskar turned his face away from Yossel. "Egon let me go this morning. He told me there were complaints that some of the meat I was cutting tasted spoiled. It was a lie. I saw the disgust on some of his customers' faces when they saw me at the chopping block. They didn't want their meat touched by the dirty Jew." He swallowed hard, the acid memory burning his throat. "But you know something? Why shouldn't they be afraid, why shouldn't they hate me? I am death walking. I am their dark, guilty hearts, if they have any. I told that right to Egon's face, too." He shook his head. "Probably shouldn't have said that. It was the excuse he needed to let me go." Oskar felt Yossel's hand on his shoulder.

"Ahh, don't let it get to you. Do you think I like working for that *schmuck* Krauss in my own shop? Every day I'm reminded of my humiliation and everything I've lost. Today he told me not to use so much powdered sugar on top of the Linzer tortes. Imagine! Krauss barely knows how to boil water." Oskar nodded begrudgingly and Yossel gave him a solid pat on the back. "You know our lot as Jews is to suffer for God and choose life, to overcome our suffering and be a light in the world."

"I feel more like a boxer who keeps getting flattened and refuses to stay down and take the count. At what point do you throw in the towel?" Oscar cracked his neck as if to ensure no lingering resentments were lodged in his spine.

"You and I don't have much of anything, Oskar," Yossel pointed toward the ceiling, "but we've got Eva. We've got the chance to help her get out of here and live again, to realize her dream and make her beautiful music. Can you imagine Eva playing in an elegant concert hall before an adoring audience?"

Oskar thought about being dressed up and sitting in the audience of a fancy Budapest concert hall, watching Eva perform. He gave a great sigh, letting the anger drain from his body. If he couldn't improve his own life in this uncaring town, maybe he could help Eva get out. At least it was something. If that were all he could ever do in this miserable life, he would feel content.

Oskar walked out the back door of the hotel carrying food scraps. As he approached the bushes he heard the squeak of rats fighting over the chicken guts. His fleeting feelings of hope for Eva vanished and he threw the can toward the noise.

"Damn you to hell! I am going to kill you! I am going to kill every one of you!" He raged on for a few minutes and sat down against the lone garbage can, defeated by rats and men.

"Oskar? Are you alright?" Oskar looked up to see the station master's worried look. "I heard you as I was coming down the hill. So did everybody who passed by. It sounded like you were in a brawl back here."

Oskar blinked several times before the anger and desolation cleared from his vision. "Oh, Josef, it's you." The station master reached out and grabbed the butcher's forearm, pulling Oskar to a standing position. Oskar told his tale of trying to find a shovel and the humiliations he had experienced. "And today this." He pulled a piece of paper out of his back pocket. "A violation notice from the town for not keeping all garbage in closed barrels. They are trying to drive me out of my mind, or at least out of Laszlo, I swear."

The station master smiled sympathetically. "Oskar, I have a shovel not two hundred yards from here at the station. You can use it anytime you like."

"Nah. If people see me walking away with a shovel they'll think I stole it. Jews steal everything, don't they?"

The station master grimaced. "Oh, Oskar, I am so sorry the situation has come to this. This ugliness, this sickness that has infected so many people. But Oskar, it hasn't infected everyone, believe me. There are still many good people who know you and think kindly about you here in Laszlo. Come, come with me back to the station. I will give you the shovel so there will be no question that it's all right for you to have it." He sprouted a mischievous smile. "And perhaps a sip of *palinke* or 'schnoops,' remember? That's what we called it when we stole a bottle from my parents and drank it under the bleachers at the basketball games. That was our secret code name."

Oskar was taken aback. He peered at Josef. He realized that since his return, he had walked around in a fog. He had blocked any good memories of Laszlo. Now, a trickle of recollections resurfaced. He had known the station master since they were children, through two World Wars, a communist takeover, the mass influenza that killed more people than any war—and this man remembered drinking together as young men at the basketball games. Later on, as fathers, they had sat on the sidelines at high school games, patting each other on the back or giving solace depending on the outcome, always rooting for each other's sons. Oskar had attended the funeral of Josef's first wife, struck down by the Great Influenza in 1918, and the burial of his second wife when she died of women's sweating disease shortly after delivering their second son.

The men walked toward the station, conversing about their wives and children and the sad ends to both their families over the years. Oskar's heart ached, but he realized it felt good to talk about better times with an old friend. When Josef mentioned the name of his own lost son, Michael, Oskar remembered the boy, and another rush of memories flooded in, bursting his defensive dam further. He'd had a life in Laszlo. A good life, and the station master was part of it before it was so brutally betrayed. Oskar realized that this conversation was the first act of kindness and humanity anyone in Laszlo had shown him since before the deportation. Maybe he needed to control his anger. Not everybody hated him. There must be more people like the Josef left in Laszlo. If he didn't chase everybody, away he might feel more welcomed, might reconstruct his shattered life.

After a few rounds of *palinke* in the office, Josef gave Oskar a bewildered look. "They come every night, Oskar. I have to be here and see each one pass by. How many Jews did the Germans take away? How many are left?" He held his hands tight over his ears as if to block out a stern verdict. "Why do these trains come night after night?"

"What trains are you talking about?"

The station master grabbed Oskar's shoulder. "The big black German DR trains. They come every night. They sit on the tracks inhaling and exhaling like giant beasts. No one ever gets off. The conductor never calls back to me, but sometimes someone summons me from the cars. Then they just leave."

Oskar looked at the empty bottles in the waste basket. "Josef, you need to go easy on the *palinke*. You need to get some sleep."

"I need forgiveness! I need to beg God to forgive me!" He squeezed his head in his hands. "But what could I have done? I'm not to blame."

Oskar tried to think of Josef as an innocent victim, but knew in his heart that the man hadn't had the courage to resist. Nobody in Laszlo did. The man's whimpering grated. Oskar couldn't hold back the angry question any longer. "Josef, how could you let this happen? How could anybody in Laszlo let this happen?"

The question hit Josef squarely in the face. He rambled on about how the murder of the Jews all over Europe had not happened in Hungary. It couldn't. Hungarians were too sophisticated to believe that propaganda garbage on the radio. Hungarian Jews were so assimilated. They served honorably in the Great War. Hungary had secretly tried to get out of its pact with Germany, but the Germans discovered the deception and invaded. The Russians were already deep inside Hungary and within one hundred miles of Laszlo. Everybody thought the war was ending. Then the deportation was ordered. They said Jews were going to work camps, like the labor battalions, like Oskar's oldest son, like the Getz pharmacists. He put his head down, shame reddening his face as he cried. "It all happened so fast."

Oskar walked up the hill to the hotel with the shovel over his shoulder. Maybe Josef was right. It did happen so fast. They all were caught off guard, even the Jews of Laszlo. But he also remembered the crowds the day of the deportation. Some of the people who

lined the street from the town square to the train station seemed
stunned, some sad. But many, too many, cheered or jeered. It was
almost a festival, watching old people prodded along by a triumphant
Sergeant Ritook. Older Jewish men in their suits and fedoras retained
their somber dignity as if they were attending a hearing or a funeral.
Mothers tried to comfort their frightened children as angry or
laughing neighbors confronted them. He saw himself lifting his wife
and younger son onto the train before climbing aboard, using his body
to shield them from the police and the taunts. If he had known what
awaited them at the other end of the tracks he would have fought back,
he would have died to protect his family. But he didn't know.

No, the station master may have been sincere, but what did his
guilt and sincerity accomplish? Nothing. He didn't speak for all the
people of Laszlo. The small comfort Oskar found in Josef's contrition
began to evaporate. The butcher tried to classify his former neighbors
and customers into those who knowingly acted, those who helped
and those who simply ignored what was happening. Should he feel
differently about each of them? And how soon after the deportation
did the citizens of Laszlo steal everything the Jews owned? Did they
wait a few months for them to return, or did they rush in before
the train had faded from view? It was too much to hold in his head.
Oskar turned his thoughts to the rats.

As Oskar rounded the hotel people cleared the street, avoiding
the burly Jew swinging a shovel and growling "I'll kill you all."

CHAPTER 18

Viktor watched as his father poured the golden Tokaji wine into a small glass. The family sat at the elaborately carved claw-footed cherrywood dining room table Sergeant Ritook had grabbed from an apartment building when the Jews were deported. His father held the amber liquid up to the light.

"I am happy these vineyards are in the hands of true Hungarians now, not Jews. It makes the wine all the sweeter." Ritook motioned to his young son. "Viktor, take this to your grandfather."

Viktor's mother put her fork down forcefully. "You know it's bad for his heart."

"Son, do as you're told."

The young boy dutifully got up from the table, avoiding its powerful, clawed feet. He was certain the table came alive at night and prowled their house because of Jewish magic. He took the glass and delivered it to the old man in the wheelchair at the other end of the table. His mother went into the kitchen. She returned with a large bowl of noodles and beef in a cream sauce, serving her disabled father-in-law before placing it on the table.

"What did you do today, Viktor?" Ritook asked his son.

"The Scouts built a fort in the woods behind Gyorgy's house. Then we made some spears and knives to protect it from attack."

"Ha! That's my boy!" cried Viktor's grandfather, spilling some of the wine on his pill-covered brown cardigan sweater. "Get ready for the next battle! We need to get the land back that was stolen from us after the Great War. Two-thirds of our country! Gone!"

"The Treaty of Trianon! Agreed to by traitors and cowards!" Viktor stood erect and recited, just like in school.

Grandfather wagged a finger at Viktor. "How many of our Hungarian brothers are under the yoke of the Romanians and Czechs now? We must free those lands and become Greater Hungary once more!"

Viktor beamed at his grandfather. "Yes sir! We will beat the Jews and the Russians again."

The old man's clouded eyes shone brightly. He looked around the room suspiciously and spoke to his grandson in a conspiratorial tone. "We have to be careful, my boy. Those Jews are treacherous. Ever wonder why great empires come and go but the Jews always remain? It is not because they are intelligent. They can't write good music and they've never invented anything. No, the secret lies in their cunning. Do you understand that?"

"Yes, Grandfather," Viktor said, hoping to get it right. "Their secret lies in their cunning."

"Exactly! They let others do the fighting and make sure they back the winning side. Then they come in and grab the spoils of the war. That's why there are so many Jewish counts and barons. They get titles from the emperor for giving him money after every war. Never trust anybody but a true Hungarian. We are Magyars, boy. We must restore our glory. Like we did in the Great War until we were betrayed."

"Don't worry, Grandfather. I will fight for the honor of our country!"

"That's my boy. I am proud of you." He sipped his wine and leaned back in his chair, closing his eyes. Viktor could tell from Grandfather's twitching eyelids that he was reliving the battles old men never lose. That's what his mother had told him. Grandfather spoke to Viktor's father without opening his eyes.

"Son, I read in the paper that the Jews have come back to town. Is that so?"

"Yes, Father," Ritook said. "Just a girl and a few older men. Nothing to worry about."

Viktor glanced up at his father. He knew he was lying to Grandfather. He was always telling Viktor's mother scary reports about the Jews. The butcher was menacing people with a shovel, threatening to kill them. The baker had taken over Krauss's shop and was planning to bring in Romanian Jews to work there. The farmhands were starting fights at Karosi's farm And the girl was bewitching the townspeople, lulling them asleep. He said she was worming her way into their hearts, confusing them into thinking that Jews were just like we were. Viktor clutched his chest. The image of a girl turning into a worm and burrowing into someone's heart terrified him. More Jewish magic.

"Nothing to worry about!" the old man shouted. "It doesn't take many Jews to cause problems. I lost my leg in the Great War because a few Jews gave the king bad advice. We lost all our land because a few Jews sold us out. We suffered under the Red Terror because a few Jews helped the Russians overthrow our beloved sovereign." He rubbed the stump where his left knee should have been. "I will never be whole again, but we can make our nation whole again." He shot the wine down his throat and set the glass down firmly. "Son, it was your job to get rid of the Jews when the government ordered it last year. You better make sure the job is finished this time."

Viktor's mother gave the sergeant a hard look, then turned sweetly to her father-in-law. "Father, please remember your heart. How would you like to show Viktor your maps? He has become so smart. He knows more about Hungarian history that any boy in his class."

"Any boy in the whole school," Viktor added as his chest expanded. Especially since the Jews were taken away last year. He hoped none of them came back. He liked being the smartest. At the same time, he missed having Jews at school. In the last year before they went away, the teachers would turn their heads in the schoolyard and Viktor could kick the Jewish boys or pull the Jewish girls' hair without being punished. He felt important. What was the use of being smart if you couldn't push other students around? That's what a real leader did.

After helping clear the table, Viktor pushed his grandfather back to the old man's room. Either he was getting stronger or his grandfather was getting lighter, but Viktor no longer struggled maneuvering the old man down the hallway. Viktor loved to be invited into that room. Maps of Hungary's former glories festooned the walls. Red arrows showed attacks and counterattacks, colored dotted lines illustrated the shifting borders of empire thanks to Hungary's ever-treacherous neighbors and the scheming Jews. His grandfather always regaled Viktor during these visits with heroic stories of fighting men on horseback, and doomed charges by the enemy. What an empire it had been! Viktor's eyes searched above the metal-framed single bed for the photo of Grandfather with the former king. There also hung Grandfather's medals from the army and Viktor's favorite—the Order of Vitez. Grandfather said the Order was a recognition of his gallantry and bravery on the battlefield, and he was now a knight. The knighthood could be passed from father to son. Viktor hungered to see it passed down to his father and eventually pinned on him. Viktor, the Valiant Knight of the Order of Vitez. For Hungary. While staring at the medals he accidentally bumped into a table where his grandfather kept lead soldiers arrayed in strategic formation. Viktor turned pale when he realized more Hungarian than Russian soldiers had fallen over.

"I am sorry, Grandfather," he pleaded.

The old man wheeled himself over to the table and began to right the soldiers. "That's alright, my boy. Just pray when it is your turn on the battlefield you are standing when the world stops shaking." He rustled the boy's cropped blond hair, then leaned over and kissed his forehead. "We will need you, Viktor, when the time comes to restore our rightful place in the world. I know you will do the right thing."

The four White Stag Scouts sat in their fort, a lean-to made of fallen branches in the woods behind Gyorgy's house. They whittled away, making swords and daggers under the direction of Viktor Ritook. Viktor snorted at the dagger little Janos was fashioning.

"You call that a dagger? It's not sharp enough to go through a piece of paper. If you want to defend yourself or defend Hungary, it needs to be sharp enough to go through skin." He hefted his own work in progress. "Here, give me your arm. I'll show you how sharp mine is." He grabbed for Janos's thin arm but the boy wriggled free.

"C'mon, Viktor, leave him alone," pleaded Gyorgy as Janos started to cry.

Viktor grinned down at the boy. "What's the matter, Janos, did I hurt you?"

Janos sniffled and wiped a tear. "No, it's just that I miss making swords with Hugo and Lajos. They were my best friends."

Viktor gave a dismissive grunt. "Stupid little boy. They weren't your friends. Jews can't be your friends. They were just pretending so they could get something out of you."

The little boy suppressed a sniffle and looked hopefully at Peter. "When are they coming back?"

Peter put his hand on Janos's shoulder. "We don't know, Janos. They went away to the work camp and maybe they've moved now that the war is over."

"They're probably dead," said Viktor as he casually sharpened his wooden blade.

"No!" Janos wailed. "They can't be. They were scouts like us. They knew how to survive! They had merit badges!"

Peter faced Viktor with clenched fists. "Why did you have to say that, Viktor?"

Viktor shrugged his shoulders and admired the sharpened tip of his dagger. "Well, that's what my father said. All the Jews were dead. Men, women, children. So I figure that Hugo and Lajos are dead, too. No sense getting upset about it. They were only Jews, not real Hungarians."

"They were our friends. They were White Stag Scouts. We're supposed to look after each other," Peter said as he comforted Janos. "Tell Janos you don't know where they are and you don't really know if they are dead."

"Sure, sure." He thought about his grandfather's table of lead soldiers, how easily they fell when the table shook. "Who knows anything about all those missing people from the war? What happened to your older brother who worked at the train station, Peter? When is he coming back?"

Peter stammered and looked down without answering.

Viktor jammed the dagger into the ground. "Anyway, we've got work to do. My father said the mayor stole all the girl's treasure. The baker is the only one left with any real treasure and it's hidden in the old Jew town." He pointed toward the fortune in the distance. "Gyorgy! What is your report on the Jew and his treasure?"

Gyorgy leapt to attention. "He went to the brick factory again this morning. He stood in front of the big field and put the blanket over his head. Then he started to say strange words. He did it for a long time, so I left."

Viktor sat back on his haunches and thought about what Gyorgy said. "He's probably repeating some magic formula to protect the treasure. We'll have to keep a close eye on him and see if he tries to dig any up. We should also set a lookout when he is not there so we can search for ourselves." He stood and stretched his back. "That treasure is almost ours. When we find it, the whole town will look up to us."

Naftali lowered the prayer shawl from his head, letting it come to rest on his shoulders. He carefully unwrapped the one *tefillin* from his left arm. He took a profoundly deep, almost painful breath. His recitation of the Mourner's Kaddish over six hundred times was finished. Although the Kaddish was an exhortation to the magnificence of God, Naftali could not stop seeing the faces of the people murdered and buried there at the brick factory. He turned and left the site, trudging back up the road toward Kosveg. When he saw the wreckage of the town he stopped and looked back, his mind unable to encompass the magnitude of the horror of the place and the meaninglessness of the massacre. For the fifth—or was it the fiftieth—time that day he cried, looking directly into the sun for some wisdom he could uncover. He stared, the white-yellow blare searing his pupils as he prayed and pleaded.

Naftali noticed a dark spot in the center of the sun. As he strained it became larger and larger. He felt certain *Ha Shem* was opening His eye to him at last. He put out his hands and beseeched the Lord for direction. The eye of *Ha Shem* got larger until it nearly blotted out the sun. Naftali heard the flutter of wings and the soft coo of a bird. A weight landed on his outstretched left hand. He blinked hard several times until the sun blindness receded. There on his hand sat a brown and white pigeon with a familiar black spot on its forehead. Naftali's eyes widened.

"Beersheba?" He reached over and stroked the bird that nested so comfortably in his hand. His father's favorite messenger pigeon. When Naftali had inspected the shed behind his parent's house he found the pigeon cages smashed and empty. But Beersheba had survived, her small, beating heart a sweet gift from *Ha Shem* to ease his heavy burden. He walked down into Kosveg carrying the bird and stroking its head. As he sat on the ruined porch of his home he noticed a small piece of paper attached to Beersheba's leg in the little metal band his father used to fasten messages that he sent to other Hassidic villages. He pulled the paper out and unrolled it. His father's tiny but florid handwriting appeared. Naftali held it close to his face to read the message:

    The Beast is loose. Bury your treasures.

The Rabbi must have sent this out a day or so before the Germans and the Laszlo police swept into Kosveg, destroying everything in the old man's world. However, there was no one to receive Beersheba because all the other *shtetls* were raided and destroyed in that same operation. Kosveg was a poor Hassidic settlement. It had no treasures. What was his father talking about? Naftali put Beersheba into the least damaged cage in the shed behind the house. The bird could have easily escaped, but she acted as if she had finally come home and wanted nothing more than to roost in her comforting space. She settled in and began a steady and sonorous cooing. She was asleep. The young Hassid envied her peacefulness.

Naftali leaned against the shed. What did Beersheba's return mean? His father couldn't have gone far to bury the treasure he referred to. The neighbors would have seen him, and the gossip would have buzzed between the windows of Kosveg like summer mosquitos. He noticed an area of grass that had been disturbed and regrown just past the shed and behind the far corner of the house. Is that where his father buried whatever treasures there were in Kosveg? He went back into the shed and found a broken-handled shovel. He removed his dirty black suit jacket and hung it on a nail in the shed. He laughed at himself for trying to retain any semblance of dignity given the circumstances. But his father always said that even if there is no one to observe your behavior, *Ha Shem* was always watching.

After fifteen minutes of steady digging in the disturbed area, Naftali hit a wooden box. He dug around its perimeter and hauled his father's old traveler's trunk to the surface. He dragged the wood and leather crate into his house, undid the strap and lifted the top. Inside were layers of fresh clothing from his father and a few prayer books. He thanked his father silently for the gifts in the trunk, which would allow Naftali to pray and appear before *Ha Shem* in dignity. Putting on his father's clothing would make him feel held by the rabbi, wrapped in his love and wisdom.

Underneath the clothes he found a bulky, wrapped object. He took it out and removed the blanket that covered it. He had found the true treasure of Kosveg—his father's Torah scroll. Hugging the scroll tightly, Naftali whirled around in a dance of bittersweet joy. Then he sat and went silent inside. He saw Moses receiving the Ten Commandments on Mount Sinai. He could hear the lamentations of the Israelites as they were forced into exile. He felt the cool waters of the Sea of Reeds parting to allow his ancestors to escape from bondage. All the learning, all the stories came flooding into him again. Even though he stood alone in Kosveg, not another person or family alive, Naftali reconnected with thousands of years of Jewish agony and ecstasy. For the moment, the brick factory and his time in the camp seemed like drops of water in an unending ocean. For the moment, anguish and doubt dissipated into the fragrant air around him. He lay on his back clutching the scroll and relaxed into a profound and sweet sleep.

Hineni. Here I am.

CHAPTER 19

In the days following the revelation of Professor Sandor's death, Eva cleaned and practiced mechanically. On Thursday she walked past the park without stopping, feeling the pain in her heart when she heard the whistle of the Special Train passing through. In the late afternoon, Eva lay unsettled on her bed, alternating once more between beautiful memories of her years with Professor Sandor and the fear of a dark future without his guidance. How could she improve to the level required by the Academy without him? Beyond that, she lived in a universe of one. Her mother and father were gone. The professor had been the only other person who knew and cared for her. All she had left was the dream of the Academy.

In the past, she only thought about becoming a great technical pianist. Now she wanted something deeper. She wanted to dedicate her study at the Academy to the professor and her parents. Even with all the tragedy in her life, she felt grateful to have a future at the Academy. The fruit of the vine. *Borei p'ree ha gafen.*

She sat up and wiped her tears and her nose with her sleeve, noticing the tattooed number as her sleeve rode up. 3742-A. The tattoo weighed her arm down like a thick iron manacle. It represented everything awful that had happened to her, her family, everyone she knew and cared about. Fear and doubt about her future came crashing over her. How long would the aid money last? It wasn't very much, certainly not enough to pay for the Academy. What could she possibly do in Laszlo if she couldn't attend the Academy? Should she continue with the piano as the center of her life or give up and join the other uprooted Jews around Europe who had to move on with their lives? Without the professor she didn't even know how to approach that decision. Who could she turn to? Yossel had his bakery and never wanted to talk about the past. Oskar was so angry that he only wanted to dwell in the past. The mayor, who wore her father's clothes and lived in her house, was clearly sympathetic. Yet he, like everyone else, appeared to have an agenda for Eva that had nothing to do with who she was, what she needed. He wanted to use her to help Laszlo move beyond the war. Yossel and Oskar wanted her to be the child they lost or never had. Her former high school friends had no understanding of her despair.

Eva got up and pressed water onto her face. She was being selfish. Before worrying so much about herself, she should at least find a way to show respect to the professor, even if he wasn't there. She used to take lessons at his apartment in town. She should go there. If she asked politely, the people living in the apartment would let her come in and say goodbye in some way. Maybe there were old books or sheet music she could take to have a physical remembrance of their years together. She put on a clean blouse and skirt from the donations boxes and hoped that the people who opened the door were not the ones who provided the clothes.

As Eva started to leave the hotel, Oskar's voice boomed behind her. "Eva! Where are you going? It's almost dinner."

"I am going to Professor Sandor's apartment to say goodbye."

Yossel came up behind the butcher, frowning. "It's almost dark, too. It isn't a good idea to be wandering the streets right now."

Eva bridled at their attempt to stop her from doing what she had to do. She was beginning to feel claustrophobic living at the hotel with these kind male strangers. "Thank you for your concern. I will be careful, but this is important to me."

"Let us go with you," they implored in unison.

Eva's hand was on the doorknob. She turned to face them. "No. This is personal. I want to do this myself. I will be back soon."

Professor Sandor had lived in a quiet neighborhood of brick apartment buildings and small shops. It had always been a Jewish neighborhood but once again Eva noticed that no Jewish names remained. The shops were run-down. No *mezuzahs* hung in the door frames. A small restaurant several blocks before the apartment building had deteriorated into a rough looking workingman's bar. Eva hurried past on the opposite side of the street. She scanned the list of names of the tenants at the professor's former apartment block. Once every name was familiar; now they were completely unknown to her. His apartment was listed under *Gombos*. She rang the bell for the superintendent and waited until an older man she recognized came down the hallway and opened the front door. He looked her up and down and spoke gruffly.

"What do you want?"

"Hello, Mr. Gardony. It's me, Eva Fleiss. I came to visit Professor Sandor's apartment and sort of say goodbye to him."

The superintendent looked closely at the gaunt girl standing before him. His eyes widened and he smiled broadly. "Eva! I remember you. You were one of Professor Sandor's favorite students. He always talked about you after your lesson. It is good to see you again. The owners of the building let his apartment out months ago. They said they couldn't wait any longer to find out if the professor was coming back." He looked at her expectantly, but averted his eyes when he saw the sad look on the girl's face. "Oh, I'm sorry." Silence hung in the air for a moment until the superintendent got back to business. "The Gombos family lives in the apartment now. They are from the countryside and moved here to get away from the Russians and to get better work than they could find in their area." He cast a glance over his shoulder and up the stairwell. "All the apartments were taken over by country people and returning soldiers. A different clientele than before the war. But they are very nice. Of course, I need to ask permission for you to go up and see the professor's old apartment. I am sure they will be fine with that."

The older man grunted up the stairs to the third floor. Eva remained nervously in the entranceway, her fingers tapping an exercise the professor insisted she do daily. What if the tenant was an ex-soldier who hated Jews? What if they told her to go away like the people in Oskar's apartment? Mr. Gardony returned shortly with a smile and beckoned Eva to follow him to the apartment. The door was open. Eva was immediately struck by the sounds and smells of a family instead of an aging bachelor professor. The Gombos family had three young, fair-haired children who ran around the small apartment with abandon, but were quickly herded into the tiny back bedroom when Eva entered. The apartment reeked of paprika and onions. Potatoes boiled away and chicken sizzled on the stovetop. As she peeked into the living room of the one-bedroom flat, Eva noticed that all the professor's bookshelves, old leather chairs, his beautiful cherrywood claw-footed table and other furniture were gone. So was his Steinway piano. Another Jewish life disappeared. Shabby tables, chairs, and cheap furnishings took the place of the professor's fine possessions. Behind a standing lamp, Eva noticed a hole puncturing the horsehair plaster wall. Was it an accident when the professor's furniture was removed, or had somebody sought his "Jewish treasure" there? A thin woman came out of the bedroom with a pleasant, yet apprehensive look on her face. Her mousy brown hair was slipping out of a bun. Eva could hear the whining of a child barricaded in the bedroom, complaining that she didn't want to stay in that room, she wanted to see the horns on the Jew.

Mrs. Gombos put out her hand to Eva, frowning at the disappointment on the younger woman's face. "I am sorry, Miss, but as you can see there is nothing here from your professor. When we got here everything was gone and the apartment was what they call 'broom clean.' He sounds like he was a wonderful man. Please walk around if you'd like."

Eva held back tears as she took a few steps forward and looked around the completely strange apartment. There was nothing to honor the professor's memory in this place. No furniture, no photographs, not a single piece of the sheet music that used to blanket the apartment like a symphonic snowstorm. Like everywhere else in Laszlo, it felt like all traces of her life, the lives of all the Jews, were being swept away. Yossel was right, by the time those children were her age, no one in Laszlo will even know a Jew. The realization left an ache in her heart. She began to whisper the Kaddish prayer but realized she didn't know the words. The first time she'd heard it was for her mother, when her parents' friends came and prayed at the house. How embarrassed she and her father were because neither could recite the prayer. She regretted never learning the words, but her family were not what they called "practicing Jews." Eva tried to hum the basic funereal melody but it died in her tight throat. She thanked Mrs. Gombas, turned, and fled from the apartment.

Locks clicked and doors cracked opened behind Eva as she trod heavily down the stairs. She stopped and listened as several tenants ran to the professor's old apartment, demanding to know if the Jewish girl was trying to get the apartment back. Mrs. Gombos assured her neighbors that the girl's visit was harmless, but fear clogged their ears and the rumors flew through the building like germs in a cough. Eva ran down the remaining flights, suppressing a scream.

Eva was reaching for the front door handle when the superintendent called out to her.

"Eva, wait, please. I have something for you. When the town came and cleared out the apartment, they left papers and music scattered everywhere. They told me to get rid of them. I don't know what they are, but I thought I should keep them in case he returned.

They are in the basement. Let me get them for you."

Eva had nothing except memories and the skills the professor tried to impart. She desperately wanted some of his old sheet music, something to hold in her hands.

The superintendent huffed up the basement stairs carrying a small wooden box full of papers. "Here, I hope they are of some use to you." He shrugged. "I don't know what else to say. I hope you play the piano again. I used to enjoy hearing your music echoing through the hallways. Professor Sandor was a great man. You are blessed to have known him."

Eva hugged the musty box to her chest and thanked the superintendent. She was saving a small part of the professor's life from the abyss where so many Jewish memories had disappeared. As the front door closed behind her, she knew she would never come back to this place.

It was twilight when Eva left the apartment building. She sneezed as dust from the box of papers was disturbed by the lithe evening breeze. The moon created a silver light in the street. Eva felt in the soft glow that Laszlo could be as it used to be, a safe place. Memories of the professor sitting next to her at the piano, encouraging her, correcting her so gently, pushed out all other thoughts as she walked back toward the town square. She passed the former restaurant and realized she hadn't gone to the other side of the street. A burst of rowdy laughter came from the bar. She quickened her pace.

"Hey, beautiful, where ya going?"

Eva stiffened. She didn't look back but heard footsteps rapidly approaching. A hand brushed her shoulder.

"What's the hurry? C'mon and have a drink with us."

She turned in fright to see a squat, powerful-looking man in a short sleeve shirt leering at her. She held tightly to the box and managed a shaky reply. "No thank you, I have to get home."

"Hey, wait a minute," a second slurred voice added. A young man in an army shirt and dirty pants stepped into view. "Aren't you the Jewish girl who was with the mayor at the coffee house a few weeks ago? I saw you there. You're pretty cute." He looked at the box of the professor's papers. "Here, let me take those. I'll carry them to your home. Where do you live?"

"Back off, Marco," the first man interjected. "I saw her first. I never kissed a Jew before. Now that I think of it, there aren't many left. This might be my only chance." He belched and looked at Eva with glazed but hungry eyes. "How about a kiss for a brave soldier?"

The men spoke in the same haughty, dangerous tone as the guards in the camp. Eva quickly looked around. She could never outrun them, especially holding the box of memories she would never release. If she bought some time with these men, maybe someone would come out of the bar and urge them to go back inside. "No, I really have to get home," Eva managed to say through a dry throat. "Aren't your friends waiting for you inside?"

The stocky man sneered and spit. "Typical Jewish girl. Thinks she's too good for us Hungarian boys. I'm gonna show you what you're missing." He lunged toward Eva, who backed away enough to keep him at an arm's length.

"Stop right there!" A strong voice ordered from behind the men. Eva recognized the young policeman who had met the returning survivors at the train station. Would he help her or join the men in harassing her?

The soldier put his hands up in front of him. "Officer, we didn't mean anything, we were just having fun with this Jew. No crime in having fun with a Jew, is there?"

"There is a crime in harassing a Hungarian citizen. Now, go back to your drinking and leave this young woman alone." The men scurried apologetically back into the bar. Rough laughter met their return after the door closed. Corporal Miklos turned to Eva with concern. "Are you alright, Miss Fleiss?"

Eva was shaken by the encounter with the men, but was surprised by the policeman's politeness. "Yes, yes. Thank you. I was just coming back from my teacher Professor Sandor's old apartment. I guess I shouldn't have walked in front of the bar like that."

Miklos glanced back toward the bar. "You have the right to walk down any street in Laszlo you choose," he said in a formal manner. Then he lowered his voice. "But, of course, there are going to be drunks and fools like that here and there. A girl must be careful."

"You mean a Jew must be careful," she said darkly.

"I meant a girl, but you are right. A Jew must be especially careful these days. It is very sad, but true." He looked at the box. "Are you going back to the Armin Hotel? I could walk you there." Eva remembered the guards at the camp who feigned friendliness, only to rob or abuse the women. She hooded her eyes, giving the policeman a guarded look. "Just to make sure you get there with no more incidents. It is getting dark." Eva hesitated a moment, then gave him the box.

They walked together through the square and toward the hotel in silence. Eva began to relax. He didn't seem to have any motive other than to help her. She noticed the street signs as they walked beneath them. Polgar Street. Hadik Street. Maybe Corporal Miklos could help her make sense of the changes in Laszlo. Nobody wanted to talk about these things except Oskar, who had a grim opinion about everything. She spoke tentatively.

"I noticed that all the street names in the Jewish section of town have been changed." She pointed toward the signs. "Polgar used to be Klein. Hadik, that was Kertesz."

The corporal hesitated before answering. "I think the town did that to confuse the Russians. Changing street names is a typical partisan tactic."

"Then why only the Jewish streets?"

"I don't know," he replied, turning his head away from Eva.

"Do you really believe that?"

The corporal sighed. "No, I don't."

Eva decided not to press the matter further. She knew the answer as well as he did. Eliminate the memory of the Jews in Laszlo. The young policeman seemed kind, but what was his involvement in this?

They were nearing the hotel without further conversation when Miklos spoke. "I used to take piano lessons with Professor Sandor when I was younger. He was strict. Too strict." He chuckled to himself. "He said that corn had a better ear for music than I did. He told my parents to save their money and put me into sports clubs instead. That's how I became a policeman eventually. I guess he was a big influence on both our lives."

Eva cast a sideways glance at the young officer. This policeman was trying to be friendly, telling her something personal. She relaxed slightly but a bubble of fear was still lodged in her stomach. "I have to ask you something else."

"Please," he said with sincerity.

Eva took a deep breath to ensure the question came out without betraying the emotion she felt. "I don't remember seeing you on the day of the deportation." Was he really a decent man, or was he just like the others, like the guards in the camp, following German orders without feelings? She swallowed and continued. "Were you there?"

Miklos's face reddened as he gave a flustered reply. "All of us were called out and ordered to follow the SS officers' instructions. I didn't have the heart to push old people or yell at our own citizens to run faster toward the train. Captain Szabo knew that, and he allowed me to remain at the police station in case there were any messages. He saved me from having to disobey direct orders." He added quietly, "He did that twice for me."

Eva digested his answer. So the police weren't a monolith—even the captain had human feelings, at least for the other policemen. Yet seeing the young policeman as an ordinary person only made things more confusing. She understood the monsters for who they were, but how could decent people herd the Jews of Laszlo onto that train? How could good people cheer them on? The questions always loomed at the edges of her awareness, dark and unmoving. Who had the answers? She wasn't ready to forgive anyone, but if she knew more about this policeman, maybe she could begin to understand.

"When was the other time?"

"I don't want to talk about it." Miklos squirmed and hung his head slightly. "But I can tell you Captain Szabo took a lot of heat from the SS for it. Even some of the other policemen said I was weak and shouldn't be given any special treatment." The corporal glanced up. They were at the hotel. He had a troubled look on his face. "Maybe I shouldn't be a policeman."

Eva realized he was the only policeman she didn't fear. "Maybe all policemen should be like you."

CHAPTER 20

Eva sprinted up to her room as soon as she finished the plate of chicken paprika with broccoli and onions from Karosi's farm that Yossel had prepared. She put Professor Sandor's papers on her bed and took a deep breath, praying that his words would bring her solace, rekindling more of the beautiful memories that had been smothered on the Laszlo train platform. Hopefully, the professor's papers would help her find the courage to move forward, even without him. The first handful were standard printed scores from Mr. Schenk's music shop. She relaxed her tight shoulders into a comfortable position as she read his handwritten notes on the scores. Some of the notes were directions to students, or critical comments about their playing. She could hear his voice in the critiques, and remembered how she would wince every time he corrected her. Some were cryptic, referring to Jupiter, Mars, or some vibration between chords. Eva always enjoyed the professor's eccentric, private relationship with music. He often waxed on about the planets, but she didn't have any idea what he was talking about. He was a firm yet fair teacher who drew something out of Eva that she didn't know existed.

Under the scores Eva found a letter from Anna Nagy, his sister in Budapest, describing her work with a group called OMIKE. She was organizing concerts and plays with Jewish musicians forced from their teaching or symphony jobs. Eva wondered why she never knew that Jewish musicians, artists, actors, and singers had been prohibited from working by the Hungarian government since 1939. She was so sheltered in Laszlo. The professor had spoken of his sister often and with such affection that Eva felt she knew her. Eva realized Anna Nagy, if she was alive, probably didn't know of her brother's fate. She determined to find her and tell her as a way of honoring the professor. The address on the letter, 36 Wesselenyi Street, might not be current, given the chaos of Budapest and the dislocation of the Jews there, but it was a start.

Further into the box Eva found a manila envelope. A brief letter was folded and attached to the envelope with a paper clip. She nearly tossed it aside when something caught her eye. She blinked hard to make certain her desperate desire to reconnect with the professor wasn't distorting her perception. Her name was scrawled across the top of the letter. The Professor was reaching out. She closed her eyes and held the letter to her cheek, then hungrily plunged into his words.

> *Dearest Eva*
>
> *Congratulations on graduating from Laszlo High School. This is a very important milestone in your life. In the fall, you will attend the Ferenc Liszt Academy in Budapest and I could not be prouder of you for this accomplishment. I have always known you had a special gift for music, a gift you yourself most likely do not completely appreciate. It is in this spirit I give you your graduation present. It is a manuscript I have worked on for years along with other faculty at the Academy. I trust when you read it many of the mysteries of our work together will be solved, or at least a path toward understanding will have opened. Think kindly of me when you attend the Academy. Alongside your heavy course load, please find time to delve into this manuscript under the tutelage of the professors named within it. Your work will have much more meaning than you are currently aware, and you will have made my life's work complete.*

To that end, I have also written a piano concerto specifically for you. You will see it incorporates many of the etudes and arpeggios you have worked on for so long. Your ultimate mastery of this piece will ensure you will join the many great musicians who have helped to maintain the beauty and integrity of music as a Pure Form in our often-dark world.

I look forward to the day when I will be with you in the Grand Hall at the Academy and hear your wonderful performance of this piano concerto.

Most respectfully,

Professor Aladar Sandor

As tears streamed down her cheeks, Eva eagerly turned over the manila envelope and untied the string closure. Inside was a thick, typed document entitled *Guide to the Music of the Spheres*. The name struck an unidentifiable chord inside Eva. Had the professor mentioned this? Had she listened? Had she understood what he was talking about? Usually when he flew off into metaphysics at the close of their lessons Eva's mind slipped back to the details of her daily life. She flipped the document open and read the first page.

Music is a fundamental form. It is one of the pillars, identified by Plato as Pure Forms, along with beauty, truth, and others, that hold the universe on its moral course. All things great and small make music by the very nature of movement. All things manifest and unmanifest, from the ocean's waves to the human soul, are connected by the vibrations of a moving universe, and those vibrations are discoverable as musical notes. Throughout human existence, philosophers and scientists have tried to grasp the higher meaning and expression of music. What is the power of music to transcend temporal and spatial reality to a place understood by the universal human soul? Why is music used to worship gods, celebrate joyous occasions, and mourn the dead throughout all time? Music helps humans make sense of the unknown. Music expresses emotions we don't know are within us until we hear it. Music can inspire us do brave things—comfort and strengthen us to face horrors—yet it can also incite us to heinous acts.

This manuscript is the result of a lifelong study by the author, along with other members of the faculty of Ferenc Liszt Academy, to map these fundamental notes and their interconnections in the hopes of embracing and supporting music's role in maintaining universal harmony and goodness. Exceptionally gifted and properly trained students should be able to utilize music as a transcendent and inspirational force.

We, the authors, acknowledge that this manuscript is a continuation of the works of Pythagoras, Plato, and many of the ancients from cultures around the world who recognized the importance of music in keeping the world in balance. We are indebted to mathematician and astronomer Johannes Kepler for advancing the work of the ancients through mathematical and scientific rigor. In light of the current use of music by fascist and authoritarian forces to distort the harmony of the universe and pervert music for evil ends, it is essential selected students be made aware of the contents herein and trained to uphold music as a Pure Form . . .

White lightning surged up Eva's spine. That was why the professor had her practice apparently random notes and patterns. He was training her in his theory that music could be harnessed as a transcendent force that could impact human behavior. Yet Eva sensed it wasn't a theory. She somehow understood his introduction perfectly. She also understood that just as the Nazis had tried to deny her of her womanhood, they tried to crush the music out of her soul. They had not succeeded.

Eva thumbed through the manuscript. It was a series of commentaries about music in relation to objects, planets, emotions, the human soul, and other subjects. It discussed ancient philosophers whom Eva had heard of and many she had not. It revealed the thoughts of civilizations in India, Persia, and even the medieval Jewish world. Each essay was illustrated with musical annotations, in some cases scales marked Ionian, Dorian, and others she was not familiar with. There were exercises like the ones Eva had practiced for years; those odd, atonal passages that made no sense. Eva wondered if the manuscript would finally explain them.

A fully scored composition entitled *Piano Concerto for the Music of the Spheres* lay at the end of the manuscript. Professor Sandor's personal gift of music to Eva. She beamed the way she did when her father brought back special gifts from his travels. The concerto was divided into three oddly named movements. "Sentience," "Communion," and "Transcendence." Even a cursory glance told Eva it was a difficult piece. Sets of notes here and there corresponded to her practices, which gave her some comfort. She let out a deep breath. She knew it would be the hardest work she had ever done, but she was determined to honor the professor's gift.

Eva found another letter folded and clipped onto the concerto. It had obviously not been sent, as there was no stamp on the envelope. It was addressed to a Professor Karady at the Academy. Although it was not meant for her, Eva longed for any other piece of the professor to hold on to. She considered the letter for a moment, then opened it.

Dear Professor Karady,

I believe my student, Eva Fleiss, is not only technically proficient but has a strong intuitive sense of the vibratory presence in things through her music. The patterns she casually identifies are often aligned with those of Pythagoras and Plato, as well as by the Kabbalists and the Islamic House of Wisdom. You would think she was the heir to Johannes

Kepler himself! Although she is too young to appreciate what this attunement with harmonies signifies and needs much continued training, I am certain she is well-suited to join the other students and carry our work forward under your tutelage at the Academy in the fall. I have created a piano concerto for Eva that stands alone as a performance piece yet includes all the elements of our work. As you know too well, the Pure Form of music has never in history been under assault like this. I fear that dark shadows will obscure the Pure Form for years to come.

I hope you agree with me about Eva.
Sincerely yours
Aladar Sandor

Eva turned off the light and laid back on the bed, embracing the manuscript. In Auschwitz, Eva found that music was an escape, a doorway beyond the pain of the present into her fantasy world of safety and beauty. Yet now it wasn't a fantasy at all. The professor had opened the doors of the Academy to her, passing her hand from his to a new mentor. She would be safe there, where music was the construct itself. No more hiding her emotions, no cleaning her own house or feigning politeness when she wanted to scream. More than a refuge, the Academy would be a place for Eva to find and fulfill the deep purpose of her life and now that of her cherished professor as well. She would honor him by creating music to manifest his wisdom that music holds up the world to its brilliance and potential. The spirit of Professor Sandor pulsed through the room. She was warmed by the thought that he had put so much faith in her, that he felt she was worthy to carry on his lifelong project. In her hypnogogic state, Eva was at her Bosendorfer in her home the way it used to be, her father in his armchair and the professor on the bench at her side. A thread, delicate yet strong, spun out of the past, through her heart and into the future. The manuscript and the professor's loving note gave Eva an indescribably embracing comfort. She closed her eyes as tears fell freely, and a blessed sleep came upon her for the first time since before the horror began.

Over the next week Eva attacked the cleaning of the house, barely touching the increasingly nice lunches Mrs. Kodaly prepared for her. She ignored the mayor's compliments on her improved playing. She practiced on the Bosendorfer as if she were possessed. The professor's manuscript opened her mind and her ears to music as more than the creation of beautiful sounds. At its essence, music was a force so powerful that it could lift a person from misery and grief to a place of peace, serenity, and hope. Is this why some people chanted and sang on their way to their deaths at Auschwitz? Is this why her mother rested so peacefully without pain when Eva played Chopin?

Music inextricably linked all things through its vibrations. The manuscript took her on a tour of the universe, where the planets gave off an evolving musical sequence as each passed along a wobbly elliptical orbit around the sun. Johannes Kepler found that when a planet was at its perihelion, closest to the sun, it created a major scale. When it was farthest from the sun, at aphelion, it created a minor scale. He also measured how the planets passing each other in their orbits combined notes and chords, creating harmonies or discordant combinations. At rare moments, some of the planets were in conjunctions that created one exquisite and perfect sound, the epitome of the Pure Form. Eva realized all of this was going on as an unheard background symphony of life.

How did Pythagoras and the ancients of such different cultures— Greek, Indian, Arabic, Jewish—sense any of this, and how did they associate planets with emotions? How did Kepler turn those philosophies into mathematical equations and connect the distances to harmonic relationships? Eva could not fully understand Professor Sandor's references to the analogies of Plato nor the formulations of Kepler, but she felt a visceral knowledge of the musical relationships between objects, sound, and emotions. It was like a language she had grown up with; she was evolving from a child's use of it to a more sophisticated understanding.

One afternoon she wandered through the library after practicing as Mrs. Kodaly insisted she stay for lunch. Before the deportation, Eva always meandered around the bookshelves, running her fingers across the leather-bound volumes. Many of the authors were unknown to her, as her father had commissioned Hungarian translations of obscure legal and philosophical texts, bound in leather and tooled in gold leaf. The books gave her a feeling of security, surrounded by so many important thinkers and fortified by her father's love and intellect. She should have talked to him more often about these books, but her teenaged interests lay elsewhere, in music and her friends. Her hand stopped on a slim volume. *Harmonices Mundi* by Johannes Kepler. She opened the book to a random page. It contained illustrations of major and minor scales and the planets associated with many of the notes. The neighboring volume was a translation of *The Life of Pythagoras* by Diogenes Laertius. Both were mentioned in the professor's manuscript. Had he given these books to her father? Did her father have them translated for the professor? Eva wished she had paid closer attention when the two most important men in her life had huddled in animated conversations over brandy after Eva's lessons. She gathered the volumes and sat in her father's brown leather chair.

As Eva thumbed through Keppler she found the theories beyond her comprehension. She would have to rely on the summaries and commentaries in the professor's manuscript to understand this Music of the Spheres. The Pythagoras volume was more accessible, and Eva read the long opening chapter telling of the great philosopher's life in Greece and Italy more than five hundred years before the Christian era. A scribbled comment appeared in a margin. Eva recognized her father's hand. The note observed the irony that Pythagoras evolved his theory of the cosmos in musical harmony at the same time the Jews of the Holy Land, the only people who believed in a unitary God, were being torn from their land and exiled into slavery in Babylon. Her father had then written in large letters *HARMONY DISRUPTED.*

Eva closed the book and leaned back in the chair. Throughout Europe, the Jewish people had just suffered an even greater destruction than the exile. Did her father believe that the professor's work could restore harmony to the Jewish people in some way through music? Might Eva contribute to this? If so, she was a strange choice for the task. She was not that Jewish and not that good a musician. But she did feel an affinity with the Music of the Spheres and she was improving technically. Her time at the Academy would help her develop. She also felt a growing awareness of being Jewish, although she didn't know much about the religious practices. In Auschwitz, Eva felt like part of a continuum of suffering that reached back thousands of years. Yet beneath, there was an even deeper connection. It was like the vibrations of music, something cellular that holds things together beyond the conscious.

Mrs. Kodaly entered the library clattering a tray of cold meats and fruit. Eva looked up to see a puzzled expression on the woman's face.

"I was just looking at a few of my father's books. I think I will take these back to the hotel with me," Eva said.

The mayor's wife stiffened. "But, Eva, you can read them here whenever you'd like. You don't have to take them away."

Eva wasn't sure if Mrs. Kodaly wanted her to stay around more, using the books as an excuse, or if she didn't want Eva to take ownership of anything in the house. Either way, Eva felt a rush of anger, but held back a sharp reply. "Thank you, Mrs. Kodaly, but I like to read late into the night, so I should take them with me."

"I'd feel better if you left them here."

Eva's eyes flared. "I didn't know you were so interested in the classics." She gripped the volumes tightly in her hands and held them out before her. "I can wait until you are finished reading them."

Mayor Kodaly walked in as the women bristled at each other. "What's this?" he asked as he took off his suit jacket. Mrs. Kodaly spoke quickly.

"Eva wants to take these books to the hotel, but I thought she should read them here."

The mayor put out his hands in a placating gesture. "But, dear, they are her father's books. She can certainly take them if she would like."

Mrs. Kodaly turned red and began to breathe rapidly. She slammed the lunch tray onto a side table and fled to the kitchen. The mayor looked at the girl. She shrugged a feigned lack of understanding as she walked past him and out the door.

Eva ran back to the hotel, passing the daily gathering of her former friends in the park. At the hotel, she grabbed some brown bread and slices of *kolbasz* and raced to her room, nibbling the sausages as she went. The late June evenings were cool, the air sweet with the scent of red *pipacs* and violet *gerbics* that grew wild along the roadside. Eva opened her window wide, inhaling the vernal delights. She leaned back on the creaky metal-framed bed and became immersed in the manuscript, learning from mystics and mathematicians how all objects created sound and in combination formed harmonies and melodies. The pages took her into the mysteries of sound from the passage of worms through the soil to the continually shifting mathematical and melodic intervals between planets.

Besides his own examples, the professor gave short passages on a range of composers who consciously sought to integrate celestial harmonies into their works, such as Rimsky-Korsakov's "Games and Dances of the Stars" and Dvorak's "Song to the Moon." He demonstrated how Debussy's *La Mer* and Beethoven's *Pastorale* Symphony intuited the powerful forces of the natural world to affect their audiences. Professor Sandor's words stretched the thin membrane between Eva's reason and her intuition. She digested every word and concept, stopping only when the notes and letters on the page swam and swirled beyond her ability to read or hold a thought any longer. Soon she would be at the Academy, under the tutelage of Professor Karady, where she would live and breathe this new awareness and learn how to manifest it into the world.

When she was certain everyone else in the hotel had gone to bed, she slipped outside and stood in the dark street, listening for every sound she could hear, feeling every emotion evoked. She tried to block out the distant sounds of the town square, where the buildings argued with each other in urgent whispers about whether the Jews should have come back. Eva felt the loneliness in the buzz of the streetlamp, the impatience in the rustling of the leaves. The light wind carried feelings of possibility and the gentle rain brought her thoughts inward. Each sound became a note, the notes merged into chords, phrases, and sequences. Eva detected the professor's musical patterns everywhere. She looked up and saw silver clouds scudding across the moonlit sky and felt the ephemeral coming and going of joy.

She also felt profound loss. As her musical exploration deepened, the solid barrier of self-protection she erected since being deported from Laszlo was dissolving. Eva was able to acknowledge her father was not merely gone. He was dead. So was the professor. So were all the shopkeepers, her Jewish classmates, teachers, and the children who ran past her on the way to school every day. That recognition made Eva's legs and arms so heavy she could hardly make it back to the hotel. All of her non-Jewish friends were still alive. But the wall of experience that had grown between them during the last year was insurmountable. She walked past them as if she were in a different world, like the *muselmann* in the camp, the ones who were dead but kept walking unaware. Eva watched families on the streets and in the park. It was painful to see them go in and out of houses and shops that belonged to quickly forgotten Jewish people.

Turning her gaze upward and away from Laszlo gave her some comfort. When she tracked the stars and moon sailing along the velvet blue horizon, she sensed movement and sound far below any

octave she could hear. It soothed the anxiety that was always beneath
the surface of her awareness. Yet even then, surrounded and engulfed
by never-ending sound, Eva felt cosmically alone, a spark of light
seeking a flame in the currents of a dark world.

Greta Kodaly also felt alone. Every day she hovered around Eva
like a moth drawn to a flame. The girl's intensity was frightening at
times. Mrs. Kodaly no longer had the smug feeling of an overlord,
living in plenty and looking out over the vassals who surrounded her.
She felt lesser than Eva. The girl had found a strength, a certainty
that baffled the mayor's wife. Eva's playing bordered on the insane,
or at least too modern at times for her tastes, yet for some reason she
could not tell the girl to stop. After all, she was playing something
created for her by her lost professor. Mrs. Kodaly often leaned
against the kitchen wall while Eva practiced. With her eyes closed,
she drank in the music. It unleashed an intermittent moodiness in
her or a rare giddiness just beyond her reach. The girl's music also
seemed to induce vivid dreams. She never remembered the dreams,
but always awoke with unsettled feelings. Muddy emotions were
stirred up inside her. She slowly sank deeper and deeper into despair,
not alone in her big house, yet ignored and lonely.

As Eva played on, Greta searched for a reason for this newfound
melancholy. After the incident with the menstrual pads, she began
to warm toward the poor girl. She had tried to show more kindness
by leaving bowls of fresh raspberries and blueberries on top of the
piano. She offered exquisite dinners if Eva wanted to stay, which she
never did. Greta felt left behind when the girl seemed to lose herself
completely in that mad whorl of notes that didn't appear to lead
anywhere. She reluctantly realized she had come to rely on the girl,
not so much for cleaning an impeccably clean house, but for a certain

companionship that didn't seem to be there. The house, the jewelry only occasionally took her mind off the fact that she and Ferenc had no children, nor could they. Her loneliness confronted her like one of Eva's dissonant, unresolved chords. She began to cry. The girl noticed, stopped playing and approached her with a worried look.

"It's nothing," Greta said, quickly trying to compose herself. "Just a momentary wave of ennui. It happens to women of my age now and then. Brought on, I'm sure, by your dreadfully sad music."

But the girl's intense attention and sincerity broke through the older woman's reserve.

"All these beautiful things I am surrounded by. They are wonderful. I never had them before. When we first moved into the house, I was in awe of all that your family owned. It was everything I ever wanted. But over time I realized beautiful things didn't make the mayor come home any earlier. They didn't make my friends have more time for me." Mrs. Kodaly paused. "They don't bring a child into the house." The mayor's wife was twirling the pearl necklace as she spoke. She looked down at her fingers enmeshed in pearls and gold—Eva's mother's necklace—and slowly, self-consciously, slid her hands to her sides. She stared at Eva through watery eyes. "They don't even make you stay longer than your practice sessions. I don't know what has happened to you lately. When you sit down at the piano you go someplace I can't follow. You seem to disappear. I suppose I have come to think of you as a niece, albeit a very willful one," she said through her sniffles and tears. "But one I cherish nonetheless." She threw her arms around a surprised Eva and hugged her tightly.

CHAPTER 21

The station master's head lolled from side to side on his desk as he mumbled incoherently. Four empty *palinke* bottles lay on the desk before him, lined up end to end on their sides to imitate a train. The bottles were clear glass, so the Josef could speak to them without the fear he held for the black DR trains. "Leave me alone. I'm not responsible," he pleaded quietly as he poked at the bottles with a finger.

He struggled out of his fog when he heard the brakes of the DR train as it slowed and stopped before the station office. It was 2 a.m. Tuesday. Beyond the door he saw it, the large black creature inhaling diesel and exhaling gray, choking fumes. The miasma oozed down the platform, obscuring the dim light from the few naked bulbs that sought valiantly to illuminate the scene. The station master approached the panting beast cautiously, peering into the engine cab. No one was there. He tentatively walked toward the cars and called out. No reply from the cavernous darkness that lay beyond the windows.

Suddenly the sharp screech of a train horn pierced the air, causing Josef to cover his ears and recoil in pain. The doors on the cars rolled open. Mist seeped from the cars, gelling into phantasmal wisps of horrendously thin men and women.

"You can't get off the train!" he cried. "Go back on the train!"

But the shapes paid no heed to the aging station master. They stood facing forward, then simply evaporated into the moist air on the platform. The train horn shrieked its banshee noise again. Josef ran frantically back to the engine. He shouted for the train to go away and take its cargo with it as the train expelled its fetid breath and left the station.

"Damn you, leave me alone!" He fled the train. He ran blindly down the darkened platform and into the corner of the Laszlo Station sign that hung off his office, gashing his head and knocking him to the ground. He lay on the hard surface as the sound of the train faded, replaced by images of Jacob Fleiss, his daughter, Oskar, and the rest of the town's Jews being shoved onto the train. Blood trickled into his tearing eyes as he moaned repeatedly. "The Jews, the Jews, the train. I swore to them it wasn't my fault."

Oskar heard the hard rapping on the door of the hotel. When he opened it, Sergeant Ritook commanded the threshold with Oskar's bloody shovel in hand and a raptor's concentration in his eyes. "Oskar Lazar, is this your shovel?"

"I borrowed it from the station master," Oskar stated in a guarded tone.

"And why did you borrow the shovel?"

Oskar worried that he would get in trouble for burying the chicken entrails and other garbage without a permit. He knew the police and the entire town were looking for any excuse to come after him. Jutting out his jaw, flexing his fists, he stared back into the eyes of a thousand years of torment. He glanced at the dried blood on the shovel and sneered at the policeman. "Let's just say I did what I needed to do to get rid of that vermin."

CHAPTER 22

On Tuesday afternoon, Eva concentrated her practice on "Sentience" and "Communion," the first and second movements of the piano concerto. "Sentience" was like an emotional warm-up, and Eva readily accessed her feelings while playing the piece. She thought about the mayor's wife. Eva had been startled by her emotional opening. Since their first encounter, Eva saw Mrs. Kodaly as an obstacle to regaining her home, her music and as much of her old self as was possible given the realities of postwar Laszlo. Yet she was moved by the woman's honesty. If she was changing, what would be the harm in showing her a little kindness. The more Mrs. Kodaly felt positively about Eva, the harder it would be to deny her the house at some point. But how long could that take? Eva had to resolve this before leaving for the Academy. As painful as it might be, she could sell the house to pay for her schooling. She had no other money and the pittance from the World Jewish Congress was running out.

"Communion" required a deeper connection, confronting emotions, feelings, and mental images that hid behind her chest, her guts, her heart. It was harder to perform because it was more difficult for Eva to confront those darker places. She noticed that each movement contained chord combinations that Pythagoras and Kepler had identified with different planets and the professor had tied to different emotions. She also recognized certain runs and sequences as being similar to passages from Beethoven, Schumann, and other great classical composers. How much were these giants aware of the Pure Form and consciously employing the Music of the Spheres to affect their audiences? The professor's manuscript mentioned a few of these connections but never went into detail. Eva would have to wait to work with Professor Karady at the Academy to learn more.

As she left the house, Eva noticed a stack of folded clothes by the door. Blouses and skirts from her room. A note on top of the pile stated briefly *For Eva.* Eva happily scooped up the clothing and called out to Mrs. Kodaly, but there was no answer. She wanted to reciprocate, to keep nurturing whatever was evolving between them. Perhaps she could learn some popular music to perform for Mrs. Kodaly's friends, who assembled each Thursday for lunch and gossip. She knew this would make the mayor's wife feel better and raise her status at her insipid luncheons. Where could she find music in town? Mr. Schenk's shop was abandoned. It would be useless to ask Oskar, who usually had nothing but angry retorts to offer, or Yossel, who only listened to classical music on the small kitchen radio. There might still be sheet music at the Jewish Home for the Aged, where she used to play. The Home was farther out of town than her house. She headed up the hill.

The Home was an old brick mansion donated by a Jewish family for the aged and infirm, regardless of their religion. Eva had enjoyed performing for the quiet, older residents who always became energized by her playing, opening faucets of memory that had rusted shut. Her mother told her that *bikkur holim*, visiting the sick, was an important act of charity. She knew there would no longer be Jews at the Home, so she was not surprised when she saw the new sign announcing the *Laszlo Veterans Hospital and Home for the Aged.* She climbed the familiar stairs and approached the front desk, where a receptionist shrugged and permitted her to go the second-floor lounge and play piano for the residents. She passed nurses and doctors moving through the corridors, but didn't recognize anyone. Of course, she thought. The staff was primarily Jewish before the deportation. As she walked through the sea of Gentile faces, her heart became heavy. She couldn't hear the booming laugh of stocky Nurse Ullman. Nor would she see the kindly smile of Doctor Borowski, who had been her family doctor since childhood and who had taken care of her mother during the illness. But she was becoming less and less shocked by such changes in Laszlo. The town was disappearing from her consciousness.

Eva entered the large, airy lounge and sat at the old upright piano. A few residents dozed in chairs about the room, taking in the sun through the glass windows on the southwestern side. She tested the keys to see how the piano sounded. Not bad considering there was no one left to keep the piano tuned. As she began to play a supple variation of Schumann's *Butterflies*, more residents came into the room. They were a mix of elderly men and wounded soldiers. Hardly anyone spoke as Eva played. She heard occasional comments among the residents asking if she was the Jewish girl who used to play piano here, and would their Jewish doctors and nurses be returning soon? She modulated to Schumann's *Scenes of Childhood*, glimpsing the far away looks of old people plucking at fleeting memories. When she finished several of the residents applauded weakly. Eva wondered whether her music actually helped alleviate their pain and loneliness, or merely provided a momentary distraction.

Some of the younger soldiers mumbled incoherently, twitching as they listened. Eva assumed they were wrestling inner demons or fighting their last battles in their minds. Soldiers unnerved Eva, but as she observed these men between pieces she felt pity for them. A nurse noticed Eva's troubled look and stood next to her at the piano. She explained that the soldiers were suffering from something called "shell shock." As the nurse talked about the causes and symptoms, Eva was horrified to learn that concussive sound had caused their condition. Might her playing trigger memories, her music cause the young soldiers pain? The torment caused by the war was felt by so many in such different ways. She didn't know the circumstances that brought about each man's trauma, nor did she want to know. Eva had plenty of demons of her own. Even so, she modulated her touch on the keys to soften the impact on their ears. The young pianist cast her music out into the audience freely and lovingly to ease their suffering in whatever way it could.

Corporal Miklos sat on a metal stool at the foot of the hospital bed as the station master snored rhythmically. The doctor said Josef should be coming around sometime today as he was more drunk and concussed than seriously injured. Why would the butcher strike this old man? Probably revenge for signaling the deportation train to leave Laszlo. The corporal worried that the growing incidents and hints of anger brewing under the surface in Laszlo were getting perilously close to erupting.

Miklos heard a beautiful piece of music playing on a piano from the other end of the hallway. He leaned back and let it wash over him. The music temporarily assuaged his inner turmoil as he struggled with the shame and the helplessness he had felt at the deportation and Kosveg. A low moan from the station master interrupted the corporal's reverie.

"It's so beautiful," he murmured. "It is like my friends from childhood calling to me."

Miklos sat up and went to the head of the bed. "Station Master, are you awake?"

The older man stirred and opened a rheumy eye. He struggled to sit, gave up, and collapsed back to the bed. "What happened? Where am I?" He became agitated. "Who is watching the trains?"

Miklos spoke in a soothing voice. "It is alright, sir. You are in the hospital. We brought you in last night with a head wound. According to your record book there is nothing scheduled to come through Laszlo today." He watched Josef digest the information and calm down. "We think you were attacked last night. Apparently, Oskar Lazar, the Jewish butcher, hit you in the head with a shovel. He is in custody." He felt the greasiness in his gut. "Sergeant Ritook is interrogating him."

"Oskar did no such thing! He is my friend," Josef shouted. "I lent him that shovel last week." He grimaced and touched his bandaged head. "I think I hit my head against the station sign when I was running away from the night train."

Miklos frowned. "What night train?"

The station master closed his eyes. "The one that comes every night, black and silent. It rolls through the station and condemns me." He grabbed for Miklos's arm, a look of urgency in his bleary eyes. "I couldn't have stopped them, you know."

After playing for almost an hour, Eva stood, stretched her hands gently and opened the piano bench. She looked through the few bundles of sheet music that were there. She recognized Lajos Kiss's "Gypsie Violin" scores, Vera Rozsa's upbeat modern tunes, several songs by Vali Racz (Mrs. Kodaly's favorite actress), and Rezso Seress's worldwide hit "Gloomy Sunday," with English words by a man named Billie Holiday. More than enough material to surprise and entertain Mrs. Kodaly's friends. Eva practiced all the songs, knowing that even if they weren't performed perfectly, she had an appreciative audience at the Home. She also found the popular pieces surprisingly enjoyable to play, particularly after hours of intense study and practice of the professor's surreal manuscript.

"Eva?"

Eva startled at the sound of her name. Hanna stood awkwardly nearby, wearing a white apron with a small red cross over the left breast pocket. Eva was unsure how to react after their uncomfortable meeting in the park. She spoke evenly. "Oh, hello. What are you doing here?"

"I'm volunteering for the summer." After a brief, self-conscious silence, Hanna added, "I'm really sorry for the way we talked in the park. It's just that I don't know how to talk to you about everything that's happened. It was like this strange nightmare that came and took you away. But once you were gone there was no one to talk to about it. It was like the earth just swallowed up all the Jewish people in the town and the war forced us to move on. My parents said they felt the same way. Then when you returned they were full of guilt and really sad." Her voice became constricted and emotional. "I missed you a lot, Eva, and had no idea what happened to you. Now I just don't know what to say."

Eva couldn't hold on to her anger in the face of her friend's contrition. She spoke gently. "There is nothing much to say. Or there is too much to say. I guess it will come out over time. I felt invisible in the park, as if my disappearance didn't mean anything to you . . . or Andras."

Hanna winced and tentatively touched Eva's arm. "Please forgive me, Eva, for everything." After a pause, Eva nodded her head slowly with her eyes downcast. "And as for Andras, he is feeling bad, too. He was so surprised to see you and then had to face everything that's happened since you left." She stopped and corrected herself, "I mean since you were deported. He talks about you every day when we get together in the park. Will you come and join us again?"

Eva felt a stab in her heart. There were so many different kinds of pain. How could her loneliness and isolation in Laszlo even momentarily eclipse the memories of Auschwitz? Was she being disloyal to her father and to Professor Sandor being so disquieted by the petty interactions with her friends? No. In the camp she had to lock away her feelings to prioritize survival over human connection. But standing in the safety of the sunny solarium, with friendship just within her reach, she felt more vulnerable than ever. She looked up at Hanna and allowed her longing for companionship to wash over her. She took her hand. "Of course I will."

A stern-faced nurse approached Eva and Hanna. She planted her hands firmly on her hips. "Young lady, it is time to stop."

Eva blinked with confusion. "But the patients are enjoying the music so much."

The nurse was unmoved. "You are agitating them. They need to calm down for their evening meals and medications." Orderlies and other nurses descended on the patients in a practiced maneuver. They ushered or rolled them quickly out of the solarium. "Please leave."

Hanna was still holding Eva's hand. "I am working for another hour. Please, let's talk soon."

"Yes, I would like that." Hanna's touch was so warm. It made Laszlo suddenly feel like a safer place.

By the time Eva left the Home it was too late to stop in the park. She hurried back to the hotel. Yossel was setting dinner dishes. She waved to the baker as she went up the stairs to her room. She wanted to plunge into the manuscript again, but stopped before the mirror first. Her skin was losing its roughness, probably due to the good food she had been eating at the hotel and her house. She took off her blouse and looked at herself. She was still so bony and angular. Eva stared at the number on her arm with revulsion. Would she have to look at it all her life? She retrieved the foundation from her make-up bag. She repeatedly patted the skin-colored powder against her tattoo. As the layers thickened, the number disappeared. Eva appraised her newly reclaimed forearm. The number would no longer define her. She would never let the tattoo show again.

A loud commotion downstairs startled Eva. She put her blouse on and ran down the stairs. Oskar sat at one of the dining tables. His face was puffy. Purple welts rose on both cheeks. Oskar looked like the men who wandered the camp with fresh bruises daily, victims of sadistic guards or the struggle for food with other prisoners. Eva felt a hollowness course throughout her body. Her hand flew to her mouth. Is this how the mayor would take care of them? She found herself sinking inwards. Oskar's firm voice brought her back.

"I told them to do their worst. After what we experienced they wouldn't be able to break me, especially since I didn't do anything wrong. I am used to being brutalized for being innocent. That's what being a Jew is all about, isn't it?" Oskar was subdued yet defiant. "When that young policeman—what's his name, Miklos?—came running in to say that the station master told them I was innocent, you should have seen the disappointment on that bastard Ritook's face. He was looking to hang one more Jew. I said to him, 'not this time.'"

Eva's pulse raced. Oskar's bloodied face, his smell of anger and sweat made her nauseous. She grasped the back of a chair as her vision began to tunnel. The tattoo burned under the make-up. She took long, deep breaths until the light in the room returned. Laszlo was not safe.

CHAPTER 23

The town clerk counted the assembled men. "There are sufficient members for a quorum," he intoned. "It is Wednesday, June 27, 1945. The meeting of the Business Promotion Council may begin." He sat down next to the mayor. Ferenc looked around at a sea of ill-fitting suits. Many of the men in attendance had obtained their businesses or increased their wealth by plundering Jewish properties. A new middle class had been created overnight by the state, a safety valve to head off unrest and another worker revolution. Give the working class more businesses and income and they will be quiet. Give the poor land to farm and they will be too busy to revolt. The state had made the Jews a social experiment—the outlet for people's anger, feelings of unjust treatment, even for their raw greed.

The mayor knew there were not enough Jews left to right all these wrongs. He was also aware he was seeking justice in the face of indifference and hostility.

"As we all know, the few Jews who survived the war have returned to Laszlo. They are in a sorry state, having lost their families and their property. This is a terrible legacy for Hungarian citizens who have been part of our community for centuries." The mayor felt the ripple of self-consciousness in the room and hastened to add, "I am not here to assign blame—there's enough of that to go around—but to figure out how we as a business community want to deal with this situation."

The furniture man, Mor, cut into the mayor's words. "Sure, sure something should be done. But we shouldn't move too fast. We need to let things settle down and give our people time to adjust."

Istvan, the coffee house owner, raised his hand. "I couldn't agree with you more, Mr. Mayor. I think we need to do something soon. I hear so much talk in the coffee house. My patrons have mixed feelings about the return of the Jews. We need to make a positive statement and give the town some guidance on a way forward."

Andor, the banker, tapped the table with his pen and spoke. "Let's get more specific, gentlemen. Mr. Mayor, what sort of things are you thinking about?"

Ferenc looked around the room for a moment, trying to gauge how his suggestions would be received. "Well, first we could consider bringing in more Jews from other areas of Hungary to try and restore a small, vibrant Jewish presence again. I have recently heard from the mayor of Aszod, which had two hundred and thirty Jews before the war and now has twenty-one. Munkacs had eighteen thousand, Veszprem around a thousand. Only a handful have returned to each. The list goes on. Maybe consolidating some of these populations here might reinvigorate our Jewish community." He had received several requests from other towns hoping to get rid of their returned Jews, to avoid the property issues, to finish what the Germans had started. They were all dealing with the same issues as Laszlo.

A man in the back of the room spoke. "Can't we put them together somewhere else? Maybe a reservation like the Americans did with their Indians. They never had to give back any land to the Indians, did they? That way they can be with their kind and we can be with ours."

Mor got to his feet. "Wait now, Mr. Mayor. It's been the policy of our government for over a decade to limit the number of Jews in business, the universities, and the professions to their percent of the overall population. We need to keep spaces open for Hungarians. You start letting Jews back in and they'll take over. We can't have Jews replacing us again."

"Those laws have been revoked, Mor," Ferenc replied evenly.

"Besides, we've lost the majority of our lawyers, our accountants, dentists, and doctors. There are simply not enough other citizens to replace them and our community has suffered for it. We need to stop seeing Jews through the propaganda of the recent past and remember how much they contributed to our lives." He looked around the room into each man's eyes. "And remember how many of us had close friends and business acquaintances, even family who were Jewish."

Gabor, a newly minted apartment block owner, pulled at his stiff collar and trembled as he stood to speak. "I'm sorry, Mr. Mayor, but I agree with Mor. As much as I had many Jewish friends, we must think of the social tension more Jews would cause. The lower classes would have to compete for housing with the poor Jews, or even lose their housing to new Jewish landlords making way for their own."

A guffaw came from the back of the room. "Nice words, Gabor. You just don't want to give up the apartment building you stole. You were nothing but a superintendent a year ago, now you own it."

Gabor turned bright red and shot back. "So? You managed Meir's factory and took false ownership when the law required him to sell the business. Now there's nobody to give the shares back to. Don't be so high and mighty, you're no different from me."

"You're out of order, Mor," said the town clerk. "You, too, Gabor. Everyone, please raise your hand and wait to be recognized. Continue, Mr. Mayor."

Ferenc realized how much these men feared losing the properties and position they had acquired. Personal gain mixed with long-held negative attitudes made a heady brew, one that would not be overcome easily. Maybe a less direct approach would be more acceptable. "So that is one idea. The second is compensation. Obviously there aren't enough Jews to receive the fair market value for all the businesses and properties taken in their absence. Perhaps a general fund could be created to support those who have returned."

The banker's hand shot up. "That is an admirable suggestion, Mr. Mayor. But what about all our wounded veterans, the widows, and orphans? What about the business owners whose properties are now being confiscated by the Russians as war reparations? I think there will be trouble if we put the Jews ahead of other deserving citizens." He stroked his chin. "But we could consider a small fund by subscription for those who feel strongly about it. We could set up an account in our bank for the purpose. Of course it would not be interest bearing."

Istvan raised his hand. "I feel very strongly about it. Jacob Fleiss helped me start and expand my business. Jews were among my best customers right up until they were taken away. We have to make amends somehow. I would be happy to contribute."

"And I'm sure there are many good-hearted, liberal citizens of Laszlo who feel the same as you do," Mor broke in. "That should be a personal choice, not something forced on us by the government. You let the Jews push too hard for compensation, property return, or other special treatment and who knows, it could even lead to violence."

The man from the back of the room shouted. "That's one way to end the Jewish problem!" Scattered laughter and clapping followed.

The mayor was startled by the resistance in the room, the laughter, and the number of heads that bobbed in approval. This was going poorly. He cleared his throat. "Then let me suggest something else. Why not repair and reopen the synagogue. It is a house of worship. Let's be honest, it was defaced and looted by our own citizens, not the Germans. It would be a proper use of town funds and a gesture of community contrition for that act."

The room pulsed with guarded conversations. The town clerk raised his hand. "There are problems with that from a legal point of view, Mr. Mayor. The former synagogue is listed as surplus property on the town rolls. It is no longer a house of worship. If the Jewish community wished to reopen, they would have to file a new application. That requires at least ten signatures from resident members of the congregation, as well as the creation of a board. There aren't ten Jewish citizens here. Actually, only two qualify as the girl is legally underage and only the baker and the butcher live in town otherwise." The town clerk pursed his lips. "There is another solution, however. The synagogue could be opened as a cultural center commemorating the Jewish presence in Laszlo. That would only require a standard nonprofit operating license that anyone could apply for."

Mor snapped his pencil in half. He stood and addressed the council. "Hardly any Jews went to that synagogue before the war. They mostly used it for socializing. How can we be sure they won't use it for politics or organizing? Jews and communists are very close. We don't want to encourage more Jews to come to Laszlo and we certainly don't need any communists. The Russian are setting up bases and confiscating businesses all over Hungary as we sit here. We need to crush this Soviet-Jewish conspiracy before it takes hold and grows." Discontented murmurs hummed through the room. Mor turned and pointed a finger at the mayor. "Why are you so interested in this, Mr. Mayor? The war is over. The Germans did what our laws failed to do—limit Jewish influence. What's done is done. We need to move on."

The mayor lanced Mor with a sharp look. "Why? Because I oversaw the destruction of a centuries-old peaceful and prosperous part of our community, Mor. That is not what I want to be remembered for." He thought of Jacob and of Eva. He couldn't even get his own wife to agree to return the house. How could he convince these men, who had covered their sins with a thin legal veneer? He tried to calm himself, but his words were carried on a knife's edge. "And I am sure there are people in this room who don't want to be remembered as the vultures who picked the bones of their deceased friends and neighbors. We need take at least a modicum of responsibility here."

The room went cold with shock. Mor opened and closed his mouth several times but ultimately said nothing. Ferenc had known Mor since childhood. He had never heard the man utter hateful words about Jews, not until Mor had the chance to grab Weiss's furniture store. The room was full of decent, ordinary men. He wondered how such bloodless, disdainful things could spill off their tongues. When did all their Jewish friends and neighbors, business partners and customers become less than human, not worthy of respect? How did extremist, marginal notions that seemed so ridiculous to educated people become common parlance? It should have ended with the war, but it didn't. The soul of Laszlo was deeply infected.

Ferenc once again wondered how much of this was his fault for not standing up to the ugliness earlier, or not warning Jacob and the other Jews to leave as soon as they could. He thought he was a resister, but ended up a bystander. He knew, but didn't believe it could happen in Laszlo. Then he believed, but it was too late. He wondered if he was making the same mistake again.

After the meeting ended Mor grabbed Andor and pulled him aside. He smiled and nodded as others left the room, then spoke to Andor in an urgent hiss.

"This is going too far, Andor. We have to stop it."

Andor looked around and whispered. "Ferenc is like a man possessed. He won't be deterred from bringing back the Jews or helping them take back their old property. And Tomas is right there with him. I don't know what we can do to stop this."

Mor scratched his chin. "It's the girl. I think the mayor's smitten with her. She can get him to do anything she wants." *A woman could always bewitch a man if he was not careful,* he thought. *Especially those young, pretty Jewish girls, like Weiss's daughter. Always thought she was too good for me.* "Well, it won't be stopped from the top down, that's for sure. But maybe it can be stopped from the bottom up."

"What do you mean, Mor?"

"I think the Jews are a threat to public order. If other people can be convinced to feel that way, maybe they will take matters into their own hands."

Andor's eyes widened. "Are you suggesting violence? I don't support that. The war is over."

"I'm not suggesting anything, but if the word gets around that the Jews are causing trouble, things might just sort themselves out. It's already happening in Poland and right here in Hungary. People are tired of the demands and the disruptions the Jews are causing. They are forcing them out. The old blood libel rumors are starting again. You know, Jews taking Christian children's blood to make their bread, like we used to hear about in church, remember? There was an incident in Chelm last month, now all the Jews of that town are running to America."

Andor scoffed. "No sane person believes those old tales anymore."

"Maybe not, but just after Chelm there was another riot in Rzeszow, then one in Pryzemysl. Jews are fleeing by the thousands. These incidents spread like brush fires. There's a smoldering resentment here in Laszlo. We both know it. We just need to blow on the embers a bit and let the fire take hold."

The banker squirmed and rubbed the knot that had formed in the back of his neck. "Maybe, Mor, but the thing about brush fires is, once they're lit they're hard to control."

CHAPTER 24

The mayor's visit to the bakery in the morning delighted Yossel. The baker wiped the flour from his hands and took off his apron. He grabbed two loaves of the morning's rye bread and headed out the door, telling an anxious Krauss to take the breads from the oven before they burned on the bottoms. He liked the idea of opening the synagogue again, even if it would only be a "cultural center." Something positive to commemorate the Jews of Laszlo, but not too provocative. He knew Oskar would hate the idea. The surly butcher would hate any idea that didn't damn all Hungarians to hell for their role in the death of the Jewish community. It really didn't matter, though. Neither Oskar nor Yossel knew anything about running a synagogue or a cultural center. They had no idea how to reconsecrate the building or repair what was essential to keeping it Jewish. Only the Hassid, Naftali, might know—if he was willing to help. Yossel had told the mayor he would visit Kosveg and talk to the young man. He also thought it might be nice to breathe clean country air, and get away from Krauss's constant interference in the joy Yossel took in baking every morning. Still, he dreaded seeing the destruction of Kosveg that he had heard about.

Yossel walked through the town. Laszlo was certainly familiar. The baker had been born and raised there. Yet it was strange and different at the same time. So many new faces as the town became a magnet for rural poor looking for work or cheap Jewish properties.

Before the deportation, Yossel would catch a smile from everyone he passed. Back then, he was the town's most popular baker. Now the reception was mixed—smiles, frowns, glares, grumbles, self-conscious silence. But Yossel was determined to remain positive. He had hired three new assistants as business picked up. The shortage of sugar forced him to use molasses and cinnamon, creating a distinct taste to all his pastries. The lines were often out the door in the morning. They may not have liked him as a Jew, but they loved him as a baker. Happy, well-fed customers were the best defense against a possible resurgence of hatred and violence.

As he walked through the forest, up and down the rolling hills beyond Laszlo, Yossel realized he had never been to Kosveg. Yossel never went into the forests surrounding Laszlo. They were full of wolves and Hassids. The Hassidic villages that surrounded Laszlo were like foreign countries, full of strange people with different clothing and customs, and the familiar yet difficult to understand Yiddish language. He thought it ironic that in the eyes of the Germans and apparently many Hungarians the Hassids were lumped together with the assimilated Jews of Laszlo. They had so little in common. But irony was no longer acceptable. It had died in Auschwitz.

The baker crested a hill and looked down into the valley. He gasped at the burned-out wooden structures that lay below wrapped in a hint of recalcitrant morning fog. Yossel felt as if he were peering into a fairy tale past, a withered village captured by an ill force.

He shivered and walked down the road. Yossel was nervous to meet Naftali again. It had been over a month since Naftali walked out of the hotel. Yossel had heard from customers who traveled this road that Naftali was living in the ruined *shtetl*, but never came into Laszlo. The synagogue as a cultural center. It was a brilliant idea. A place for Jews to gather, but really where they could pray in a sanctified space right under the noses of the Gentiles without their knowledge. Yossel didn't like subterfuge, but he had to confess that Jews needed to tread carefully right now. Just because the fire was out didn't mean you could stick your hands in the embers. If the Jews of Laszlo showed their friendliness and willingness to reintegrate into Laszlo again, maybe the Gentiles wouldn't feel threatened and would begin to accept him and the others. It was happening in the bakery, why not for their small community as a whole? But they simply couldn't do it without the young Hassid.

Yossel called out, not wanting to surprise the young man. Shortly, a black-clad shape stepped from one of the decrepit dwellings and began ambling toward the baker. Yossel noticed that Naftali's eyes were shining and feral. There was no hint of the self-consciousness or awkwardness that had marked his face in the DP camp or on the train back to Laszlo. His white shirtsleeves were rolled up over his black jacket, and his sinewy arms and neck gave Yossel the impression of a taut sapling. Yossel looked around at the destruction and realized that there was no place here for casual conversation or pleasant, polite greetings. What could he say? *So, how are you doing, Naftali?* The two men stood with eyes fixed on each other in silence for a long time. Finally, Yossel remembered the loaves of bread under his arm and offered them out before him. Naftali looked blankly at the breads, then gave an imperceptible nod and put his hands on them. They stood holding the loaves in an unspoken act of connection. The Hassid mumbled the *motzi* blessing over the bread.

Ha motzi lechem min ha'aretz

Yossel noticed the number on Naftali's forearm. 4635-A. It added up to eighteen, the value of *chai*—life. Irony was alive, after all.

"Have any more people returned?" Naftali asked.

"No."

The silence grew between them. Finally, Yossel asked gently, "What are you doing out here, Naftali?"

The younger man shrugged and looked back at the wreck of his village. "Waiting for *Ha Shem*'s plan to be revealed to me. *Hineni.* Here I am."

"I don't know what God's plan is. I never did. But I have come to ask your advice."

The Hassid snorted. "My advice? The Jews of Laszlo always looked down on us. You ignored us unless you wanted something we were selling or mourners for your funerals, or needed defending from drunken soldiers."

"It's true," Yossel admitted. "And you thought of us as useless people, especially the well-off. You didn't think we were godly enough. You thought our seeking acceptance into Hungarian society was a betrayal of our Jewishness."

Naftali nodded slowly. "Yes, but tell me. Did joining the Christian world make you any safer in the end?"

"No," Yossel sighed. "But you tell me. Did cutting yourself off from the rest of the world make you any safer in the end?"

Naftali hesitated for a moment. "No."

"Naftali, you and I have both survived the darkness and returned from *Sheol*, the abode of the dead. Our time in the camp burned away any differences between us. Perhaps this is the rare time when we both need each other. Do we want to rebuild our Jewish world with the same bitterness and division as before? *Hineni.* I am here, to ask for your help."

"What do you want of me?"

Yossel paused and rubbed his chin. "We want to reopen the synagogue in Laszlo. Right now it is a shell of a building. No stained glass, no candlesticks, no Torah. And we don't know the rituals for reclaiming the building or even how to do a proper prayer service."

Naftali closed his eyes and appeared deeply pensive. "The temple is destroyed again. We thought our synagogues were our holy places. We thought our *shtetls* were our sacred places. Yet each time, *Ha Shem* destroys them. Why should we rebuild the synagogue? *Ha Shem* purifies these places to remind us that He resides in the heart, not in a building. Our relationship to *Ha Shem* exists in spaces that are no longer stone and mortar. Even Jerusalem is a state of mind, a yearning for some perfect place in this world."

Yossel raised an eyebrow and smiled. "But that's the thing, Naftali. In the eyes of the Christians it won't be our synagogue. It will be what they call a *cultural center.*"

"What is that?"

"A cultural center will be a commemoration of the Jewish history of our area. It is also a place where they can see us and remember what they did to us, think about their actions, and hopefully repent."

"Commemoration." Naftali shook his head slowly and twisted his fingers into his beard. "That means to adapt the truth of memory to the needs of today for the comfort of forgetting."

Yossel was growing frustrated with Naftali's philosophical musings. Maybe it was a waste of time trying to convince this lonely Hassid to help him in Laszlo. One last try. "Maybe you are right. To you, a synagogue is not necessary. To them, a synagogue is threatening. But a cultural center is a neutral place. Everybody takes into it what they will. For us, even if only in our secret hearts, the site will always be a synagogue. We can go in and hold services or ceremonies there. We can pray there. But we need you to guide us in making it happen. Will you at least think about it?"

Peter and Janos watched the men talking a short distance from the broken-down house where the Jewish man lived. They crept from the bushes behind the house and looked inside through a glassless window. They saw the silver candlesticks and the ancient scroll.

"Is that his book of magic?" Janos whispered as he trembled.

"Shhh," Peter said. "Yes, and it looks like he is starting to dig up the treasure. We should get back and report this to the Scouts." He turned and began to walk back to the bushes, keeping low.

Janos began to follow, then stopped. He reached into his pocket to feel the hard-boiled egg he had brought for the sad, hungry-looking man. He glanced at Peter, then dashed up the steps and placed the egg next to the candlesticks on the table. He ran back to his glaring fellow White Stag Scout. Peter grabbed him by the collar and the two disappeared into the forest.

Naftali walked back toward the house, pondering the strange request from Yossel. If this was part of *Ha Shem*'s plan, he thought, it would be revealed. The world was uncharted for Naftali. There were no longer any comforting guideposts for him. He looked down and noticed the tufts of grass pushing through the baked earth. It was early summer, something was sprouting, even in Kosveg. Was life returning to the Hassidic world elsewhere? Should he go to Palestine or America, like so many of the surviving Hassids? That is what the Hassids of Debrecen told him in Auschwitz. Europe was nothing but a graveyard for Jews. Was he finished with his work here in Kosveg? Would helping open the synagogue in Laszlo, even as a "cultural center," be a small act of *tikkun olam*, healing the world as required by Jewish law? Could he help reignite the light of Torah in a town where Jews were so fallen and hatred ran silent and deep under the surface, as always?

He mounted the steps lost in confused thought, longing for clarity from a God who seemed to be so distant and cold. As he entered the house, he noticed something next to the candlesticks. An egg. He picked it up and examined it. He spun it on the table. It turned like a top. It was hard-boiled. He held it up before him and closed his eyes. During a time of grief and mourning, such eggs were a symbol of life, affirming hope in the face of death. Naftali dropped to his knees and wailed his gratitude to *Ha Shem* for this small miracle of guidance.

CHAPTER 25

When the mayor got home, he found Greta humming and smiling. "Hello dear, did your tea party go well?"

"Yes, yes, yes! Eva played wonderfully and my friends were so impressed with her. She played Vali Racz, my favorite. They all thanked me for giving them such a beautiful afternoon."

"You did a good thing, my dear." Ferenc smiled. It was comforting to see Greta so happy. Just as important, he was certain that as more people in the town came to know Eva and the other Jews as people again, face to face, the harder it would be to dislike them. If it succeeded with Greta's shallow friends, it should work on a larger scale. Eva was the key. Her music was so pure and heartfelt, it reached inside and warmed you. "Greta, what do you think about having a house party for all our friends and some of the business leaders in town? You entertain so beautifully and Eva can perform. I think it would go a long way toward the healing Laszlo needs."

"We haven't had a party since before the Germans came. I love the idea." She looked around the living room. "We may have to move some of the furniture, and of course the piano could be the centerpiece of the evening. But wait, Eva has nothing nice to wear."

"Why not take a dress or two from the wardrobe in her old bedroom?"

Greta frowned. "I've given her some clothes already. I'm afraid bringing her performance dresses might be painful to her."

Or painful to you, the mayor thought, then admonished himself for being so judgmental. Greta seemed more accepting of Eva lately. One day at a time. "Perhaps, but it might also be a gentle way to help her feel more connected to her life before . . . all that happened. And you have been developing such a nice relationship with Eva. You have really helped her to come back to life."

Greta's eyes sparkled at her husband's observation. She tapped her pursed lips with a finger. "She's still so thin. I guess I could take in a seam here and there. Yes, Ferenc, you're right. It would be a nice gesture and she certainly needs to be dressed appropriately for a house party." She twisted the string of pearls she wore. "I suppose I could find a nice necklace to go with her outfit."

Eva entered the library nervously and alone. She didn't want to miss the little weekly *Shabbos* ritual at the hotel, but the mayor had set the date and time of the house party without consulting her. Yossel said that Jews lit the candles to dispel the darkness of this world and enter the pure light of the Sabbath, where everything was at peace. For Eva, who was asked to light the candles each week, it meant letting go of the slights and disappointments, the loneliness and alienation she suffered daily. The ritual helped, but music was the only thing that offered her real solace and escape. Yossel urged her to go and perform at the mayor's house party, advising her to "keep the door open." Oskar warned her not to let it hit her in the back on her way out of the party. When she asked the mayor if Yossel and Oskar could attend the party as they had not heard Eva play since they returned, he mumbled an evasive reply. He wanted the guests to focus on Eva and not be distracted by the presence of the others. But she suspected it was because of Oskar's trouble with the police, even though he hadn't done anything wrong. The mayor always expressed his concern for the situation of all the Jews in Laszlo, yet he only seemed to pay attention to Eva. He had even told her once that she was the key to healing the town. As much as she wanted and needed his help, she didn't want to abandon Yossel and Oskar. They had suffered and lost with her, protected and supported her. If she performed well and made Mrs. Kodaly and the guests happy, it could bring her a step closer to regaining her house, and help Oskar and Yossel find greater acceptance in Laszlo.

The gold necklace Mrs. Kodaly had given her for the event sat heavily around Eva's neck. She looked down at her brown dress, squeezing her fingers to suppress her anger. The dress and jewelry were hers and her mother's. Mrs. Kodaly flitted about the guests, making cheery small talk. Eva's eyes narrowed as she watched the mayor's wife place a tray of food on top of the Bosendorfer and walk away. She ran major scales in her head to control her agitation at the sacrilege, then approached Mrs. Kodaly, who was busy directing servers and guests.

"Excuse me, Mrs. Kodaly," Eva said, suppressing the volcano boiling inside. "Would it be possible to remove the food from the piano? I need to open it for the sound to carry through a room full of people."

Mrs. Kodaly looked over to the piano in embarrassment. "Oh, of course. It must have been the servers." She adopted a confidential tone. "There are not too many of us in Laszlo who appreciate a quality instrument." She breezed off to have the situation rectified. When a server removed the tray, Eva quickly raised and propped up the top board to prevent further insult to her beautiful piano.

Eva timidly took a glass of sour cherry juice and seltzer from a passing tray and glanced around the library. She remembered many times her parents had gatherings like this. Small tables where men played poker or women played whist. Huddles of hushed conversation where gossip was the currency. A bluish haze of cigar smoke that always made Eva think of pictures she had seen of a

Turkish bazaar. She thought she recognized a few faces in the room. Some of her father's clients, perhaps. Several eyed her with sympathy. Others' thoughts were guarded by hooded eyes and frosty smiles. Who had been in the crowd at the deportation? Were they jeering or saddened? She pushed the clouded memories and the familiar faces away. Faces no longer mattered to Eva. Her long hours of practicing from the professor's manuscript mixed with hurt and anxiety made her acutely aware of the tiny sound each person gave off as he or she spun through the air, moving from place to place. Laszlo itself made a collective hum, a fused cacophony of individual notes. When Eva passed people in the street or wove through crowds in the square, she was aware of the sound. But tonight, in such a small, crowded space with so much pressure on her, she felt unmoored by it. The sound wasn't particularly pleasant. For the first time since entering the professor's musical worldview, Eva wanted to turn off the music.

Eva took her seat at the Bosendorfer. While she warmed up, she watched the mayor trying to keep the atmosphere light with witty banter and generous, if waning supplies of her father's bourbon, scotch, and elderberry. She performed a series of classical pieces interspersed with popular tunes. She was clearly an object of fascination or judgment, but she was not included in the party. Did the mayor or his wife even notice? At least he had taken a step to normalize Eva's presence in Laszlo before some of the town's leading businesspeople and socialites. That could do a lot for the Jews in general. They might be seen as ordinary Laszlo citizens again. Eva was unhappy with her uninspired but proficient performance. It didn't matter as long as Mrs. Kodaly was happy with the party and the mayor felt his plan to use Eva was progressing. As the evening slowed, Mayor Kodaly clinked his glass with a spoon to command attention.

"Ladies and gentlemen. Greta and I are so happy that you could join us tonight to celebrate peace and normalcy in Laszlo after a long war." Scattered clapping and murmured agreement floated through the house, as Mrs. Kodaly came and stood by his side. "We have a special guest, as you are aware. Eva Fleiss has returned to Laszlo and I hope you will join me in a round of applause for sharing her amazing talent with us tonight." Polite, muted applause. "Eva, would you like to say a few words?"

The mayor's invitation to speak surprised Eva. She had so much that she wanted to say, even to scream, but as she looked around the room she could not penetrate the masks or bring light to the shadows. She was aware that her music did not seem to affect the guests in any way. Nobody broke from what they were doing to close their eyes and swoon, or express that dreamy demeanor she had seen at the Home. Nobody came up to talk about her father, thank her, or listen closely. They talked right next to her as if she didn't—or shouldn't—exist. She felt uneasy at the way the furniture man, Mor, looked at her from time to time. She couldn't read what lurked behind his dark, troubled eyes.

Besides, hearing her words might only make the guests' animosity or guilt worse. Among the prisoners and even some guards at the camp she saw how people punished the object of their guilt rather than face their own responsibility. Who in this crowd of adults was sincerely interested in what she had to say? Eva felt as if the memory and meaning of her life were being erased as she stood there, like the slow erosion of rich soil by an incessant wind. What could she say when she felt so unsure and unsafe? She could barely pronounce the only words she could think of. Her insecurity came out sounding like humility.

"Thank you."

The room filled with a collective sigh of relief, followed by strong applause. Eva bowed in acknowledgment and went to the kitchen to calm her nerves. Someone turned on the BBC. Benny Goodman's *Carnegie Hall Jazz Concert* played and the conversation swelled again. As the music filled her head, she warmed at the memory of her father learning the swing dance to Goodman's "I Got Rhythm". As a lawyer his thoughts were always organized and coordinated, but his feet never followed suite. Shortly she heard the *clink-clink-clink* of the mayor's glass again. She poked her head around the kitchen door to listen without entering the room.

"I would like to thank you all for coming again, and I hope the friendship and the music made for a lovely evening. I do want to let you all know that Eva will be attending the Ferenc Liszt Academy of Music in the capital this fall. She is the first person from Laszlo ever to attend our nation's most prestigious institute of music. Soon she will walk the same halls as the greats of Hungarian music—Bela Bartok, Ferenc Liszt, Zoltan Kodaly, and so many others. Please show your appreciation for this amazing accomplishment by a daughter of Laszlo. Eva Fleiss."

A loud applause and cheer arose, compelling Eva to reenter the library and take in the accolades. The mayor raised his hands to quiet the crowd. "Of course, the Academy is expensive, and the war has not been kind to the Fleiss family, whom all of you have known as friends or in a professional capacity." He scanned the room, making eye contact with as many guests as would meet his gaze. "Therefore, the town is starting a fund to support Eva's studies. I hope you will see it in your hearts to join us in putting Laszlo on the musical map of our great nation." His comments were met with vague sounds of assent. Eva was impressed. She had no idea this was his secret agenda for the party. It was only fair that the town pay for the Academy as partial restitution for what it had done to her family, her life. "In addition, we must recognize that Jacob Fleiss was a treasure in Laszlo. His great work helped the well-off and the indigent alike. In the course of closing out his law office we came across a number of open invoices for legal work performed by Jacob Fleiss for many of you. I have taken the liberty of putting those invoices in envelopes marked with the name of the client on the secretary's desk in the foyer. If you find an envelope with your name on it as you leave, please take it and send in a bank draft as soon as possible. What better way to honor your obligations and honor both the man and his talented daughter? Thank you and good evening."

There was a cascade of grumbles and whispered imprecations after the mayor's closing remarks. Eva was stunned and embarrassed. Money owed her father might be recovered for her education, but the angry looks on the departing guests probably meant they thought Eva was a part of this plan. Things were tentative enough for the Jews in Laszlo. This might backfire on all of them. The mayor stood firm next to the secretary's desk to ensure that all the envelopes were taken. He had chosen his guest list well for the evening. Not a single envelope remained after the last guest left. Mrs. Kodaly stood frozen with a glass in her hand, purple with rage.

Mor fled the party, stuffed the invoice into his coat pocket and stomped across the square to the coffee house. He shot down the coffee and whiskey in his cup. Even though he had been told it was past closing time he yelled to the waiter for a refill and glared across the table at Sergeant Ritook. "He humiliated us into giving the girl money to go to the Academy."

Ritook pulled slowly on a cigarette then stubbed it out into the ashtray on the table. "Then she'll be leaving Laszlo soon. One less Jew. You should be happy. I know I am."

"Yes, but I don't like the way she manipulates the mayor. Obviously she was behind his little stunt tonight. Jews are good at that. I wouldn't be surprised if she is using her, how shall I say this delicately, her feminine wiles to cloud his judgment." He thought he detected a reaction from Ritook, but the sergeant didn't take the bait. "I have heard from my niece, a nurse at the Laszlo Home, that the girl stirred up the patients into a near riot. Now they are demanding the return of the Jewish doctors and nurses."

Ritook snorted. "That's not going to happen. They are all dead.

The patients will settle down and forget about it once the girl leaves town."

Mor tried a different approach. "And you've probably heard how she helped saboteurs in the work camp she was in blow up some German equipment."

"So?"

"At the time, Sergeant, Germany and Hungary were allies. That means her sabotage was treasonous. She should be arrested for treason."

"Mr. Mor, I agree with you that the girl is the most dangerous of the Jews, but I doubt the captain will support a charge of treason. Besides, she's leaving Laszlo soon. Let her go. The Jewish girl is nothing more than a headache."

Mor gripped the edge of the table in exasperation. Didn't Ritook see how serious this was? "But those other Jews. They've been trouble since they returned. The butcher attacked the station master, they're threatening people and trying to take back properties." He gave Ritook a knowing look. "They even convinced the mayor to open the old synagogue again."

Ritook's face hardened at the reference to Oskar. "That trouble-making butcher got off easy. Anyway, I can't arrest the Jews for opening a cultural center. They've got a permit."

"But we don't know what they are doing in secret—what they're planning," Mor pleaded. "Everybody knows they are either conspiring with the communists or plotting to bring more Jews to Laszlo. Maybe both. You've seen the Russian trucks driving past town. Jews and Russians once again plotting to take over our great country." He looked the sergeant squarely in the eyes. "I fear the Jews are a threat to public order."

"Why don't you take that up directly with Captain Szabo?"

Mor threw his hands in the air, then gulped down his second cup. "Captain Szabo is a functionary. He blows with the prevailing wind of the state. He winked at the mayor's inaction when the Jews were declared a different race. He cracked down when the Arrow Cross came to power. Now he's a friend of the Jews who've returned because they are legally Hungarians again. But you, Ritook, everybody knows about your good work at the brick factory," he raised his empty cup. "You are a man of principle."

Ritook eyed Mor with suspicion. "I am just a policeman. I uphold Hungarian law, nothing more. I will go after them like a hound out of hell if they break a law, but I can't throw people in jail on your suspicions."

Mor chuckled. "I know your father, Ritook. I know about his Order of Vitez. I know his feelings about the place of Jews in Hungary. I believe you are your father's son."

CHAPTER 26

Eva wasn't sure what to expect as she entered the house the morning after the party. Mrs. Kodaly probably thought, like the guests, that Eva and the mayor had conspired, manipulating the guests into giving money to Eva. At least that's what Oskar moaned after Eva told him. Inside, everything in the house seemed covered in a thick, translucent film, as if it had been polluted by the behavior of the guests and the mayor's intrigues. Eva's good memories were being crowded out by her constant mental battles with his wife. She was losing interest in her house. All Eva wanted was to play her piano and get to the Academy.

Both Mrs. Kodaly and the mayor were waiting. Mrs. Kodaly seemed swelled with anger. The mayor looked contrite. His wife nudged him with an elbow. "Go ahead, Ferenc."

"I am sorry about last night, Eva. Your music was wonderful, and I am afraid I spoiled the evening for you. I didn't mean to embarrass you. However, I want you to know that when I went over your father's ledgers, I found that the people who were coming to the party last night owed his law office almost five thousand *pengos*. That is enough to pay for your tuition and your room and board the entire time you are at the Academy. I didn't want those people to get away with denying you your chance because they chose to ignore their debts."

Eva realized with relief that Mrs. Kodaly was furious at being embarrassed by the mayor. She didn't seem to associate Eva with his stunt.

Mrs. Kodaly softened at her husband's apology. She looked around the room, noticing the ashtrays, glasses, and small plates scattered about. "All right, please help me straighten up from the party. Then practice all you'd like." Mrs. Kodaly glanced at the mayor, who nodded to her. "There is something else, Eva. We don't want you to work today after helping straighten up. Instead, you can go up and visit your bedroom. It hasn't been touched since the day you left. When you first came here we thought it might be too much for you. But we think it is time for you to go inside it again. When you are ready, the door is unlocked." Mrs. Kodaly's eyes glistened as her words took a few moments to emerge. "And welcome home."

After quickly clearing the dishes and cleaning the library and kitchen, Eva rushed up the stairs and stood before the door. She wanted to run around the house, touching everything. But in her mind, her bedroom was the beating heart of the house. Every day she passed the door she chafed at being kept out of it. For some reason, Mrs. Kodaly had changed her mind about letting Eva into the room. Was it their apparently thawing relationship, or the way Eva was treated by the guests? Why did she think entering her own bedroom would be "too much" for Eva? It didn't matter. She hesitated for a minute to control her racing heart. Then she turned the knob, pushed the door open and entered the room.

It was as if time hadn't ticked forward since the deportation. All the pain and sadness disappeared for a brief moment as Eva stood captured by this frozen past. Cream-colored wallpaper with a pattern of small repeating plums still adorned the walls. She immediately sat on her bed, which she had made up that last morning, thinking she and her father were coming back shortly. She buried her head in the pillow, expecting to inhale the familiar scents of shampoo and skin cream. Instead, she coughed out the dust and musty odor of an abandoned warehouse of her memories. She rolled over and admonished herself for expecting anything different after a year of neglect.

The ornately carved wardrobe loomed large in one corner of

the room. Through the opened door, Eva could see a rack of her old dresses, a gap where Mrs. Kodaly had removed the brown party dress. She walked to the wardrobe and touched the fabrics, remembering the times she wore each, the happy memories they evoked. She threw off her donated clothes and eased into the green taffeta dress with fine pearl buttons her mother had made for her last successful regional competition. Her parents had been so proud when the audience gave Eva a standing ovation. The dress hung on her sadly, no longer carrying the pride of her achievement. She wiggled into her favorite black patent leather shoes, noting how her feet had shriveled and flattened. At least they were still comfortable.

Eva's eyes were drawn to the wall shelves that encircled the room just above her head. Her collection of ceramic-faced dolls given by her father smiled benevolently down at her from between framed photographs of Eva and her family on summer vacations, school events, and different music competitions. In one photo, Eva and Professor Sandor sat together at the Bosendorfer. She took down a photograph of her family with the Danube behind them. If she took the photograph from the silver frame, would the water continue flowing and her parents keep smiling and hugging her? When she realized none of this would happen, the longing came roaring back worse than before. Eva fell onto her bed. Her body convulsed with crushing waves of grief.

She must have slept for a long time. The sunlight had shifted noticeably, highlighting the lilac blossoms outside her window. Eva sat up and rubbed her eyes. She went to the desk to find a tissue. The algebra textbook she used in her final school year lay open to the last chapter. She glanced at a page of practice problems. How simple the world would be if all the variables of life could be put into solvable equations. But Eva had learned in the camp that the world was not algebraic, that the most solid equation could be disrupted and destroyed despite the supposed rules.

In the top drawer of the desk she found the blue silk make-up kit her mother had given her for her sixteenth birthday. Her chin quivered below a sad smile as she rummaged through the kit, thinking of the many times she used it with her mother's guidance. It was one of the few things they could do together after her mother became bedridden. She remembered how they laughed as they puckered into the mirror and applied lipstick together before her first high school dance. Here in her room, Eva's mother came alive to her. Holding the kit and touching the cool silky fabric, Eva realized that she hadn't thought about her mother much in this past year since the deportation. Tears burned her cheeks as she remembered her mother's face, her laugh and her touch. Two winters ago, after her mother's death, Eva was numb with grief. How was she to know what horrors lay in wait for her in the spring? She felt a bittersweet relief that her mother had died peacefully at home in her bed rather than suffering and perishing in terror and humiliation. Eva closed the kit, putting the make-up and her grief back in the drawer for the moment.

In the large bottom drawer Eva found a box of letters. She took it out and returned to the bed. It was mostly filled with birthday cards from her parents and news clippings of her concerts. Toward the back, Eva found an envelope containing her high school diploma. In the upper right corner the school had pasted a yellow star as the law required. Eva recalled her first innocent thought that the stars must have rained from the night sky onto Laszlo while the town slept, turning yellow in the earth's atmosphere. By morning, the fallen stars had latched on to lapels and sleeves, storefronts and apartment buildings. It was more mystifying than frightening at first. Parents were somber, knowing they had sewn an unknown but frightening fate onto their children's clothes. At school, the younger children marveled at the stars on their classmates. Many realized for the first time they were members of a special club. The yellow stars had a different impact on some of the Gentiles, however, transforming the Jews of the town from neighbors into strangers, from friends into enemies.

Eva's chest ached as she relived her hurt and the confusion that followed. She hadn't changed at all, but she wasn't the same in many people's eyes. She peeled the star off her diploma, crushed it and threw it into the wastebasket next to the desk. It left a shadow of gluey residue, just enough to remind Eva of its former presence. She put the diploma back in the envelope and filed it away in the box.

Another envelope was from the Academy. Eva opened it and read her acceptance letter. It was comforting to see the letter after a year. She was amazed to realize that she could almost recite it, having repeated it like a daily prayer of hope in Auschwitz. She looked up and saw the professor smiling at her with approval from the frame on the wall shelf. A second, unopened letter from the Academy sat behind the acceptance letter. Eva thought it must be the details of admission. The envelope was stamped June 15, days after the deportation. Although it was a year old, the letter would contain the information she needed to begin her study at the Academy. Perhaps this was why the Academy had not responded to her two recent letters, she thought happily. They had already replied.

Eva grabbed the Waterford Glass letter opener her father had given her and slit the envelope. She laid back against her pillows to enjoy the letter and fantasize about being at the Academy. The letter was surprisingly brief:

> *Dear Miss Fleiss:*
>
> *As you are aware, there have been significant changes in Hungarian law toward certain racial classes that limit our ability to offer admission based on merit alone. It is with great regret that we must inform you it is necessary for us in accordance with the new law to withdraw our offer of enrollment at the Ferenc Liszt Academy of Music.*
>
> *We wish you all the best of luck in finding an academic home that will allow your fine talents to flourish.*
>
> *Most regretfully,*
>
> *Mrs. Irma Rakoczi*
>
> *Assistant to the Director*

Eva's breathing became shallow. Her heart hammered fiercely against her ribs. In spite of everything she had lost, she always had the dream of the Academy to hold on to. Now the last shred of her past and her only plan for the future had been torn away. She curled up on the bed and looked up at the professor. He was no longer smiling. The plums on the wallpaper began to seep purple blood. Her fingertips then her hands prickled as the room darkened and tilted. Eva was falling down a dark well, her fingers scraping and clawing at the wall to slow her mad descent. She hit the black whirlpool at the bottom. She spun and sank, engulfed in the hot, primordial ooze that fed the loathing above. The war was over and the Germans had lost, yet the eternal hatred that crept up from the well remained unvanquished. It had wiped out her past and stolen her future.

Mrs. Kodaly became concerned when Eva didn't come down for several hours. She and the mayor mounted the stairs and called the girl. They looked at each other when there was no reply and ran to the bedroom. Eva lay curled in a fetal position on the bed in a baggy green taffeta dress, a letter gripped in her outstretched hand. Mrs. Kodaly's fear subsided when she noticed the deep rise and fall of Eva's breath. She took the letter from the girl's hand and read it softly aloud. Ferenc exhaled audibly.

"That's why they didn't respond to Eva's letters."

"My God, Ferenc, what can we do?" Mrs. Kodaly stared down at Eva, seeing the sleeping innocent and feeling a lump of pity lodging in her throat.

The mayor reread the letter. "This letter is a year old. The law has changed. The quotas are gone. Jews are free to attend any university they can get into. She was already accepted. I'm sure I can get her back in." His hopeful tone became a sigh of despair. "But I don't even know if the Academy survived the siege of Budapest. Last night, one of the guests told me all of the bridges were destroyed and most of the city is in ruins. And the Jews? I've heard that over a hundred thousand from Budapest alone were murdered in the Auschwitz camp after the deportation. A hundred thousand."

Mrs. Kodaly grabbed her chest in shock at the figure. "I hadn't known. And all these Jews from Laszlo. Gone. Dear God, how did this girl survive?"

"I have no idea. It's a miracle." The mayor folded the letter and tucked it tenderly under Eva's hand. "But I promised Eva, I promised all those poor, misbegotten people at the hotel they would be taken care of." He gently stroked Eva's brow. "Let's let her sleep for now."

Eva opened her eyes in darkness. A sliver of moonlight came through one of the bedroom windows, illuminating eerie fixed smiles on the faces of her ceramic dolls. Her mind filled with conflicting currents of fear, helplessness, and confusion. No family, no professor, no Academy, no future. It was too much to think about. She closed her eyes and found herself walking up a broad, winding way that spiraled into a velvet sky. The steps were large piano keys, and as she advanced each key gave off a barely perceptible note. Planets rotated and whirled above and below, responding to sounds created by her footsteps. Angels and diaphanous souls flew past, harmonizing with the notes, as well. Eva saw the Academy far ahead. It filled her heart with soft clouds of peace until she came to a chasm in the keyboard path. She looked down into the blackness. A guttural chant rose toward her, pulsing closer and closer. She felt her happiness, her very life force, draining away. Eva knew she had to get beyond the gulf and continue on her path, but it seemed too wide to cross.

Eva had no idea how long she was in her bedroom, but she stirred herself and realized the mayor and Mrs. Kodaly must be wondering what was going on. She stepped heavily down the stairs to find them sitting anxiously in the library. Her pretty green dress hung limp and crumpled in defeat on her body.

Mrs. Kodaly leaped up and took her arm, guiding Eva into a leather chair and kneeling beside her. "Eva, dear, we read the letter. We are so sorry. Is there anything we can do for you?"

Eva shook her head slowly, her unfocused eyes staring ahead. Her right hand scratched at her left forearm, stripping away some pancake and revealing the outline of the tattooed numbers. Mrs. Kodaly flinched at the sight. "No," Eva said. "I wrote them twice." She held up the letter that was folded in her left hand. "It's finished." She closed her eyes as if the lids were made of lead.

The mayor rubbed his chin and clenched his jaw. "Eva, let me contact them. Perhaps the mail isn't getting through. After all, Budapest is still recovering from the pummeling it took from the Russians and the Germans during the siege." He spoke rapidly, as if reaching for every reasonable explanation he could. "Also, it's summer. Maybe there aren't many staff there at this time. I'll try the telephone tomorrow. If that doesn't work I will send a telegram to a banker I know in the capitol. He can send one of his men to the Academy to see what is going on. We can't jump to conclusions. We are going to do whatever we can to get you into the Academy."

Mrs. Kodaly stroked Eva's arm gently. Eva tensed slightly, but didn't resist. "Would you like to stay here tonight, in your own room?"

"In my own room," Eva whispered. "I have waited to hear those words for such a long time. It's odd, they don't matter that much to me right now." She slowly emerged from her fog, blinking her eyes.

"No, Yossel and Oskar must be worried about me. I should have returned to the hotel by now. I'll come back tomorrow to clean and practice." She left with leaden footsteps and a heavy heart.

Mrs. Kodaly closed the front door behind Eva, her hands lingering on the highly polished wood. The mayor called to her softly.

"Darling, are you all right?"

Mrs. Kodaly turned, her make-up smeared by tears. "That poor girl. She has suffered so much." She dabbed her eyes with a pink handkerchief. "You must do everything you can to get her into the Academy."

"Raising all the money she will need was a good start." The mayor gave a helpless shrug. "I will keep trying to contact the Academy."

Mrs. Kodaly nodded absently. "I also can't stop thinking about the house party. Did you see the way the guests treated her, Ferenc, as if she were a servant or not there at all? There was so much hostility toward her."

"I think many of them were finally feeling shame. They saw this innocent young girl who suffered so much while they reaped their bounty. They didn't know how to react." He shook his head and frowned. "But it may have made some of them angrier. Even though our guests agreed to repay what was owed Jacob, few of them would consider returning what they have stolen."

Mrs. Kodaly exhaled a low sob as she stared at the piano. She put her hand to her neck and felt for the pearl necklace she wore. "I loved all these things I never had. They filled an empty space in my life."

The mayor reached tenderly for his wife's arm. "Greta, don't bring up the past. We've tried so hard to move on."

"I can't help it, Ferenc. I think about our baby boy every day. The beautiful little soul we created and lost. And we can't have another."

"My love, it was a complicated delivery. You know that. He couldn't survive childbirth. We were lucky you did."

"When Eva came back, I was so afraid she would take the house and everything else away. I was afraid the emptiness would return." Mrs. Kodaly shuddered and remained silent for a moment. "Then her music became so inspired. It moved me in a way I can't explain. It softened my heart and somehow I came to accept that losing our boy was not my fault. It's so strange, Ferenc. Somewhere in the music, I felt our little lost son blessing and releasing me." She thought about those hours of listening to Eva's music from the next room, and how the sounds at first evoked melancholy. Yet as she listened more carefully over time, Mrs. Kodaly allowed herself to be embraced and transported by the sounds. She wanted to thank Eva, but began to feel uncomfortable wearing her mother's clothing and living in her house.

"Then I realized how owning all these things actually blinded me. At the party I saw all the greed in others, I saw all the pain of that poor child who has lost so much. And when we offered to let her stay in the house, she refused. I feel as if I am waking from a dream." Her body clenched as she moaned loudly. "I am no different from the guests, Ferenc. Oh, look what I have done, what I have stolen from the girl!" Mrs. Kodaly put her hands on her temples, the misery plain on her face. "How could I? All I have done to her when she gave me so much." She fell backward against the polished door, doubled over and wept.

The mayor put his arms around his wife and held her until she relaxed. They sank to the floor together. She felt a surge of long buried love arise toward her husband. His voice was gentle. "We don't need all this, Greta. We can give it back."

Swirls of ground fog softened the road back to the hotel. Eva struggled to hear any sound. She wondered if the music of the spheres had been real or imagined, fired by painful longing for a connection with the professor. Every muscle in her body ached. She was so tired of struggling for her dream. She passed the park, hardly noticing the cigarette glow and the muted conversations. Hanna called out to her, but Eva ignored her friend. Andras's entreaty sounded hollow and distant. She tried to move her fingers and play something comforting, but her hands rebelled and hung listlessly at her side.

She entered the hotel, noticing the smell of sadness and defeat that she now associated with the bodies of old men. Worried looks on the faces of Yossel, Oskar, and the two farmhands greeted her. She told them about the letter from the Academy. Nobody asked about the party.

Oskar scratched his unshaven neck and shook his head. "Maybe it's time to face it, Eva. This music thing is such an uphill struggle. Every time you take a step forward, they shove you back. It's too much for a young girl to deal with. You should have a family to help you. There's nothing for you in Laszlo, there is nothing for you in Hungary." He hung his head and exhaled heavily. "Maybe you should leave. Maybe we should all just leave."

Eva considered Oskar's word. He was right. She had no family, no real community to support her. What did she have left in Hungary?

Herschel aimed a moon-faced, sad smile at Eva. "You could come with us to Palestine. We're gonna sell Zsuzsa to buy the tickets. Then we're gonna work on farms and find good women to marry."

Mendel broke in. "We saw it in a Jewish newspaper from Budapest. There's lots of ads from women in Palestine who want to marry."

Oscar grunted. "Palestine. It's illegal to go there. The British aren't letting anybody in unless they have some kind of permission. And I heard only Zionists can get permission. You know, those Jews who believe God reserved the Holy Land for them."

Eva mustered a sad smile. "Thanks, Herschel. You are very kind.

But I am no farmer. And I don't even know what a Zionist is." Maybe she should go to New York, in America. She didn't know anybody, but so what? The newspaper said many Jews were going there. She couldn't clean her house and play her piano in Laszlo for the rest of her life. The money the mayor had raised would get her started. She could teach children, like the professor did. Oskar was right. Leave Hungary. Get a new start.

"Eva, come to the synagogue with us tomorrow," Yossel said. "We will meet the mayor there and look at what needs to be done to restore the building. It will get your mind off this sad business for a while."

Eva sighed. Her heart beat with the heavy, slow cadence of a funeral procession. "I don't want to get involved in that project. I didn't go to the synagogue much before. Maybe a few times for a *bar mitzvah* or *Yom Kippur* service." Eva hesitated as a profound realization surfaced. "To be honest, I don't really think of myself as that Jewish, even though it's my heritage. I still think of myself as a Hungarian first."

"Yeah, lots of us feel that way about being Jewish," Oskar said. "But it doesn't matter. They won't let you *not* be a Jew, whether you practice or not, wear a Hassid's black clothes or the latest fashions from Paris." He looked around at the silent, diverted faces. "Well, that's what we learned from all this, right? You're a Jew in their eyes if only one of your grandparents was Jewish. You can't escape through time; you can't escape through conversion. And you know why? Because Christians need us as a scapegoat for their anger at their kings, their generals, their governments. They feel helpless, unable to control their own lives so they blame us. Damn them. It's been that way for centuries."

"Oskar, please!" Yossel said, motioning subtly toward Eva. "Not now."

Eva was not interested in that kind of talk. She was still struggling with Oskar's remark about leaving Laszlo. She stood and walked toward the stairs. "I want to go to sleep. I am going back to my house tomorrow to practice."

"Why?" Oskar demanded. "It'll just bring you more pain. Why not take a break?"

Eva stiffened. She realized that even without the Academy, her life in music was not over. Professor Sandor had reached out from the grave to gift her life with meaning in the chaos of a meaningless world. She couldn't quit now, although she was unable to see ahead. She turned toward Oskar. "Music has helped me hold on through everything that's happened. It has given me a purpose in all this darkness and misery. I need to hold on to that purpose. The professor created something good for me. Something good is waiting for me." Tears pooled in her eyes. "I'm not going to abandon it because we're not in the camp anymore, or because my perfect path isn't clear anymore." She turned and walked up the stairs, but heard Oskar's low, rumbling voice.

"Poor child. She doesn't know. We're all still in the camp."

Eva woke to a sunny morning, which lifted her spirits somewhat. She got dressed and made her way back to the house. Odd, she thought of it less and less as her home. Mrs. Kodaly was solicitous when Eva arrived. They spent an hour rolling the piano aside and taking the Persian carpet in the library outside to beat the dust out of it. Eva found it comforting to have something to focus on that was neither music nor memories, although the beater was shaped like a clef note. The mayor had strung a line between two trees. The two women struggled to hoist the heavy carpet over the line. Eva took pleasure in thumping the carpet. Her muscles worked hard, relishing the physical outlet for her jumbled feelings. Mrs. Kodaly slapped haphazardly at the carpet beside Eva, making neutral comments and eventually quieting down as Eva ignored her.

When they finished, Eva entered the house and approached the

Bosendorfer with apprehension. Without the professor and without the Academy she was unsure what the future held. But without music she had nothing at all. She had to continue. Eva sat on the bench and placed her hands gently on the keys. She stilled her racing mind, waiting for the familiar tingle and vibration. Nothing came. She fought back a rising panic, determined to play. *Please, please, save me. You are all I have.* Her fingers mechanically ran a simple scale. She didn't hold her father's outstretched hand as they hurried to the deportation train. It was too embarrassing for a girl her age to do that. She felt the heavy regret lodge in her chest. Another scale. The professor and the bumblebee children ran down the platform. A whorl of shadowy images, thin phantoms trembling in fear, hanging bodies, death, death. She banged chords from Wagner in anger, seeing the faces of the police at her return and the disguised or blatant dislike from the mayor's guests. It was time to stop and breathe. Stand up, stretch, and shake the cramping negativity out through her fingers.

Eva returned to the piano. She played a few of the strange chord combinations from the professor's manuscript and from her early practice. She ran the D-major scale, where the moon was A, Saturn F-sharp. No planets spun into view, no stars hummed in harmony. But there was a slight tingle at the tips of her fingers. *Come back, please.* She continued to play the notes and chords over and over until slight ripples of electricity went up her arms. Soon, they enveloped her. Mars E, Jupiter F, Mercury B-flat. She alternated between major and minor scales, encompassing joy and sorrow. The room disappeared and Eva was swept into the cosmos, dissolving into a star-splattered night. For the first time she fully embodied the transcendent quality of music that Professor Sandor had tried to explain to her when she was too young and inexperienced to understand. She merged with the music without cognition, letting go of the temporal to a timeless Pure Form. Music for its own sake, captured by its ability to shape feelings, experiences and reality from grief to liberation. Elated, light, ecstatic, fearless. No up, no down, just constant movement and reverberation. No memories or images. Only pure sound.

Eva came out of her reverie and unity with the music. She was exhausted and alone. She looked around the library. The same books, rug, and furniture she had known all her life stared back at her. But now she perceived them as little more than slightly vibrating objects. They had no true solidity. She knew it was time to let them go.

CHAPTER 27

Yossel left the bakery to walk to the synagogue. He carried his old *matzo*-making rectangular cutter and perforated roller. The tools served no purpose at the bakery. Maybe he would make *matzo* at the hotel. Most of the people he passed smiled and acknowledged him by name, and he reciprocated their pleasantries. Sometimes he stopped to explain what the tools were, as very few Gentiles in Laszlo knew about *matzo*. It couldn't hurt to begin educating the populace about Jewish culture, they were sure to be more sympathetic if they understood Jews better. He felt good to be feeding the town again. Even the police had resumed their unofficial but not unwelcomed freeloading. The underlying hum of anger or resentment he sometimes detected appeared to be abating. He stood on a precipice, a turning point for the Jews in Laszlo.

The baker stared meditatively at the broken chandelier until the farmhands noisily hefted an overturned bench back into place. He was happy they had gotten their jobs back and were coming to the hotel every Friday for the *Shabbos* meal. Mendel and Herschel never talked about the scratches and bruises they carried with increasing frequency. Yossel assumed such was the lot of farmworkers. He noticed the new purple welt on Herschel's forehead and thought of the mark of Cain. Was it a sign of God's protection or a badge of shame? Two ancient rabbis offered opposite interpretations and left us to struggle with the meaning. Typical of our tradition, Yossel thought.

Oskar collected damaged prayer books, muttering curses of biblical proportions at whoever defaced the synagogue, everyone in Laszlo and the whole of Hungary. He kept his voice low as he complained to Yossel. "I still don't like this. They are trying to make us more Jewish than we are. They want us to be 'good Jews' so they can point to us and say 'see how we treat good Jews?' But one false step by us or one shift in their fortunes and we're finished."

Yossel didn't want to acknowledge the truth of Oskar's comments. He knew their neighbors' acceptance often seemed to depend on 'good' behavior. Please them and don't offend. It was conditional. He fought against the feeling they were only allowing the synagogue to reopen to show their generosity, not their solidarity or their contrition. But he couldn't control their thoughts or motives. He could only smile and be docile, giving no cause for animosity. He chose to believe in their ultimate goodness. He had to. The mayor wandered the main room, directing the few town volunteers in the sweeping and collection of trash and interrupting Yossel's thoughts. The baker took in all the action around him, and consciously returned to his positive outlook. He thought of the *challah. Hands working together will heal this place and braid something new and beautiful.*

The mayor approached Yossel with his hat held before him respectfully. "There is a lot to be done but it seems mostly cosmetic, except for the stained glass and the chandelier. I think we can get the repainting and the replacement of the wallpaper in a week, two at most. What do you think?"

"It's a start. It will take a lot longer for the deeper scars to heal." The baker gave a long exhale, shrugged, and forced a wan smile. "But every journey starts with the first step, right?"

"Yes," said Ferenc. "One day at a time. I agree. Will you be in charge of the clean-up?"

Yossel shook his head. "I have to be at the bakery every morning."

"I'll do it," Oskar said. "I'm going crazy sitting at that hotel every day fighting rats and boredom."

"Wonderful," Ferenc replied. "I will have the town garbage men come and haul things away."

"Hah! If they see my face they'll turn and run." Oskar explained the garbage problem at the hotel.

The mayor looked down in embarrassment. "I didn't know. Believe me, from now on they will come and haul your garbage every week."

Oskar smiled and bowed humbly. "Thank you, Mr. Mayor." He turned to leave, mouthing to Yossel privately, *Mayor Saves Town from Filthy Jews Again.*

"Yossel, Oskar," the mayor said in a tremulous voice. "I don't have words to express how sad and ashamed I am about all of this. I—"

"Naftali!" Yossel's exclamation echoed through the building.

The Hassid stood framed in light in the doorway of the synagogue. He took off his battered black hat, revealing the handmade cloth *yarmulke* he wore underneath. As Nafthali entered, sad tears rolled down his cheeks, getting lost in his wild beard. Yossel made a quick apology to the mayor and approached the young man. They grasped each other's forearms.

"You came. Thank God you came. We can clean the building but otherwise we are lost."

The Hassid's eyes adjusted to the dim light inside the building but retained their far away visage. "I received a sign from *Ha Shem.* This is my path to reentering the world." He walked away from Yossel and into the synagogue, staring at the damage, picking up a page from a prayer book. "So much sacrilege, so much hatred." He stepped onto the *bima,* noticing the wooden scrollwork around the raised prayer platform was still intact, but the silver caps on the posts were gone. He approached the *aron ha kodesh,* the sacred Ark where the Torah scroll was housed before being taken out for services or being joyously paraded through the congregation at the end of the yearly Torah reading cycle. The red velvet curtain that kept the sanctuary from view was missing. The two doors of the cabinet hung askew, torn off the top hinges but hanging from the bottoms as if tenaciously refusing to abandon their posts. The Torah scroll was gone, either lovingly buried somewhere on the synagogue grounds before the deportation, or stolen shortly afterward. He silently gave thanks to his father for burying the Kosveg Torah. The sacred scroll would bring the light of *Ha Shem* into this sorrowful place once more. The young Hassid churned inside at the destruction around him, yet he felt the ancient connection that coursed through every synagogue in every country where they existed. The building may have been greatly damaged, but the web of history and communion with *Ha Shem* remained—a still, small voice only Naftali could hear.

Naftali was aware that Yossel and the others watched as he examined the Ark, but they left him alone. They had their own work to do to restore the synagogue of Laszlo. The Hassid knew that his mission was on a different plane from theirs, at least for the moment. Hopefully, they would converge in joy and splendor when the synagogue reopened.

Eva stood outside the synagogue. She thought about the weekly Sabbath ceremonies at the hotel. How she would miss the candles, the sense of awe and intimacy—the first time in her life she felt a conscious connection to the tradition. Yet that was not enough to keep her in Laszlo. It was time to move on to Budapest and do whatever she could to gain entry into the Academy. She heard the voices inside but hesitated to enter. Yossel and the others knew about her ambivalence toward her Jewish heritage and the restoration project. If she walked inside they would assume she was there to help and she didn't want to disappoint them. But she also didn't want to wait any longer before sharing her decision with her unintentional family in Laszlo. She needed to tell them before her resolve weakened.

"Hello?"

Everyone turned at the tentative sound of a young woman's voice.

"Eva!" Yossel said with a wide smile. "You came after all."

Eva held up her hands to stop Yossel from going further. "I am here, but only to say something really important." She took a breath. "I am leaving Laszlo and going to Budapest."

A stunned silence gripped the room. Yossel was the first to speak.

"But Eva, why?"

Eva steeled herself and spoke in a firm, gentle voice. "You have all been so good to me, but you know there is nothing left for me in Laszlo. I want to go to Budapest and visit the Academy. I want to try and get admitted again. I need to move forward with my life."

The mayor stepped toward her. "But Eva, we haven't heard from the Academy yet. At least wait to hear from my contacts in Budapest. We need to know as much as we can before you make a decision."

"And where would you stay?" Oskar said nervously.

"I was hoping to contact Anna Nagy, the professor's sister. She lives in the Jewish district somewhere near the Academy."

"But you don't know if she survived the war or stayed in Hungary," Yossel replied. "And nobody lives in their own apartment anymore. Most of the buildings were destroyed."

Herschel called out. "Eva, you have to wait until we open the synagogue. We have to celebrate together, don't we?"

"It should only be two weeks or so." Yossel pleaded. "We're going to have a small service just for us. Won't you stay to see our community reborn?"

Eva took in the hopeful, concerned faces surrounding her. She sensed the poignant bond that had formed between them, the last Jews of Laszlo. She also realized she hadn't thought through any practical details of travel to Budapest. If she waited until the synagogue opened, she could gather contacts, collect her father's money, and allow more time to hear from the Academy. Eva looked up at the broken chandelier. She would wait for the light to return.

CHAPTER 28

Viktor listened to Grandfather's labored breathing coming from the other room. He knew Father was going to yell at him because Mother was walking so stiffly around the apartment. Viktor didn't like it when Grandfather got ill, especially when they talked about his heart, which they said was getting worse. At least it kept Father occupied. He cringed when Father entered the room with a scowl on his face.

"I told you not to go to the brick factory, didn't I?"

The voice fell on Viktor like a thunderclap. His eyes widened with fear. How did Father know? It had to be Janos. Yes, Janos must have told his father, Corporal Miklos. Then his father told Viktor's father. Viktor gulped and spoke meekly. "Yes, Father. I did go. We all did."

Sergeant Ritook slowly took off his belt and wrapped the buckle around his hand. "Why did you disobey me?"

Viktor felt relieved. He wouldn't get the buckle, only the strap. "We were watching the Jew. We followed him to the brick factory. He was guarding his treasure there. We wanted to find it and dig it up like you and the other men did when you sent the Jews away."

Ritook lowered the belt, sat on the couch, and put an arm around his son. "Look, Viktor, there are no Jewish treasures out there anymore. Whatever those village Jews had was found long ago. There wasn't much. They were very poor. They were nothing like the rich

Jews here in town." He glanced around the apartment. "I want your word, young man. You will never go back there."

Viktor was quick to reply. "I promise, Father."

Grandfather's voice carried weakly from the other room. "Son, any news of your brother yet?"

Ritook's voice was flat. "No, Father, many of the men are still stationed in Romania."

Viktor knew it was a lie. He had overheard Father saying Viktor's uncle died in the slaughter of the Hungarian Sixth at Leningrad. It was wrong to lie, but Father told him lying was allowed sometimes to prevent Grandfather from having more pain.

Viktor's mother called out from Grandfather's room. "Erno, come quickly. It's getting worse." Viktor's father jumped up and ran to the room. Viktor sat frozen on the couch. He heard the urgency and anger in his mother's voice. "What are we going to do? You took away the only heart doctor in Laszlo."

"All the Jews had to go. We had to follow orders."

Viktor thought he must have misunderstood. Grandfather's doctor was a Jew?

His mother's voice was biting. "If you hadn't deported the doctor, your father wouldn't be on the verge of dying, would he? Is this apartment and that big table worth losing your father?"

The Jewish table, Viktor thought and looked at the table. The clawed feet stretched restlessly. *I knew it was cursed. Now it's killing Grandfather.*

Viktor's father spoke coldly. "You didn't object when we got this apartment, did you?"

"What choice did I have? I was happy where we were, but you and everyone else in town went crazy with greed when the Jews were deported. You wouldn't listen to anything I said."

Viktor's father ignored his wife's words. "And if the Jews hadn't monopolized medicine there would be plenty of good Hungarian doctors."

"That is really stupid, Erno."

Viktor poked his head into Grandfather's bedroom. His parents didn't notice him until he spoke. "Why can't the doctor come to the house like he always does?"

"Because the doctor is dead like all the other Jews," his mother said. Her tone was oddly pleasant, but Viktor knew that meant she was holding a lot of anger. It would come out later when she banged the pots and slammed the cabinets in the kitchen. She always did that after supper.

Viktor's father was standing over Grandfather with a helpless look on his face. Viktor had never seen that look. It was nothing like his angry face. It frightened Viktor.

"We've got to get him to Debrecen," his father said. "It's the closest good hospital."

Viktor's mother stroked Grandfather's head. "It's too far. The ride will probably kill him. We need to hire a full-time nurse to watch him."

His father snorted his mean laugh, the one he gave when he didn't actually think something was funny. "Where the hell are we going to get the money for that?"

Grandfather was suffering, maybe even dying. Viktor was a White Stag Scout. He knew how to help.

The scouts huddled together in the fort. Viktor was angry.

"Look, Janos, you little rat, I know you told your father."

The little boy shrank. "He asked me what we were doing every day. I couldn't lie to my father. White Scouts don't lie, right?"

"Okay, I won't bust your nose this time but listen up. All of you. The Jew is in town every day because they're fixing their old church. That means we have lots of time to look around the brick factory for the treasure."

Peter objected. "But you just told us you promised your father not to go there again."

Viktor stood up. He was taller than Peter by the height of the front of his crew cut. "Peter, when you are older you will understand. Sometimes you have to make a promise you know you won't keep for the greater good. Like when the government promised to protect the Jews and then sent them away. We need to get that treasure to save my grandfather's life. Are you in or out?"

The boys reluctantly agreed. Viktor sketched out his plan in the dirt.

"There are three buildings at the brick factory. We will check them one at a time, only going every other day so it's not suspicious."

"But I heard that the buildings are haunted." Janos croaked. "My father told someone there are dead people in there."

"Then you can be the lookout. That's what cowards do. We older boys will do the searching." Viktor gave Janos a malicious grin. "Of course, that means you get the smallest share. We follow the railroad tracks down to the brick factory and back. We can say we were checking the tracks for safety or looking for metal to collect for our merit badges. If there's nothing in the buildings, we move on to here." He stuck the tip of his stick into the dirt. "The fields."

CHAPTER 29

The week slipped by as Eva concentrated on the professor's gift, becoming lost in the intricate melodies of the *Piano Concerto for the Music of the Spheres*. She felt near to mastering the first and second movements, as they contained many of the arpeggios and chord combinations she had been taught by the professor. The third movement, "Transcendence", remained an enigma. The atonal passages were new, and Eva could not reach into the music and connect with the movement. The Professor's manuscript notes for "Transcendence" described a conjoining of the sounds of the piano and the celestial harmonies. An ultimate connection with the Pure Form. Eva had briefly experienced a connection, but did not understand it. How could her small fingers connect a chord on a piano to the sounds of a massive planet millions of miles away? How did that maintain beauty and balance evil on earth? At times while practicing the third movement, she detected some sort of shimmering presence around her. Was this the vibratory connection? Were they angels or Pythagoras's transmigrating souls? They disappeared if she tried to focus on them, like the shadowy movements in the corners of her eyes sometimes. Even so, Eva always sensed Professor Sandor's spirit close to her at the keyboard. She also sensed Mrs. Kodaly's presence. Although the mayor's wife was never in view, Eva could hear slight moans and quiet weeping from the kitchen or the upstairs.

Eva was now free to roam the house after she did the few chores

Mrs. Kodaly now asked of her. She took clothes from her bedroom every day, but didn't want to stay after practicing. Each foray through her bedroom and the other rooms brought poignant memories of her mother and father, but steeled Eva's determination to go to Budapest. The mayor had not received a reply to his telegram and the Academy continued to be unresponsive. Yet Eva felt confident that going would solve the mysteries of silence and result in her readmission. At the very least, it would get her out of Laszlo and mark some forward progress in her life.

As she said goodbye to Mrs. Kodaly at the end of the week, the door opened and the mayor entered the house.

"I have news, Eva. I got a telegram today from my banker. He heard from the Academy. They were closed most of last term because of the siege but expect to be fully functioning by fall." His eyebrows arched sympathetically. "Unfortunately, the application date is past and the incoming class is full. You will have to wait until next year."

Eva was stunned. "I can't wait. What would I do for a whole year?"

Mrs. Kodaly spoke in a hopeful tone. "You could stay with us and keep practicing."

Eva held back her anger. Mrs. Kodaly was only trying to be helpful. "I can't stay in Laszlo. There is nothing here for me." She saw the hurt in the older woman's face, and quickly added, "Of course, you have been so kind and I would love to live here with you, but I need to move on and start my career. I am already a year behind."

The mayor struggled to find words. "There is more. The Academy said they had no record of your application. You have no choice but to apply again for next year."

"But I have my admission letter. I have the letter rescinding the offer."

"I don't understand it either, maybe the records room was destroyed," Ferenc said.

Eva paced the library, her fingers twitching aimlessly. Her future was evaporating. No professor, no Academy. "I need to go to the Academy and bring my letters. I can explain what happened."

"Eva, Budapest is in ruins. It's a rough, occupied city. Let me take you there for a few days—"

"No! I will go by myself!" Eva let loose a burst of fury. "I will make them listen to me!"

Eva stormed out of the house and down the hill. She consciously played music in her head that might calm her down. She entered the park humming Mendelssohn. Its sweetness matched the pleasant late July weather and slowly improved her mood. She would be leaving for Budapest in another week. The mystery would be solved. Now, however, she wanted to say goodbye to her former friends, hoping to close this episode of her life on a peaceful note. She looked toward the bench. Only Andras was there. Eva sat next to him and exhaled the last of her ire. He handed her his lit cigarette. She took a perfunctory puff and returned it.

Andras dropped his head and spoke quietly. "I heard you are leaving Laszlo."

Eva wanted to rage about the situation with the Academy, but she had to think it through first and Andras was not the best listener. "Good news travels fast," she said with feigned cheer. She desperately wanted to touch that feeling she had when they almost kissed, to feel anything that would ground her. Every touchstone of her life had disappeared.

"I hear Budapest is pretty much destroyed and it's full of Russian soldiers." He flicked the butt of the cigarette into the grass. "Aren't you nervous?"

Eva absently batted a fly away. "Not really. I've seen worse."

"Oh, of course." Andras sat in silence for a moment, then he brightened. "I'm working at the cinema this summer. I could get you in free. We could watch the movie from the projection booth. It'd be fun."

Eva needed to break out from the tightness that gripped her

heart. She had not done anything simply for fun since her return. She would be alone with Andras. A last chance to create at least one sweet memory from her time in Laszlo. She sighed. "I'd like that."

Andras warmed to her smile. "We're showing an American film called *Arsenic and Old Lace*. Cary Grant's two spinster aunts murder old bachelors by poisoning their wine with arsenic." He chuckled. "They think they're putting the old gentlemen out of their misery."

Eva winced.

"It's a comedy."

There was nothing comic to her about death. "I'm pretty busy this week, but I'd love to see something with you before I leave. Maybe the next movie." She wondered why Andras never seemed sensitive to what she had gone through. Was he embarrassed, ashamed, or were all boys his age this dense? As much as she longed for a relationship, maybe even a boyfriend, Eva decided that music remained the wiser path for now.

The work on the synagogue continued at a solid pace. Windows were replaced, walls painted and the *bima* polished and shining. A new red velvet curtain protected the empty Torah Ark. The building seemed to glow with hope. The mood among the volunteers and the Jews was upbeat. Yossel fueled the good feelings with daily doses of hot *bilkalach* buns and an ever-changing assortment of pastries. Shop owners visited to offer food, extra chairs, or anything else needed to support the effort.

One evening, a box was left at the synagogue containing its charity collection can, candlesticks, a silver *bima* post cap, and other looted objects. More boxes followed full of clothes, small paintings, watches, and a host of goods from Jewish homes. Notes inside apologized for taking these things. Letters told of guarding objects at the request of the Jewish owners, and now thankfully having a place to return them. Laszlo was doing collective penance for its sins. Yossel wondered if it had something to do with Eva's music. The girl was performing at the old hospital and the mayor's house, and customers at the bakery talked about how wonderfully she played. Eva was upholding beauty and light in the world, a real *Tzaddik*.

"See?" Yossel said over his shoulder to Oskar as the men went through several newly arrived boxes. "The goodness is coming back."

"Maybe. I think it's an easy way out for them. They keep the stuff they want and return what they don't. Not exactly a burnt offering." Oskar pulled a small object from the bottom of a box. "No!" he grunted as if struck in the stomach.

Yossel turned quickly to see Oskar's bulky frame curled over a brown stuffed bear. He moved to the butcher's side and grabbed his shoulder. "Oskar, what is it?"

Oskar hugged the stuffed bear and sobbed heavily. "This belonged to my little Mihaly."

Yossel tried to soothe the big man. "Oh, Oskar, how can you be sure? All stuffed bears look like that. It could be anybody's."

Oskar wiped his nose on his sleeve, blinking heavily. "I bought the bear from a salesman at the Armin Hotel a year before the deportation. It's from the Streiner factory in Germany. Mihaly nearly chewed the right ear off with happiness when I brought it home. He also managed to bite through one of the black button eyes. See here?" He showed the bear to Yossel, who tried not to flinch. Oskar exhaled slowly. "I've got to see this as a sign that some goodness is coming back like you say. Otherwise I'll go mad." He hugged the bear tightly, stuffed it into his pocket and cleared the anguish from his throat. "At least I have something to help me remember my little boy."

The private ceremony for the Jews of Laszlo was to take place on Friday night, July 13, only a day away. Naftali scoured the remaining prayer books and the few surviving tomes to put together a service appropriate for the reopening of a synagogue. At first, he thought the girl should sit in the balcony, behind the modesty screens. He envisioned the scene and saw the girl, who had lost her family, sitting alone and miserable. Hadn't there been enough sadness in her life? Technically, he reasoned, the synagogue wouldn't be officially opened until the service was ended, so maybe it was acceptable for her to sit with the men during the ceremony. He sighed, thinking of his father's scowl at the arrangement. But it was a new beginning, wasn't it?

Naftali left Kosveg early Friday evening and walked through Laszlo. He wore his father's long black caftan, his prayer shawl over his head and carried the Torah scroll. The *niggun* he hummed hovered between joy and mourning. He noticed but ignored the troubled looks cast at him by the townspeople he passed. His eyes and his heart focused on the holy work ahead, on the resurrection of the synagogue of Laszlo. It was *Tisha B'Av*, the ninth day of the Jewish calendar month of *Av*, the date Jews lament the destruction of the Holy Temples of ancient Israel. Naftali fasted and wore hard paper slippers he had made, as wearing leather was forbidden on this date. To the west, the blood sun was setting below the clouds in a tongue of fire. Naftali turned his gaze toward the deepening blue of the eastern sky instead, noticing the first star in the firmament that heralded the coming *Shabbos*. He arrived before the others and placed the Torah in the reconstructed Ark. He stood on the *bima*, reverently voicing gratitude, praise, and blessings to *Ha Shem* for providing a chance to manifest holiness in this Jewish space once more. He looked up to see the four men enter and silently take their seats. Where was the girl?

Eva walked nervously toward the synagogue. She didn't know what to expect from the ceremony. She had so little experience with Jewish services. More troubling, her ears picked up disconcerting vibrations from the few people that walked past her on the street. As she neared the synagogue she spied the cinema marquee further up the road. She would have gone to the movies tonight with Andras instead, but the cinema was showing an old silent movie called "A City Without Jews" which was supposed to show how awful life would be if all the Jews were gone. Eva didn't want to see a film about Jews or remorseful townspeople. The film was the mayor's idea, of course. Andras had been hurt that Eva turned him down twice, especially since she was leaving for Budapest on the Saturday afternoon train. It was their last chance to be together.

A soft glow of electric candles from the ornate wall sconces greeted Eva as she entered the synagogue. She walked up to Yossel and he welcomed her to sit next to him after looking toward Naftali and receiving a subtle nod. Naftali said a few words about the joy and sorrow of reopening the synagogue.

"How curious, yet how miraculous that we renew our Jewish spirit here this *Shabbos*. For this is the *Shabbos* of *Tisha B'Av*, where we lament the abominations and trials that *Ha Shem* has placed upon our people over the centuries. We lament the destruction of the first and second Temples on this date. Yet, as if this was not enough tragedy, we also remember and cry for disasters that have befallen our people throughout time. We wail for the Israelites doomed to die in the desert. We weep for the last of our people expelled from Spain during the Inquisition and from France, England, and Italy before then. Ours is a history of blood and sorrow." Eva listened intently as

Naftali let the long history of affliction to befall the Jewish people settle like a heavy hand on the heart of all who sat in the synagogue. She knew he wasn't trying to diminish their recent suffering, only to remind them of the legacy of injustice that is the lot of every Jew. The remembrance of *Tisha B'Av*. She thought of her father's margin note in the book about Pythagoras—*Harmony Disrupted*.

Naftali continued. "And we have our own sorrow, the terrible suffering in our time, worse than anything that has happened before. But the Talmud says there is nothing more whole than a broken Jewish heart. For it is only through a broken heart that we let go of the illusory promises of this world to feel our devotion to a higher calling. We must not allow our pain to obscure the ideals of justice and righteousness that are our birthright as the descendants of Abraham. The destruction is over for now. Our lamentations of today must give way to hope for tomorrow."

He invited the group to pray along with him, recognizing that few of them were observant. In a kind voice he shared that in the Jewish tradition, reciting prayers opened the gates of Heaven, but for those who didn't know the words, humming along with *kavanah*, pure intention, knocked the gates down.

> *Al naharoth babhel shâm yashabhnu gam—bakhiynu bezakherenu'eth—tsiyyon . . .*
> *By the rivers of Babylon, there we sat, sat and wept, as we remembered Zion . . .*

Yossel and Oskar joined in a halting recitation, while the farm hands and Eva emotionally, wordlessly battered down the gates of Heaven. Naftali continued the service with long chants and songs. He *shuckled*, bobbing forward and backward as he intoned the *Shehechiyanu* prayer of gratitude for new beginnings:

> *"Baruch Ata Adonai, Elohainu Melech ha Olam*
> *Shehechiyanu v'kiyimanu v'higiyanu lazman hazeh."*

The mellifluous, haunting melodies filled the Jews of Laszlo with longing and hope for a new life. The sounds floated out the door and onto Kossuth Street, beseeching an ambivalent world for peace.

Andras came out of the projection booth at the end of the film and leaned against the wall in the lobby to enjoy a cigarette. The cinema was filled on a Friday night, as usual. He liked to listen to the comments the moviegoers made on their way out, trying to guess someone's opinion from the way they were dressed or the look on their face. The people were either very quiet or mumbling under their breath to their companions.

"Damned Jews. I'm sick of hearing about them."

"I don't want to give back the apartment. It's ours now."

"Watch them seek revenge. We should be ready."

"I'm not going to welcome them back like in the movie, like they were heroes or something. This is just propaganda from the mayor."

The comments troubled Andras. He walked outside. People were gathered in front of the cinema. Ordinarily, they just went home or out for a drink. He heard the mournful sounds from down the street. The Jews were having their service. Eva was with them. The sounds came toward the cinema like a creeping fog, swirling around the feet of the moviegoers. The fog began to darken as it snaked up to envelop the crowd. Passersby stopped to listen to the strange language and tonality. Some were saddened, some remorseful. Some became angry. Remarks got louder, sharper, more menacing in tone. Andras felt a rising tension, ready to burst like a weakened heart.

Naftali replaced the Torah in the Ark as the Jews of Laszlo wept. Nobody except Naftali knew all the words of every prayer, yet the power of the pleas to God and the resuscitated inner connection between the Jews and their ancient history brought out unfathomably deep feelings in all. Even after the Ark was closed and the last chant faded from the air, everyone sat still, lost in the mist of some spiritual or familial remembrance.

Naftali stayed behind as the others began to leave the synagogue. No words were spoken after the powerful ceremony, but everyone was aware that something had awoken, both inside each person and in the wood and stones of the building itself. The community was birthed anew.

Eva and Oskar walked out the door first, cocooned in warm thoughts for those they had lost. Eva also realized that she was identifying with the long history of Jewish suffering for the first time. In the camp, the suffering was immediate and all-consuming, nobody put it into perspective for her. But tonight, on *Tisha B'Av*, she was profoundly aware that she was part of a continuum that began millennia ago. As painful as it was, Eva found comfort in that. They stopped on the front step to admire the clear and untroubled evening sky of Eva's last night in Laszlo. Oskar sighed and turned a misty gaze on Eva.

"I am happy we could share this, that your last memories of Laszlo will be so peaceful."

Something whistled past their heads and smashed against the doorway. A crowd was fast approaching. Oskar grabbed Eva's arm. "Get back inside!" he shouted. Before she could move a man wielding a tire iron ran at her. She threw her hands up protectively as the iron bar came down hard, smashing her left hand. Eva screamed at the sharp tear of soft flesh and the crack of bone. Oskar pushed the man away as Yossel and the farmhands charged out of the synagogue. Stones and debris rained down on the men as Oskar tried to cover Eva from the barrage.

Amidst the shouting and rude laughter of the crowd Eva could hear the chants. "Jews out!" and "You will not return!" and "Arrow Cross!" Between the pain and the fear her head began to spin and she vomited. The faces of the mob were grotesque masks, their features distorted by the hatred from the bottom of the well. She looked up through Nazi-style salutes and saw Andras at the back of the crowd. He had a cigarette in his mouth.

She screamed at him in anger and hurt. "Andras! How could you!" The young man visibly recoiled. He dropped the cigarette, crushed it out and walked heavily away. How could he betray their friendship and join that mob? Her hand and heart throbbed in painful synchronicity as she watched him leave.

The honking of the police van and the sound of the loudspeaker blaring "Desist!" broke the surge of the crowd. People threw one last stone or bottle and walked away as if they were casually leaving a performance. Nobody was arrested.

Corporal Zoldy and Officer Boros pushed through the milling crowd. The two officers stood protectively on the synagogue steps as the Jews cautiously reemerged. Zoldy inspected Eva's bloody hand and told her to go to the van, where Corporal Miklos would drive her to the hospital. He ordered the others into the van for an escort to the hotel.

Eva sat in the front seat with Miklos, her hand wrapped in a shawl she had brought to the synagogue, unsure of the proper protocol for a woman. She struggled to reconcile this evening of Jewish communal bonding with the mob attack. Jews were supposed to be Hungarians again, but she was attacked and beaten for being a Jew. She rambled on frenetically about the crowd as Miklos listened sympathetically.

"I thought the war was over. I played my music for people. I thought we were accepted again. But they were so hateful. I wanted my last night to be beautiful, but it feels like Laszlo is pushing me away."

Miklos spoke in a calming voice. "That mob didn't represent the town. People get crazy in a crowd situation. Something set them off. There were probably some drunks from the bar, too. You know what a problem we have here with alcohol. Maybe they were the ones who threw things and hit you. Most people in Laszlo are cheering for you."

"But I saw my friend Andras in the crowd." Her heart now hurt worse than her hand.

Miklos gave her a quizzical look. "Andras? The young man from the cinema? He was the one who called and warned us about the mob headed toward the synagogue."

Naftali waited inside the synagogue for the crowd to disappear. The shouts and chants echoed inside his head, evoking the police raid on Kosveg. He tried to push the images out of his mind but didn't succeed and he found himself back on the train heading away from the brick factory with gunfire echoing through the air like harsh laughter. *Tisha B'Av.*

He looked back toward the Ark where the sacred Torah stayed safe for now. Was he truly being guided by the hand of *Ha Shem*, or was he being duped by *Ha Satan*, the Evil One, in delivering the Torah—the last shred of holiness in Kosveg—into the maw of Hell for its final destruction in Laszlo? Naftali couldn't let it remain in this building. He slid down to the floor and looked up. The chandelier was suspended above, its lights shining through the dim building. He had done what he said he would do, held a prayer service in the synagogue. But Naftali knew this was not his world, this was not his true mission from *Ha Shem*. How foolish and self-righteous he had been to believe he was destined for something wonderful in Laszlo. He went to the Ark and opened it. The Torah scroll stood pure and holy before him. He lifted it from the Ark as he said a blessing. He used his back to close the Ark. The street outside was quiet and empty. He held the Torah tightly to his chest and secreted it back to Kosveg in the darkness unseen.

Eva slept fitfully, and dreamed of planets whirring around her until a searing black sun rose and melted them all. The death of the planets yielded an ugly, harsh sound. She woke in the middle of the night, drenched in sweat, twisted and trapped in her blanket. She kicked and kicked at the covering, her fear, anger, and confusion too much for her body to contain. Her illusion of safety flew away with the blanket. She lay feverish, exposed, and unprotected on the mattress. Her fingers began to twitch out a melody to calm her, but sharp pain seared her left hand when She tried to move it. She couldn't play piano with a fractured finger and six tight stitches. Eva had gone to the synagogue to honor her heritage and help the small Jewish community come back to life. Instead, Laszlo's parting gift was the ruin of her reborn hopes.

An intense argument from the kitchen below interrupted her despair. Oskar was shouting and Yossel was pleading. Shards of phrases sliced into Eva's consciousness. *Not safe here . . . Want to bury our memory along with our bodies . . . Protect the girl.* She tried to keep the words away, but realized it didn't matter. The seeds sewn in an ancient past and baked hard into the soil of Laszlo had sprouted again. The ugly harvest was bigger than Yossel, Oskar, or the mayor could contain. How could she ever believe it was over, or that somehow she was protected from its fury by her music? Would she find safety in Budapest, or was she doomed to be followed by the legacy of persecution of Jews? The lesson of *Tisha B'Av.* Yet even if all of this was true, Eva had learned a greater lesson by surviving Auschwitz. Persecution never stopped the Jews from living, surviving, and moving forward with faith and resolve. She couldn't let the hatred render her helpless, she would still go to Budapest.

CHAPTER 30

Eva was surprised and self-conscious at the size of the crowd that flooded the train station the next afternoon. The mayor must have spread the news of her departure. The sincere smiles and friendly faces took her mind off the shock of the synagogue violence and the wound throbbing beneath the bandaging on her left hand. The mayor had also arranged for a church choir to come to the station. They sang "A Hymn to the God of Abraham," which the choirmaster announced as "an old hymn born in a synagogue" because it was based on Hebrew prayers. Their beautiful voices spread wings of peace over the station. Eva tried to hold onto the spirit of the hymn, but the growing noise of the crowd began to sound like the violent mob from the night before. She focused on the many familiar faces, everyone she knew in Laszlo except Naftali and Andras, to allay the coming of the frightening vision.

Mayor Kodaly produced a golden sash with *Laszlo* printed on it, and urged Eva to wear it. She understood he was trying to rally the town spirit in support of the Jews, as always. But the color of the sash was a sharp reminder of the yellow star she and the others had been forced to wear. She whispered this to the mayor, who grimaced and put the sash away.

Eva watched the station master hand her lone suitcase up to the coachman. Mrs. Kodaly had packed several of her dresses from the bedroom closet along with other items of clothing and a few sanitary pads. Photos of Eva and her parents and one of the professor were tucked inside her suitcase as well, along with the manuscript and the letters from the Academy. She tried not to focus on the fact that she was abandoning her house, her piano without any resolution. Who knew what would happen with all of that? Moving forward, going to Budapest was the most important thing right now. The station master ran up and down the platform, pleading with Hanna, Ilona, the doctor, the other Jews, the mayor, and the many citizens to clear the platform so that the two o'clock to Budapest could leave safely.

As the crowd thinned, Eva glimpsed the mother of the child she thought was Izidor. The woman approached with a contrite demeanor and took her aside. She looked at Eva's hand with concern, then spoke quietly. "I wanted to tell you that the boy is Izidor, but we call him Karl. I know I treated you rudely the day you returned and I have avoided you in town, but I didn't want to confuse the child. The night before the deportation his mother begged me to take him and raise him as my own. She knew what was going to happen. Her last words to me were that the worst thing a mother can do in this world is raise her child Jewish." She blushed and looked down. "I know that sounds harsh, but she wanted to protect her boy then and for the rest of his life. I am sending him to live with my sister in America, away from this never-ending hatred. He will never know he was born a Jew."

The words shocked Eva. Hatred had won again. Or had it? The boy might never know about his mother's excruciating sacrifice, but her courageous deed had saved him from the gas chamber. His mother had chosen life. Didn't Yossel say that was the greatest *mitzvah*? But did he have to abandon being a Jew to be safe? Perhaps Jews in America didn't experience the subterranean loathing they did in Europe and could have normal lives for generations.

The woman held Eva's gaze for a long time before she cleared the emotion from her throat and spoke. "One last thing. I want you to know that Karl remembers you. You played piano for him once and he never forgot. He says he wants to play the piano when he grows up." She reached out to stroke Eva's cheek tenderly and withdrew into the crowd.

The mayor made a brief speech about the wonderful future awaiting Eva in Budapest. He repeated several of the comments he made at the house concert. Eva remembered that he was, after all, a politician. He ended by reminding the crowd that Laszlo would always honor its first famous pianist. He privately gave Eva a small leather pouch.

"Mrs. Kodaly put together a collection of jewelry for you, including the pearl and gold necklace she always wore. She knows it was your favorite and she hopes that when you wear it to perform you will think kindly of her."

Eva opened the pouch and beheld the necklace. Her mother had promised the necklace to Eva, and after the war and the dislocation it had finally come to her. She only wished her mother could be there to put it around Eva's neck when she performed at the Academy. The mayor coughed into his hand and seemed to struggle to speak.

"Eva, I know how hard it has been for you, being in your own house with strangers. And I know Mrs. Kodaly was not always kind or understanding of your situation. She had gotten used to the house and the fine things your family had, but she also felt terrible about what happened to you. Over the times you helped in the house and practiced your music, she came to care about you deeply."

Mayor Kodaly took an envelope from his suit jacket. "I set up an account at the National Bank in your name and deposited your father's money in it. Mrs. Kodaly and I have also signed the house over to you and given ourselves a lease, renting your house for three years. I hope you don't mind. I thought that when you turn twenty-one you can sell the house, as I'm sure you won't be coming back to live in Laszlo. Maybe we can buy it for real then."

Eva realized how much he had put at risk to support her in the face of his wife's initial resistance and the animosity of many of his friends and colleagues. She reddened at the realization that she had never fully trusted the mayor and that she had let Oskar's harsh judgments color her view. Yet in the end, he had proven his integrity. She tried to control her tears as she hugged him with her right arm. "Thank you for honoring my father and helping me. I realize it's been hard for you and Mrs. Kodaly, as well."

The mayor stammered through a tight throat. "Good luck to you, Eva. Your father would be so proud."

Yossel and Oskar pushed up to see Eva as the mayor walked off to shake hands with people in the crowd. Yossel spoke for them. "Eva, go to Budapest and be somebody. We could have been, except the hatred keeps us down. As your uncles, we wish you all the best. We will be cheering for you and thinking about you every *Shabbos* when Oskar tries to make *challah* as good as yours." He handed her a fresh loaf wrapped in paper. "This is a special gift to remember us. We made it together."

Oskar's eyed glowed like the embers of a dying fire. Eva couldn't tell if he had given in to the world-weariness beating down his spirit or he was emotional at their parting. He stuck out his jaw and nodded sagely. "You are a strong young woman, Eva. I am very proud of you. I have a good feeling about you and Budapest." He blinked back a tear. "And you know I don't have good feelings too often."

Herschel jumped up and down behind Oskar, trying to get Eva's attention. He waved his huge hands and yelled to her as Mendel tried to keep his brother from accidentally clubbing people around him. "Eva! Next year in Jerusalem!"

The last Jews of Laszlo stood together on the platform. Eva tried to stay focused on the warm feelings between them and their unbending support for her since they returned. They were as much of a family as she could claim. They had taught her the deeper meaning of *Shabbos.* The lighting of the candles dispelled the darkness. The blessing over the wine helped her feel gratitude when she often didn't feel there was anything to be grateful for. The *challah* opened her awareness to how many people participated in creating the things and the opportunities in this world. The weekly ritual showed Eva there was a place to find peace in the chaos of her life. Yet troubling thoughts nipped at the periphery of her mind. She worried what would happen to Yossel, Oskar, and the others after she was gone.

Eva looked over the crowd one last time as the choir began a final hymn. She closed her eyes and felt the hum of so many different bodies, their euphony harmonizing and embracing her. She wanted to hold on to that feeling, to carry the sweet peace she felt as her final impression of Laszlo, not the madness of the night before.

"Please, Miss Fleiss!" the station master pleaded. Eva opened her eyes and caught the confusion of emotion and professionalism in his face. He bowed with reddened cheeks and offered her a red flower. "It is time for you to leave Laszlo."

The train was only half-full as it huffed through the countryside. Most of the other passengers were elderly women. Eva wondered if they were all widows. But how do you ask people about death and war? She shook her head to dispel the thought. She was eighteen and had never gone anywhere by herself. This was a rite of passage of sorts. She remembered the annual trips to Budapest she took with her parents and Mira since she was five to listen to classical music at the Academy. It had been like walking into a fairy tale palace. The chandeliers, the paintings of mythical musicians and nymphs, the orchestra in tuxedos and gowns. Eva was sobered by the contrast between her dream of the Academy and the ravaged towns beyond the window. How much damage had the war done to that magical place? Regardless, she knew it would be her sanctuary—if she could get in. She flexed her throbbing hand. She watched the landscape roll by from her cushioned bench and was lulled into a light sleep by the rocking motion of the carriage and the intermittent passing shadows.

Eva woke abruptly to raucous laughter and the slam of the door between carriages. Three soldiers sauntered through the car, sizing up each passenger. Brown, rough woolen Red Army uniforms, the same men who had liberated Auschwitz. She felt some comfort at the thought. Hungarian soldiers hadn't treated her well.

The soldiers approached Eva and mumbled something to each other. One sat on each side of her on the bench and the other placed himself in front of her. They smiled and began to talk to her in soothing, low voices in Russian. The voices reminded her of the SS *basso profundo* that used to overwhelm her dreams. Although she smiled in return, Eva felt a knot in her stomach as the men loomed close enough for their thighs to touch hers. She was soon drowning in the smell of alcohol and rotten teeth. One of the seated soldiers grabbed the loaf of *challah*. The other snatched the small bag that contained her jewelry. Eva began to have difficulty breathing. She cringed protectively into the seat; the camp guards were taunting her again. Color drained from her vision and the world turned the dreaded ashen gray. But she wasn't in the camp. This wasn't a dream. Panic turned to anger pulsing through her body, pushing back the grayness. She would not be victimized by soldiers again. She grabbed the jewelry bag and screamed at the soldier. He was startled by her action and released the bag.

"Hey, you! Leave that girl alone!" shouted a thickset, elderly woman across the aisle in Russian.

"Where is your respect?" another, almost her twin, yelled. "Is that what your mother taught you?"

The two women leaped from their seats and began to harangue the soldiers. "Give back her bread! Shame, shame!"

The soldiers backed away from the angry elders. The first threw the *challah* back to Eva. "Here," he belched in broken Hungarian. "Take your dirty Jew bread. I wouldn't eat it anyway. It's probably made with the blood of good Christian children." They hurried out of the car laughing and slamming the door behind them.

Eva's body shook with adrenalin. Pain lanced her hand from grabbing the jewelry bag. Blood seeped around her bandage and began to drip off her fingers. Her feeling of comfort leaving Laszlo disappeared. Eva wondered if she should have stayed there or let the mayor accompany her to Budapest. The two women came and sat with her, stroking her arms for comfort. One of the women bent down and tore a long strip of fabric from the hem of her dress. She quickly wrapped Eva's bleeding hand and held it in compression and compassion for a few silent minutes. Eva tried to object that she didn't want the woman to ruin her dress. The woman laughed.

"I went through three dresses during the siege." She fluffed the edge of her dress. "Lots of women do this. It is more like a medical kit than a dress."

The women were cousins from a small farming village. They were making their weekly trip to the outdoor market on Andrassy Street to sell the beets they grew. Eva recognized the red and green leaves sticking out from the lumpy burlap sacks on the seats next to them. The normality of their conversation and the gentleness of their rough hands calmed Eva. When the chemical taste of the adrenalin left her mouth and pulsed out of her chest and arms she spoke to the women.

"I thought the Russians were our saviors. They took us out of the camp. They defeated the Germans."

"I have been through many wars," said the woman whose salt and pepper braid was tied in a rag about her head. "Soldiers are rarely friends to women."

"Once they win they act like all the others before them. Russians, Germans, Hungarians, Turks. They're all the same. Maybe the Americans are different. We will see." She pulled out a hand-rolled cigarette and offered it to Eva. When the girl refused, the woman shrugged and lit it for herself. "You be careful in Budapest. The Russians are like rutting pigs on the street." She thrust out her hips and made a grunting sound. Eva turned as red as their beets at the rude gesture, but laughed heartily along with the women. "You are brave, but you may not be so lucky again. A Russian may just as soon shoot you as give up his loot. It happens a lot in Budapest."

The second woman reached over Eva for the cigarette, took a long drag and returned it. "And always have something to offer them—a watch, a necklace, anything—before their pea brains have time to think about what they really want from you." Her hoarse voice revealed a lifetime of cigarettes and suffering. "It may save your virtue, maybe your life."

Eva thought about that. What was wrong with the world? Why was someone always trying to hurt her, to take away her life? She reached over and took the cigarette from her neighbor. They sat together for the next three hours. Eva asked the women what they knew about the condition of the city, and where a single woman might board safely for a few nights. They gave her an address, saying she would be safe there and the owner might be able to help her find the professor's sister, if she was alive and still in the city.

The train arrived at a small station outside Budapest. There, Eva helped the women wrestle their sacks of beets onto the platform. They all mounted a horse-drawn wagon that took them to the main station, as the war-damaged tracks prevented the train from going further. The wagon bounced over the potholed road to the station. Eva offered the *challah* to the women in appreciation for their help and companionship. The women demurred but agreed to share the bread. Eva held one end and the two women grabbed the other. She silently mouthed the *motzi* blessing Yossel had taught her.

Ha motzi lechem min ha'aretz. Amen

The women did not know the prayer, but they respectfully helped tear the bread in half. A fat roll of *pengo*s tumbled out onto Eva's lap.

CHAPTER 31

Eva stood alone on the platform. She thought Budapest would look like the Emerald City of Oz from the book her father bought her after she won the Carpathian Regional Competition four years earlier. That's how it had always appeared when she strolled through the city holding her parents' hands on their way to the concerts at the Academy. Elegant clothing shops, crowded outdoor cafes, and overflowing food markets lined the clean, wide boulevards while crowds of well-dressed men and women sauntered past. Instead, debris and dust blew by on this sunny day. Photographs and pleas to help find missing relatives and loved ones plastered the remaining walls of the station. Legless men sitting on cardboard begged from anyone who would look in their direction.

She braced herself to walk down her Yellow Brick Road, wide Andrassy Boulevard, toward the Danube that ran through the heart of Budapest. But the road was pockmarked from Russian and German artillery during the fierce 100-day siege that had ended the war. The women on the train said the siege had lifted only five months earlier and the city had not come close to recovering from the shock and physical destruction. Eva had feared she would be frightened to walk down the streets of Budapest alone. The city vibrated with a jumble of strange notes. Yet none of the sights or sounds troubled her greatly. It was odd, but her horrid experience in Auschwitz had steeled her to the agonies of life, revealing an internal fortitude that she unknowingly possessed all along.

The beet sellers had told her it would be easy to find the Jewish ghetto, even though it was hidden from view. She was to walk down Andrassy until she saw the big cement building on her right, flying many Hungarian flags. That would be the headquarters of the secret police, as it had been under the Germans and the Arrow Cross. Now that the war was over, it was the Arrow Cross members' tortured cries that echoed through the streets. They advised her to cross the street before then so as not to get caught up in anything going on. Anyone could be grabbed off the street, tortured, and made to confess whatever the current government demanded. Soon she would come to Erzsebet Road, a major thoroughfare. The boarding house was at 37-01 Erzsebet, on the corner with the smaller Dob Street. The ghetto was sandwiched between Kiraly, Erzsebet, Dohany, and Karoly streets. An eight-foot wood and stone wall topped with barbed wire snaked through the small streets inside the area, hidden from any of the four main avenues. The women told Eva there were only four entrances to the ghetto during the war, one accessible from each main street, although there might be more now. The entrances had been tightly controlled, preventing people coming out and food or medicine going in. Toward the end of the war, the area reeked of rotting bodies the Germans and Arrow Cross would not allow to be removed. Although the bodies were gone and buried, the moist nights often released their vapors as the last ethereal evidence of their agony. The women believed most of the remaining Jews of Budapest still lived within the ghetto. Their homes in other parts of the city were either destroyed or taken over by different families by now. If the professor's sister was alive and still in Budapest, she would almost certainly be in the ghetto.

As Eva walked along Andrassy she couldn't find a building that wasn't at least partially destroyed by the fighting. Her passage was difficult as she picked her way past burned trucks, rubble piles and smoldering garbage. Municipal workers pulled two bodies from the ruins of one building. She realizcd she was not upset at the sight. She held her nose as she passed a group of elderly men carving up the long-gone carcass of a dray horse. It gave off an all too familiar scent of death and decay. No, this was not the Emerald City she had envisioned.

She avoided the secret police headquarters and turned left on Erzsebet Road at the Oktagon, a broad, eight-sided intersection that had been beautiful before the war. Now, a massive rubble pile stood in the center of the Oktagon, turning it into a giant traffic rotary. Eva was surprised to see a functioning electric streetcar running down Erzsebet on tracks somehow spared the barrages of the siege. The overhead lines crackled with blue sparks as the streetcar passed.

37-01 Erzsebet was a stately three-story residence. Its marble facade was bullet-scarred yet standing. Eva walked through the courtly cast-iron gate and noticed two entrances, one grand and one modest. Probably a servant's entrance. She approached the larger entry, mounted the three marble steps to the door and rang the bell. As she waited, she could hear laughter and animated conversation inside. A young woman in a stylish, sleeveless black dress opened the door and looked Eva up and down with surprise.

"You're a young, pretty one," she said.

Eva thought that was an odd greeting. "I was told you let rooms to single women here."

"Ohh," the woman replied. "Try the other door. This one's the business." She closed the door before Eva could say another word.

Eva went to the smaller door, but was startled to see a sign posted:

SCARLET FEVER—DO NOT ENTER

She returned to the large door and knocked again. The slightly annoyed woman told her the sign was a ruse to keep soldiers away. She went back to the smaller door. A large, friendly woman asked her business and, apparently satisfied, invited her in. She led Eva up a narrow stairway and unlocked a small room with a single iron bed, a side table, and a dirty window. She advised Eva that the water closet was down the hall, and to pay no attention to the women in the other rooms.

"They work here. You're the only paying guest. There's a common sitting room at the end of the hallway, if you please. It faces the lot next door where another building used to be. Now it's very sunny and bright." After collecting ten *pengos*, she gave Eva a key to the room and the front door and said goodbye.

Eva relaxed on the lumpy horsehair mattress for an hour or so, watching the afternoon light play against the soot-streaked window. In the safe haven of a locked room after her first view of Budapest, she wondered how to find the professor's sister and how to approach the Academy. She fell into a light sleep until women's voices from the hallway roused her. She peeked out of the door to see three well-dressed young women going into the common room. She thought it would be nice to have someone her own age to talk to, so she smoothed down her hair, closed the door behind her and walked down the hall. As she approached the common room she could hear female voices chatting and laughing. She shyly poked her head in and was surprised to see an ornate drawing room. Sconces gave the red velvet wallpaper a soft glow. Half a dozen women in various degrees of dress and undress lounged on leather chairs and beautifully upholstered sofas. A blue Persian rug with a border of hunting dogs chasing deer graced the polished wooden floor. One of the women noticed Eva and smiled broadly.

"Come in, you must be the new girl." She looked down at Eva's bandaged hand. "Looks like you might have a little trouble playing for a while."

Eva glanced at her hand, wondering how the woman knew she was a musician. "It hurts but I need to play as much as I can. I desperately need the practice." When the women burst out laughing she blushed with a rush of annoyance. "I don't see what's so funny."

The door opened and the large woman who had admitted Eva entered the room. She frowned at the young women, who quieted at her stare. "Ladies, this is Miss Fleiss. She's taking a room for a few days. I didn't think you'd mix with the girls during your stay, but I suppose I should tell you. This house used to belong to a businessman. I was his housekeeper. He didn't survive the war. I turned this side of the house into a boarding room. The other side is a bordello."

"A what?" Eva asked. The young women suppressed laughter.

"A house of ill-repute, to use the common phrase, although we have an excellent reputation. Most of the girls here are Jewish. They survived the deportations and the camps. They have no families. They are accountants, an engineer, shop clerks, and a few housewives who prefer our company to that of their husbands." The room buzzed with affectionate teasing. The matron continued. "There is no work in Budapest. This is not their preferred way to live but it provides a safe place and some income until the girls can sort their lives out. Oh, and there are some non-Jews, too. After all, we are all Hungarians first. We are like the Catholic Sisters of Charity, right, ladies?" The women laughed. She looked at Eva. "Does that offend you?"

Eva contemplated the mostly Jewish young women around her. They had suffered as she had. They lost their families. She knew what they went through in the camps. They were trying to put their lives together as best they could, just as she was. She only felt warmth in her heart for them, not judgment. "No. I was in Auschwitz. I understand."

A thin woman who seemed barely more than a child sat up from a sofa. "I was in Auschwitz, too. My family and everyone in our building." She looked down and mumbled, "I am the only one left."

Eva felt an intense pain in her heart, and an instant bond. She quickly responded. "Me, too." Their eyes met and they shared their experiences in silence.

"Are you from Budapest?" a blond woman in a silk oriental robe asked.

"No, I am from Laszlo. It's in the east, near the Romanian border."

"The east?" the woman asked. "I didn't know any Jews from the east survived."

Eva considered the pitiful handful of Jews in Laszlo. "Not many did."

"What are you doing in Budapest?"

"I am supposed to attend the Liszt Academy of Music. I play the piano."

There was a flurry of animated conversation. Several of the women got up and led Eva to the end of the room. They opened a door that led into another large room. Even in the late afternoon, dusky light poured through the huge glass windows, softened by floor-to-ceiling sheers. A Steinway grand piano dominated the center of the room. Eva walked to the piano and touched the keys. They emitted a low, grateful vibration.

"Will you play for us? Please!" the young Auschwitz survivor cried. "We miss music so much. Anything!"

Eva sat at the Steinway. Her pinky was immobilized by the bandage and the stitches. It caused a dull, stretching pain as she reached for notes. She hesitated to play when she found that several of the keys stuck and were out of tune. Another women pleaded with her.

"Please play anyway. It is better than being alone with my thoughts."

She played Chopin, thinking that the fluid, feminine melodies would bring some comfort to these women. One by one, women wandered in from the other room as she played. They sat at the bench by her side or on the rug while leaning against the piano. Eva noticed how each one swooned or grimaced, smiled or cried softly, lost in her own painful or sweet memories. They dreamed their own dreams of lives crushed and buried in the rubble of that meaningless war. The words of the professor's manuscript came gently to her.

> *One does not have to know the mysteries to be affected by them. Your task is to open the pathways that allow your*

audience to hear, to feel, to be moved. There is a hidden instinct in the grandest Duke and the lowest peasant that longs to embrace the Pure Forms behind the shadows.

Eva regarded the women while she played. She felt their emotional states and tried to play something that would ease a painful memory, comfort a lost soul, or strengthen a bruised heart. She moved from Chopin on to the first movement of her piano concerto. "Sentience" was a gentle piece that allowed the women to acknowledge their feelings, without the deeper confrontation of the second movement, "Communion." For the first time, she was consciously applying what she learned from the professor's manuscript. Could this be her contribution to restoring some sort of harmony to Jewish people, to offer the healing power of music to Jews who suffered the atrocities of the camps? She had never performed in such an intimate way for a group of women, let alone so many her age who had survived such similar horrors. If she couldn't connect to some grander cosmic order, she could at least bring solace to these wounded souls. She let go of her thoughts and allowed the music to flow. She was giving a gift of pure love to them and, she realized, they to her as well.

CHAPTER 32

Naftali sat on his ramshackle porch, viewing the destruction of Kosveg. His foray into the world through Laszlo had been ill-advised. What a fool he was to listen to Yossel and his scheme. He needed to get back on the path of righteousness as a Hassid. That way, he could be a lamp unto their feet, not another confused participant in the illusion that was their modern society. He thought about the angry crowd outside the synagogue. The people of Laszlo were not inherently evil like the Nazis. They had lost the necessary balance between *gevurah* and *chesed*, judgment and compassion, allowing the scourge of hatred to infect them again. Wasn't his role as a Hassid to strive constantly to restore the balance through prayer and good works? It was clear he could not do that in Laszlo or in any part of the corrupted and broken world alone. In Auschwitz, he heard of a large community of Hassids going to start fresh in America, in a place called Brooklyn. That name, Brooklyn, was repeated over and over until it had gained the same mystical significance as the land of milk and honey. He would not be alone there. He would be safe. After all, wasn't America a land of immigrants? There could be no outsiders if everyone came from somewhere else. The plague could not follow him across the ocean.

He walked to the shed where Beersheba cooed contentedly. He took a small scrap of parchment from the rusty nail banged into the side of the shed where his father had left paper for making messages.

He wrote a note to no one in particular:

Gone to Brooklyn America

"Come, Beersheba," Naftali said gently as he picked up the bird. "One last flight for you, then you are free." He attached the note to the metal clip on her leg and took her outside of the shed and into the sunshine. He kissed her sweetly on the head and threw her into the air. Beersheba flew around the dead village in ever-increasing circles, looking back at Naftali, who cried on the ground below. She turned upward and flew directly into the sun until she was gone.

Naftali returned to the shed and tore the cage door off its rusted hinges. He overturned the cage and stomped on it again and again until it was a mangle of wire fencing and splinters under his feet. If Beersheba ever returned to Kosveg, she would not be caged again.

The Hassid returned to the shell of his family home. He contemplated the Torah scroll. Perhaps he should rebury it where his father had laid it to rest before, but who would find it? It was more likely to be dug up by some treasure hunter from the town—maybe destroyed—than to shine its loving light on a Jewish face again. He decided to take it to Brooklyn. He packed the scroll in the traveler's trunk it had lain in, protected and waiting beneath the earth. He added his prayer shawl, the single *tefillin* and the few threadbare clothes he possessed. *There must be a train to Debrecen in a day or so*, he thought. He would stay at the hotel in town until it came, explain himself to Yossel and the others, and say goodbye to Laszlo and Hungary. He felt for the wooden Aleph block he carried in his pocket at all times. It reminded him of sweet beginnings, and that the spark of *Ha Shem's* light would always be within him.

The White Stag Scouts walked up the railroad tracks toward the station, obscuring their path from the brick factory. They kicked at cans and other debris along the tracks and threw stones from the rail bed into the surrounding woods, downhearted at having spent another day fruitlessly searching for the Jewish treasure. They could see the tail end of the train at the station as it huffed in preparation to leave.

Viktor looked toward the station and stopped abruptly. "Hey! Isn't that the Jew from the village?"

"What's he doing at the station?" Gyorgi asked.

Viktor squinted toward the black-clad figure. His eyes widened. "He's getting on the train. And look! He's got a box with him. He's escaping with the treasure! We've got to stop him!" Viktor began to panic. He needed the treasure to pay for Grandfather's doctor.

"Calm down, Viktor," Peter said. "He couldn't fit much treasure in that little box. He probably grabbed what he could carry. Let him go. Now there is nobody to catch us at the brick factory."

"Yeah, I guess you're right," Viktor said as he kicked at a loose rock. "But we better double our efforts and find the treasure."

"What's the rush if he's gone?" Peter's tone of authority grated on Viktor. After all, he was the leader, not Peter. "Maybe we should take a break for a week or so. I wouldn't mind doing something else. Besides, I have to lie to my father every day we go there. We all do."

Viktor watched the Jew climb aboard the train as it began to move slowly from the station. He had to push the scouts harder. They had to get that treasure soon.

Mor stood at the far end of the platform, supervising his two employees as they loaded several heavy wooden crates into the store truck. His weekly shipments were bringing beautiful surplus furniture from all over the country into his shop. Carved, painted folk furniture from the western regions came and went quickly, as did the popular bentwood chairs and bed sets from the Ungvarer factory and J&J Kohn. He had never made so much money. Weiss had taught him well. Of course, his cash flow was helped by not having to pay the outstanding invoices he had inherited from Weiss from Jewish furniture factories that had closed or been destroyed during the war. Jews had such discerning taste—the rich ones anyway. He signed the receipt for the crates and looked at the powerful train that had delivered his newfound bounty.

"We live in a marvelous age, don't we, Josef? All this cargo, all those passengers rumbling around the country so quickly. These trains have changed our lives."

"Yes, sir," the station master said, but seemed distracted by the sight of the lone young man dressed in black on the platform. "They have changed many lives."

Mor coughed into his fist to get Josef's attention. "I know you love trains. As with most things we love, we have to overlook some actions that make us uncomfortable. Still, as a railroad man you must give the Germans credit for an amazing feat of organization. Half a million Jews shipped out of Hungary in only eight weeks, and with no prior notice! And such efficiency, getting thousands of cattle cars, scheduling hundreds of trips without a single derailment or accident." The station master didn't seem to be listening. He should have more respect for a leading member of the business community. Mor motioned his chin toward the black-clad young man. "That young man down there. Isn't he the Jew from the village?"

"Yes he is, Mr. Mor."

"Where is he going?" Mor knew Josef was not permitted to share passenger information. However, Mor was becoming the most important merchant in Laszlo. The man would not refuse his request.

The station master hesitated, chewing his lower lip nervously. "He's on his way to Debrecen. It was a one-way ticket."

Mor considered this intelligence. The Soviets had taken Debrecen near the end of the war and were administering it. They had tanks, trucks, and thousands of battle-ready troops there. The Red Bear had already swallowed three counties in Hungary and annexed them to Soviet Ukraine. They could easily take over Laszlo if they had an excuse. The Americans and British were exhausted and would not gamble lives over his small town in eastern Hungary. Mor knew that many Jews had communist leanings, at least the ones who didn't own large estates or factories. The young man at the end of the platform had nothing. He most certainly was a communist. He was going to report the little scuffle at the synagogue to the Russians, make a bigger deal of it than it was. The Russians might confiscate Weiss's furniture store and all Mor's new wealth, maybe even ship him off to a labor camp. That's what they were doing in the annexed areas, giving Jews their revenge against those who innocently took over abandoned businesses. Mor decided he should warn his friends at the coffee house about the coming Jewish-inspired Russian invasion. It might be just what was needed to wake people up to the danger of the Jews returning to Lazlo. The station master, flipping a few pages on the clipboard in his hand, interrupted Mor's thoughts. "I also need to advise you that the noon train a week from Thursday will be delayed by an hour. You won't have to come down so early for your next shipment. We have a Special Train coming through."

"A Special Train? I thought we were done with all that."

"The passengers are Romanian Jews on their way to Budapest and then out of the country. Those poor people are in bad shape."

Mor knew that thousands of destitute Romanian Jews had been storming the border for months, trying to escape desperate hunger in their own country. The radio called it "the Famine Flight." Mor thought they would be diseased, maybe carrying the plague. They should not be allowed to stop in Laszlo. He had to tell Sergeant Ritook.

"Thank you, Josef. You are a true patriot." He tipped his hat and got in the cab of the truck, knowing the station master would appreciate the compliment from the most important man in Laszlo.

Josef gave his little bow and tipped his cap in return.

Oskar leaned against a station lamppost as the train carrying Naftali departed. Even though the young man had given a stirring sermon at the synagogue, the butcher didn't particularly care if he left. In fact, Oskar was certain it was Naftali's presence at the synagogue that led to the attack. He never had good feelings about those Hassids. Their odd clothing and looks made them easy targets for people's anxiety and hatred. They looked dirty and unkempt, so people said they brought disease. They lived apart, so they were suspected of disloyalty to the country and plotting with outsiders— foreign Jews, Communists, whoever. Oskar thought they gave ordinary Jews like him a bad name, a guilt by religious association. In Auschwitz, he had conversations with Jews from other countries who felt the same. They were different from the Hassids. They were assimilated, educated, safe. The Hassids were primitive. But in the end it happened to everybody. Doctors, nurses, businessmen, lawyers, and Hassids all burned in the gas-fueled flames of hate. Of course, Oskar felt horrible about what had happened at Kosveg, but at the same time he didn't mind seeing Naftali go. Maybe it would take some of the bad air out of the town, but probably not. As the train disappeared down the track, Oskar considered boarding the next one and leaving Laszlo for good. No family, no house, no job. What was in this sad little town for him?

He straightened up and grabbed the shovel he wanted to return to the station master. He knocked on the office door and waved. Josef came out and took the shovel. He smiled at the butcher.

"Oskar, I've been thinking. I know you don't have work. I need an assistant and there is no one I trust around here. The young soldiers are more interested in drinking, women, and pitying themselves than working. How would you like to work with me? It's a respectable job."

The butcher stared at his old friend. He was desperate for something to do and it was a good job. People in town would have to respect him. Or would they? Oskar didn't trust the people of Laszlo. He had also developed a fear of trains. It hurt him to turn down a good job, even more to disappoint Josef, who was trying to be kind. But it wasn't for him. "I'm sorry, Josef. I do need the work but to be honest I can't stand to hear trains anymore, let alone get near them. When I hear them from the hotel I start to shake." He smiled awkwardly and left the station.

Josef frowned as he watched Oskar head up the hill. His whole life had been about trains. It was ironic that Jewish bankers had made this railroad system possible. He owed his career and comfortable life to them. It was hard for him to accept that someone didn't want to be near trains. But he remembered Oskar was deported on a train that the station master himself had switched to this very station. That's why he had offered Oskar the job. Maybe if he helped at least one Jew, those damned night trains would stop coming. He looked down, embarrassed, weighed down by the shame of his participation on that sad day.

CHAPTER 33

Before Eva ventured out in the morning, she gave the matron the name and address of the professor's sister. The matron promised to seek the woman's whereabouts through her connections in the government, the military, and the embassies. Anna Nagy. It was a Herculean task, she said. "We can search the records of those who left the country under Swedish or other protection. Many did. We can also look to see if she returned from the camps and is registered with the Joint Committee." A shadow crossed the matron's face. "She may have never left Budapest, and that we can't trace yet."

Eva thanked the matron for her kindness. She was eager to go to the Academy, certain the sight of the beautiful building would bolster her courage to take the next frightening step of going in and advocating for her admission. It was only a few blocks away, down Kiraly Street, one of the borders of the Jewish ghetto. She buttoned up her blouse, straightened her skirt and set out.

Kiraly Street was an old Jewish commercial street, much narrower than the grand boulevard of Andrassy or Erzsebet Road. The scars of war along Kiraly seemed more prominent and ugly. All of the overhead business signs that should have jutted out over the sidewalk were gone. Only mangled metal frames and bare electric wires remained. Few of the Yiddish store names survived intact. On her left, she could see the stone wall topped by barbed wire that snaked out of sight between buildings and enclosed the ghetto. Here and there, the wall had been smashed by a bomb or torn down by human hands. Impromptu checkpoints of rubble and wood guarded these entries to the ghetto. Eva wondered if the Jews of the ghetto required protection from the war's lingering hatred. Gargoyles stared down malevolently at the ghetto from the roofs of adjacent buildings, crouched and seemingly ready to spring. Budapest didn't feel that different from Laszlo.

Young men in civilian clothes huddled at each entrance to the ghetto. They eyed Eva warily as she passed by, their thoughts perhaps straying from guarding their small enclaves to what might be in the manila folder she clutched or what was under her clothes. These were the first tough, confident young Jewish men Eva had seen since before the deportation. She realized that she was identifying with them as Jews for the first time in her life, without being forced to by the Germans or by the people of Laszlo. She felt a heady mix of pride, attraction, and fear. Her emotions rose, crested, and subsided in waves as she approached and passed each in turn until she became used to the sights and the brazen stares.

She neared a checkpoint and was confronted by four little boys wielding sticks. They asked what her business was. She told them she was looking for her aunt Anna, who lived somewhere inside the ghetto. One of the boys, ten-year-old Abraham, was dispatched to accompany Eva on her search. She had no plan other than to ask the managers of each building she passed if they knew Anna Nagy. As they entered the area, Eva looked up at the wounded remnants of ghetto buildings. Many outside walls were gone, gored by the gods of war, splayed open as if in vivisection to reveal the pulsing of life within. An older woman wearing a skirt and a brassiere washed clothes in a tub and hung them on a line tied between buildings. A couple sat at a small table, sharing a meal. Children ran around the rubble piles at the base of the buildings, playing whatever games their imaginations provided, normalizing the abnormality of their young lives.

Most of the buildings had gated walkways leading to an interior courtyard. A wooden or metal door on the street side of the gate indicated where the manager lived. Abraham led the way and knocked on each manager's door. If a manager answered at all, he would let them in and tell them to wait. He asked the tenants if they knew the woman or if she lived in any of the crowded apartments that rose to four or five levels surrounding the courtyard. Each inquiry was long and ultimately frustrating as Eva waited in the hot sun for a positive answer that never came. After a dozen tries, Abraham announced he was bored and wanted to go back to the checkpoint. Eva felt tired from walking and emotionally drained from her lack of success. She realized that with hundreds of buildings and thousands of apartments in the ghetto she was more likely to find a piano floating in mid-air than to locate the professor's sister. She hoped the matron had fared better.

Eva continued walking down Kiraly Street. After several blocks she noticed the intact side of a beautiful granite building beside a small plaza filled with rubble from the shattered building across from it. Eva looked around the front of the building. Her eyes widened at the sight of towering statues of four men holding a podium on their broad backs. In a throne atop the podium sat another statue. A name was etched under the god-like black marble figure—Ferenc Liszt.

She had found the Academy. Eva put her hands to her chest as her breath shortened and her vision clouded with tears. All her life the Academy had represented the beauty of music and the joy of her family. In Auschwitz, it transmuted into a distant place of safety, one she longed for but feared she would never reach. Now she was here, yet her elation was ephemeral as Eva considered what she had to do next. The statue of Liszt stared down at her, challenging her talent and commitment. She held his stony gaze, determined to obtain an audition and prove her worth.

She walked up and pushed repeatedly on the massive glass and steel front doors. They were locked and nobody was visible inside. She peered through the glass, seeing the blue marble columns topped with gold friezes within. She wanted to get closer, but that would come in time. Eva backed up through the gray cement dust of the plaza to take in the entirety of the building. Six giant columns stood between the second and fourth floors, making the upper part of the building look like a Greek temple. The raw physicality of the Academy snatched away her breath. A grunt of effort caught her attention. She turned around to see a bearded, white-haired man in a dirty work coat trying to lift a heavy piece of rubble into a cart. He looked like a prisoner in the camp, being worked to death at hard labor. She walked over to him.

"May I help?"

He nodded through labored breathing. Together, Eva and the man hefted the jagged piece of cement into the rubbish cart. After they had pushed the piece over the edge of the cart, Eva asked why he stopped to pick up such heavy pieces instead of simply sweeping the lighter debris. He wiped his brow with a dusty sleeve. The motion reminded Eva of her father in their garden, and pain shot through her heart. She always thought she would watch her father age.

"I am used to carrying heavy loads. It is difficult for me to let go of them." The man started to thank her when he noticed her hand. "Young lady, you are bleeding."

Eva looked at her bandaged hand. It had begun to seep blood again. "I must have strained the stitches moving that cement," she said, flexing her fingers and feeling the pain on the side of her hand.

The man took a white handkerchief from his coat pocket and handed it to Eva, who shook her head. She didn't want to bloody it. "You have done an old man a kindness. You will be rewarded in the next life if not in this one," he said, pressing it into her hand.

Eva smiled. That was something the professor would say, maybe an old Jewish expression. She looked up at the Academy. "How can it be that the Academy looks completely untouched when all the buildings around it are battered and crumbling?"

The man shrugged his bushy white eyebrows. "Who can say?

Perhaps God prefers Brahms to bombs. Are you a student there?"

"I was accepted before the deportation but, it's very confusing. I need to speak to someone, but I don't know anyone and I can't get in the building."

"The deportation." His brow furrowed and his eyes lost focus. "So you are Jewish." The man took off his work gloves and leaned against the cart. He had elegant hands. "Students come and go every morning through that side door you passed." Eva detected empathy in the corners of his slight smile. "Perhaps you will have better luck if you join the throng tomorrow, Monday, when classes begin. Come back around ten. Young musicians do not seem to get up very early. If you do not have an instrument, carry some papers to look like you belong."

Eva thought how her new life in Budapest was unfolding—young prostitutes and old street sweepers. No, that was unfair, an observation from another place and time, a place of privileged ignorance. These were all people who suffered, cared, and had self-worth and dignity. They deserved respect for living every day with what life had given them.

A military jeep carrying four Russian soldiers slowed as it passed the Academy. The soldiers regarded Eva. One of them turned to his comrades and said something that made them laugh crudely. Eva stiffened at the attention. The old man's face soured as the jeep roared away. "And always keep your eyes open for those soldiers. They come out of nowhere like hawks snatching up mice."

After another frustrating afternoon of talking to building managers in the ghetto, Eva returned to the boarding house. She sought out the matron, who said the address Eva gave her for Anna Nagy was no more than a bombed-out shell. Nearby residents told her the Jews in that neighborhood had been moved during the war to housing near the factories and airports to dissuade the Allied bombers from targeting those installations. They had all been dispersed since the war ended. The matron had contacted the Swedish, Swiss, Spanish, and Chinese embassies but was unable to find Anna Nagy's name among those spirited out of Hungary by the brave diplomats of those countries. Nobody at the Jewish agencies could find her name on the camp returnee lists. Either Anna Nagy perished as so many others from Budapest or she was alive in the ghetto somewhere. When Eva described her search of the apartment buildings, the matron scoffed.

"There are seventy thousand Jews crammed in there. The government is trying to do a census, but it won't be completed for a year. It won't be accurate anyway. Most Jews don't ever want to appear on a government list again." She held up her hands when Eva tried to speak. "I don't know what else I can do to help you." Eva felt her chest deflate. "If you want to stay here while you search I won't charge you, provided you play the piano for the ladies every night. I thought most of them were dead inside. Last night your music kindled some kind of spark. It seems a balm for their poor souls."

Eva decided that rather than try to storm the Academy the first day she would watch the comings and goings to understand the flow of students and faculty into the building. She stopped at a small bakery on Kiraly Street and bought two rolls with butter. She would share them with the old man if he was still there. He was pushing his broom, cleaning the dust and minor debris from the plaza. The two sat together on one of the few surviving benches that faced the Academy.

"My name is Eva," she said as she handed him the roll.

The old man took off his gloves and accepted the offering with the slight bow that older gentlemen always give. "You can call me

Uncle Zoli." He proceeded to describe the activity they observed. The students came through the side door, which had direct access to the practice rooms on the floors above. The professors and administrators entered through the front doors and were let in by the staff. The only way Eva could get in was through the side door. She would have to try her luck crossing from there through the lobby, past the guards and the doorman.

"Look, Eva," Uncle Zoli said, pointing toward a tall, distinguished-looking man headed for the front door. "That is Ede Zathureczky, the director of the Academy. He's the man you need to see about your status. And the man with him is Gyorgy Kosa, one of the piano instructors. He was sent to a labor battalion last year, but as you can see, he survived." He winced. "So many didn't."

Eva was stunned. "He's Jewish?"

"Yes, several of the Jewish professors came back last semester when the Academy reopened after the siege." He lowered his voice. "Actually, most of the Jewish staff and Jewish students remained here during the war, even though the law required them to be dismissed. The director and staff worked hard to protect them. It is one of the proudest and best-kept secrets of the Academy."

A spark of hope flared within Eva. How different from Laszlo, where so many people cheered and jeered at the deportation, and the anger seethed there still. "How did the Academy manage that? There was so much hatred."

"Ede Zathureczky was very firm in his support for his staff and students. He even hid some of the Jewish students in his private apartment on the first floor. It is amazing what one man or woman can do if they have the courage to stand up." He looked up at the giant seated statue of Ferenc Liszt. "The Academy is a citadel of music, and the director would not let its walls be breached by its enemies." His jaw tightened as if a sharp pain had stabbed a tooth. "He mostly succeeded." The old man stood and stretched his back. He grabbed his broom and stared at the people entering the building. "And yet, there is still some rot within."

Eva looked quizzically at the old street cleaner. "How do you know so much about what goes on there?"

He looked down wistfully at his bare hands as he put his gloves on. "I have worked around here for a long time."

Eva left the Academy and returned to the makeshift ghetto entrance. Abraham stood with his hands folded across his chest, his curly brown hair fringing around his cap. He didn't look interested in helping Eva again. But his hardened young eyes revealed their innocence when Eva produced a piece of sugar candy from the bakery. She promised to give it to him if he accompanied her again. He eagerly agreed. They retraced their earlier searches down Akacfa Street and continued questioning building managers. They turned right onto Dob Street and stopped when they came to Klauzal Square. The broad, open square had been cratered by artillery during the siege, yet people had turned it into an outdoor market selling and bartering everything from furniture to food. They wandered the market for a while as Abraham gave Eva a tour of the goods and named some of the sellers. They sat on one of several packing crates that had been set up as benches and evening shelters for the homeless. Abraham sucked greedily at the candy while Eva observed the buildings around the square. Like the ones on other streets, most buildings were pitted with bullet holes and several torn open to expose the private lives of the apartment dwellers. An old upright piano hung precariously over the edge of a third-floor apartment. Eva gasped and clutched her throat. A little girl in a black-sequined dress pecked a two-fingered version of a *Brandenburg Concerto*, oblivious to the crumbling floor inches from her feet. The girl stopped playing. She looked directly at Eva and playfully twirled around too close to the edge, her black sequins sparkling in the sunlight. The girl curtsied before retreating into the shadows of the apartment. Eva rubbed her eyes. Was that another vision? The girl was gone but the piano remained.

After finishing his candy, Abraham abruptly announced he was done for the day and ran away. Eva slumped on the crate, thinking of how she might find Anna, if she was anywhere to be found. She looked up again at the piano suspended between light and dark in the ruined apartment.

The iron gate at the front of the crumbling apartment building was open. No manager came to challenge Eva as she entered the courtyard. The narrow, ancient elevator was clearly not working and looked too much like a cage for Eva's comfort. She visualized the piano being on the left side of the building on the third floor, so she turned and walked to the left stairwell. The wooden stairs creaked under her feet as she slowly spiraled upwards. The handrail wobbled slightly. Eva thought she heard the muffled crackle of a radio as she passed the second-floor landing. She avoided a splintered step as she reached the third floor. The dead quiet made her shiver. She wondered if anyone at all lived in this building.

A girl's faint laughter came from the apartment to Eva's right. She pushed the door open and called inside. When no one replied she entered the apartment. At the far end she could see the outside light where the wall had given way. She walked further in and found the piano, with the market of Klauzal Square framed in the sunlight behind it. She took in the movements in the market for a moment, then stepped tentatively toward the piano. One corner of it hung out into the air while a second lay just on the brink. A dusty, red Persian carpet covered the room and hid the rough edge of the floor that merged into empty space. Eva took a deep breath and eased onto the piano bench. The floor had a slight sponginess under her. She feared it could give way at any moment. Her fingers sought out the keys and began to play a Bach sonata. She glanced outward occasionally, noticing marketgoers staring upwards and starting to gather near the base of the building. Some shouted warnings against her foolhardiness. She played several more classical pieces until the crowd in the square was quite large. When she finished there were scattered applause and comments.

Eva looked out over the crowd—a throng of Jews who had suffered terribly, lost loved ones and all they possessed. She thought about her mother, her father, and the professor. Her sadness poured out and merged with the profound grief she felt from the crowd. The emotion throbbed through the air like an off-key note. She began to play "Gloomy Sunday." She didn't play it at Mrs. Kodaly's party or at the mayor's house concert. It seemed inappropriate to sing about despair to the point of contemplating suicide in those settings. She didn't want to reveal the depth of pain that she and the other Jews were carrying in Laszlo. But this crowd of survivors would understand. The choices were stark when there was nothing left—leap into the dark void or seek the light. From the crowd below a lone female voice began to sing.

> "It is autumn and the leaves are falling
> All love has died on earth
> The wind is weeping with sorrowful tears
> My heart will never hope for a new spring again
> My tears and my sorrows are all in vain
> People are heartless, greedy, and wicked . . ."

A dozen, two dozen, then a hundred voices joined in creating a cathartic dirge that echoed throughout the ghetto.

> "Love has died!
> The world has come to its end, hope has ceased to have a meaning
> Cities are being wiped out, shrapnel is making music
> Meadows are colored red with human blood
> There are dead people on the streets everywhere
> I will say another quiet prayer:

People are sinners, Lord, they make mistakes . . .
The world has ended!"

Eva stopped playing. Her hand and heart throbbed wildly. She looked through wet eyes at the crowd below. Many people gazed up at her with tears, smiles. and faces twisted by harsh or beautiful memories. A clap from one person led to a surge of applause. Eva turned to see people clapping from windows and balconies in all directions. She had received applause from many audiences in her life, but nothing touched her as deeply as this wave of affection from the sea of Jewish faces that engulfed her. Ordinary people, survivors who understood each other's tragedy without asking. They were not diplomats, officials, or aid workers. If anyone knew where Anna Nagy was, that person would be in this crowd. She stood, careful to avoid the ragged edge of the floor.

"Please help me!" she shouted. "I am trying to find Anna Nagy! She worked with OMIKE during the war. Some of you must know her. I am sure she lives here somewhere!" There was no reply from the crowd, although several people turned and murmured to each other. Eva continued, "I will come back tomorrow and the next day and play again. Please tell your neighbors and friends. Help me find Anna Nagy!"

She returned every afternoon that week. The crowds got larger and larger, the applause more heartfelt and widespread. People approached her and requested music from their past, a song from their wedding, the tune they danced to on their first date, a late husband's favorite waltz. They brought her photos and sheet music from their homes, pastries and sweets from their stalls in the market. They chatted with her about life and loss in the city and in their former small towns. In these conversations, Eva found the comfort and safety to talk about her life, as well. She sensed she was being accepted by the people of the Klauzal Square market, and by many of those who leaned out their windows to listen and sometimes to sing along. Before the deportation, she was a high school student who cared about her family and friends but had no wider sense of identity. Now, being in the ghetto gave her a feeling of belonging to a large community, one of shared heritage and experience. Yet nobody could help her find Anna Nagy. She knew she should be resting her injured hand, which continued to hurt and weep daily. Each day, the piano inched closer to the edge of the crumbling building. Eva knew the vibrations were weakening the integrity of the floor, but she had to keep playing.

CHAPTER 34

Yossel was humming along to Mozart's cheerful "Turkish March" on the BBC while doing the breakfast dishes. It had been over a week since the synagogue violence. Things were peaceful and the baker had returned to his optimistic outlook. He glanced out the small window over the sink. People were lining up and down the street, laughing and cheering as if a parade were about to begin. Oskar put down the butcher's knives he was sharpening and the two men poked their heads out the front door. The crowd started to sing "Himnusz," the Hungarian national anthem.

> "Isten, aldd meg a magyart
> Jo kedvvel, boseggel,
> Nyujts feleje vedo kart,
> Ha kuzd ellenseggel . . ."
>
> (O God, bless the nation of Hungary
> With your grace and bounty
> Extend over it your guarding arm
> During strife with its enemies . . .)

Oskar glanced around nervously. "This feels damned familiar." He shouted to a man marching by with a small boy perched on his shoulders waving a little flag. "Hey! What's going on?"

The man responded gleefully. "The Germans are being

deported!" He continued with bouncy steps down the road toward the train station.

"What Germans is he talking about?" Yossel asked Oskar.

Oskar scratched his head. "I don't know. Maybe they found some soldiers in the woods who didn't know the war was over. It happens."

The men looked past the crowd to see Corporal Zoldy leading a small, downcast group of men, women, and children as they hauled their luggage down the street. Yossel recognized some of them as customers from the bakery. He saw Eva's friend, the blond boy Andras, accompanied by his parents. Corporal Miklos walked along the side of the street. The baker swallowed hard and called out to the young policeman.

"Excuse me, Corporal! What's happening?"

Corporal Miklos stopped and turned to Yossel with a stricken look. "The government is deporting ethnic Germans, anyone of German ancestry. They are confiscating their homes and businesses. We are taking them to the train." He shrugged helplessly and moved on.

"Not again!" Yossel cried out, his heart beginning to pound wildly.

A man standing in front of Yossel spun around angrily. "Shut up or you can join them." He resumed enjoying the pageant. "Traitors! Hungary for pure Hungarians!"

Oskar spit on the ground. "Good, let them go." He laughed and shouted over the crowd. "Kick them out!"

The butcher's words were a punch in Yossel's gut. He put his hands on his stomach protectively and turned to Oskar. "How quickly you've become a good Hungarian again."

Oskar's face showed a mixture of anger and glee. "What do I care about them? Their cousins murdered every Jew they could. Good riddance."

Yossel sighed. "Collective punishment? Guilty because of their ancestry? Who knows that better than we do?" He watched as the dozen or so confused and frightened families were herded past. His eyes moistened. He mumbled sadly. "Are we the bystanders now?"

"At least they're turning their hate on somebody else for a while." Oskar whistled the "Himnusz" as he watched the spectacle. "Hey!" he blurted out. "Isn't that Krauss, your boss?"

Yossel scanned the marchers and found the limping man, still wearing his flour-caked apron. He broke through the crowd to get Krauss's attention. The man saw Yossel and waved dejectedly. He kept walking.

"Yossel! I've deeded you the bakery! It's under the cash register!" He pulled his crying young son along as they passed. "It was never really mine, was it? Good luck with it, Yossel! Quick, give me some *pengos* to make it legal!"

Yossel ran up to Krauss and tried to thrust the bills in his hand. A shove from a scowling Sergeant Ritook pushed Krauss out of Yossel's reach. The *pengos* sailed in the wind through the street, chased by delighted little boys waving flags.

A woman in the crowd pointed to Yossel. "Look at that Jew, always trying to make money off someone's misfortune. Shame on you!" Derisive laughter rolled through the crowd. Yossel stood frozen as the citizens of Laszlo swallowed up Krauss and his son and continued toward the train station. Oskar walked over and put his hand on the baker's shoulder.

Yossel pulled at his hair in lamentation. He wiped his eyes and nose with his sleeve. "I prayed so hard to get the bakery back, but I never asked God to punish poor Krauss and his little boy."

"Guess God still has a sense of irony," Oskar said flatly. He slapped Yossel's back. "Let me help you with the dishes. Then we should go to the bakery and make sure it's safe." He led the miserable baker back toward the hotel. "Hey, maybe I can work with you. I need the job and you need the help."

Yossel and Oskar walked in silence through the town square. A few small Hungarian flags rolled past, urged along by intermittent gusts of wind. A broken suitcase spilled its meager contents where the Jewish headstones had been. Few of the people they passed offered a smile or a hint of greeting. One couple crossed the street as they approached as if to avoid something contagious. The men stopped in front of the synagogue to pay silent respect. The wind moaned a lonely plea for remembrance through the shattered stained glass and the cavernous interior. Oskar peered deep inside the deserted building and cried out when he saw the empty Ark.

"The bastards! They stole the Torah!" He searched the street for the culprit, his hands clenching and opening repeatedly.

Yossel tried to calm the butcher. "We can't be sure what happened. Maybe the police took it for safekeeping. Maybe Naftali buried it again." He watched as Oskar's internal volcanic rage bubbled toward the surface.

"It's gone." Oskar stroked the scarred synagogue door. "Everything Jewish in Laszlo is gone except us."

"We've got the bakery now. At least we can support ourselves, even if only until we figure out what to do next." Yossel retrieved the keys to the bakery from his pocket and jingled them in his hand as they continued down the road.

The baker was surprised by the large padlock and chain that prevented him from putting his key in the door. He wondered aloud if Krauss had put it on when he closed up for the deportation, to protect the shop from looters. Oskar called Yossel over to the large shop window. An announcement from the town was posted, obscuring the view of the empty wooden pastry rack inside.

Confiscated by Town of Laszlo Pursuant to Order of Sale
Contact Town Clerk for Bidding Details

Oskar growled and punched the window. It bowed and vibrated, but didn't break. "That's it. We need to leave this town right away. I feel like I'm being strangled."

"Let me talk to the town clerk. We can figure out a way to make this work." Yossel forced the words past his heavy heart. "There are still good people in Laszlo."

"Why don't you wake up, Yossel? They don't care. We are dead to them."

"Because, Oskar, like the Torah commands, I choose life."

The butcher bit his hand in frustration. "You didn't choose life. Some SS guard chose life for you, just as easily as he could've chosen death. If you're gonna be grateful to God for anything, be grateful He stayed the hand of the beast when it came for you and let a lot of better Jews die. Neither of us might be so lucky the next time."

"Wait, explain that again." Yossel was exasperated as he tried to follow the town clerk. "You are going to file paperwork to give me my own bakery back because the government has ordered German property to be seized and distributed to Jews who lost property? Why such a legal maze? It's my bakery. Just take the lock off the door and look the other way."

"I can't do that!"

Oskar was looking out the office window, playing with the blinds. His voice was numb. "You did it when we were deported to the death camp."

The town clerk cast his eyes downward until he regained his composure. "It's not that simple. We are supposed to sell it to the highest bidder. But the mayor and I have been thinking that under these special circumstances we could try to use the Jewish compensation law instead. We *might* be able to give it back."

Oskar yawned. He hadn't had his second cup of coffee yet. "He means they're doing you a favor."

The town clerk flinched, "We don't do *favors*, sir. We are trying to find the right legal standard to see justice is done. You must know the town wants justice for our Jewish citizens." He turned back to the baker and adjusted his tie. "Now, Yossel, I will order the compensation forms today. It is a new application. The one you filled out two weeks ago has been superseded due to the new regulations. You only need your national identity card proving your Jewish heritage and a copy of your original title."

The baker was dumbfounded. "But Mr. Kadar, you know who I am. You've been giving me business licenses for twenty years. You know we lost everything in the camp. None of us has any papers at all."

The town clerk's face reddened. "Oh, of course, right. Well, you need to have the identity card to participate in any new government program. You can apply for one here. Just bring in your birth certificate." He smiled benevolently. "We will waive the filing fee."

Yossel and Oskar argued most of the way back to the hotel. Oskar wanted to pretend he was a Zionist and go to Palestine with the Fischer brothers as soon as possible. Yossel urged him to wait and see if the baker could get his shop back. They had plenty of time.

A small crowd was gathered around the front of the hotel, talking and gesturing toward the forlorn building. Yossel and Oskar approached cautiously. The crowd parted so the men could see what was so interesting. Three large green crossed arrow symbols were painted on the walls and the door, alongside angry graffiti: *No Jews!* and *Jews out of Laszlo!* Yossel stood immobilized.

Oskar grasped the baker's arm and pulled him inside, slamming the door behind them. "So much for the good people of Laszlo."

They both shook with fear. It was happening again. All afternoon and evening Yossel and Oskar paced the hotel lobby, unable to concentrate on anything but a menace that loomed larger as the hours passed. Neither man could sleep when darkness descended, so they kept watch together in the lobby. When Oskar's head dipped he dreamed of Auschwitz, but all the guards looked like Ritook. Yossel stayed awake ruminating about the otherwise decent people who stood by and let these things happen. He listed the small acts of kindness he had experienced at the bakery. He refused to let these little lights of goodness be overshadowed by the darkness of the graffiti.

"I know I will get the bakery back. I know I will." Yossel repeated the words like a sacred Hebrew chant to protect him from the infection he knew was growing and spreading throughout Laszlo in spite of his positive outlook.

"Keep dreaming, Yossel," the butcher mumbled from his hypnogogic state. "Maybe one day I will have my own slaughterhouse and a big packing plant. I will employ hundreds of the townspeople who persecuted us. May we live and be happy."

They took turns peering out the windows at the moon-cast shadows and straining to hear danger in the sounds of the night.

Oskar jerked awake at the clank of metal hitting the ground. He heard voices outside the window above his head. His heart pounded fiercely as he raised himself off the sofa and moved the curtain enough to peek outside. Only a few shabbily dressed men were there, but the butcher could see others approaching from up the hill. At that distance he couldn't identify the weapons they were carrying. Oskar knew the loathing that was permeating the town had bolstered the attackers' courage. It was broad daylight. They were finally coming to get him.

"Yossel!" he whispered harshly. "Get up! Hurry!"

The baker fell out of a chair mid-snore and blinked rapidly. He crawled beside the butcher and squinted out the window. "Oskar, what can we do?" the baker pleaded. A hard knocking at the door brought both men to their feet. They ignored the sound and grabbed the small end tables that were scattered in the lobby, huffing with fear.

"Open up, Yossel! It's Mayor Kodaly!"

Yossel put down the end table, unlocked the door and opened it slightly. Mayor Kodaly stood there, holding a bucket and scrub brush. Behind him, a small crowd of townspeople mixed a tub of whitewash. The station master stirred the paint with his shovel. Yossel recognized Eva's friend Hanna, who had been at the station to wish Eva well. Several of the volunteers who helped restore the synagogue were there. The mayor stepped beside the baker and put his arm on his shoulder. He addressed the gathered townspeople.

"On behalf of the town I want to apologize for this appalling act. We have come to repair the damage to the hotel and to our reputation." He turned to Yossel with a smile. "Don't ever doubt it. You are valued citizens of our town. You have good friends in Laszlo."

Townspeople chatted sympathetically with Yossel and Oskar as they worked together to scrape down the painted surfaces as best they could. The green paint had seeped deep into the long ignored, pitted concrete surfaces. Yossel brought coffee and some pastries out to the group. The mayor sipped the coffee, complimented Yossel on his *kiffles*, got in the large red Chrysler Imperial, and left to applause and cheers. After coffee, people cheerfully painted over the green crosses and slogans. It became obvious that one coat was not enough, as the malevolence seemed to burn through the thin whitewash. The crowd began to apply a second coat. Yossel watched the volunteer painters. His heart filled with gratitude.

"You see, Oskar?"

"I know, I know. 'There are good people in Laszlo.'"

Yossel smiled. "You can joke, but I think there are only a handful of really hateful people in Laszlo. There are many more good ones."

The sound of a police siren arrested the work and conversation.

Yossel and Oskar greeted Sergeant Ritook and Corporal Zoldy, explaining about the vandalism and the kindness of the townspeople. They thanked the police for coming down, but told them everything was calm.

Sergeant Ritook stepped up to examine the green crossed arrows and turned toward the crowd. The arrows emerged from his back like the wings of a harpy. He jerked a thumb at the symbols.

"This is an act of vandalism. We will find the criminals and bring them to justice." There were shaking heads and murmurs of approval in the crowd. "But these drawings and words are evidence. Do not paint over them. Anyone caught doing so will be arrested for destruction of evidence at the scene of a crime. Am I understood? Do not paint over them. Now please disperse."

The policemen left with their siren screaming. People gathered their brushes and buckets and trickled away from the hotel to words of praise from Yossel and sullen nods from Oskar. When everyone was gone, Oskar cursed the town loudly and retreated into the hotel. Yossel tried to summon his positive attitude. If they kept a very low profile this too would pass, and they could keep building good will in Laszlo. He stared at the wall. The whitewash had nearly dried, yet Yossel could see the shadows of the arrows and the hateful speech smoldering in anticipation below the surface.

CHAPTER 35

Eva stood nervously by the side door of the Academy on Monday morning as students came and went. She held the professor's manuscript tightly against her chest as if it were a good luck talisman. The old man was not there last week, which made her feel uneasy. Was he ill? He was somehow a comforting presence. Without him, Eva had vacillated for several days between rushing into the Academy or waiting for some opportune moment. She couldn't wait any longer. She focused on the door and charged in with three female students who twittered gaily as they entered. The guard seated inside the doorway glanced up briefly before returning to his morning paper.

Once inside, Eva followed the girls down a darkened hallway. They disappeared through a heavy, blood-red velvet curtain. Eva peeked through the curtain and caught her breath. The magnificent multicolored marble lobby of the concert hall lay before her. Orchestral music poured silkily from the Grand Hall. Vivid memories came to her of her father holding her hand as they walked through this very hall, he in his best black suit, she in a pretty blue dress her mother had made with lace at the neck and sleeves. A sharp laugh from one of the students in the lobby shattered the memory. Two guards shifted their positions and stared at her. Eva put a hand to her forehead, as much to shield her face from the guards as to anchor her into the present again. She quickly turned and headed up the stairwell to the second floor. Students practiced in the rooms that lined the hallway. Piano, violin, cello. Eva stopped and reveled in the music, embraced by the sounds at once cacophonous and harmonious. The vibrations of the music pounded against her chest, so much more compelling than music from a radio. She felt as if she were finally home.

A silent room whispered welcome, and Eva slowly opened the door. The parquet-floored room was empty except for a baby grand piano in front of large windows that let joyful sunlight pour in. Eva hesitated. This was not part of her plan for the day. She didn't have permission to sit down and play this exquisite piano, but she could not stop herself. She entered the room, closing the door quietly behind her. Her feet drew her closer and closer until she touched the lid lightly. The beautiful piano hummed quietly as Eva sat carefully on the bench and put up the professor's piano concerto. She realized that she needed this time badly. Although the piano at the brothel was good, it wasn't professionally tuned and maintained like this one. She enjoyed giving impromptu concerts to the young Jewish women, but performing for them didn't enhance her technique like practicing etudes and arpeggios. Nor was she practicing Professor Sandor's piano concerto at the brothel. She was afraid of what emotions the otherworldly piece might evoke among the traumatized women.

In the privacy of this practice room she could finally float away. No one was watching. She was not performing for anyone. The soft, swirling melodies of "Sentience," the opening movement of the *Piano Concerto for the Music of the Spheres*, swept through the room and she with it. The first step, the awareness and acknowledgment of emotions. It was just Eva and the music, rising and falling, exploring the soft breath of a blade of grass, the sparkle of sunlight on water, the brooding of thunderclouds before a storm. As she practiced, the music drew her inward, expressing emotions she had kept inside, had feared sharing—love and grief, longing and rage. She finally understood the depth of the professor's concerto, why it was at times melodious and at others, discordant and seemingly off key. It reflected the universal, conflicting currents that lay at the core of being human. Just as her music had a calming effect on the old soldiers in the Home and the young women at the brothel, it affected Eva, too. Losing herself in the music, fear and sadness evaporated and in their place hope and courage came alive. She cried as she played, laughed aloud, and let the music soothe her like the shower of lilacs in her yard. She came to a soft close, exhausted and exhilarated. As the final notes faded away, it occurred to Eva that if she came every day the guards might think she belonged and she could continue to practice undisturbed.

Eva was startled as the door opened and a young woman about her age entered. A tangle of long red hair framed an annoyed expression.

"Excuse me, but this is my practice time. Didn't you see my name on the reserved list?"

Eva flushed and stuttered. "I am so sorry. I am new here. I didn't know how to reserve the room."

The student tucked the fiery bush behind her ears. "Next time, just put your name on the list outside the door. There are only ten minutes left for this time slot, so you might as well finish up." She backed out of the room and started to close the door. She stopped and looked at Eva curiously. "There are only four of us in the piano group this summer. I don't recognize you. My name is Hedy."

Eva averted her eyes. "I'm actually not starting until the fall term." She was not comfortable lying, but this was hopefully true.

The student smiled indulgently. "Then just invent some name so if you get caught it won't be a black mark against you when you come." She winked. "It's still summer session and nobody knows everybody here yet. But what was that music you were playing? It was so unusual. I was really affected in some strange way. And, I must say, you played it with such heart."

Hedy's words touched Eva deeply. It was the first time anyone had commented on her performing the professor's work. It was especially meaningful coming from a fellow musician. *A fellow musician.* It had been so long since she felt welcomed and understood. She yearned to get into the Academy. It was like a home, a safe haven. Eva decided to take a chance and tell Hedy her story. The student came and sat beside her on the bench and held her uninjured hand. Eva spoke for a long time, unburdening her soul through a torrent of tears to her new friend. Silence swaddled the young women like a warm blanket when she finished.

"I need to see the director, Ede Zathureczky, but I can't walk around the halls without an ID card. I can't call him because the lines are down. I can't write him again because he doesn't respond to my letters. I don't know what to do."

Hedy sat silently for a moment, frowning. Eva couldn't tell if her expression of indignation was due to Eva's mendacity or a response to what she'd been through. "I am not Jewish, but I lost a lot of Jewish friends. I will help you. Let's meet here again next Monday morning." She smiled at Eva. "I will put my name down to reserve the room for you."

Eva left the Academy in a gaggle of students, buoyed by her meeting with Hedy. She returned to the ghetto entrance and continued walking to Klauzal Square. She crossed the square, chatting with some of the market sellers whom she had seen every day that week and had come to know. They tended to be older women and younger men, as most of the middle-aged people were deported to labor camps or Auschwitz and did not return. Children dodged between stalls showing no scars of war, only the exuberance of childhood. Most of the vendors called her Miss Eva. A toothless old fruit seller named Geza gave her sour cherry or apricot sponge cake, *lepeny*, every day. He called her "his piano *malach*," explaining that the Yiddish word meant both "angel" and "a channel between worlds." Her music connected him to family and friends now gone. One woman set up dazzling displays of colorful flowers in the ruins of the Klausal fountain. They were not for sale, she told Eva. Rather, they were her daily means of reminding people that beauty lived amidst the destruction. Her words reminded Eva of the Pure Form, the cosmic music that harmonized beneath all the mayhem of the manifest plane.

Eva was learning the vendors' names and their stories, developing a kindred bond with them. She noticed the different reactions the sellers and their customers had to their liberation. For some, the joy of survival and a feeling of optimism outweighed the sorrow of their losses. For others, the wounds were too deep to find much pleasure in the revival of life. She began to understand why Yossel and Oskar behaved so differently from each other. They had their own ways of dealing with their grief. She wondered which path she would have followed if she didn't have her music, if her Bosendorfer had not been waiting for her return.

While conversing with a woman over a pair of shoes, Eva glanced up toward the piano. It wasn't there. Her stomach clenched. She dropped the shoes and ran to the base of the building. The piano lay shattered on the pavement. She searched out the exposed living room where the piano hung over the ledge the day before. The little girl with the black-sequined dress looked down at her sadly, then turned and faded into the crumbling apartment.

She bent over the ruined piano. Many of the keys were twisted upwards on the keyboard like little gravestones. She tapped at a few. No hammers flew to the strings, no sound emanated from the busted body. Pianos were living things to Eva. They responded to touch, expressed emotion. This one was dead, lifeless. It had given her something precious—recognition and a connection to the people in the ghetto, breathing a little more life into her. Yet another thing of beauty in her life destroyed. Eva battled tears of frustration and defeat, finally sobbing uncontrollably, keening, rocking. Through ragged breath, she choked out the words to "Gloomy Sunday" as she fingered the mangled keys.

"Excuse me, miss?"

Eva turned and looked into the face of a young man. He was sharply dressed. His hair was freshly cut in the shaved-sided modern style and slicked down with Brilliantine. The electric blue sparks of the streetcar danced off his engaging smile. He carried the faint citrus smell of aftershave.

"Were you the girl playing the piano up there yesterday?"

Eva stood up, brushed the tears from her eyes and the cement dust from her skirt. She looked away from the handsome young man and down at the shattered piano. "Yes, but obviously I won't be playing anymore."

"I heard you. You moved me."

She wasn't sure if he meant her playing or her. Eva was unnerved by the way his green eyes held hers without a hint of self-consciousness.

"I am Jeno," he said with a generous smile. Eva felt her body grow warm. "I have come to take you to Anna Nagy."

The young man bowed gallantly and gestured toward the other side of Klauzal Square. Eva said a silent goodbye to the piano, thanking it for bringing her this far. As they crossed the square, he talked about how good it felt now that the war was over to walk freely through the city when no one was going to turn you in to the police.

"You can relax when nobody around wants you dead."

Eva was struck by the phrase. Of course, that was true in the camp, but it had also been true in Laszlo, where the constant fear of insult or violence kept her on edge much of the time. Here in the ghetto, surrounded by other survivors, she felt more relaxed, even safe.

Jeno waved and nodded to many of the sellers in the square. He appraised the goods on offer, noting their value before and after the war and the best things to own as a hedge against the increasingly worthless *pengo*. He told stories of buying and selling everything from meat to mink stoles, confiding that his profession was the black market. He had no time or interest in university or training programs. He stopped to light a cigarette and offer it to Eva.

"It's a Gauloise. It's French. Really hard to find. But I can get anything I want." She reached for it but withdrew, thinking fleetingly of Andras. Boys and their cigarettes only led to dashed dreams and trouble. Jeno put the pack away.

"I guess you don't approve. But the way I figure it, life is too short to play by rules that only serve the wealthy and powerful. *A pokolba veluk!* To hell with them! I live my life by my own rules, one full day at a time."

As Eva followed Jeno through the jumbled and confusing back streets of the ghetto, she wondered if following this cocky young man was wise. She didn't know him and had no idea where she was. They turned down a very narrow street, where the tight formation of the buildings blocked sound and sunlight. She started to hold back and slow down. Jeno turned and smiled. In the dark shadows, Eva couldn't judge if his smile was sweet or sinister. Did he really know Anna Nagy?

"Almost there."

It was a dead end, terminating against one of the high ghetto walls. They could go no further. Eva looked up at the barbed wire that topped the bricks. The buildings began to crowd in on her. Her breath quickened and her skin tingled. She was trapped. There was no one else in the alley, and a bend in the street hid them from the main road.

"It's just in here." Jeno pointed to an old wooden door close to the wall.

The sign on the door where the camp guards took the women loomed beyond Jeno's shining hair. *Eingang Verboten*. Entrance Forbidden. Eva braced herself against the wall, as the wave of panic crested. "She lives in there? Why doesn't the building have a gate and a courtyard?"

"It's just the back entrance to our building. It's the quickest way to get to her apartment." The young man tilted his head. "What are you so nervous about?" He shrugged his shoulders, turned, and unlocked the door with a key. Eva peered over his shoulder and saw the usual stairwell and the light of a courtyard behind it. She exhaled and rubbed her arms to calm herself, but was determined to stay alert.

They entered the stairwell and began to climb. Jeno gave a casual assessment of the refugees who lived in the building. So many people forced into so few apartments. Old rabbis shared rooms with young women. Doctors lived with janitors. There was too much trauma and dislocation for social class to resurface yet. Eva was moved by the stories Jeno told of people recreating the families they lost by living with older survivors and orphaned children. Could a real household be an accidental collection of people, the residue of destroyed families? The ghetto did seem to be filled with people thrown together with no place to go, people who had a sense of belonging because they desperately wanted to belong somewhere. Her family was gone. Her eyes moistened as she wondered what a new family might look like.

Jeno had a small private room in an apartment, he said with a hint of invitation that Eva chose to ignore. A family with four children lived in the larger room. The bathroom was down the hall, shared by several reconstructed families on this floor.

"I lived in that room growing up. But the others wanted to move in after I lost my family." Pain etched his face briefly, which the young man seemed to will away. "I told them they could stay in the other rooms if they behaved themselves. I'm never going to share a room again." He grinned slyly. "Except perhaps with a girlfriend or wife. I don't want to hear strangers snoring and crying all night." He said he was glad to live next to Anna Nagy, though. "She is a great lady."

Jeno tapped respectfully on the bruised wooden door. A woman's voice called him to enter. Eva followed him into the apartment. It was probably never a grand place, even in its heyday. A faded, green velvety paper hung limply on the walls as if urgently needing to lay down and rest. The floor was covered by the most worn rug she had ever seen. An ancient divan, side table and chair were the only furniture. A pile of faded *Parisi Divat* fashion magazines splayed across the side table. Yet the room was enlivened by the dozen posters that adorned the walls, their pins offering support to the sagging wallpaper. Each announced an OMIKE performance, highlighting the famous Jewish actors, musicians, directors, and playwrights forbidden by law to perform anywhere but in the OMIKE venue at the Goldman Hall, and only to Jewish audiences. She stood spellbound by the faces, the costumes, and the broad range of productions. Literary readings and cabaret competed with operas such as *Carmen, Traviata, La Boheme* and *The Magic Flute*. Classical performances and jazz shared the stage with great Yiddish theater like *Dybbuk* and *Der Golem*.

Eva heard a woman's voice behind her. "That last poster is dated March 22, 1944, but the Germans closed us down three days earlier." The woman went to the wall and touched the poster. "All this beauty, presented by our most acclaimed Jewish performers, came to a dead stop. It is ironic. We were to perform *Moses*, who delivered us from evil."

The woman appeared to be in her fifties. Her beautifully tailored dress and pearl necklace seemed so out of place in the dilapidated apartment. Her long hair swept behind her in an elegant chignon and she wore make up as if she would be leaving for the theater any moment.

"Mrs. Nagy, this is the pianist I told you about," Jeno said.

Eva started to speak but her throat swelled shut. Anna Nagy looked so much like her brother, Professor Sandor. The same inquisitive, sweet smile and knowing eyes that greeted her every time she met the professor for a lesson. Eva wanted to tell her everything at once but was overwhelmed by the tide of emotion that welled up from deep within her. She stood before the woman and sobbed.

"Dear girl, no no." Anna Nagy hurried over and put her arms around Eva. The girl relaxed into the older woman's embrace. She stayed there for a long time, melting into a cocoon of touch she hadn't known for over a year. She came out with blinking eyes to see Anna Nagy's radiant and strong face. Only then did Eva notice that both the woman's hands were twisted, the fingers huddled together protectively like beaten children. Eva pulled away slightly, shocked at the sight. Eva's hands were her connection to music, to moving forward. She felt a stab in her heart at the thought of not being able to use them.

Anna followed the changed expression on Eva's face down to her mangled fingers. "I was the head seamstress at Goldmark Hall, our theater. When we were forced to close in '44, I organized secret house concerts to keep the musicians employed. You know my family is dedicated to the arts, *the Pure Forms*, my brother Aladar would call them." She held up her hands and gazed at them lovingly, but sadly. "We held concerts for several months, until we were betrayed by someone in the organization. I still don't know who. I was taken into the torture house on Andrassy by the Arrow Cross. They thought I would give names in exchange for my hands. I will never sew another costume, but I have a clear conscience. So many of our great artists were taken away from us forever anyway." She nodded at the posters. "Fortunately, some survived."

Eva's entire body tightened. Would Anna Nagy expect that her brother had survived as well? She bowed her head and took a deep breath. "My name is Eva Fleiss. I—"

"Aladar's favorite student! I know exactly who you are." She laughed and went into the small back bedroom, the only other room in the apartment. She kept speaking while she rummaged around, saying that Professor Sandor rarely talked of anything else besides Eva, the one who would keep the Pure Form of music alive. She returned with a framed photo of Professor Sandor and a younger Eva sitting at a piano, smiling from an impossible past. She pulled her to the divan and made Eva sit beside her. Anna smiled broadly and looked at Eva with wide, expectant eyes. "Aladar always said you were like a daughter to him. So tell me, my dearest Eva, what good news do you have of my beloved brother?"

Saying it aloud, telling the only other living person who cared about Professor Sandor caused Eva's heart to break anew. Although they had just met, they clutched each in shared sorrow as if they were family. Eva helped Anna change and get into her bed. She sat with the distraught woman a while, watching her radiance dim and sputter like a candle tired of burning brightly. She promised to return every day and talk with her. Eva and Jeno went down the stairwell and out into the street in silence. Jeno took out a cigarette and offered it to Eva. This time she took it, glad to have something to do as the vast sea of emotion from her visit slowly began its ebb.

Jeno lit both his and Eva's cigarette, cupping his hand so that it casually stroked Eva's cheek. "I think she took it pretty well, considering."

Eva was focused on the lingering feeling of lamb's wool against her cheek. She blinked. Jeno's comment seemed so insensitive. Her eyes flashed. "Considering what?"

"Considering she lost her husband and her daughter in the last year as well. He was a great director. Lily was so beautiful, and what a voice!" He looked into Eva's eyes, studying them with a sincerity he hadn't shown before. "She wasn't much older than you."

That evening Eva sat at the Steinway in the boarding house, plucking absently at the keys. Her heart was too burdened to concentrate on patterns of notes. Several young women from the bordello wandered in and sat around her. The dark-haired woman asked Eva why she was so sad. Eva could not hold back the gush of tears as she told Anna's tale of the crushing of OMIKE and losing her husband and daughter. She explained her relationship to Anna's brother and the mutual loss the women shared over his death. The blond woman put her arms around Eva. Other women surrounded her on the bench and enveloped her in empathy borne of profound understanding. Eva had never known the comfort of a community of women. She felt a longing for what these women had in each other. Even though their bond was through sorrow, it was better than the coldness and isolation of Laszlo. In the odd safety of a brothel, in the company of other survivors, each woman dared to touch her own raw nerve once again. Hands searched out hands, lips found cheeks and foreheads. Whispers soothed whimpers. The tears that splashed on the keyboard combined with the sobs and caresses of the women, creating a symphony of mutual support that lasted until the pink morning light kissed them gently awake.

After a long morning practice on Tuesday, Eva joined Jeno on a visit to the large outdoor food market on Andrassy Street, near a temporary pontoon bridge, the only functioning way to cross the Danube. It was Eva's first foray into Budapest beyond her walk from the train station. She was excited to see more of the city, especially on such a sunny, warm summer day. Many of the buildings along Andrassy were reduced to rubble or had lost their exquisite granite facades to the shelling. Large, shattered wooden frames gave hints of the grand displays of food, clothing, and culture that should have been in the ghostly shops along the boulevard. Eva gasped at the destruction of the beautiful Danube bridges, their ornate metalwork twisted and granite statuary blasted to rubble during the siege.

The bustle of the market dispelled the sadness of the city. The stalls were slapped together from salvaged building materials, shaded by old bedsheets and blankets. Eva had never seen so many different kinds of fruits and vegetables in one place. It was the height of the season for strawberries, cherries, raspberries, and blueberries. Her fingers became stained a rainbow of colors from their overzealous sampling. The riot of hues from the beets, asparagus, broccoli, and carrots announced that farmers beyond the city were producing again. Even the butcher stalls were overflowing with chicken and pork, alongside wild-caught boar, deer, and rabbits. Jeno presumed to do the haggling, but backed off and bowed when Eva stepped in to break an impasse over the price of some meat-stuffed cabbage called *kaposzta*. They laughed and chatted as they carried the groceries up the stairs to Anna's apartment to prepare a surprise meal for her.

Eva was stunned when Anna opened the door, wearing an old housecoat and no make-up. Her hair hung limp and defeated past her shoulders. Jeno quietly took the groceries into the small kitchen and began to prepare their meal. Eva felt awful—she had done this to Anna, even though she had only told her the hard truth. Should she have feigned ignorance? Maybe it was better to wonder forever. Maybe the intensity of knowing was worse than a soft, fading ache over time. Eva didn't know. She had nothing to compare. All the death in her life came abruptly.

Although Anna's condition was a shock, Eva was fortified by the love she had received from the women the night before. She reached out and hugged Anna, wrapping her in the same compassion and comfort the professor's sister had given her on their first meeting. Eva felt drawn to Anna Nagy by more than their shared love for the professor. Anna was elegant and loving, just like Eva's mother. Could the professor's sister be the seed of her new family? She guided Anna to the divan, where they sat together as Jeno quietly left the apartment. Eva tenderly held Anna's crippled hands and glanced at the posters that surrounded them. She spoke softly. "The costumes are so brilliant. Did you make them all?"

Anna's eyes came into focus. She surveyed the posters. "Yes, but that was a long time ago. Making costumes gave me such joy, but now these posters are a graveyard of old friends and fading memories."

Eva searched for something to pierce Anna's sadness. "It must be so difficult to create those designs, cut the pieces and sew them together. If I tried I would probably stitch my fingers to the fabric."

Anna squeezed Eva's hands and smiled. "No, my dear, with those beautiful fingers you would be a wonderful seamstress." She frowned at the bandage on Eva's left hand. "Although you will have to wait for that wound to heal."

"I may need a new profession if I can't get into the Academy. At the very least I could repair my own clothes. Maybe you could teach me the basics." She lifted up the edge of her skirt. "This hem has given way. Can we fix it together?"

Anna brightened a bit. "Hems are easy to repair. I could get my sewing kit out and show you some beginning stitches." A shadow crossed her face. "But I can't thread or work a needle anymore."

Eva bent over and kissed Anna's twisted fingers, her chest warming with emotion. "Please, let my hands be your hands."

CHAPTER 36

A week after first entering the Academy, Eva struggled to practice the professor's piano concerto as she waited for Hedy to enter the room. She was so nervous about Hedy's plan to spirit Eva across the lobby and up the stairs to the director's office that she was unable to concentrate. She could not touch the emotions she had unlocked in the arms of the women at the brothel, or while holding Anna's tortured hands. Eventually, the door cracked open and a familiar bushel of red hair appeared. Two other girls came in with Hedy, carrying cases for violin and clarinet. They shared Hedy's conspiratorial look as one student passed Eva the violin case. Eva gathered her score and letters from the Academy and the girls marched out together. They went down the stairwell and out into the lobby among the other students. The guards paid them no heed until Eva stopped before the large doors leading to the Grand Hall. Between the doors, an elaborate painting of four Muses with lyres seemed to mediate the space between the world of matter and the ethereal plane of pure sound within the hall.

Someone pinched Eva's arm when one of the guards began to approach the group. Hedy smiled sweetly at the guard as the four young women began crossing the lobby again.

"We have an appointment with Director Zathureczky about our quartet."

The guard nodded and returned to his post.

Hedy prodded Eva along. "If you want to see a really wild painting, go up to the first floor. It's all Egyptian and Greek things. It always gives me a chill. And the inside of the Grand Hall looks like a scene from *The Phantom of the Opera*."

The girls hurried to the elegantly winding staircase on the far side of the lobby. Eva was surprised when they stopped and each touched a dark blue crystalline ball that sat atop the newel post at the base of the stairway. Hedy took Eva's hand and put it on the ball.

"It's a tradition here that the ball contains the spirit of music. It's infused with all the great music that's been performed here over the years. We touch it for luck and inspiration."

Eva gazed into the crystal. The deep blue ball gave off a slight hum.

"Especially around exams," another girl chimed in. They laughed and raced up to the third floor, stopping at the ornate oak door of the director's office. Hedy took back the violin case and touched Eva's arm.

"You are on your own. Good luck."

They left Eva alone, staring at the imposing barrier. Her future lay beyond this door. Eva needed to make the strongest case to the director why she should be given an audition. She pushed back the fear at the thought of not attending the Academy. Would she have to wait tables or join Uncle Zoli cleaning the streets? She tapped on the door and waited. When there was no reply, she knocked more firmly. Footsteps approached from the other side and the door opened. A short, rotund woman with frizzy gray hair peered at Eva pleasantly through thick glasses. She squinted continuously.

"Yes? Do you have an appointment?"

Eva knew she had to be bold. "I need to see the director. I was admitted before the deportations but then was told it was withdrawn."

The woman adjusted her glasses. She spoke with great kindness. "And you were never notified that you were reinstated?"

Eva was startled. "Reinstated? No, I was told my application never existed. But I have the acceptance letter right here." She passed the letter to the woman, whose eyes bulged wide behind her glasses as she slowly pronounced Eva's name. She told Eva to come into her office and wait. Eva noticed the nameplate, *Mrs. Irma Rakoczi, Assistant to Director*. The name seemed familiar. It was the name on the letter withdrawing Eva's admission. The woman disappeared into another room behind hers and closed the door. Eva heard voices for a short while before the door opened again. Mrs. Rakoczi came out, followed by the man Uncle Zoli had identified as Ede Zathureczky, the director of the Academy. Eva was awestruck by the tall, distinguished man. His eyes were sharp and his hair was a thick shock of white that crescendoed at his forehead in a pompadour. His imperious demeanor forced Eva to shrink back into herself before she regained her composure. The director invited Eva into his office and closed the door. He motioned her to a leather couch as he sat stiffly behind his large, well-organized desk. Eva handed him the admission and rescission letters.

The director reviewed the letters and sighed. "You were not alone in this, Miss Fleiss. When the Arrow Cross took over, they forced us to deny admission to Jews. We resisted as best we could, but it was a struggle. Several faculty supported the government and made it difficult for us. I am afraid that not all musicians are openhearted and compassionate. A number of our most promising Jewish students and even some faculty were arrested and never returned. There is still a sadness that sits over the Academy from this." He let the words linger. "As soon as the war ended we sent letters to all Jewish students whose offers were withdrawn, I think there were twenty, readmitting you subject to a new audition."

His expression turned apologetic. "We required a new audition because of the time that had elapsed and the difficult circumstances of the admitted Jewish students, yourself included. Frankly, we didn't know who survived and what their physical and mental conditions would be. We must still consider ability along with justice." The director tapped his thumb on his chin pensively, then looked directly at Eva with his piercing dark eyes. "You say you never received the letter of reinstatement?"

"No, sir. I wrote two letters in the last month trying to understand what was happening. I never received a reply, but I did receive this." She gave him the telegram to the mayor stating that the Academy had no record of Eva's application.

The director appeared puzzled as he read the telegram. He reached over to his desk and pressed a buzzer. Mrs. Rakoczi entered the room.

"Mrs. Rakoczi, did we ever receive any letters from Miss Fleiss about attending the Academy?"

Mrs. Rakoczi blinked several times. "Why, no, sir, but you know how disrupted the post has been since the war."

"Did anyone from administration send a telegram to the National Bank or the mayor of Laszlo about Miss Fleiss?" He showed her the telegram. Mrs. Rakoczi read it with twitching, widening eyes.

"No, sir, of course not. Someone must have put the wrong student name on the telegram." She returned it to the director and shook her head. "There's so much confusion in the administration since the siege ended and classes reopened. It's a wonder more mix-ups like this don't happen."

"How many of the rescinded Jewish students have responded to our letters of readmission?"

The assistant scratched her head and adjusted her thick glasses. "Actually, sir, I don't think any of them have, but I'd have to check."

The director tapped his finger on his chair as he considered this. "When no one replied immediately I assumed that with address changes and . . ." he chose the word deliberately, "disappearances, it would take a while and at least a few would respond. But none at all?"

"Only our dear Miss Fleiss, it appears, sir." Mrs. Rakoczi smiled kindly at Eva.

"But she never received the letter. She only came here because she is so tenacious." He looked thoughtfully at Eva, who blushed and put her head down. "Something is not right." The room was silent for a moment until the director spoke again. "In the meantime, we have Miss Fleiss here. She is an admitted student for the fall term, pending the audition. When can we schedule her in?"

Eva controlled her face but fidgeted energetically in her seat. Regardless of all the past struggles and confusion, she had made it happen. She was getting her audition at last.

Mrs. Rakoczi flipped fretfully through her notebook. "Unfortunately, sir, this is the last week of auditions and all the slots are taken. Summer term ends Friday. The judges will be leaving on Friday night after the last audition. Perhaps next year—"

Eva bolted out of her seat. The blood rushed to her face as she shouted. "I can't wait until next year. I held on in Auschwitz because of my music—because I knew I was coming here. I need to honor Professor Sandor and keep the Pure Form alive."

The director stared wide-eyed at Eva. "The Pure Form?"

Eva reached inside the score and produced Professor Sandor's letter to Professor Karady. The director took his time reading and digesting the contents of the letter. He sat back and expelled a long breath. He asked Mrs. Rakoczi to leave the room so that he might have a private word with Eva. "But make sure you schedule her audition. Make it the last one on Friday night, regardless of the time. Tell the judges to be prepared to stay late."

When the door closed behind Mrs. Rakoczi, the director smiled softly at Eva. "Sorry if Mrs. Rakoczi appears a bit flustered. She's a war widow. She only started working with us in June of last year, and we were closed during the three months of the siege. She's quite sweet, but doesn't know our systems well yet."

He turned pensive. "Miss Fleiss, as you must know, Professor Sandor and Professor Karady worked for years on this theory of theirs. I must tell you, it was rather controversial among the faculty; most thought it a foolish enterprise. Between the wars, Gustav Holst wrote an entire symphony on the music of the spheres, *The Planets*, but said it never did more than move his audiences emotionally. Shostakovich and many others tried, as well, with no illuminating breakthroughs. In spite of that, Professor Sandor insisted that more could be attained through music than mere emotionality. Personally, I think it is interesting theory, but I don't believe in it. I trust if you attend the Academy you will focus more on your technique than on Professor Sandor's intellectual exercise." Eva back stiffened but she held the anger she felt at the dismissal of her teacher's work. She quickly told herself his opinion didn't matter. Perhaps he was jealous of the professor's brilliance.

The director must have taken notice of Eva's agitation. His tone softened. "Regardless, Professor Sandor was a towering intellect and a dedicated teacher. It is obvious that he believed in you, that you had the aptitude and inner calling to participate in his work. That honor was reserved for very few students, all of whom achieved great things at the Academy and beyond."

The director's words unlocked a gate deep within Eva's heart. She had an intuitive knowing that something beautiful, something powerful had been washing over her for years through her study with Professor Sandor. Her work on the piano concerto had unfolded her wings of perception, yet until now she thought it simply a special bond, a Jacob's ladder between herself and the professor's spirit. Now she understood, emotionally and intellectually, the honor that he had bestowed upon her by bringing her into his small circle of students, and the loving respect he had possessed in helping her develop her understanding of the Pure Form. Music as a transformative, transcendent force. She would continue under Professor Karady, but dedicate her work to Professor Sandor.

"I was so terribly sorry to hear about Professor Sandor," the director continued. "He dedicated his life to exploring his music theory. Who knows? Perhaps he actually did hold back the deluge, to the extent it was held back." He struggled with a thought. "Regrettably, Professor Karady has left the faculty. He was terribly distressed by his inability to save some of his most talented Jewish students during the war. Several were being trained as you were. To be honest, I think his heart was broken. He was the last faculty member who was part of this special group of theirs."

Eva felt panic rising. She was so close to entering the Academy, but who would guide her? "There is no one else? No professors? No other students?"

The director gave Eva a sympathetic look. "No one. The last two students were studying under Professor Karady. Jusztus Bardos and Arpad Unger. Those poor young men. So dedicated, so much potential. We hid them here through most of the war. They were arrested last autumn as they left my office. I don't know how they were discovered, but that doesn't matter. I am afraid you are the last student to have studied this body of work." He got up and walked to the window. "It is sad about Professor Karady. When his students were taken, he lost all control. He locked himself in one of the practice rooms and played those strange compositions of his for days, calling their names, shouting, pleading for the students to come back. Then he simply walked out the front door and has not entered the Academy since." The director's lips torqued as if reliving Professor Karady's pain. "He seems to be suspended in purgatory. He won't return to the faculty, yet he can't leave the Academy."

Eva did not understand the director's cryptic comment. "I'm sorry, what do you mean?"

The director motioned to the plaza below. "There he is every day, sweeping and keeping the grounds clean as if he is honoring the Academy with his service, yet he won't come in. In my experience, musicians confronted with such deep loss have a choice. They can use their pain to break through to greater levels of understanding, or they can become lost in their grief and never find a way out." He lowered the window blind. "Frankly, like many before him, Professor Karady may have gone mad." He shook his head and turned back to Eva. "But there are many wonderful teachers who can mentor you in classical music here. You are still welcome to attend the Academy since you were admitted last year." He looked doubtfully down at her bandaged hand. "Provided you can pass the audition."

Mrs. Rakoczi smiled at Eva as she left the director's office.

"I'm glad things are working out for you. I am going to find out what happened to your letter. You and all the other Jewish students should get what you deserve." She offered Eva a piece of paper. "Here are the requirements for the audition. Now before you leave I need to update your file. Where are you staying?"

Eva stammered that she was at a boarding house on Erszebet Road, not wanting to say it was part of a bordello and shock the sweet, older woman. "But I spend every afternoon with my aunt who lives at 340 Kazinczy Street in the Jewish quarter. You can reach me there. Her name is Anna Nagy."

Mrs. Rakoczi blinked rapidly and adjusted her glasses again. She quickly wrote down the information. "I'm happy to hear that. It is nice that you have family nearby."

Eva warmed to the secretary's kind words. "Mrs. Nagy's not my real aunt. She's the sister of my piano teacher. But she lives alone and can't use her hands. They were injured during the war. I am very fond of her, so I think of her as my aunt."

Mrs. Rakoczi smiled sadly. "She is lucky you found her. We all lost so much during the war. I know how hard it is to live alone. Perhaps one day I will meet her."

CHAPTER 37

E va left the Academy through the front door, bowling past the surprised guards. Her mind was spinning. Only four days to prepare for the audition. With the director's permission slip she could access the practice rooms every day. Yet even her excitement about the audition was tempered by the void that loomed ahead. How could she manifest the transcendent power of music or reach the professor's Pure Form if she had no mentor? She could be a great technical pianist, but there would always be a piece of her unfulfilled, a sacred duty not performed. She also wondered what had happened to the other Jewish students.

At the far corner of the plaza, the old man was sweeping debris. Eva ran to him. She breathlessly told him about the audition scheduled for Friday night. She told him what she had never revealed to anyone except Ede Zathureczky, about keeping the Pure Form of music alive and how without Professor Sandor no one was left to mentor her. She delivered the letter to him from Professor Sandor, certain that this reaching out from his old friend and colleague would energize the former professor. Uncle Zoli read the letter slowly. The old man shrugged his shoulders wearily several times, his mouth twitching as if he were arguing with himself internally. He passed Professor Sandor's letter back to Eva.

"I am sorry for you, young lady. I understand what it is like to have your dreams shattered suddenly. So many of us lost all hope during the war. You have a good heart. You will heal in time." He turned and continued sweeping. Eva stood there, waiting, hoping for more.

"But you worked with Professor Sandor to keep the tradition alive at the Academy. There is no one else. I need you."

The old man seemed to shrivel inside his long work coat. "The truth is, young lady, music can be emotional, but there is simply nothing to transform or transcend. I don't believe in the Pure Form and the Music of the Spheres theory. They are just an old man's fantasy of hope for a better world. Look around you. There is no better world to be had."

Eva shook with emotion. She clenched her fists to calm herself. A stab of pain coursed through her left hand from the pressure against the fracture. "Uncle Zoli, Professor Sandor once told me that the whole of history was a battle between darkness and light, between people trying to control others and people fighting back. He said sometimes the darkness wins but then the light returns. It is a never-ending struggle."

Zoltan Karady stopped sweeping and stood still, not facing Eva. "Yes, yes, I know. Plato, Pythagoras, the others. It is merely a theory. Some of the greatest composers have tried and failed to hear the planetary harmonies, the great Pure Form, and manifest them through their music. Beethoven, Bach, Mozart, Dvorak. The list goes on. They have moved audiences to tears, but never made the greater connection, transformed people, never held back the darkness. Tchaikovsky believed he heard the harmonies once but could never find them again. He ultimately killed himself. I tell you, it is just a theory."

She stepped around to see his face and pleaded. "I know you have suffered, so have I, so have so many. We have lost our most beloved, our parents, our students, our friends." She saw the pain in his face. "If we don't fight to bring back the light, to restore the balance, the darkness triumphs. You wrote the *Music of the Spheres* manuscript with Professor Sandor. I have played the piano concerto. I have sensed the planets and heard their tones, their harmonies. I have seen the souls hovering above the piano. I believe in the Pure Form. I know its power to balance the world but I can't develop it alone. Please help me."

"You think armies will return to their barracks when you play? Planes will stop bombing cities? Young lady, if the greatest men of the music world have been unable to find the Pure Form and manifest it through the Music of the Spheres, how could an innocent girl do so?"

Eva felt like she had been slapped in the face. "Innocent? I was innocent before Auschwitz, before my father and every Jew in my town was murdered before my eyes! I have seen and experienced the worst horrors imaginable. Tell me, Professor, did any of those great men of music have to survive a death camp?" She turned from the old man and breathed deeply to regain her control. When she had calmed down, she faced him again and spoke softly. "Professor Sandor once told me that deep loss allows for profound understanding. Maybe I hear the harmonies and see the souls because of Auschwitz, because of all that I have lived through."

The old man's shoulders heaved as if he had put down a burden carried far too long. He spoke in a cracked voice without looking at Eva. "Perhaps you are right. I am sorry to have judged you without knowing your experience. I have been lost lately." He disappeared into thought for a moment, then looked at Eva with desperation. "You have seen souls? Tell me, are you certain it wasn't a dream?"

Eva felt a tingle of optimism. "I didn't exactly see them. I felt them as a presence, then I saw these shimmering orbs of light. That was during "Transcendence," the third movement of the piano concerto. It was beautiful."

Zoltan Karady stood still for a long while, seeming to ponder Eva's words. "More of Plato's shadows against a cave wall. I don't believe in the Pure Form anymore." Then, without any acknowledgment to the young woman behind him, he bent over and began to sweep again, pushing away the debris of his spent life along with Eva's fading dream.

Jeno intercepted Eva as she left the Academy plaza. He offered to walk her to Anna's apartment. She was happy to see him, but could not return his wide smile. She was too confused and hurt by the director's attitude and Professor Karady's dismissive lack of interest.

"No, not now. I need to get this morning out of my mind before seeing Mrs. Nagy. I don't want to carry my burdens into her life."

Jeno gave her a sympathetic pout that broadened into his electric smile. His eyes danced mischievously. "Then let me take you someplace fun for a change. It will take your mind off your worries. Afterward, we can visit Mrs. Nagy."

"Seriously, Jeno. My heart is too heavy to do anything fun."

"That's the perfect time." He put out his hand. "Just trust me. Please." Eva hesitated for a moment. He knew how to break down her resistance. She tentatively reached out and took Jeno's hand, enjoying its warmth. It made her feel that they had a real friendship.

They entered the ghetto and became lost in the side streets. Soon they came to a bombed-out building. Jeno started to enter.

Eva was hesitant. "Where are we going?"

"To a party that never ends."

As they clambered deeper into the building, Eva could hear voices and a hint of music. They dropped to the basement level and entered a large, cement-walled room full of colored lights and young people. Eva had never been with so many people her age before. They were dancing to records, drinking, laughing, sharing whispered secrets. Jeno called it a "ruin bar." He told Eva that most of the young people here had lost their families. They came often because they needed the joy of living to balance the hollow ache of mourning. Eva understood immediately. Budapest was so unlike Laszlo. Here, she could be with others who understood her pain and loneliness, whose worlds had similarly collapsed. The women at the boarding house, the sellers at the market, Anna, even Jeno. She didn't need to explain anything. They all just *knew*.

Jeno took her arm and guided her to the bar, ordering a small bottle of cherry *palinke*. He offered it to Eva, who declined. He feigned indignation. "I will forgive you because you are so young, but refusing to share *palinke* is an insult to our great country." Jeno shrugged and took a gulp, then turned to Eva with a sloppy grin. "I am celebrating tonight."

"Why? Did you barter for an automobile?"

"No, even better. I bartered for a future." Jeno told her how he had traded a bottle of premium Russian wheat vodka for the name and address of a man in New York who was helping Hungarian Jews emigrate to America. "I am to say that he is my uncle on my mother's side. That makes the family name harder to trace. He will vouch for me. The World Jewish Congress will make the arrangements." He glanced around at the bombed-out building. "If it all works out, I will leave this place and start fresh in America."

In Laszlo, Eva briefly imagined going to America like thousands of other surviving Hungarian Jews. But here at the ruin bar, surrounded by life and possibilities, the idea felt more tangible. Maybe it would be good to go to a city unscarred by war, without so many ghosts and memories. She swam for a moment in the pictures of New York she had seen in *Kepes Kronica*, then let the images evaporate. No, she had to finish her training and honor the professor's work. Besides, America was full of gangsters, cowboys, and hustlers like Jeno. Eva preferred to be surrounded by the musical heritage and culture of Hungary, even if, as a Jew, she had a fraught relationship with it.

She also thought of Anna, her last living link with the professor. No, Anna was more than that, it was as if Eva's mother had reached out and blessed Anna to care for her daughter. And what about all of the people in the ghetto with whom Eva felt a kinship of experience and maybe even some kind of . . . shared *Jewishness*? Jeno looked at the ghetto and only saw broken people and chaos. Eva saw wounded, resilient people. A community seeking renewal. If only she could be a part of it. That would be better than New York. The gentle touch of a hand on her shoulder chased away her thoughts. Jeno smiled sweetly at her.

"Shall we dance? You have to help me celebrate."

Eva hesitated. She knew ballroom dances but this was some sort of folk dance. She had seen it but never danced it. The music was fast and the steps undecipherable.

"It's the *czardas*, our national dance. Aren't you patriotic? We are all Hungarians again. Come on, let me show you."

Jeno took Eva's hand and led her onto the dance floor. He stood next to her through a line dance, then a circle dance, and soon Eva was kicking and stepping along with the other young people. The music shifted from time to time, settling on a fast, spinning couples dance that Jeno called "the courting dance" with a mischievous smile. He put his hands on Eva's hips and directed her hands to his shoulders.

"You must keep looking at my eyes the whole dance. Don't think about your feet, they will follow. And don't worry about anybody else. They don't care how badly you dance."

They swept around the floor, laughing and whooping when the others did. She never got the steps right, but like Jeno said, it didn't seem to matter. Eva was light-headed from the whirling, the prolonged physical contact, and the scent of Jeno's aftershave and sweat.

When the dance ended they went back to the bar. "I think I'm ready for that *palinke* now," Eva said as she allowed her breathing to calm. Jeno laughed and ordered another bottle. He reached into his pocket and pulled out something wrapped in a handkerchief.

"Here, I have a present for you."

Eva unfolded the cloth and found a man's gold wristwatch inside. She looked at it with curiosity. "It's very kind of you, but it's not my style."

Jeno chuckled and shook his head. "It's not for you to wear. It's to have if you run into any Russian soldiers. They love wristwatches." His face became grim. "It may save your life."

"Did you steal it?"

Jeno looked offended. "No, I traded a small Cossack dagger for it."

Eva raised an eyebrow. "And how did you get the dagger?" When Jeno put both hands in his pockets and looked down, Eva handed him the watch. "Here, I don't want the fruit of a poisonous tree. I am trying to bring beauty to the world, not add to the misery."

Jeno scoffed. "That's foolish. A little theft and a lot of barter makes the world go around. Soon all the *pengos* will be worthless. The paper will be good for nothing but starting fires." His tone turned hurtful. "Even at your dear Academy, students pay fees with sugar, beets, or whatever food they can find sometimes." He laughed. "But what would a young musician from the countryside know of such things?" He took a long swig from the *palinke* bottle.

The barb pierced Eva. She looked down at her injured hand. "Music has its own value."

"Ha! It's not food or fuel. You can't eat it or heat your home with it. It disappears as soon as you are done with it. What real value does it have?"

Eva's eyes flashed. How could anybody challenge the value of music? "Music gives us hope. It helps us aspire to be better people, to touch our deeper emotions so we can become more humane and compassionate to others." She waited for a response from Jeno, but the young man just blinked at her without comprehension. She realized her description was too abstract for a practical young man like Jeno. Music was everything to Eva, nothing to Jeno. But she didn't want to lose his friendship, he was a wonderful companion and her only male friend in Budapest. They still had possibilities. She softened her tone. "Music is food and fuel to me. It fed my soul and kept me alive in Auschwitz. It warmed my spirit during the frozen winter when there was no other source of comfort. And now the

Academy is my only hope for shelter tomorrow. I have nothing else. If I fail the audition, I am totally lost."

Jeno looked deep into Eva's eyes. "You are beautiful, Eva. But I don't understand anything you're saying, except about touching emotions." He leaned over to kiss her. She turned her head and frowned. He laughed. "Didn't you learn anything from the war, Eva? We are all Lost Children now, like Peter Pan and Wendy. There is no guarantee there will be a tomorrow. Let's have fun now."

"No, I don't want to." She pushed his hand off her shoulder. She had waited so long for her first real kiss, one where she freely and joyfully leapt at the embrace. Jeno's cloddish attempt at romance wasn't it. "Leave me alone." She turned to leave the bar. Jeno grabbed for her arm, sincere alarm on his face.

"Eva, please, it's dangerous to walk alone at this time. Let me go with you to Anna Nagy."

"No."

"Please. I am sorry. I truly am."

Eva saw the repentant look on Jeno's face. She thought how boys her age weren't as mature as girls. They were like bread in the oven. They looked finished on the outside, but when you poke a fork in them you realize they are not done baking. Unlike Andras, however, Jeno was sensitive to Eva's feelings, even if clumsy about it. She relented. They walked out of the ruin bar and into the bright afternoon sunlight. Even though the square was filled with the usual sounds of children, hawkers, and gossipers, Eva and Jeno walked to the apartment in silence.

Jeno left Eva at Anna's building, saying he had an errand to run. She was happy to see Anna Nagy dressed and made up when she entered the apartment. Anna appeared to have regained that ebullient spirit she exuded when they first met. The woman walked into the bedroom and returned with a tattered costume sketchbook and a file of musical scores. She placed them on the side table next to the divan.

"I was only able to save the scores from the house concerts, everything else was destroyed when the Arrow Cross ransacked the theater." She looked back at one of the posters, smiling longingly at an old friend. "I want you to take them. Maybe there is something useful for you." Anna flipped through the sheets of music as Eva looked over her shoulder. She pulled out a few pages. "This one, Ravel's "Kaddish," was important to us. We ended each house concert with this. It brought some comfort as we honored the musicians who had disappeared since the prior performance."

Eva picked up the score. Someone had written the words to the Kaddish prayer under the music. She was grateful to have it. She could learn the prayer at last, and express it through her playing.

Anna invited Eva to look through the sketchbook as she commented on the plays and performances, the actors and musicians for whom she had created such intricate, amazing costumes. The technical details of the outfits mixed seamlessly with the theater's history and gossip. Anna's eyes sparkled and her hands gesticulated sewing and cutting and expressive movements particular to famous actors. Eva felt she was backstage with Anna watching the bustle of performers coming on and off, removing vests and wigs for costume changes. Music always played in the background.

Anna leaned back and sighed. "Then the Germans closed our theater and we went underground. We lived a tentative but almost normal life until the Arrow Cross swept into power and unleashed their fury. Who were they? Our neighbors, factory workers, intellectuals, even fellow artists, united by a twisted ideology that considered Jews less than human. They were just a minor party, a fading collection of hooligans and malcontents, until the Germans lifted them from the dung heap and installed them as our government. Toward the end, they took away the hosts of the house concerts and many of our performers. I don't know how the Arrow Cross found them. Most were hiding in attics and basements. But the thugs charged into the ghetto and rounded them up, as well as anybody unlucky enough to be nearby. They shot twenty thousand Jews in the streets in a matter of weeks. So many bodies rudely dumped into our beautiful Danube. I can't look at the river anymore without seeing them drifting by." Eva thought about the photo of her family with the Danube behind them. Could she ever see the photo the same way again?

Anna seemed to reach out into another world. "Oh, Lily, my beautiful girl." She stayed in that ethereal realm for a long time, seeing her daughter through tightly closed eyes.

Eva felt a well of nausea. She took Anna's hands while the older woman lingered in her daze. Finally, Anna came back, sighed, and looked lovingly at Eva.

"I'm sorry, Eva. I was so lost in my own grief, I forgot how much you must have suffered, too." She stroked Eva's hair, lingering at the ringlets that were starting to emerge at the tips. "Please tell me your story. Do you have family back in Laszlo?"

Eva began to shake. She thought she had accepted her parents' death, but another psychic wall collapsed. As she tried to describe losing her mother, then her father as well as every Jew she knew in Laszlo, she wept openly. She fell into Anna's arms again.

They hugged and rocked back and forth until the light disappeared from the window. Afterward, Anna led Eva to a nightstand that supported a pitcher of water and a large ceramic bowl. "Put your hands over the bowl, my darling." Anna poured water over Eva's hands with difficulty. "My husband and I shared this ritual every week after *Kiddush*, the blessing of the wine during *Shabbos*. We intentionally wash away the cares of the week. I know it's only Monday, but this seems appropriate tonight." She poured the water three times as Eva envisioned her parents, the professor, the women at the brothel, and Professor Karady.

Let it all go, Eva thought, *just for one night*.

Eva in turn poured for Anna, who spoke aloud the names of her husband and daughter, and several people Eva assumed were from her theater work. Her crippled hands relaxed into the flow of the warm water. Then Anna asked Eva to open the window. The older woman managed to hurl the water out, reciting a prayer in Hebrew.

"*Tashlich al Ha Shem yeh halcha*. Cast off to God your burdens."

They returned to the divan and sat together. Anna told more stories of OMIKE as she reflected on the posters on her walls, bringing the theater to life once again. Eva asked Anna if they could visit the Goldmark. Anna frowned.

"The building is just a shell. All of the furniture, sets, everything was broken up by the Arrow Cross. It would be too painful to see."

Eva persisted gently. "But the war is over. Maybe there is a chance to rebuild. We could go there and dream together." *Dream together.* This was the first time since returning from the camp that she had expressed a hope, a dream bigger than playing the piano.

Anna stared at Eva for a moment, then smiled. "I can certainly see Aladar's influence on you. 'Focus and willpower,' that's what he always said, wasn't it? Our parents said that was the secret to our resilience, the key to Jewish survival during all these millennia of struggle." She looked up to the posters. "In the arts we know it is necessary to harness the pain of our lived experience to excel." Anna seemed to wrestle with a thought. "Perhaps it would be good to visit the Goldmark."

Later, Eva answered the knock on the Anna's door. Jeno entered the apartment with a large pot of beef and potatoes in a thick broth. The tang of paprika filled the apartment.

"Compliments of the Russians."

Jeno went to the cupboard and took out three bowls. As they began to eat, Anna puckered her mouth.

"Jeno, this is not beef. It's horsemeat."

The young man took a bite of the meat. His face soured and his ears turned red. Eva put down her spoon, frowned, and raised an eyebrow at him.

"I hope you didn't trade anything valuable for this. You can barely eat it and you certainly can't heat your home with it." She smirked triumphantly. "I prefer music."

Anna spoke in a consoling voice. "Let us hope it had good grass for grazing."

They continued the meal in bemused silence. Jeno kept glancing at Eva with an apologetic expression. She let him stew in anticipation before she grudgingly gave him a smile.

Eva talked about the audition. She had passed it before and had been practicing hard, but the stitches in her left hand were still weeping and a slight infection had set in. It hurt to play. Without any professors to help her prepare she didn't know if she could be ready in time. Anna asked Jeno to retrieve some tincture of iodine from the bathroom. She removed the bandage and squeezed the infection from the wound with the palms of her twisted hands as Jeno poured iodine on the stitches. Eva tightened her shoulders and squeezed her eyes shut at the stinging, but relaxed as Jeno wrapped a small cloth bandage around her hand. His gentleness was such a contrast to his rough worldview.

The small, round teapot Anna had placed on her coal brazier began to whistle. Its shape reminded Eva of the stout little woman with the thick glasses and frizzy hair who worked for the director. She related how the poor woman was so flustered about Eva's missing file and why none of the Jewish students had replied to their readmission letters. Anna moved the kettle to the counter and cocked her head at Eva.

"Did she constantly twitch her eyes?"

"Yes," said Eva in surprise.

"Do you know when she started at the Academy?"

"I think the director said around June, just after we were taken away."

"What did you say her name was?"

"Rakoczi, Mrs. Irma Rakoczi."

"It's very odd. A woman named Irma Kovacs volunteered with us organizing the underground concerts. She had a unique appearance, just as you described. She disappeared during one of the round ups. In May, I think."

Eva thought Anna would be happy that an old coworker survived, but Anna looked troubled. "What's wrong?"

"It's curious that Irma disappeared as our members were rounded up, then this other Irma appeared at the Academy when they started losing students and faculty. And then your files and letters get lost."

Eva recalled the many times she had heard about former Arrow Cross members hiding in plain sight by simply changing their clothes. Could Mrs. Rakoczi have been an Arrow Cross informant? "Do you think she's the same woman? She seemed so sweet."

"I don't know. It's just a queer feeling." She let the frown fade. "Let's change the subject. What are you going to wear to the audition?"

Eva was startled, but glad to move away from Anna's painful memories. "I hadn't thought about it. I have some dresses from high school. I guess one of them will have to do."

Anna pursed her lips and gave Eva a motherly scowl. "First impressions are everything in performance, young lady. You need to exhibit your professionalism and commitment through your presentation as well as through your music." Eva looked downcast, she didn't want to spend her money on dresses, but Anna was right. Anna told her to follow her into the bedroom. She pulled an old leather-covered trunk from under her bed and instructed Eva to open it. Bright fabrics and lace shone out. Anna rummaged through the material and held up a beautiful, sky-blue gown. Eva gasped. It was the same heavenly color as the dress her mother had made for her high school graduation concert. The one she wore in so many of her vivid dreams.

"I made this for my Lily. She was supposed to wear it in Handel's 'Judah Maccabee' one year ago. She was to play the role performed by Vera Rozsa. Such an honor." Anna stared off, eyes misted, watching her daughter and friends under the bright lights on the Goldmark stage. "It wasn't to be. The Germans had ordered us to perform their version of the opera. Instead of a small band of Jews resisting a large enemy, it became a propaganda piece to German strength and that beast Hitler. I don't know how they found out we were going to perform the original, but they stormed the theater just before the curtain went up. Lily never had the chance to wear the dress."

Eva ran her hands over the gown. "It's the most beautiful gown I have ever seen." She clenched her jaw to hold back tears. "I will be honored to wear it."

Anna held it up against Eva's shoulders and gazed at her as if she was seeing another young woman. She blinked back the vision and cleared her throat. "Of course, it will need to be taken in at the waist. Perhaps a few darts around the bust."

Eva's arms encircled the gown and Anna, hugging them both tightly. "Please let me help you."

CHAPTER 38

Eva entered the Academy on Tuesday morning with her pass from the director, no longer having to hide. She tried hard to push from her consciousness the pain of Professor Karady sweeping in the plaza and ignoring her entreaties. The guards greeted her politely as she passed through the lobby. The memory of a beautiful painting on the floor above drew her up the staircase to the first floor. She wandered between the red and brown speckled porphyry columns topped with gold friezes that populated the foyer like a well-tended orchard.

A large fresco of nymphs kneeling at a pool of water flowing from a marble font claimed the wall between the entrance doors to the Grand Hall. It looked like an illustration from one of the mythology books her father had read to her at bedtime. She heard the gurgle of water as the laughing nymphs called her to join them. A dozen women and a few bearded men stood nearby, dressed in medieval, hooded garb. Above, sky-robed angels with trumpets and lyres perched on blue clouds serenading Apollo, the Greek god of music and light. Eva noticed that the ethereal blue was the same color as the dresses her mother and Anna had made. An inscription surrounded the painting:

Those who are looking for Life, come to the fountain of Art

Eva desperately wanted to join the nymphs by the pool and, adorned in a blue gown, ascend to Apollo's realm of pure music and light.

She detected a full orchestra's untamed warm-up. She had not heard that harsh, discordant mixture of sounds since Auschwitz. Back then, the violins cried as if in pain for lack of good strings and with broken hearts. Here, they sounded of infinite possibilities. Eva followed the sounds through the doors and into the Grand Hall. The concert hall soared three stories in the splendor of gold-adorned classical imagery. She gaped at swans holding wreaths of gold and lyres in tribute to this temple of music. Laurel trees set their dark roots on the ground, grew up the sidewalls, and covered the vault with golden foliage. Towering temple maidens supported the corners of the hall, while cherubs played instruments in the clouds atop it all. Thousands of pipes from an immense organ shot skyward at the far end of the Grand Hall. Beyond the chandeliers, six stained-glass light fixtures were embedded in the ceiling. Eva strained to read the one word etched in each. *Melody. Fantasy. Rhythm. Poetry. Beauty. Harmony*. She sat in the cushioned seats to catch her breath. She felt as if she had transcended the boundary between the profane and the sacred. She did not want to return.

"Excuse me! You're not allowed in here!"

Eva whipped her head around to see a glaring guard. She apologized red-faced and scurried out. Her practice that morning was inspired, full of heart and longing. The stiches pulsed and pulled, causing sharp pain whenever Eva extended her left hand. Yet Eva had overcome so much to be here at the Academy at last, she was not going to allow the pain in her hand to interfere with her performance. Professor Sandor's voice whispered in her ear. *Play this part soft and slow like a classical guitar. Light arms and fingers, soft touch.* She went through each of the pieces on the audition list. They ranged in difficulty, but Eva was familiar with all of them. She didn't have time or energy to practice the *Piano Concerto for the Music of the Spheres*. The piece was irrelevant for the audition. She would have to wait until she attended the Academy to immerse herself in its odd yet compelling sound.

As Eva climbed the stairs to Anna's apartment, she wondered how last evening's talk of Lily and the theater had affected the older woman. Would she be sad, reliving the loss of her beloved, talented daughter and the world of Jewish theater she had worked so hard to protect? Eva tapped gently on the door. It opened quickly, revealing Anna in a long beige dress with a low waistline and sequined shoulders. Anna beamed at the surprise on Eva's face.

"Let's get out of the apartment and go for a walk," she said. "I wish to visit Goldmark Hall."

Eva's eyebrows furrowed in concern. "Are you certain? You told me it was pretty torn up after it was closed. It must be full of sad memories for you. Maybe we should wait a while."

Anna waved dismissively. "Nonsense. I don't have time in my life to avoid the light for fear of shadows. It is time to live again."

Anna and Eva linked arms as they walked the five long blocks down Wesselenyi Street from Anna's apartment to Goldmark Hall. Anna wore a jaunty pillbox hat with a half face veil. Eva felt like she was accompanying a cinema star. Wesselenyi Street did not show the same level of destruction as Kiraly Street. Food vendors, furniture stalls and a sizable afternoon crowd enjoyed the bright summer sun along the street. People passed and greeted Anna, who in turn gave Eva some background or shared a little gossip. Several people asked if Eva was Anna's daughter. At first both Eva and Anna looked awkwardly at each other as Anna said no, but after a while Anna responded positively, saying Eva was her new daughter. Anna's remark was always received with a smile and a knowing nod. Like Jeno had said, families were being recreated in the Budapest ghetto.

Anna stopped and gazed sadly at the remains of a grand house. She hummed a quiet melody. Eva recognized the address carved in the mantle above the crumbling door frame—36. The address on the professor's unmailed letter to his sister. Eva asked if this had been her house before the war. Anna slowly nodded.

"It was a beautiful house, always full of light and life. So many parties, so many people. But we were evicted and forced to move into a Yellow Star house by the train station." Eva looked at her quizzically. "Those were houses where Jews were forced to live together as the government rounded us up and took our homes. A Yellow Star was posted on the front of those houses." Anna shuddered, then looked up at her ruined home. "We were out of our house three months when an artillery shell hit. All the Christian families who had moved in were killed. When the Germans invaded we were jammed into the ghetto and the wall constructed. Fortunately, Goldmark Hall and the Dohany Synagogue next to it were within the ghetto walls. That helped us keep the culture and the spirit of our people alive." They walked in silence for a block until they came to the shell of an old brick building. Anna held Eva tightly, taking long breaths through her clenched jaw.

"I thought somehow there would be more left. I wanted to show you the two small dressing rooms, the old stage, the scrims that flew the painted scenery in and out. But it is all gone."

Eva's chest tightened. Anna's entire world had disappeared, from people to institutions, even to the buildings. Eva was young, she had a house in Laszlo, time to rebuild and create new dreams. Poor Anna had nothing. As she wondered what to say to Anna, the older woman heaved a sigh and spoke up in a firm voice.

"Well, my dear, it looks like we have a lot of work to do."

Eva was shocked. How could Anna rebuild this bombed-out wreck of a building? Anna must have noticed her demeanor. She smiled.

"I don't mean rebuilding Goldmark Hall. That will take years and more money than God has. I mean rebuild OMIKE, rebuild the Jewish theater again. Anna's eyes shone at Eva. "Of course, it is too much for me to manage alone, but if you were here with me, we could accomplish so much together." She took Eva's hand in both of hers. "And I want you to open at the first performance."

Eva began to tear up. Anna was offering her the honor of helping resurrect the Jewish musical heritage of Hungary. She would play for the professor and all of the lost musicians and actors of OMIKE. Perhaps she would perform *Piano Concerto for the Music of the Spheres*. It would give her the chance to do something for the Jewish community which had made her feel so welcome.

They both turned at the sound of music in the street. A block away, three musicians playing an accordion, a violin, and a clarinet were entertaining a small crowd. Anna began to smile and hum. "That is an old Yiddish tune, *Di Mezinke Oysgegebn*, it means 'My Youngest Daughter is Getting Married.'" The crowd clapped along with the quick tempo and laughed at the singer's Yiddish lyrics.

> *Hekher, beser! Di rod di rod macht geser*
> *Groys hot mich G't gemachto, glik hot er mir gebracht*
> *Hulyet kinder a gantse nacht*
> *Di mezinke oysgegebn!*

> *Higher, better! The circle is getting bigger*
> *God has made me great, He has brought me happiness*
> *Rejoice, children, all night long*
> *My youngest daughter is getting married!*

As they returned to Anna's apartment, they could hear the band playing "Rivkele," a Yiddish tango. They looked back to see couples performing the elegant, slow movements in the street. Anna sighed, "Jews and hope."

Eva asked Anna gently. "Are you very religious?"

Anna shook her head. "Not really. Our parents were observant, but neither Aladar nor I continued the formal practices. But I am profoundly committed to our Jewish culture and ethics. I believe in doing *mitzvah*, conscious acts of empathy, *tikkun olam*, healing the world, and *tsedakah*, giving back to the community. It is living these values and my feeling of connection to who we are as a people that have kept me going through all of this. Always remember, Eva, we are a resilient people. We draw our strength from a very deep well. And of course," she said with a twinkle, "we all need a good sense of humor."

That evening, after sharing a meal with Anna and fitting the gown, Eva and Jeno went out on the balcony. Jeno lit a Gauloise. He asked Eva why she was so quiet.

"Did Anna seem preoccupied tonight?" she asked, taking a drag of Jeno's French cigarette.

"A little, I guess. Why?"

"Her face changed when I talked about the Academy. She's probably troubled about that woman, Mrs. Rakoczi. I'm sure she thinks Rakoczi and Kovacs are the same person. Maybe it's no coincidence she worked with Anna when the performers were targeted, then started working at the Academy when their students and staff began to disappear."

Jeno shrugged. "Maybe, but lots of people disappeared. I was around the whole time, too. You don't think I had anything to do with it, do you?"

She punched his arm. "Don't be so clever—or so thick. Then there's this business with the new Jewish students. Not a single one replied. Mrs. Rakoczi was supposed to send the letters. Mine never went out. I wonder if any of them did."

"It's all pretty circumstantial, don't you think?" Jeno yawned and stretched his arms.

Eva continued, undeterred by Jeno's apparent lack of interest. "I also asked the librarian today if I could send a telegram from the

Academy. She told me that all telegrams come through the director's office and that Mrs. Rakoczi was in charge of all correspondence. She must have been the one who sent the telegram to the mayor saying they couldn't find my file. You know how people say the Arrow Cross disappeared, but remain in plain sight? Maybe Mrs. Kovacs changed her name before she was caught and kept informing on Jews once she was safely at the Academy. She seemed so nice to me, but now I just don't know." She looked at Jeno. He prided himself on being a hustler and a man who could do anything. "Do you think you could check her out, maybe follow her after work?"

Jeno looked dubious. "I don't know. What will you give me?"

Eva's eyes flared. She couldn't believe his selfishness. "Why is everything a transaction with you?"

Jeno's face registered the sting of her words. "I was only joking. I thought maybe I could get a kiss."

So Jeno wants to barter with me. Time to teach him a lesson. Eva leaned her head back and raised an eyebrow. "You're a fearless man," she taunted him playfully. "And if you are going to be an American, you must be brash, like Humphrey Bogart, and suave, like Robert Taylor. If you want a kiss, why don't you simply ask for one?" She enjoyed having the upper hand for once.

Jeno swallowed hard. He moved closer. "Eva, may I have a kiss?" The warm, humid air shimmered off the wrought iron balcony.

"Yes," she breathed. Closer. Eva looked deeply into his eyes and smiled. Then she put her hand firmly on his chest. "After you find out something about Mrs. Rakoczi."

"Dante Sonata," the Liszt piece she had chosen, was particularly difficult Wednesday morning. The pain in her hand and the sinking feeling that she simply was not proficient enough to pass the audition pummeled Eva's confidence. She decided to play very slowly to ensure she hit every note. She performed mechanically, more concerned with her technical proficiency than her artistry for the moment. Speed and finesse would come later. She heard the door squeak open. Hedy usually stopped in to say hello and comment on her playing. As much as Eva enjoyed Hedy's visits, she didn't want casual chatter this morning. She ignored the sound.

"Ferenc Liszt used to say 'Technique should create itself from spirit, not from mechanics.' You need to be a bad artist, not a good student. Slow practice doesn't help. Do it again, faster."

She looked up in surprise. Zoltan Karady towered in the doorway. He wore a dark suit instead of his workman's coverall and coat. His beard was trimmed, although his long gray hair remained wild. He held up a finger to silence Eva before she could respond.

"Do not think I am here because of my work with Professor Sandor. I am only here to help you prepare for the audition. From what I just heard, you need my help." He briskly approached the piano and sat next to Eva. "Your crescendo wave destroys the tension of the piece. Instead of crescendo, use an extra accent on the last note. Like this." His fingers efficiently demonstrated. Without explanation or niceties, the professor launched into a running critique of Eva's playing. He forced her to repeat sections over and over.

"A little better already, but still lazy . . ."

"No. This is like touching fire. Short fast touch . . ."

"F—A—B—A. See? Like this . . ."

"Why so soft? This is how Liszt did it . . ."

Eva put what she could into the practice. She was touched by Karady's presence and wondered if her outburst in the plaza had helped him break through his own pain to come back to the Academy, even for a day. However, he was a harsh teacher, very unlike Professor Sandor. It made her self-conscious, which undermined her passionate connection to the keyboard.

Karady stared intently at Eva. "Why are you holding back? I know what you have gone through. Use your experience to reach deep into your core. Use the emotion."

It was one thing for Eva to use her music to soothe others, but she couldn't consciously use it to plumb her own emotions, to try and soothe herself. The memories were like solid walls of stone. Immovable. Impenetrable. "I can't go back there. I have tried so hard to get past the images and feelings. It is too painful."

"Until you do and use the energy of the experience to propel yourself forward, you will never reach your potential. Now, follow Liszt and Dante into hell or don't do this piece. Again!"

Eva could barely catch her breath for the next two hours. She ended the session physically and emotionally drained. Her head and heart hurt from pushing back the images of her parents, the professor, and the non-stop rush of dark memories that Liszt's exploration of hell forced into her consciousness. But Karady never gave her the time to process any of it.

"You are technically proficient, but Budapest is full of waiters and fruit sellers who are better. Control your power. Channel your passion." He slammed his fingers down on a final chord. "Good." He turned to Eva, the struggle for words creasing his face. Eva looked at him questioningly. "Eva, I must admit that when you were playing so fiercely I felt the heat of Dante's Hades. I could hear the screams of souls in hell." Eva's eyes widened. "But don't misunderstand me. These are common reactions to music performed well. Your music evokes mood and emotion. That is good, but that is all—the awareness and connection of the first and second movements in the piano concerto, "Sentience" and "Communion." I don't know of anyone who has taken the Music of the Spheres beyond this level. Do not confuse this with manifesting the supposed planetary harmonies. I still do not think that can happen." He let his face relax, gave Eva a kindly nod and strode out of the room.

Eva sat motionless at the piano. Professor Karady's help was important for her audition, but he couldn't mentor her if he didn't think there was more to the music than mere emotion. Why did he stop believing in his work with Professor Sandor? A student knocked on the door and said it was his time to practice. Eva went out into the hallway and dropped to the floor. Holding her throbbing hand, she let go of her confusion about Professor Karady and sank into the muted sounds of a dozen instruments seeking harmony.

CHAPTER 39

The station master began to perspire as the crowd gathered late Wednesday morning, growing in size and intensity. The police were there as well, fanned out down the platform between the crowd and the tracks. As the train carrying the Romanian Jews rolled in, a collective growl rumbled through the station. Fiery shouts of "No more Jews!" and "No plague!" and "Jews won't replace us!" were hurled toward the train like Molotov cocktails. The conductor leaped from the cab and rushed to the station master.

"There are ten Jews on this train who have to get off in Laszlo. They have passes from the WJC to stay here at the Armin Hotel for a week until the processing center in Budapest isn't so backed up." He glanced nervously at the people massed on the platform, and thrust the clipboard at the station master. "Sign here, Josef. I want to get them off the train and be on my way. This crowd looks ugly."

Captain Szabo reached over and grabbed the clipboard. A tremor of nervousness surfaced in his voice. "I've heard this train may be carrying plague. Is that true?"

The conductor gave an apologetic look. "These are Romanian Jews, Captain. They look worse than the Jews who came back to Laszlo. I guess some of them could be sick." He shrugged his shoulders. "I don't know. I don't have that kind of information."

"We can't allow disease to spread into our community. Passes or no passes, they stay on the train. It's a matter of public health.

Be on your way." Captain Szabo handed the clipboard back to the conductor. He turned to see a man in rags leap from the last car and bolt toward the woods. "Ritook! Miklos! Get that man back here!"

Ritook ran toward the end of the train, but was hampered by the crowd. "Miklos, grab him! Shoot him if he resists!"

Corporal Miklos sprinted into the woods. He caught a glimpse of the man between trees. The policeman was young and strong. He easily caught up to the man as he lay on the ground, panting and holding his side. He flinched at the man's skeletal, feral appearance. The war was long over, why would anyone look like this now? His mind struggled between letting him run deeper into the woods and following the captain's orders. "You have to come back to the train. You can't stay here."

The man cast wild, pleading eyes at Miklos. "Please, don't send me back. They took everything. Our food, our money, even our clothes. They beat us every day."

"Who did? The Germans?"

"No, not in the camps. When we got home. Our neighbors. They took everything. They forced us to live like animals on the streets, naked, eating garbage. Then they called us dirty Jews." He looked down at his rags and cried. "I was an accountant. An honest man. I survived the camps. Now look at me."

Miklos took his hand off his holstered pistol. He sat on his haunches next to the quaking, desperate man. His mind filled with visions of old Hassidic men and women, begging for their lives at his feet in Kosveg, while children stood by, holding their grandparents tight and blinking with incomprehension. He saw them lined up three across at the brick factory with police pistols placed at the base of their necks. SS officers adjusted the angles of the policemen's guns to ensure accuracy and not waste a second bullet.

He held out his hand and spoke softly. "Come back with me to the train. You will be safe in Budapest." *Probably safer than here*, he thought. He helped the defeated figure to his feet and they walked together back to the last car. Miklos had to shield the man from the stones and hurtful taunts of the crowd. Although he recognized many of the townspeople, looking at their faces contorted by rampant hatred he realized he didn't know them at all.

Sergeant Ritook slapped the man forcefully on the back of the head as they passed and pushed him into the car. "We have enough Jews in Laszlo." He turned to Miklos with an appraising grin. "I'm surprised at you. I thought you'd let him go. Impressive. You're starting to act like a policeman." He looked into the train window at the man as the train began to roll past. "Personally, I would have shot him."

Miklos stared hard at the sergeant. Was Ritook merely taunting him, or would he have shot that harmless, unarmed man like he had so many in the brick factory? Miklos clenched his jaw and his fists. "They don't all have to die, do they, Ritook?"

Yossel looked up from preparing dinner to see Mendel and Herschel enter the hotel lobby. "It's only Thursday, *Shabbos* isn't until tomorrow night. What are you doing here?" He noticed the bloody bandage on Herschel's head. "Herschel! What happened to you?"

The large man stared sadly at Yossel and put his head down. "They shot Zsuzsa."

Mendel patted him on the shoulder and cast a distraught look at Yossel. "The other farmhands wouldn't give us back our mother's quilt and some other things they stole from us while we were in the camp. We filed those papers you helped us fill out with the town clerk, but he said it would take a long time to process. Karosi's son said that Zsuzsa belonged to him because Herschel had abandoned her."

"I never 'bandoned Zsuzsa," Herschel mumbled miserably.

"So Herschel got into a fight with the guy and knocked him out. Later the son came back with a pistol. He shot Zsuzsa in the head and killed her." Herschel wailed as his brother recounted the tale. "Then Mr. Karosi came to our bunkhouse and told us we had to leave because he found out we filed the papers with the town clerk. He said we were troublemaking Jews, if we didn't go right away he would call the police. So we came here." Mendel hugged his big brother as the man started to cry out the name of his lost cow over and over.

"More violence," groused Oskar as he entered the room. "The town is getting uglier by the day."

"I guess there is nothing left for us now but to go to Palestine." Mendel said. "We got the papers from the WJC last week anyway, so all we have to do is show up at their office in Budapest. I'll check the train schedule. We want to leave right away. I hope there's a train tomorrow morning."

"Please stay for one last *Shabbos*. It's only tomorrow night," Yossel implored. "We can let go of all the pain we've experienced since returning. We can light the candles and wish you well from a sacred, safe place."

The farmhands were reluctant, but after Yossel promised them a box of fresh pastries for their trip they agreed to stay until the Saturday afternoon train to Budapest. They got the key from Yossel and went into their old room to wash Herschel's cut. Yossel watched them go and let out a sigh.

"It's a sad thing, Oskar. They are moving on to start a new life in Palestine. They'll create families, have new stories to tell that have nothing to do with the war. But the memory of our families stops in Laszlo." He looked at his friend and smiled. "That is, unless you get married again."

Oskar moaned. "Who's gonna marry a man with a face like a pickled herring?"

"Lots of Jewish women like pickled herring."

"Ever the optimist, Yossel."

Yossel turned to check the chicken stew on the stove. "It's down to you and me, Oskar. I pray Eva's grace still protects us."

Oskar grunted. "Forget about us, we have no future. I pray Eva's grace protects Eva."

CHAPTER 40

Piano practice on Thursday morning was not going well. Eva's injured finger throbbed and had difficulty filling out left hand chords. Her timing was off just enough to be noticed.

"You are not concentrating!" Professor Karady glowered. "Music played for music's sake keeps the form alive like an empty rite. It does not infuse it with the life energy needed to arouse an audience," he hesitated, then continued, "let alone keep the world in balance, if you believe such things."

"I am sorry, Professor, my thoughts were elsewhere." Eva's mind kept wandering to Mrs. Rakoczi. Jeno said that he followed her to her apartment last night. She then went to a tavern known to be frequented by fascists and toughs. What would a sweet old secretary do in such a place? "I need to push these thoughts away. I don't want to be in the world right now."

"That is the wrong attitude. You are not escaping from the world. You are purposefully going into a temple to serve, to uphold the beauty in that world. The Academy is a sanctuary of music, yes, but it is only a temporary place of refuge." Karady sat at the keyboard and shoved Eva aside more roughly than she was prepared for. "If you don't focus, if you don't give yourself completely, if you don't draw on every ounce of pain and experience you have had in your short life, how will your work balance the demonic energy that the fascists give to their performances?" He seemed exhausted by his exhortations, mopping his face with a handkerchief. "I know you think music is pure, but there will always be those who contort music into a tool of manipulation. Here is an example. You know Beethoven's "Coriolan Overture," yes? It is a thing of beauty, but listen."

He began with an F-minor chord. "This is how most orchestras begin the piece. Audiences become entranced by this. Hitler loved Beethoven as much as he loved Wagner. Furtwängler, Hitler's favorite conductor, morphed the beauty that Beethoven intended of the overture into something very different. F-minor now represents the lament over Germany's loss, its humiliation. The Germans shake off their lament by unleashing a furious attack here. F-major." He smashed at the keys. Eva felt the twisting of the sound and the geological shift of the world around her. "And now B-major. Harsh, strong, seething passion. This is how the Nazis created the maelstrom, the sense of catastrophic power that perverted the beauty of Beethoven's music." He poured his own rage into the piece, then stopped abruptly.

Eva realized that her heart was pounding and her palms were moist. She loved the "Coriolan Overture" but this version brought back dark memories of screaming crowds and powerful, vicious men. She shook the images out of her head. Music had never made her fearful before.

The professor sat quietly for a moment, his ragged breathing ultimately slowing. "To some, the effect is more battering than uplifting. But if people are constantly bombarded with propaganda that preys on fear and insecurity then many will be drawn to the power the music promises. The Nazis used this music to rouse people to ugly actions that served their purposes." Karady's hand went to his forehead as he seemed to disappear into a dark pit.

A question burned inside Eva. Even if Professor Karady wouldn't mentor her in the Music of the Spheres, he clearly understood the power of music.

"Professor, why does it seem easier to bring people to hatred than to compassion?"

Karady's eyes widened as he looked out over the piano. Eva wondered if she had overstepped an unspoken boundary with this professor. She knew she could have asked this of Professor Sandor, but they had a long relationship and he was like family. Eva began to regret asking the question and started to backtrack. "I'm sorry, Professor. It's just that I—"

He held up his hand to silence her. "I am not offended by your question, Eva. I have struggled with it many times." He stood and walked around the practice room, following the patterns in the parquet floor. "But the question assumes people are a blank slate. That is not the case. People are the products of their culture as much as their current situation. Here in Hungary and most of Europe there is a long history of prejudice against Jewish people." Karady appeared to wander into a private world again. He blinked and continued. "People fear whatever threatens their sense of security. It could be a coming storm, a disease, or even the presence of people who are different from them. The hateful stories, the subtle or overt attitudes are passed down through the generations until there is no real reason anymore, just a buried cultural attitude. So, the Nazi propaganda of hate supported by a symphony of anger and righteousness finds a predisposed and receptive audience. It seems easier to bring them to hatred than to compassion because they are already primed for it, whether they are aware of it or not. It is like a dry forest floor waiting to be ignited by a dropped cigarette."

Professor Karady calmed himself and spoke in a soothing, poignant tone. "As Plato taught, beauty, like all values, is in constant, agonizing conflict with its opposite. Our lot is to be vigilant, to dedicate our lives to the Pure Form. Music in service to beauty and its manifestations; goodness, compassion, love. To use this gift is a choice, and sometimes there is a heavy price to pay. Are you ready to do that or are you not?"

Eva realized Zoltan Karady must have been thinking of his lost students. Their work trying to balance the evil in the world through the Music of the Spheres had only resulted in their deaths. No wonder he had been so resistant to her in the beginning. He was mourning his lost students and Eva was asking him to put her in the same danger. She thought of Professor Sandor. He could have left Hungary, like Bela Bartok. Ultimately, the professor had died for his belief in the power of music as well. Eva wondered if more beauty in the world could have prevented the ugliness that led to the war. Probably not. Yet if more people had been exposed to hope instead of an incessant diet of hate, could the war have been less destructive? Would more people have resisted? Perhaps. Eva had a choice—to commit herself to holding back the darkness that had consumed her family and friends, or to be a bystander. She placed her hands firmly but reverently on the keyboard. "Yes. I am ready."

Their work on the audition pieces was complete. Eva felt confident that she would perform well enough to pass the audition the following night. The Sabbath. Would performing the night of the Sabbath be good luck in the Jewish tradition? Or was it bad luck because Jews were supposed to leave the world in peace? But making music was bringing beauty into the world, how could it be wrong? Wasn't that a *mitzvah*? She wished she knew more about the religion—or was it the culture? Now was not the time to get lost in the confusion of her heritage.

She wanted to share her experiences with the Music of the Spheres with Professor Karady but he always avoided discussing the piano concerto during their practices. Now she understood why. But it was already Thursday afternoon. This was her last chance to be with him before the Friday night audition. If it didn't go well she might never work with Professor Karady again. Her heart began to race, she hoped her voice would not betray her anxiety.

"Professor, now that our practice time is over, may we work on *Piano Concerto for the Music of the Spheres*? I have so many questions about 'Transcendence,' the third movement—"

"Absolutely not! Music may or may not balance hatred, but it is not possible to see souls! Souls flee the dead and do not return!" He cut her off in a voice filled with agony. Beneath it, Eva detected a note of fear.

Jeno pulled on the Gauloise and released the smoke forcefully. "She leaves her apartment at seven each night. Tonight I will go to the apartment after she is gone." The early evening was damp and hot. The dark clouds of impending rain brooded overhead.

"I want to go with you. I can be your lookout." Eva knew Jeno was bold and clever, but this was too important to leave to him alone. If Eva could prove that Mrs. Rakoczi was the informer at OMIKE and the Academy, she could bring a small piece of justice to all the lost Jewish students and performers. Even if her music could not combat the darkness, Eva could offer the solace of closure to Anna and Professor Karady.

Jeno looked at Eva with surprise. "I thought you didn't want to be a part of my world." He gave her a teasing smile. "I thought you were kind of soft."

Eva grabbed his cigarette and took a deep drag. She had survived a concentration camp. The fact that she retained or regained any softness at all was a testament to her tenacity. She passed it back to Jeno and blew three smoke rings. "I am made of tougher stuff than you know."

Jeno's cheeks reddened. "Oh, of course. You lived through . . . you are right." He stubbed the cigarette on the rail. "Well, let's be off."

They walked to Mrs. Rakoczi's apartment building off Andrassy near the torture headquarters, and sat in a café across the street. As they waited, Eva stared back at the government building. It hummed with a malignant chord. Shortly after seven, Mrs. Rakoczi left her building and trundled down the road, just as Jeno had said. Jeno told Eva to stay at the cafe until he paid off the apartment manager to tell him where Mrs. Rakoczi lived. The manager would lend him the key and look the other way as they climbed the stairs to her floor.

He came back jingling the keys. "I told you. Gold watches are better than *pengos*."

They lingered at the railing for a moment to ensure no neighbors were watching out their windows. Jeno eased open the door. Eva followed him in quietly. The apartment was crowded with furniture and books. In the early evening half-light, they prowled the main room and moved toward a small study off to one side. Jeno opened a number of drawers in a roll top desk as Eva went deeper into the labyrinthine apartment. In the darkness, she smelled the must and sweat of an older person. Just like the Armin Hotel. She turned on a table lamp in the farthest room and gasped. Jeno ran to her side. The walls around them were plastered with photos of men and women, crossed out in red paint. Manila files covered the large wooden desk under the photos. Eva picked one up and read the header: 'Lajos Glass, violin.' They glanced through a dozen folders, each headed by a name and an instrument and containing a photo with an X through it.

"What are these," Jeno asked. "School files?"

Worms writhed throughout Eva's stomach. "I think they are OMIKE people and Academy students who were murdered. She was definitely an informer for the Arrow Cross." She hesitated, then continued searching through the files, knowing but fearing what she would find. 'Jusztus Bardos, piano' and 'Arpad Unger, cello.' Professor Karady's lost students. She gazed around the room. The photographic death masks on the walls mockingly mirrored the beautiful faces in Anna's posters. Eva moved some files aside and stared at a bound pack of Academy mailing envelopes. They were unopened and the stamps had not been cancelled. She dug quickly through the pile until she found what she suspected. The envelope addressed to her. She grabbed several of the unmailed readmission letters and the files of Professor Karady's students. "I'm going to give these to the director tomorrow. He will know what to do."

"Let me take them, Eva. You shouldn't have to face that woman again."

Eva knew Jeno's offer came from his desire to protect her, but this was her work to complete. "No, Jeno. I will do it. I want to stare into her face, knowing what I do. I want to see how evil sits behind that false smile. I have seen evil face to face before. I am not afraid." She turned to leave the room.

"Wait. Look at this," Jeno hissed. At the lowest right corner of the mass of photos on the wall was a picture of Anna Nagy, cut out from a yearbook or newspaper. It was not crossed out. "It looks like Anna is still on her list."

Eva reached to tear down the photo of Anna. Jeno grabbed her arm.

"Don't. We can't let her know anyone was here."

Eva startled as she remembered her first conversation with Mrs. Rakoczi. "I gave her Anna's address!" As they hurried from the room, Eva glanced back at the people impaled on the walls. So many young musicians who would never reach their zenith, so much exquisite music denied to a world in need. The faces implored her for justice and not to be forgotten in the silence of time and obscure corners of memory. Their pleas followed her out of the apartment.

They ran as fast as they could back to Anna. Through huffing breaths, Eva explained their visit to Mrs. Rakoczi's apartment and showed Anna the letters and files. The woman became distraught, calling out the names of murdered friends and loved ones from OMIKE. Neither Jeno nor Eva mentioned seeing Anna's photo. Eva helped Anna get into bed and served her some chicken broth. She hugged Professor Sandor's sister as if she would never let her go again. Anna relaxed into her arms.

After Anna fell asleep, Jeno gently washed and wrapped Eva's oozing hand again with a clean bandage. He told her he would spend the night on Anna's divan to make sure she was safe. They went to the balcony and shared a cigarette. Eva watched Jeno's profile through the smoke. She had her music to help navigate the chaos of the world. Maybe Jeno's flip attitude and toughness were his way of coping. He certainly could be kind, even gentle, when he wanted to be. Was it the adrenaline of the evening that made her heart pump so fast and left a chemical taste in her mouth, or was she developing deeper feelings for Jeno? She put her hand tenderly on his shoulder, surprised at her own boldness. He turned toward her, captured by her soft gaze. She brought her lips to his, unexpected and delicate. For the briefest of moments the camp, the trains, and the hatred disappeared.

Jeno slid his face along Eva's and held her closely. He whispered urgently into her ear. "Eva, come with me to America. Let's start our lives again without all this fear and misery."

Eva pushed him back, floored by his comment. "What about my music? I have to attend the Academy. It's been my goal all my life."

Jeno stroked her hair and made soothing sounds. "Shhh. I have asked around. There are many good music schools in New York. Listen, Bela Bartok is there and he is calling for Hungarian musicians to come and join him. It must be an amazing scene. You belong there."

The phrase hung in Eva's mind. *You belong there.* Where did she belong? New York and Bela Bartok? In a community of young musicians from Hungary and America and who knows where? She had no community in Laszlo, and the town was sundered between rejection and acceptance. Her family and friends were gone, their ashes scattered over unknown landscapes, nothing to mark their fleeting time on earth. Only her mother's grave remained, along with the memory of her father. And her commitment to honor the professor's work through the Academy. The Jewish community in Budapest, though deeply wounded, was still large and strong. It could become her community, too. They could all heal and recover together. What about Anna? The woman was her last personal connection to the professor. When she thought of Anna her heart warmed like it did when she thought of her mother. She couldn't leave Anna. She had promised to be Anna's hands.

Jeno put his hands on her shoulders, his eyes tender and caring. "I know what you are thinking. I have already spoken to Anna." He stroked the side of her face. "Eva, she wants you to go."

Eva stood before the door to the director's office on Friday morning holding a large manila envelope containing the files and letters she had grabbed from Mrs. Rakoczi's apartment. The faces on the apartment wall urged her on. In the camp, she had learned to banish emotion from her face so she would not draw attention. Eva summoned up the courage she had when she walked past the guards as she returned from the munitions factory each day with gunpowder crammed under every fingernail. She was ready.

Mrs. Rakoczi answered Eva's knock with pleasant, blinking eyes. Nothing seemed amiss. "The director is in auditions this morning," she said, staring at the envelope. "You can leave those with me."

Eva was not prepared for the director's absence, but she couldn't give the documents to Mrs. Rakoczi. "No, no thank you," she stammered. "I will wait for the director. I need to go over some things with him." Eva watched Mrs. Rakoczi's eyes sharpen as she continued to stare at the envelope. It was not wise to allow any long silences between them. "These are the scores he asked me to prepare for him and the judges. I have a few questions about the Liszt piece, and I wondered if I might do Chopin's 'Nocturne' in D instead of C. It would be easier on my finger."

The secretary clearly did not know anything about music, so Eva prattled on in detail about the pieces. Soon Mrs. Rakoczi became glassy-eyed and let Eva enter and sit in her anteroom to wait for the director. Eva settled in facing Mrs. Rakoczi, the envelope resting on her lap. She tried to keep a casual air as the secretary ignored her and fussed with papers on her desk, but anger grew inside Eva and her pulse quickened. This woman was as much a murderer as those Arrow Cross thugs who tortured Anna and killed so many. She concentrated on her fingers, moving them in slight motions than mirrored some of the professor's exercises. Her pulse and breath slowed. Focus and willpower.

After a half hour, the director strode through the anteroom with a surprised glance at Eva. He barked "No meetings!" at the secretary and closed his office door before Eva could grab his attention. Mrs. Rakoczi looked at Eva with sympathy and whispered.

"Don't worry dear, I will get you in to see him. I'm sure what you have to say is important." She got up and knocked gently on the door, opened it, and disappeared inside the director's office. Eva heard the quick, muffled conversation and Mrs. Rakoczi reappeared with a smile. "The director will see you now."

Eva leapt from her chair, nearly spilling the files from the envelope. She rushed into the director's office and closed the door behind her.

The director frowned. "This better be important, Miss Fleiss. I am in the middle of auditions and I cannot give you any special treatment. If you have questions about the required music you should have asked before now."

"I am sorry to interrupt you, sir, but this is very important. I have proof that Mrs. Rakoczi was working with the Arrow Cross during the war, and I think she still is. She was the one who informed on Professor Karady's students and a lot of others." She pulled the files from the envelope and placed them before the director. The director opened a file and winced as the grainy, black-and-white image of Jusztus Bardos stared back at him. He continued to examine the files. Eva pointed to the letter addressed to her. "That is my readmission letter. You can see it was never mailed. I found all of this in Mrs. Rakoczi's apartment last night. There is a lot more evidence there, but I didn't want to alert her that I had been in the apartment."

The director's eyes never left the photographs of the students.

"You broke into her apartment? That is a criminal act."

Eva was surprised by the director's comment. Why was he deflecting away from the facts in front of him? "Isn't it more important that I discovered she was working with the Arrow Cross? I think that's why she wanted to work at the Academy."

The director sighed heavily and pushed back in his chair. "She took the job, Miss Fleiss, because I asked her to. We desperately needed the help and . . ." he paused, his face turning stern. "She is my wife's sister." He gathered up the files and gripped them tightly in his hands. "Leave these with me, Miss Fleiss," the director said abruptly. "You need to prepare for your audition tonight. Please go now. I am late for the next student."

Eva rushed past a grinning Mrs. Rakoczi and into the hall. It was noon. She was supposed to be at Anna's for a small Sabbath ceremony before her audition. She was confused and angered by the director's dismissal and the revelation that he and the secretary were related. Would the director bury the evidence and hide what Mrs. Rakoczi did? Was he involved? Did he keep the Academy safe by bartering away some of the Jewish students and staff? Was her audition a set-up for failure? The director had dismissed the professor's work. Was this his final act to eliminate anyone who sought to manifest the Pure Form? Was Anna in even greater danger now? Eva was nauseous with the questions swirling through her mind. She needed to calm down and sort things out before she went to Anna's, and certainly before she went to her audition—if she should bother going. Maybe Jeno was right. Go to America. Get away from all of this and start fresh.

She wandered the hall without direction. When she regained awareness, she was standing before the fresco of nymphs by the pool that fronted the main entrance to the Grand Hall. Apollo, the god of music, stared down at her with bemusement. His outstretched hand pointed to the inscription:

Those who are looking for Life, come to the fountain of Art.

No. Eva would not abandon the audition. Even if it were a sham, she would honor her father's wish that she try to get in, as well as the professor's faith in her abilities. She took a long last look at the fresco and headed to the practice rooms. There was enough time for one more session before the audition this evening.

CHAPTER 41

The farmhands scrubbed the floors of the hotel kitchen and dining area Friday afternoon, cleansing the rooms in preparation for the Sabbath. Yossel watched with mixed emotions. This was their last night together before the men left for Palestine. The hotel would be a very lonely place with all the surviving Jews of Laszlo gone, except him and Oskar. But welcoming the Sabbath was an ancient ritual among the Jewish people, performed in homes around the world every Friday night since the destruction of the Temple. It was a time to let go of the pain and sadness of the mundane world. For twenty-four hours, anyway. *What a practical people we are*, Yossel thought.

Oskar came through the front door carrying the fresh lamb he had purchased for a special final Sabbath meal with the farmhands. He laid the carcass on the kitchen counter apologetically and tied on a fresh white apron. Yossel knew Oskar's apron, as well as his arms and chin, would soon be covered in lamb's blood. The butcher was always so messy. Yossel sighed, knowing he would have to clean the kitchen all over again when Oskar was finished. However, he had become used to pitting his sense of order against Oskar's love of chaos in his kitchen. It would be worth it. Fresh *barany gulyas* was Yossel's favorite. Oskar's off-key whistling made the baker smile. He knew that working at the bakery when it reopened would give the butcher a sense of possibility, help him get past his anger and just maybe see some of the goodness in people that Yossel saw.

"I saved a lot buying it this way. I can cut it up into chops, roasts, and cubes to grind. We can use the shank bones for soup." Oskar took his large butcher's knife and began to prepare the shoulder and rump roasts.

Yossel chopped the carrots, onions, peppers, and tomatoes. He had already lined up the green beans, garlic, paprika and the cupful of black currants he loved to toss in toward the end of the long simmering stew. The smell of baking *challah* filled the hotel, just as the light of *Shabbos* would fill their hearts tonight. He would send the farmhands off to the Promised Land full and happy. The smell also reminded Yossel of Eva. He wondered what she was doing on this *Shabbos* evening. They would have to remember her in their prayers.

The afternoon rain was evolving from mist to large droplets outside the kitchen window. Yossel sipped the red wine he was saving for the stewpot. He smiled at the thought of what his grandmother always said. A Jewish belief, she claimed, but Yossel never met anyone else who had heard it, except a Swedish man once. *Rain on an auspicious occasion is good luck.*

Viktor sat atop a large rock at the edge of the field, watching for intruders. He thought no one would come out to the brick factory in the rain and just before dinnertime, so they should be safe from discovery. The other White Stag Scouts scanned the wet ground behind him, poking in the mud with sticks for the treasure Viktor knew was buried there. The silence was only broken by the complaints of the boys as their shoes were sucked off in the sticky mud or a gold nugget the size of a hand turned out to be a rock.

Janos plopped down in the mud and wiped his nose on his damp sleeve. "I'm tired and I'm getting hungry."

"Shut up and search," Viktor commanded. "You're always such a baby."

"Am not," Janos mumbled.

Peter spoke kindly to the little boy squirming in discomfort. "Hey, Janos, come look over here with me." Janos perked up at the attention and trudged over to Peter. From a distance, the boys heard Gyorgi relaying the news that he hadn't found anything yet. Viktor followed Peter and Janos to a grassless patch as the two continued their hunt for the elusive Jewish treasure. Janos squinted at something metallic poking out of the ground. He got on his knees and probed around the object. He scraped away the muddy surface. The top of a shiny golden ring gleamed before him. He waved frantically and shouted to the others.

"I've found it! I found the treasure!" The boys converged on Janos. Viktor went to grab at the ring but Peter held him back.

"Janos found it. Let him pick it up."

Janos continued to scrape the mud with his tiny fingers. He stuck them into the ground and under the ring. He tried pulling it up but the ring held fast. The rain became heavier.

"C'mon, Janos. Hurry up!" Viktor said.

Janos grunted and pulled again. "It's stuck on a root or something." He pulled with all his strength and the ring came out with a sucking sound. Janos held up the ring. The boys gathered close, admiring the glittering golden fruit of their long search. Janos passed it to Peter. The older boy scraped some of the mud away from the root to see the ring better. He screamed and dropped the ring.

"It's a bone! The ring is on a finger bone!"

The boys shrieked and began to run. The rain increased as the skies cried for justice. The red brick dust in the field became a sea of blood. Thick mud clutched at the boys' feet as they stumbled out of the field. Viktor slipped and fell. His hands sank into the mud, landing on something hard below him. As he pressed his left hand deeper into the mud to push himself upright, a shinbone was levered out of the muck directly in front of his face. He burst into tears and bawled for help. Peter and Gyorgi pulled Viktor up and they ran from the field. Janos followed at their heels, wailing about the gash on his arm from his own fall. The rumble of approaching thunder, like the laughter of an angry god, chased the White Stag Scouts away from the brick factory.

Oskar stepped out of the hotel and looked at the brooding, darkening sky. He grumbled about the rain as he carried the bloody remains of the lamb carcass in a bucket toward the garbage bin. He turned at the sound of children coming up the hill from the direction of the station. What were they doing out in the rain? They were covered in mud. The littlest one looked hurt, clutching his bleeding arm. Why should he care? The little bastards would grow up to be like their hateful parents. Let them catch influenza.

He stopped himself. *Shabbos* was so near. He had a chance to do a *mitzvah*, a good deed to help heal the world. "Damn it," he growled. "Why do I have to be Jewish?" He thought of his lost youngest son. He was about the same age as the hurt child. If only someone could have been there to save his boy. The stab of pain in his heart at the thought of his son transformed to a warm, paternal feeling for the wet, hurt little boy in the road before him. It broke through the last vestiges of Oskar's resistance to caring about others again. Maybe that was at the heart of a *mitzvah*, he pondered. It is not only the importance of the act, but also the humanity it brings out in the doer. The butcher called to the boy.

"Hey! Are you hurt? Come here, let me help you." He put down the bucket and walked toward the boys with his right hand held out. His arms and apron were covered in blood. He still held the butcher's knife in his left hand.

As the White Stag scouts limped up the hill, shaking from their experience at the brick factory and fearing what awaited them when they got to their homes, they startled at the sound of a shout. Viktor squinted through the rain and saw a huge man approaching from the Armin Hotel, covered in blood and carrying a large knife. The boy screamed in terror and began to run up the hill away from the Jewish demon. Peter and Gyorgi followed. They stopped and turned around after twenty yards and saw the demon herding Janos toward the hotel. Peter started to go back down the hill, yelling "We've got to save Janos!" Gyorgi tailed him uncertainly.

Viktor hesitated. He was the leader of the scouts. He should save Janos, not Peter. But the demon was so big and he had that knife. Viktor started running up the hill again. He shouted over his shoulder. "Janos fell behind! He's weak! I'm not gonna die for him!"

Peter stopped and aimed a wet, hard face toward Viktor. "Who's the coward now?" He ran back to the hotel.

Viktor watched through the rain as the Jew cast a spell on the boys. He must have bewitched them because Janos and the others meekly followed him inside to their deaths. He clutched his soaked shirt at the neck and ran home.

Viktor burst into the apartment, wet, cold, and muddied, wailing for his mother. His cries brought out the neighbors, who listened as Viktor told of nearly being captured by the blood-splattered Jew with the big knife. His mother asked what happened to the other boys. "He got them all. He took them into the hotel. I tried to save them but the Jew was just too big." She screamed and dashed to telephone her husband. Two of the neighbors grabbed clubs from their apartments and ran down the hall, shouting for help.

"The Jews grabbed some kids at the Armin Hotel! Help us!"

The cry was picked up as they headed toward the hotel. More people flooded the wet streets, streaming down the hill along with the torrential rain. Viktor found new courage in the shouts of his neighbors and ran along with them, his story growing in every telling. He was important. Grandfather would be so proud.

"I haven't seen that little boy Karl for weeks!" a schoolteacher yelled. "They must have taken him!"

"They tried to kill me, too!" Viktor shouted. "But I fought them and escaped!"

"Our children!" Someone screamed. "They drain their blood for their satanic rituals! I heard about it in church!"

"Where's my daughter?" Another bawled. "She should have been home by now!"

"I think I saw her through the window!" Viktor bellowed. "I will save her!"

The rumors were captured on the winds of fear and spread through the town. As they lodged in the hearts of the townspeople the number of missing and slaughtered children grew. Over a hundred citizens of Laszlo descended on the hotel carrying clubs, bricks, and a millennium of hatred. Men and women screamed for revenge and justice for the imagined crimes of the Jews. They surged toward the door, slamming against it with fists and wood.

Oskar finished cleaning the gash on Janos's arm, swabbed iodine and wrapped it gently in gauze. He told the little boy how brave he was. Janos jumped down from the bathroom counter and ran to join his friends in the dining room. Peter and Gyorgi sat at the table, happily chewing on gingerbread men as their freshly washed legs swung under their chairs. Herschel sat with the boys, matching kings, knights, and castles from a worn deck of William Tell playing cards.

Yossel refilled glasses of milk for the boys. "I tried calling the police a few times to come and take these boys home but the line's always busy."

"That's alright, it's Friday night. Probably busy with drunken soldiers," Oskar said. "The boys are safe with us."

They all jumped at the sound of pounding on the door. Yossel went to open it and was thrust out of the way by a mass of angry men and women who pushed into the hotel foyer.

"Murderers! Butchers of children!" people roared. They stopped cold at the sight of the three boys sitting with mouthfuls of cookies. But the swell of bodies beyond the door could not see the children. Rocks flew through the windows, shattering glass onto the stewing lamb. Oskar tried to push the stunned townspeople out of the door but the crush from the other side was too great. Outside, someone shouted that he found bones, blood, and guts in a bucket behind the hotel.

"Look at the blood on his apron!" someone shrieked, a thrust arm pointing at Oskar through the door. "He's the one! He's been butchering the children!"

"The other one, the baker! He showed me the tools he makes his bread with! That's what the blood is for!" a woman wailed. "Where's my daughter!"

"Just like Chelm!" cried another. "God, how many have they murdered?"

Yossel opened his hands wide and pleaded with the frenzied townspeople. "Friends, the children are here! They're safe! There's nothing wrong!" He spotted several of his customers at the bakery and tried to get their attention, but their twisted faces betrayed no recognition.

"Murderers! Murderers!" the crowd chanted.

At the far end of the dining room, Mendel and Herschel scuffled with a group of men who had pushed their way into the hotel. They tried to escape and ran up the stairs followed by a maddened host of club-wielding men. Others from outside rushed in and began to pummel Yossel and Oskar. Someone grabbed the perforated *matzo* roller and bashed Yossel repeatedly about the head. The sounds of rage and pain, breaking glass and bones echoed throughout the hotel as the boys were hustled out the front door by their saviors. Although he was terrified by the chaos around him, Janos managed to grab a final gingerbread man and a few playing cards as he ran out. A tear fell from his eye and splashed on the table, missing an immobile Golem by inches. He scooped up a small stuffed bear with one ear and a broken eye button that lay on the floor as he passed. A cheer went through the crowd as the boys appeared. People thanked the Lord for saving their children before the Jews had used them in their ungodly rituals. Somebody grabbed the gingerbread man from Janos's hand and threw it to the ground, shouting that it was made with the blood of Christian children. Janos touched the other one snuggled safely within his pocket.

The harsh scream of a siren announced the arrival of the police van. It skidded to a stop next to the furniture company truck, which was blaring Wagner's *Twilight of the Gods* on the radio as its headlights illuminated the hotel. Mor looked out the passenger window, humming the opera and waving his hands as if conducting the pogrom before him. Captain Szabo jumped out of the van, trailed by Ritook, Zoldy, Gronski, Boros, and Miklos. The captain took the boys aside and turned them over to their anxious parents. Miklos grabbed his son, Janos, and hugged the boy tightly. He held him at arm's length and looked at the bandaging on his arm.

"Janos, are you alright?"

The little boy's eyes sparkled. "Yes, Father. The nice Jewish man fixed my cut." He dug the gingerbread man out of his pocket and held it up for his father to see. "And then he gave me a cookie." A woman from town broke away from rock throwing to kindly offer to take Janos to her home for the evening. He protectively hugged the little bear he had rescued from the crowd. It would be safe with him.

The captain ordered Ritook and Miklos inside the hotel to assess the situation as he watched townspeople rushing in and out of the hotel. He saw factory workers throwing rocks and singing nationalist songs, angered at the Jews whose factories were shut down after they were deported. Ex-soldiers blamed the Jews for being communists and starting the war that took their limbs and their futures. Recent migrants from the countryside brought their rage at lost homes and loved ones due to the war. Shop clerks and store owners fought shoulder-to-shoulder, finding temporary camaraderie in protecting their newly gotten gains. Drunken, frustrated young men who had nothing else to do and no one else to blame for their unemployment and lack of self-esteem joined the carnage. Former Arrow Cross members who never acknowledged their sins from the war found absolution in this new cause, breaking windows and spewing hateful slogans again. The captain knew so many of them. They weren't bad people. Mostly ordinary citizens out of control, doing hateful things to these few remaining Jews. Many would regret it in their secret hearts later, maybe try and do something to balance their personal book of judgment. Most would simply forget and carry on as if the rampage and violence never happened and they didn't participate in it. The townspeople attacking the hotel thought they were avenging the murder of a handful of nonexistent children. Where was their outrage over the real murder of a hundred of Laszlo's littlest ones, the Jewish children deported to the ovens of Auschwitz? Captain Szabo found himself thinking of the girl, Jacob Fleiss's daughter who played the piano, thankful she was not here to witness or be hurt by this.

The captain pulled his hat further down to protect his face from the pelting rain. Usually such a downpour quelled the violence of a mob, but tonight it seemed to bloat its wrath. The crowd was not quieted by the presence of the police either. Instead, their righteous outrage swelled as if blessed by the state. Shouting and stones filled the air as the townspeople cried out for the bodies of the ten, twenty, now thirty missing children of Laszlo.

The policemen found Yossel and Oskar being beaten and kicked on the floor of the kitchen. They pushed the crowd aside and muscled the seriously injured men out toward the police van. People screamed and struck the wounded Jews as the police shoved through the mob outside. Miklos tried to defend Yossel as best he could, even appealing to the attackers by name. Ritook led Oskar through the assault without shielding him in any way. He paused as a man yelled to his wife for a club. The sergeant waited until it arrived and the man smashed Oskar with it repeatedly. The captain ordered the wounded men put in the back of the van for protection, then told Miklos to go back and find out what had happened to the farmhands.

A red Chrysler Imperial downshifted to a stop behind the police van. The mayor leaped out and approached Captain Szabo. "This is madness, Szabo. You must stop it!"

Captain Szabo glanced at the Arrow Cross symbols on the hotel illuminated by Mor's headlights. He spoke without taking his eyes off the men milling angrily around the hotel door. "It's a mob, Mayor. It has to burn itself out."

They both turned at a shout from the crowd cursing the mayor for bringing the murderous Jews back to Laszlo. Several voices growled their assent. A rock bounced off the police van. Szabo grabbed the mayor's sleeve and forced him back toward Jacob Fleiss's car.

"You'd better leave. You're inflaming the crowd."

Ferenc Kodaly climbed into the car, confused and miserable. "I only tried to heal our town."

"Maybe Laszlo's not ready to heal." The captain slammed the car door and watched as it drove away. He turned a grim face toward the tumult. "Maybe it never will be."

Miklos ran into the hotel, past rioting townspeople. The smoke from the *challah*, incinerating in the gas oven, flooded the hotel. He heard a commotion upstairs and sprinted to the second floor. He burst into the room furthest down the corridor and saw Herschel holding a man over his head by an open window. Mendel sat bleeding profusely from a gash on his head on the floor nearby. Miklos drew his revolver and aimed it at Herschel.

"No, please," Mendel pleaded. He looked up at his big brother and spoke tenderly through breath shortened by a broken rib. "Herschel, put the man down. I know he hurt me but the police are here. They will protect us. We must choose life, right? Especially on the Sabbath."

The large man scowled but hesitated as he seemed to weigh his choices. "Choose life. We're gonna go to Palestine and be safe, yes?"

"Yes, my sweet brother," Mendel wheezed. "Everything will be beautiful for us."

Herschel cast his brother an impish grin. "We're gonna get married." He brought the man down to his chest. Miklos was touched by the brothers' interaction. He lowered his weapon and sighed with relief. There would be no repeat of Kosveg here.

A bullet shot past Miklos's ear and hit Herschel in the throat. The farmhand dropped the man and fell to the ground, gurgling and grabbing the source of the spurting blood. Miklos spun around, his ears ringing with the sound of the gunshot. Ritook stood with his gun held out, ready to fire another round.

"It's a good thing I got here in time to save you." He said without taking his eyes off Herschel. "Get the other one down to the van.

I'll take care of the big one." Miklos was too stunned to protest. He helped Mendel to his feet and grabbed him gently around the waist, trying not to put pressure on Mendel's broken rib. The two men shook with disgust and fear as they struggled down the hallway, leaving a trail of Jewish blood down the stairs and out to the van.

Ritook listened as the footsteps faded. He considered the barely conscious, wounded man on the ground. If he shot him again Miklos would tell the captain. It would be hard to say the man attacked Ritook when he was so weak from loss of blood. He glanced at the bed behind Herschel and saw the new pillow the town had bought from Mor with the money from the World Jewish Congress.

The rain picked up in intensity. The crowd had gone beyond any possibility of Captain Szabo's control. They pounded on the van holding Yossel, Oskar, and Mendel. The captain shouted to Ritook to get the wounded Jews out of there, to take them to the hospital. Ritook objected, saying that the hospital wouldn't be any safer as the rumor of blood libel had spread throughout the town and more people kept coming out into the streets. The captain considered Miklos, who tried valiantly to push the raging crowd away from the van.

"Corporal, you have a farm just outside of town. Can you take these men there for the night until things are under control?"

Miklos felt uneasy about the request, but thought about Oskar's kindness to the officer's young son. He wanted to help the beaten Jews and get them away from the hotel as soon as possible. He saw Ritook behind the driver's wheel and Zoldy beside him, so he hurried into the back of the van. The men were badly hurt, but Miklos checked them over quickly and assessed they were stable enough for the ride. He watched out the rear window as the captain and the remaining policemen tried to control the situation at the hotel. He spoke calmly to the wounded men, assuring them they would be safe on his farm. He put his hand gently on Oskar's shoulder, trying to keep him awake as he wove in and out of consciousness.

"Oskar, thank you for taking care of Janos. That was a kind thing for you to do."

The butcher stirred from his bruised stupor. He put a finger in his mouth and fished out a broken tooth. He examined it and threw it to the floor of the van. "Yeah," he mumbled painfully. "I will be rewarded in the next life."

CHAPTER 42

Eva advanced nervously through the empty lobby of the Academy. It was eight o'clock on Friday night, a half hour before her scheduled audition. The late July sun had almost set. Golden light slanted under the clouds and across the lobby of the Academy, illuminating the blue marble pillars. The gentle rain of the afternoon had intensified, the thick drops creating a drumbeat against the stained-glass windows. She stopped and focused on the steady rhythm of the rainfall to calm herself. What was it Yossel had said? *Rain on an auspicious occasion is good luck.* She thought warmly about the men in Laszlo celebrating the Sabbath while she was doing the same with Anna and Jeno earlier today. Were they thinking of her, too? The memory of lighting the candles to dispel the darkness of the week while Oskar grumbled *"Gut Shabbos"* made her smile. The smile faded as she thought of Jeno. He had urged her to come to New York at the Sabbath dinner. Anna had agreed, but Eva perceived a loneliness in the woman's eyes that betrayed her words. Jeno left the dinner abruptly, saying as he always did that he had things to do, but Eva knew he was upset that she would not commit to going to America. Another young man walking out of her life.

An ensemble practicing a movement from *Twilight of the Gods* in a distant room caught her attention. Wagner, Hitler's favorite. The musical score of her nightmares. She tried to tune out the sound. A commotion broke out at the far end of the lobby. The police were hauling a thrashing Mrs. Rakoczi down the stairwell. The woman hissed and spit like a demon, cursing Jews as foul, degenerate beasts, defilers of the Magyar race. The frizzy-haired secretary foamed as she resisted the officers. She glared at Eva and screamed. "I am glad I got rid of all that Jewish scum. I'm only sorry I missed you and your aunt!"

Eva's right hand rose to her mouth as she watched the woman being pushed through the front door of the Academy. One of the police told Eva that the director had turned Mrs. Rakoczi in. Faced with the evidence in the files, the woman had confessed. The secretary would be taken to the building on Andrassy Street, where she would be convinced to name the Arrow Cross members she worked with. Hatred had clearly not surrendered with the end of the war, but Eva knew that one lingering stream had been dammed. At least the director wasn't in league with his sister-in-law. Eva shuddered and forced the image of Mrs. Rakoczi out of her mind. This was not what she wanted to witness before her audition. She turned and leaned against one of the cool marble pillars. Her fingers twitched a poor attempt at a Chopin sonata to calm her. Focus and willpower. She needed to concentrate on the upcoming audition.

She had never been in the Academy when the hallways weren't choked with students and the air filled with music. She clutched her scores to Lily's cerulean gown with her bandaged hand. The other gripped the luminescent gold and pearl necklace that Anna had placed around her neck as Eva's mother had always done. Her eyes went to the blue crystalline balls on the newel posts of the stairway. Eva ran over and stared into the oceanic abyss, sensing a minor chord deep inside the mineralized rock. She reached out and touched it to clear her mind and bolster the confidence she struggled to maintain. Did she feel a faint vibration, or was it imagination brought on by standing at this precipice in her life? She nervously opened the door of the Small Hall, where the student auditions were held. The sterile white walls and unadorned stage gave the impression of a surgical room where each performance would be dissected by the faculty, sitting in the boxes above the main seats. Yet the hall was empty, except for a lone workman. Her stomach clenched. Where were the judges, the director? The workman came down from a ladder against a wall and approached her.

"Sorry, Miss, but the Small Hall is closed now. There's a leak in the stained glass. See there?" He pointed toward a crack in the bottom of one of the large windows. "It was the only shrapnel to hit the Academy during the entire war. Funny, it didn't start leaking until about an hour ago. Heavy rain. Bad luck, I guess."

"But I'm supposed to audition here tonight."

"I don't know. Maybe it was cancelled. You'll have to ask somebody else." He went back to the ladder.

Eva turned to look for help, but no one else was there. Had the director been involved with his sister-in-law's scheme? Had he fled the Academy when the police came to arrest her? She began to perspire and breathe rapidly, confused and unsure of what to do. She left the hall to search for anyone who could assist her, but the foyer and the hallway were silent. There would be no audition. All of the practice, the dreams, the pain were for nothing. She walked heavily through the lobby and toward the entrance, her bandaged hand dabbing at the tears streaming down her cheeks.

Suddenly, the front door opened and Director Zathureczky and Professor Karady briskly entered the building. The director's face was twisted in rage. Professor Karady tried to retain his dignity but tears slipped down his ashen face. The arrest of Mrs. Rakoczi incised the deep wound around his lost students. The director spotted Eva and ordered her to accompany them.

"Eva, come, we are behind schedule because of the arrest of Mrs. Rakoczi. Your audition has been rescheduled for the Grand Hall."

Eva was shocked. The Grand Hall. She had dreamed of sitting by the pool with the nymphs, yet now she was being invited directly into Apollo's sacred grove. She sensed Professor Sandor's hand in this. They walked together in silence to the door to the Grand Hall.

The director told her to wait a moment.

"Before you go in, I wanted to thank you for uncovering the truth about Mrs. Rakoczi. I never thought to suspect her because she was a relative. I was a fool. She did much harm to the Academy and to so many talented artists, students, and faculty. You have lifted a shadow from our institution."

He put a hand on Karady's shoulder. "You have also helped us heal our long and important relationship with Professor Karady, who has agreed to return to the faculty next semester." Karady bowed slightly to the director, and gave an exhausted smile to Eva. Zathureczky took an envelope from his pinstriped suit jacket. "I also wanted to share this curious document with you. I only received it this morning. And with everything else going on I nearly forgot to read it." He handed it to Eva. "It is a petition in support of your readmission, signed by the Mayor of Laszlo and over one hundred residents. We have never seen anything like this before. It is obvious that you were well-respected in your hometown."

Eva scanned the petition and was touched to see Hanna, the mayor and Mrs. Kodaly, and a few others she recognized. Over one hundred names. Perhaps the mayor was right to use Eva to try and heal the town. She wondered briefly why Andras hadn't signed it, but considered his absence from the petition as the final word on their friendship. She smiled appreciatively and returned the document. The director had said "hometown." Although she was glad the town had become so supportive, Eva no longer thought of Laszlo as her home. In a few short weeks she already felt more at home in the Jewish ghetto of Budapest that had embraced her so wholeheartedly than she did in Laszlo. She longed to attend the Academy and pursue the professor's dream—her dream. All of that depended on what happened on the other side of the large leather-covered doors before her. The judges would know none of what happened here. They would judge her strictly on her performance. She flexed her injured hand.

Professor Karady closed his eyes and took a deep breath. "Your path to this font of the arts, this temple to music, has been long and hard. I know you have suffered and I know you are brave." He opened his eyes and they twinkled through their sadness at Eva. "I have known that for a very long time."

Eva had sensed their connection as soon as they met, but didn't understand his comment. She looked questioningly at the old professor.

He gave her a warm and loving look. "I remember a little girl, maybe four years old. She stood up in the aisle during one of my performances of the *Brandenburg Concertos* and twirled around in her black-sequined dress. After the concert her father brought her to the stage. I lifted her up and sat her on the piano bench next to me. She played so passionately with those little fingers, even though she had never touched a piano key before that night. I told my colleague Sandor that she would be a keeper of the Pure Form here at the Academy one day. Now that day has come." Zoltan Karady opened the door to the Grand Hall and bowed deeply. "Good luck, Eva Fleiss."

It was twilight when the van arrived at Miklos's farm. Ritook opened the back door of the van. He ordered Miklos to pull the men outside and lay them on the grass. Miklos protested, but Ritook reminded him he was in charge and needed to make sure the Jews had no weapons and posed no threat to the officers. After moving the men, Miklos went back and turned off the motor. Ritook laughed when Miklos told him he didn't want the men to have to breathe the van's exhaust fumes while they lay on the ground. Zoldy leaned against the van, his hands in his pockets, watching impassively. Ritook took out his revolver. He pointed it down at Yossel, then lifted it to aim at Miklos.

"It's time for you to prove you're not a coward."

Miklos stared at the gun barrel and began to shake. "What do you mean?"

Zoldy snickered from behind Miklos. He also took out his pistol, and shook it at Miklos like a finger of judgment. "You think we don't know what you did at Kosveg, complaining that your gun misfired so the captain would put you on guard duty? You thought you were better than we were, too good to do your duty. You left us to carry out the orders so you wouldn't feel guilty afterward."

The blood drained from Miklos's face. The world tilted. He put a hand on the van to steady himself. "I couldn't shoot those innocent people."

"The captain, he cried like a baby when we finished, but he wasn't a coward. He followed orders just like we did," Ritook said. "You're one of us, Miklos, whether you like it or not. You need to prove you can follow orders."

Ritook looked down at the badly injured Jews by his feet. "I don't know this one," he said pointing his nose toward Mendel. He pushed his boot down on Oskar's throat for a moment, eliciting a low groan. "This one's a really bad character." He poked Yossel with his toe. "And this one. He's a good Jew." He returned his penetrating stare to Miklos. "Time to redeem yourself."

Miklos stood firm. His fists clenched and he pushed his jaw out, even though he was quaking inside. "No. I will not kill these wounded men."

Ritook mockingly feigned reason. "But Miklos, there're already dead. Don't you remember what your friend Oskar said when he came back to Laszlo? He said they all died the minute we shoved them onto that train. And you were right there at the deportation, weren't you? You're already responsible. This is just the clean-up." Ritook and Zoldy steadied their revolvers at Miklos. "Where's your allegiance, Corporal? Are you going to follow orders this time or not?"

"Time to redeem yourself," Zoldy repeated. "And hurry up. It's way past dinner."

The three Jews lay on the wet grass as the policemen spoke nearby. They were barely able to move from their injuries. Mendel opened his mouth to catch a drop of rainwater. He let out a sigh.

"It feels so peaceful here."

Oskar's voice gurgled a reply. "It's the calm of a morgue."

Mendel tilted his head and looked at Oskar with innocent eyes. "What do you mean, Oskar? What do they want from us?"

The butcher spoke gently to the farmhand. "They want our most precious Jewish treasure. The one they could never find. Our beating hearts."

Yossel felt like every one of his bones was broken. So much pain radiated throughout his body that he couldn't focus on any specific hurt. His hand reached over to search for Oskar. The butcher's arm felt bloated and spongy. "I tried to be good, to be positive and respectful to everybody. I wanted them to know they had nothing to fear from us." He winced as he moved his back. "It was a bet, a gamble. It worked most of my life. I guess it was a good run."

Oskar groaned at Yossel's touch and rolled his head toward the baker. "Can't say my way was any better. My anger just made them more defensive. Didn't make them look at themselves. Hating Jews is baked into their black hearts and there's nothing we could've done about it. This was always going to end one way."

The silence that sits like a false promise at the eye of a storm enveloped them. *Barely time for a good life before the next tragedy,* Yossel remembered the butcher saying. He listened to his friend's labored, intermittent breathing. "Oskar, are you afraid of dying?"

Oskar barked his harsh laugh, coughing hard as a broken rib knifed against his lung. "Afraid of dying? No, Yossel. I'm afraid of living." He was quiet for a moment. "I hope Eva does alright."

Yossel struggled to grin through broken teeth. "I'm sure she will. I still think she's one of the thirty-six righteous ones, a true *Tzaddik*. God put her here to keep some beauty in the world."

Oskar grunted as pain lanced through his chest again. "You know how much I love the girl. But I still don't believe that religious crap."

The click of a revolver's hammer being set in place broke the sweet silence of the evening. The heavy rain clouds parted slightly above their heads, revealing a small patch of the velvet heavens. Yossel looked up at the twilight sky and saw the first star. A little twinkle of light in a darkening firmament. A minuscule sensation of love worked its way up from his heart and out his eye as a tear. "Look, Oskar. It's time. *Gut Shabbos.*"

Oskar felt for Yossel's hand and squeezed it gently. He followed his friend's gaze through swollen, blackened eyes. The starry outline of a little boy's face shined in welcome through the parting clouds. It was millions of miles away, yet it promised the butcher a release from all his pain. "*Gut Shabbos*, my friend."

CHAPTER 43

Eva settled comfortably on the piano bench, uplifted by the elegance of Lily's sky-blue dress. She stared up at the swans, the angels, and the other inhabitants of the sacred grove of Apollo. A few students came to watch, sitting in the empty lower level as was the tradition. Director Zathureczky, Professor Karady, and two faculty judges were settling into their box high above her. The judges were complaining in hushed voices loud enough for Eva to hear. They questioned the purpose of this late audition, given that the incoming class was full, and the girl had a damaged hand. The director silenced them, stating that Eva was already admitted pending the audition, and that both Professor Sandor and Professor Karady saw something special in her. Looking around the Grand Hall, Eva felt her anxiety rise. Even when she knew her pieces by heart, Eva was always nervous before a performance. Her father used to say her nerves showed how much she cared about doing her best. Eva's fingers twitched as though calling her to pay attention to them.

Suddenly, the doors to the lower hall opened and a dozen stylishly dressed young women strode in, herded by a middle-aged matron. Their beautifully made-up faces shone with the sisterly love they shared with Eva at the bordello. They smiled up at her and whispered to each other as they took seats. One of them stared up at the judge's box, pointed, and waved playfully. A judge showed consternation, but subtly waved back. The women were soon followed by Anna Nagy and Jeno. Eva's heart warmed at the sight of the professor's sister. It was the same feeling she had when her mother entered an auditorium where Eva was going to perform. Eva thought of her parents, wishing they could have been there to see her audition, to look at her with shining eyes of love and support. They would never do that again. Jeno looked behind himself then turned to Eva with his arms flung out in an exaggerated shrug and a broad grin. He held the door open as people from the Jewish ghetto poured into the Grand Hall. Eva was amazed when she saw the woman who owned the bakery where she bought her rolls and candy. Little Abraham and his gang followed the woman like hounds on a scent. Geza, the toothless fruit seller, played an imaginary keyboard as he smiled up at his "piano angel." Other vendors from the Klauzal Square market, young couples from the ruin bar, and elderly survivors leaning on the arms of their companions filled the empty seats. They all looked at Eva with expectation and affection. The judges gawked down in bewilderment at such an unprecedented show of communal support at an audition. Eva put her hands to her chest, feeling the warmth emanating throughout her body. She had become one of their own. She mouthed the words silently, but knew they were heard and felt by everyone there.

"*Gut Shabbos.*"

Ede Zathureczky stood astonished at the rail of the judge's box as all nine hundred seats below filled. He beamed down at Eva. "It seems you have quite a following, Miss Fleiss." He cleared his throat. "It is time to begin. I see your program will be Chopin, Liszt, and a famous composer of your choice. Are you ready for your first piece?"

As the crowd quieted, Eva took a deep breath and turned toward the piano. *Bosendorfer* was written in gold script across its face. She put a finger on the slight gash in the *B*, then blinked. The gash was gone. "Yes, sir. For my first piece I will perform Chopin's 'Nocturne' in E-minor." Her mother had loved Chopin. "Nocturne" was a simple, sweet composition that allowed for soulful expression. It was also a gentle way for Eva to prepare her pained hand for the harder pieces ahead. She played in a reflective mood, allowing a vision of her mother to drift at the margins of her awareness, smiling at her. The comfort of that image infused her playing. The melody lingered softly, then ascended to a higher register. Eva ran the trill-like final passage brilliantly. The excitement of the music subsided and the piece ended as calmly as a cloudless night over the Danube.

When Eva finished, the audience applauded. One of the judges stood up and ordered quiet, saying this was an examination, not a free public concert. Eva reddened and looked to the judges for comment. One complimented her touch on the keys, control of dynamics and the progressing lines of melody, but said there were moments when the piece dragged a bit. The other said she had to work on the nuance of the tempo. The director countered by noting the agility of her left-hand ostinato, considering her injury. Eva knew the judges were not enthusiastic. Given their earlier grumbling, were they looking for an excuse to fail her? If she was going to pass the audition she needed to impress the judges, not be a merely proficient piano player. Her hand began to throb under the fresh bandage.

"Your Liszt piece, please," one of the judges intoned dully. "And we hope to see more passion."

"Dante Sonata" was one of the composer's most exacting and important pieces. It was a powerful composition that went through nine thematic transformations mirroring the nine circles of hell from the poet's work *Inferno*. Eva performed difficult combinations of A-flat major and D-minor chords that evoked the horrible howls and tears of the anguished souls in hell. Her long fingers worked up to the spectacular conflagration Liszt captured from Dante. Her body felt seared by the heat. As the flames of hell subsided, she skillfully brought Dante's pilgrim through his arduous spiritual voyage. It was a punishing performance. Eva gasped with the lack of breath and emotional exhaustion, yet she also felt the exhilaration of surviving the voyage through the underworld. A stabbing pain shot through her left hand, and fresh blood seeped through the new bandage.

She gazed out over the audience and saw the Jews of Budapest weeping and holding each other, reliving their own hellish circles of unfathomable pain. She felt a yielding in their taut vibrations of rage and waves of denial—the psychic swords and shields a wounded, yet proud people had developed to combat their agonies.

Eva's eyes widened as the blood from her hand percolated through the bandage and pooled on the keyboard. The thick red liquid dripped off the piano and onto the stage. Throbbing rivulets sought out the centuries-old sounds of despair and weariness from the audience. The blood spread throughout the hall, covering every seat and washing up against the female pillars who held the room in their angelic embrace. Eva and the audience bled their grief together. Their catharsis was magnified by the acoustics of the Grand Hall, as if urged on by Apollo himself. When the swell of frenetic energy and psychic longing in the hall subsided, the judges sat stunned and without comment. One recovered his composure and mopped the sweat off his face with a handkerchief. In a strained voice, he thanked Eva for a beautiful performance of Liszt and called on her to continue.

Eva emerged from her dream-like communion with the audience. She stared out to see Anna's adoring face, wet with tears. Make-up and pain smeared the faces of the young women from the bordello. Even Jeno sat stupified, shaking his head slowly in a gesture Eva perceived to be an internal struggle with whether to leave Budapest or stay. Eva knew they needed to be soothed, uplifted, transported somewhere. Many heads were bowed, but more looked at Eva with anticipation and urgency. She wanted to remain in their embrace, to relish her growing bond with the Jews of Budapest and her affinity with her Jewish heritage. This was what she truly sought—to be loved and held in a family and community again.

The tingling of her fingertips against the keys brought her attention back to the piano. She realized the decisive moment that would define her life was only one piece away. Eva flipped to Mendelssohn's Concerto No. 1 in G-Minor, her personal choice, and began to perform her third and final selection. She identified with Mendelssohn, who struggled with his Jewish identity throughout his life as his family sought accommodation with the dominant culture. The concerto was fast and furious, and would highlight her speed, accuracy, and fluency. But as she played the pain in her hand increased, interfering with her concentration. Her fingers moved mechanically and by her strength of will, but her mind and heart sensed the audience's need for something more.

This piece is wrong, Eva thought. She felt compelled to help heal the wounds she had just opened. She needed to play Professor Sandor's piano concerto. If the Pure Form of music could push back against the ugliness, if hearing universal sounds in proper harmony had helped her deal with her own trauma, perhaps this music was the salve the Jews of Budapest needed at this moment, as well. Eva's rational mind warned her that she was not expert at Professor Sandor's concerto. It was an often-atonal piece, difficult enough without her injury or her lack of practice. One or two wrong notes would mean a disastrous performance. She would be jeopardizing her audition and her long-held dream of attending the Academy. But did it ultimately matter? Her only true community sat before her, there to support her, suffering more deeply than they would have if Eva had not opened their wounds. She became so absorbed in their pain that she didn't know where she was in the Mendelssohn piece. Her heart told her what she had to do.

Eva stopped playing and turned to the audience. She breathed in the agony of the Jews of Budapest, let it mix with her own, and exhaled compassion and understanding. She visualized the fresco outside the Grand Hall. Blue angel's wings unfurled behind her as she sat on a cloud the color of her gown. The young women from the bordello, dressed in blue, lounged beside her with lutes and lyres. She felt no physical pain or internal hesitation. One of the judges called out to her in concern.

"Miss Fleiss? Why have you stopped? Is your hand too injured to continue? We can consider your application again next term."

Eva aimed her radiant face at the judge's box. "I'm sorry, but I must change my program. Instead of Mendelssohn, I am going to perform *Piano Concerto for The Music of the Spheres* by Professor Aladar Sandor, whose memory I wish to honor." Ede Zathureczky nodded in somber understanding. Next to him, Zoltan Karady's face flashed the same fear and anxiety as whenever Eva tried to talk to him about the concerto. The two faculty judges looked at each other in confusion. One of them stood and faced Eva.

"I'm sorry, Miss Fleiss, but the requirements are clearly stated on the audition sheet. The third piece must be from one of the great composers."

"Professor Sandor *was* a great composer." She saw all the pleading faces on the wall in Mrs. Rakoczi's apartment. "Like too many others, the war cut short his brilliance before the world had a chance to know him."

Karady's expression shifted between apprehension and awe. The judges conferred again, animated and agitated. They consulted with Director Zathureczky. One of the judges threw up his hands and turned sideways in his seat, away from the men in the box. The other judge spoke.

"This is highly unusual, Miss Fleiss," he said, scanning the distraught audience. "As are many of the circumstances of this audition. We appreciate what struggles you have gone through to get here and how determined you are to join the Academy. However, ultimately, we can only accept students of the highest proficiency. And, frankly, your faltering performance of the Mendelssohn piece gives me some pause as to your readiness. You really should allow that hand to heal. This is your last opportunity to prove you belong here. If you wish to play an unknown piece you will be taking a huge risk." He glanced around the judge's box. His voice relented. "But the choice is yours."

Eva's shining blue-green eyes gazed out at the audience with understanding and compassion. She saw their tired, sluggish bodies tied to this plane of suffering. Just as hers was. The bright lights from the chandeliers illuminated Eva's long fingers and bruised, bloodied left hand as she began the opening movement, "Sentience," as a soft lament in C-minor. It was not difficult to connect with the audience. "Dante Sonata" had already forced them to confront their pain. The movement was an endless cycle of melodies seamlessly woven together. Eva and the Jews of Budapest swirled together in the melodies, acknowledging their shared experiences and becoming aware of something greater to come.

Eva moved on to "Communion," the second movement. Her shift to A-flat minor took them down through their suffocating hearts until the pain was unbearable. Mother, Father, Professor! B-flat minor skirted the edge of blasphemy, turning away from any possibility of hope. They languished at the edge of the abyss, full of longing for redemption. Eva veered to B-minor, the key of patience and submission to providence. The music became a pulsing chant, a purgatory giving respite, a space to breathe. Deep inside her, from a place she could not name, a still, small voice urged *Now*.

Eva began the third movement, "Transcendence," emanating a harmony that surpassed the range of anyone's hearing, but was clear to their hearts. Everything dissolved except her fingers and the keyboard, her sole anchors to the mundane realm. Her music unveiled the secrets confined in the combinations of notes and melodies in the professor's composition. His concerto evoked the full range of human experience from innocence to betrayal, from pain, anguish, death to the rebirth of hope, healing love, and the ascendancy of the human spirit.

The deep rumble of the setting sun in D-major burst a triumphant hallelujah. The soft swish of the rising moon in A-major graced her with restored trust in innocence and faith in the divine. Eva sensed tender, soothing stars and unending space in A-minor, and heard the planets humming their unique sounds as they vibrated through wobbly, elliptical orbits around the sun. Gloomy Saturn in F-sharp minor. Jealous Venus, B-major. Joyful Mercury intoned optimism in B-flat major. She played the tonalities and octaves of each planet as it passed by. The universe was displayed before her, and she saw the planets conjoined in a pattern that birthed a beautiful sound. Her whole being became suffused with an inward song. The Jews of Budapest must have heard it, too. Eva felt the release of their agitation as fire melts ice and water quenches a flame.

She heard a whirring sound above her head as spinning wheels of light showered down white sparks. The sparks covered the soundboard of the Bosendorfer and spread out in all directions at once. The air flooded with radiant, translucent beings. Some wore street clothes; others wore striped pajamas. Some settled on people in the audience, finding their loved ones and creating a multitude of vibratory hums in innumerable pitches. She saw two orbs of light tenderly encompassing Anna as she wept, and knew that she had been embraced by her husband and beloved daughter, Lily. From a universe away, she heard the strained voice of Zoltan Karady cry out "Jusztus! Arpad! I am sorry! I tried to save you. Forgive me!" As Eva transitioned to C-sharp minor, he released an agonized wail in the same key. It was a passionate expression of sorrow and deep grief, full of penance and self-punishment, as his hands reached out to touch the spirits of his lost students. Other specters continued a forlorn search, swooping through the air like bees seeking out their destined nectar. Eva was filled with love. She continued playing with increased intensity.

Eva turned toward discordant notes, and with deep anguish absorbed the images of Yossel and Oskar, reaching for her as if to bless her and say goodbye. *Them too?* she thought as her heart ached. The Fischer brothers wailed in sorrow nearby. Eva felt the pain spilling from their kind spirits. The confused, anguished form of Corporal Miklos darted erratically through space around them. Their astral presence told her the ancient, malevolent plague had risen up and stricken Laszlo once more. A long keen heaved from deep within her as she grieved for them all, then thanked and blessed them for their kindness to a lost young woman.

Suddenly, a distant chord harmonized with one she was playing. The sound was meant only for her. She saw the spirits of her mother and father. There was no pain in their faces, only a radiant, boundless love that embraced her. She felt the brush of lips like soft clouds against her forehead. Her essence joined with that of her parents. Time stalled as Eva and her parents pulsed as one. From that sweet place of joy, Eva heard another major chord. She sensed the professor in waves of pride and comfort. She kissed his ephemeral hand. The words of his letter graced the air. *I look forward to the day when I will be with you in the Grand Hall at the Academy.* Tears flowed, glowing and searing like hot lava released from her molten core. Her mother, her father, the professor.

Eva continued to play the professor's concerto—her concerto—slowly bringing it back to the chanting tempo and soft timbre of the first movement. She ended with grace.

The judge's voice was jarring. "Thank you, Miss Fleiss. That was very interesting and extremely bold of you. Well done. We appreciate your time." The two judges huddled into a conference again.

She emerged from her meditative state and looked around, sapped by her experience. The orbs of light still pulsed and vibrated throughout the Grand Hall. Her parents, the professor, and the spirits of the men from Laszlo hovered close to her, questioningly. Why hadn't they all gone on? Eva stared at the faces of the audience. The longing for their beloveds was etched in every one. She realized that their love, grief, anger, fear—all the human emotions that connect us to each other—would keep the spirits bound in limbo until they were released from the grasping of our wounded hearts. She sensed her own loved ones again. A bittersweet awareness crept into Eva. She was holding them back, as well.

"Miss Fleiss? The audition is over. You may go now. And please, take care of your hand."

Eva looked at her throbbing hand. The blood had soaked through the bandage and was smeared across the keys of the Bosendorfer. The healing was incomplete. From within her consciousness the professor quoted from his manuscript.

> *If we believe that the Soul is a real force, if nearly impossible to perceive, and that notes can be attuned to any force, shouldn't we be able to follow the sound of a Soul beyond the death of the body? Is there a Music of migrating Souls? Can the Pure Form soothe the tortured Soul and ease it along its ultimate passage? Pythagoras believed so, as did Plato.*

She bowed toward the judges and spoke in a hoarse voice.

"Thank you for allowing my audition. I do have one more piece I need to perform."

"I'm sorry, Miss Fleiss," one of the judges said in exasperation. "It's been a long day for us and a tiring evening for you, I'm sure. We need to catch the last train to Vienna tonight and must leave. The audition is over. You may go now."

Ede Zathureczky put his hand on the judge's arm. "Wait, Imre. Let her continue. You and Hugo may leave if you must." He looked down at Eva and smiled kindly. "Miss Fleiss, the judges have informed me that you have passed the audition. You may attend the Academy when the new term begins next month. Congratulations." He looked around the audience in the Grand Hall, then scanned above their heads. A beatific smile graced his face. "But please go on. You need to finish what you have begun."

Eva's heart filled with joy. She had realized her lifelong dream. She wanted to bask in the moment, savor the achievement. Her hand and back ached. She was drained in every possible way. But she was being called to give a greater performance, one that she had unknowingly been preparing for since she first touched the keys of this same piano as a child. The professor had brought her the gift of the Music of the Spheres, but it was Eva's profound pain and loss, expressed through the soundboard of the Bosendorfer, that had opened the pathway of "Transcendence" and revealed the spirits.

Yet it was only half the equation. Now she would carry the work forward to its conclusion. She opened her folder and took out the tattered score of Ravel's "Kaddish," the gift from Anna Nagy. She had always thought the Mourner's Kaddish was a series of prayers glorifying God for the sake of the departed. Looking over the audience, she realized it was meant equally for those left behind. She put her fingers to the keys, but hesitated. This could be her last opportunity to embrace so intimately the spirits of her parents, the professor, and the kind strangers from Laszlo. Her desire to hold on, never to let go, was enormous, as it surely was for everybody in the audience. She also recognized it was selfish, as it kept the souls from their journey. Eva savored the connection. *Please, please let me touch you a moment longer.* It may have only lasted seconds or minutes, but Eva knew it would remain her entire lifetime.

Slowly she pressed the keys and quietly began the haunting melody. It had the tender sound of a heartbeat. The rhythmic repetition of minor chords became a catalyst that melted the glue of grief that bound the manifest and spectral together in the Grand Hall. Someone in the audience began to recite the prayer in time with Eva's playing.

Yitgadal v'yitkadash sh'mei raba b'alma di-v'ra . . .

The *basso profundo* murmur spread throughout the crowd as more of the Jews of Budapest joined in. The sound rumbled as if from the earth itself. The deep ululation of ancient alliterative syllables and sounds infused spirit and matter.

Yitbarach v'yishtabach, v'yitpa'ar v'yitromam
v'yitnaseh, v'yithadar v'yit'aleh v'yit'halal . . .

The translucent, glowing images split open like the husk off a seed, revealing the *nefesh*, the vital soul of each spirit. Stripped of all earthly binds, they flew inward through the crystalline structure of their hearts to rejoin the spark of life, the first emanation from the divine. They soared upward past the planetary energies, as Eva's strong yet sensitive fingers released the notes, chords, harmonies, and melodies of each and all. Fueled by the chanting of the earthbound, they spiraled past the moon, freed of its cyclical pull of growth and waning; past Mercury and its power of devising evil; Venus and the illusion of desire; the impious judgment of warlike Mars; the encompassing compassion of Jupiter, and all other influences of the spheres on the soul and its human incarnation.

Eva's own soul joined the chorus, as she felt her grasping loosen and the pain, longing, and grief she carried evaporating into love. She sensed the slipping of her beloveds away from this manifest plane. Her mother, her father, the professor, the people who had raised her and formed who she was. Positive Yossel and grumbling Oskar, the gentle farmhands, kind Corporal Miklos, all had helped her transition from a lonely survivor to a strong young woman who had regained her path. Her heart went with them, stretched inward and outward until it became a single string encompassing the universe. On that string, she struck the last note of "Kaddish." It harmonized perfectly with the rapture of all those liberated souls, fusing into the oneness of the Pure Form. Her long, tortuous journey from Auschwitz to the Academy was finally ending. For a brief moment, as evanescent as the blink of the first star of the Sabbath, balance was restored. Eva's world hummed in peace.

THE END

ACKNOWLEDGMENTS

This was a difficult novel for me to write for many reasons. First and foremost, I had to overcome the feeling that I had no right to write a survivor's story, in spite of the vast literature on concentration camps and the aftermath of the war. Dr. Jack LaForte helped me identify and confront the issues holding me back. Dr. Jack Terry (*z"l*), to whom this book is dedicated, asked penetrating yet always compassionate questions about why I wanted to write *Finding Home*. He also introduced me to the music of Schumann. Jack Terry and other survivors (who wished not to be recognized here) shared the profundity of their physical and emotional experiences openly and helped insure that I reflected them accurately.

The return of Jewish concentration camp survivors to their hometowns after the war is largely unexamined in popular literature. I was fortunate to find many academic papers by Veronika Kusz, Eva Kovacs, Ferenc Laczo, Borbala Klacsmann, Naida-Michal Brandl, Erika Szivos, and Peter Apor. The works of Jan Gross first opened my eyes to the heartbreaking, little-known pogroms that scarred Eastern Europe. In Hungary, I was tutored in history by Peter Tibor Nagy, and escorted through classes and time at Ferenc Liszt Academy by Peter Barsony, Endre Toth, and Eva Szalai (who allowed me to enjoy her piano practice at the Academy).

At home, I enjoyed the amazing support, encouragement, and occasional editorial comments of noted authors Ilan Stavans, Jennifer

Rosner, and David R. Gillham. True blessings for a debut novelist.

Last, but certainly not least, my family participated in so much of the making of this novel. My daughter Aliya was the perfect beta reader as a young professional musician, offering both insight into music and a young woman's interior landscape. Daughter Sarah provided emotional support and feedback. My amazing wife Annette helped me get past my mannish plot-first approach to deepen the emotionality of the characters, particularly regarding trauma, and provided incredible insight throughout the writing.

Thanks to all of you for helping me achieve my long-held dream of bringing Eva and her world to life.

Made in United States
North Haven, CT
12 June 2025

69720583R00219